THE EMPEROR'S GIFT

Two creatures barred my way, their too-long tongues lashing across my armour in a scraping caress. The first beast died to a surge of psychic force, blasting it back against a wall to dissolve against the hull. The second staggered, its head cracked open by my return blow, barbed tongue thrashing with blind anguish. I reached for the staggering creature with my sixth sense, caught it with a telekine's grip around its throat, and dragged it closer. Its worthless struggles ended as I butted my helm into its choking face, breaking whatever passed for bone in its hideous head. With an outstretched arm, I cast it back into the void. Let it bleed its sick fire into space.

A WARHAMMER 40,000 NOVEL

Grey Knights

THE EMPEROR'S GIFT

Aaron Dembski-Bowden

BLACK LIBRARY

A BLACK LIBRARY PUBLICATION
First published in Great Britain in 2012.
Paperback edition published in 2013 by
Black Library,
Games Workshop Ltd.,
Willow Road,
Nottingham,
NG7 2WS, UK

10 9 8 7 6 5 4 3 2 1

Cover by Cheoljoo Lee.

A CIP record for this book
is available from the British Library.

UK ISBN 13: 978 1 84970 396 3
US ISBN 13: 978 1 84970 397 0

See Black Library on the internet at
www.blacklibrary.com

Find out more about Games Workshop
and the world of Warhammer 40,000 at
www.games-workshop.com

Printed and bound by CPI Group (UK) Ltd, Croydon, CR0 4YY

It is the 41st millennium. For more than a hundred centuries the Emperor has sat immobile on the Golden Throne of Earth. He is the master of mankind by the will of the gods, and master of a million worlds by the might of his inexhaustible armies. He is a rotting carcass writhing invisibly with power from the Dark Age of Technology. He is the Carrion Lord of the Imperium for whom a thousand souls are sacrificed every day, so that he may never truly die.

Yet even in his deathless state, the Emperor continues his eternal vigilance. Mighty battlefleets cross the daemon-infested miasma of the warp, the only route between distant stars, their way lit by the Astronomican, the psychic manifestation of the Emperor's will. Vast armies give battle in his name on uncounted worlds. Greatest amongst his soldiers are the Adeptus Astartes, the Space Marines, bio-engineered super-warriors. Their comrades in arms are legion: the Imperial Guard and countless planetary defence forces, the ever-vigilant Inquisition and the tech-priests of the Adeptus Mechanicus to name only a few. But for all their multitudes, they are barely enough to hold off the ever-present threat from aliens, heretics, mutants - and worse.

To be a man in such times is to be one amongst untold billions. It is to live in the cruellest and most bloody regime imaginable. These are the tales of those times. Forget the power of technology and science, for so much has been forgotten, never to be re-learned. Forget the promise of progress and understanding, for in the grim dark future there is only war. There is no peace amongst the stars, only an eternity of carnage and slaughter, and the laughter of thirsting gods.

CAST OF CHARACTERS

ANNIKA JARLSDOTTYR – Inquisitor, Ordo Malleus.

AXIUM – Executor Primaris of the Adeptus Mechanicus 'Palladium Kataphrakt' coven.

BRAND RAWTHROAT – Wolf Guard of the Adeptus Astartes Space Wolves Chapter.

DUMENIDON – Grey Knight, warrior of Squad Castian.

ENCELADUS – Grey Knight, Sepulcar of the Dead Fields.

FREDERIC DARFORD – Inquisitorial agent, former lieutenant and sniper in the Mordian Iron Guard 151st Infantry.

GALEO – Grey Knight, Justicar of Squad Castian.

GARVEN MERRICK – Inquisitorial agent, former enforcer.

GHESMEI KYSNAROS – Lord Inquisitor, unaligned.

GRAUVR – Space Marine of the Adeptus Astartes Space Wolves Chapter.

HYPERION – Grey Knight, pyrokine warrior of Squad Castian.

JOROS – Grey Knight, Grand Master of the Eighth Brotherhood.

LOGAN GRIMNAR – 'The Great Wolf', High King of Fenris and Chapter Master of the Adeptus Astartes Space Wolves Chapter.

MALCHADIEL – Grey Knight, telekine warrior of Squad Castian; twin brother of Sothis.

NADION – Grey Knight, Apothecary of the Eighth Brotherhood.

RYMIR CLOVON – Inquisitorial agent, former leader of the heretical Coppertongue cult.

SOSA KHATAN – 'The Khatan'; Inquisitorial agent, former trooper in the 73rd Attilan Rough Riders.

SOTHIS – Grey Knight, warrior of Squad Castian; twin brother of Malchadiel.

TALWYN CASTOR – Lifebonded captain of the Grey Knights warship *Karabela*.

TAREMAR AURELLIAN – 'The Gold'; Grey Knight, Brother-Captain of the Third Brotherhood.

TORCRITH – Grey Knight, Prognosticar of the Augurium.

VASILLA TERESS – Inquisitorial agent, Sister of the Order of the Scrittura.

VAURMAND – Grey Knight, Grand Master of the Third Brotherhood.

'One unbreakable shield against the coming darkness,
One last blade, forged in defiance of fate.
Let them be my legacy to the galaxy I conquered,
And my final gift to the species I failed.'

– Inscription upon the *Arcus Daemonica*,
attributed to the Emperor of Mankind

PROLOGUE
AWAKENING

I

'I don't know.'

His life could be distilled into those three words. What little he remembered of it, anyway.

'I don't know.' He said it to the voices, each time they asked him those same questions. They never asked anything else.

What is your name?

'I don't know.'

What year is it?

'I don't know.'

There'd be a pause, for exactly six seconds. He'd count the beats in his mind. Sometimes, if it was late in the questioning, his racing heartbeat would throw off his counting. It was never enough. They'd always ask again.

What is your name? came the voice from nowhere – always male, but not always the same voice.

'I don't know,' he'd say to the surrounding emptiness. His

voice didn't echo. The blackness seemed to swallow it whole. He couldn't even see his hand held up before his face. No amount of staring wide-eyed ever brought clarity to the nothingness.

What year is it?

'I don't know.'

Sometimes, as they questioned him, he'd push his knuckles against his closed eyes, trying to make bright pressure-smears just to bring colour to the darkness.

It never worked. That's how he knew he was blind.

II

He couldn't say how long it took for things to change, but change they did: first the question, and then the answer.

His 'day' began the moment his eyes first opened, no different from before. As ever, he couldn't move beyond the small confines of what he considered his cell. He checked each time he awoke, running his hands along what felt like cold, featureless stone. The stone tasted like salt, and smelled of blood. There was no door.

What is your name? demanded the voice. A low and aggressively masculine tone, today. Almost angry.

'I don't know.'

What year is it?

'I don't know.'

He wondered if he'd committed some grievous crime. Perhaps this was his punishment. That made sense, didn't it? The thought wasn't a new one, for it often danced through his consciousness, inspiring more fruitless, answerless musing.

He'd asked the voices before, of course, many times. He'd also learned quickly enough that they were extremely unforthcoming. They would ask, but never answer.

What is your name?

He sighed, slinking back to the thin blanket he considered his bed. In the sightless dark, he wrapped the rag around his shoulders, and returned to shivering.

'I don't know.'

What year is it?

'I don't know.'

He was hungry, which surprised him. He rarely woke feeling hunger. Though he couldn't remember eating or drinking anything since first waking there, he knew they fed him. Still, the only taste he knew was that the walls left a saline tingle on the tongue, so he suspected his sustenance came through an intravenous process during the hours he was unconscious. The tiny pinpricks along his forearms were always sorest just after he awoke.

He fingered them now, all the way down to the metal socket plugs at his wrists.

What is your name?

He'd answered differently, at first. He'd railed at the unseen voices, demanding answers and insisting he shouldn't be here. The latter claim always felt more than a little hollow, since he had no idea at all whether he should be there or not. He often wondered if he deserved to be contained as he was. Perhaps he did. Perhaps he was a murderer.

These thoughts granted him little guilt, for he could remember nothing of his life outside these walls. Penance was an easy trial when one couldn't recall the sin.

Eventually, the routine settled into place. He no longer invented names or spat out meaningless syllables. He abandoned the sullen silences, and the equally-ineffective shouted questions. They hurt him whenever he said anything except the truth.

'I don't know.'

What year is it?

'I don't know.'

He'd never understood just how they hurt him, but the pain would begin in his head and bloom outwards from there. A dull throb behind his eyes would leak to his ears and the roof of his mouth, creeping down his spine. The last time he'd managed to endure it until his fingers felt as if they were aflame. The pain had dripped all the way down his torso, infecting half of his body.

Pain was a catalyst for honesty. He told the truth after that moment. He told it unfailingly.

What is your name?

Was he going to die here? Did he have long left to live? These thoughts struck with greater force than any guilt. Feeling his own flesh never offered much in the way of enlightenment. With no sight for reference, he was reduced to guesswork. Despite not feeling any loose skin, scars or obvious wrinkles, his flesh was grotesquely tight to the bones beneath. That could just as easily be a sign of advanced age as it could suggest malnutrition. He had no idea if it was either, both, or neither.

It was a bizarre feeling to not even know how old he was, somehow stranger than not knowing his name, or remembering the sin that sentenced him to that cell.

What is your name? The voice snarled this time.

Was that a repetition? Had he missed an answer? The pain sparked like a second heartbeat in his head, throbbing in his sinuses and the delicate tissue connecting his eyes to his brain. He had to spit to clear his mouth of the sudden drool-flush.

Maybe they would kill him if he held back from answering. He'd tried to die that way before, back in the beginning, but the pain always broke him, leaving him weeping and panting, confessing the truth yet again.

What is your name?

He looked up, seeing nothing, already feeling the tremble in his fingers as the pain spread with pinching fire down to his jaw. A snorted breath, not quite a laugh, broke from his wet lips. He felt himself smiling, felt the welcome warmth of tears on his face. Perhaps this was what going mad felt like. Perhaps he'd been mad for months already.

What is your name?

His cheeks hurt, both from the spreading punishment and the ache of grinning. This shouldn't be funny, but it was. In a way, it really was. What had he done to belong here? It must have been something bad. Something really, truly bad.

Was he important? Did he know something they wanted to pry from his skull? If that was the case, they were out of luck; the memory-starved darkness in his head was as empty as the blackness before his eyes.

That set him laughing again, harder this time.

'My name,' he began to answer, but crumbled into childish sniggering. The pain ramped up, quicker than before, knifing to his tongue and throat in a quick pulse. He gagged, but didn't stop grinning. If there'd been anything in his system, he would have thrown it up right then and there.

What is your name?

'I don't know.' The pain receded, but didn't dissipate completely. He was still locked into a madman's smile as he drew another breath. 'I don't know.'

He leaned back against the wall, the laughter finally fading. 'My name is whatever you want it to be. My name is whatever it needs to be, to get me the hell out of here.'

In an instant, the pain vanished. The voices went with it, leaving him cold, blind, and unsure if he'd passed some kind of test, or failed it.

* * *

III

When he awoke next, his arms were sore.

His hands were leaden weights, connected to stone-heavy bones that weighed his muscles down. Even opening his eyes was a trial.

With a grunt, he reached to feel the tender skin of his fore-arms. Dots of pain marked the miniscule puncture wounds, and he wondered just how long he'd been unconscious this time. He couldn't remember going to sleep, but that wasn't anything new. He could never remember drifting off into welcoming slumber. A hollow absence punctuated his periods of wakening into the cold – he suspected they were rendering him unconscious somehow, rather than letting him succumb to natural sleep.

Your name is Twenty-six. The voice was gentler now, though still grindingly masculine. He froze, statue-still in the black-ness, suddenly trembling. *You have accepted that you must bear a new name. That is the first step. Your name is Twenty-six.*

'My name...' He had to swallow before getting the words out. 'My name is Twenty-six.'

What year is it?

He licked his lips, fearful of losing what pathetic progress he'd made. 'I don't know. I swear, I don't know.' It was the truth, but he hesitated, unsure if the truth was enough, any more. He bit his lip far too hard as panic threatened. 'But I want to know. I want to know the year. What year is it?'

The expected pause began, and stretched far longer than the routine usually allowed. He was drawing breath to speak when the voice returned.

It is the year Four-Zero-Six.

The date meant nothing to him. He wasn't sure if he was supposed to reply. 'How old am I?'

Chronologically, you are fifteen Terran standard years of age.

He almost laughed again. He was barely more than a child.

And for so many hours, he'd been thinking he was an old man. The concept was enough to leave him reeling.

Stand, Twenty-six.

Despite the nausea, he did as ordered, feeling for the wall and using it as support.

Open your eyes.

'I...'

Open your eyes.

He blinked. Trembling fingertips bumped against the cold, soft surface of his open eyes. He was getting grit in his eyes from his dirty fingers. He had to swallow again. Saliva stringed between his teeth.

Open your eyes.

'But they are open.'

Twenty-six, open your eyes.

'They're open! They are!'

Twenty-six, open your eyes.

He moaned in the darkness, beating his fists bloody against the stone wall. 'They're open!'

Twenty-six, open your eyes.

And then, in fear that bordered on feral, he tried to obey. He tried to open eyes that were already wide.

That was when he woke up.

IV

He didn't come up slowly this time. He woke with a jolt, and the very first thing he did was scream. Light knifed into his eyes with the merciless kiss of acid poured into a hole. He screamed, dragging cold air into protesting lungs.

Twenty-six, remain calm.

He felt like he was crying, but his face wasn't wet. His hands were a protective screen over his closed eyes, a guard to wash out the pain.

Twenty-six, remain calm.

'I can't see. It's too bright.'

Twenty-six, the voice said again, just as the pain began to pulse. *Remain calm.*

He rose on shaking limbs, blinking as he dared a glance through his fingers. The light poured back in, fire-keen, burning his eyeballs in their sockets and dancing down the nerves into his head.

He breathed a wordless, meaningless mishmash of curses, panting like a trapped animal.

Twenty-six. Remain still.

Not a chance. The second he heard the grind of a metal door opening, he bolted blindly towards it, one hand reaching out to feel for anything in the way.

He crashed teeth-jarringly hard into something metal, something tall, that emitted a pervasive engine-growl heavy enough to make his gums ache. After thudding against it, he fell back to the stone floor.

Footsteps. Heavy, booted footsteps, sending shivers through the ground.

'I didn't do anything.' He still wondered if that were true. 'Just let me go.'

Twenty-six, came the voice in his mind again. *Stand, be silent, and open your eyes.*

He could at least comply with the order to stand, though his legs barely obeyed. Being silent took even more effort, and as for opening his eyes...

'It's too bright.'

The illumination is set to its lowest levels. You have not used your eyes in ninety-nine days. The pain will pass.

'I don't understand.'

Your ignorance will also pass. That is why we have come.

Another voice, deeper, with an edge of irritation, joined the first. *Open your eyes.*

He tried again. It worked on the sixth or seventh attempt, though his vision offered nothing more than a slice of harsh light at first. His eyes watered continually, as if they could flush the sting from his eye sockets.

Shapes resolved at last. Three shapes, each one a man – two clad in hooded robes the rich, dark shade of dirty iron, and the other wearing a hulking suit of armour, as bright as polished steel. The painful light came from this last figure, as the overhead illumination reflected from the burnished silver plating.

All three kept their faces hidden; the former two beneath deep hoods, the latter behind an ornate helm with eye lenses of the most distressingly pure, piercing blue.

Twenty-six. He had no idea from whence the voice came, for none of the figures moved. *Look around you. What do you see?*

What indeed. Through straining eyes, he took in the chamber's details. Every dimension seemed the same as before – the only exceptions were the door's sudden existence, and the symbols inscribed in bright metal along the walls and floor.

He knuckled his eyes free of tears for a moment. Blinking cleared up the rest. He should have felt these symbols, even in his blind questing. Each one was raised in bas-relief, stark silver against the dark stone. 'These symbols, what are they?'

Wards. Again, none of the figures moved. *Hexagrammic wards. We had to be sure you were free from taint. We also had to be certain you recalled nothing of your former life.*

The second voice cut in. *You have remained here for the mandated ninety-nine nights, as we scryed into your soul.*

The ritual is complete, a third voice spoke at last. *We are satisfied with your purity.*

The armoured figure's joints growled as it inclined its head. *Though some doubts yet remain.*

'Why couldn't I feel these symbols? Where was the door?' He couldn't stop trembling, though more from adrenaline than the cold, and more the cold than any real fear. Looking down revealed he was clad in a similar robe to two of the figures, though it was once white, and now only greyed by dust.

The first robed figure reached up to lower its hood. The man was clean-shaven, and he looked anywhere between thirty and sixty, with evidence of every decade etched on his face: the smooth skin of youth; the knowing stare of experienced eyes; the fine lines of laughter and sleepless nights, with steely stubble gone to grey atop his shaven head.

The indefinable quality of his age was, however, not the most bizarre thing about his face. He was a man enhanced to imposing proportions, as if his entire body had undergone a decade more growth and development than would be natural. Even in the robe, he cut a towering figure, dwarfing the prisoner.

'Why won't you answer me? Why was I blind?'

You were never blind. We engineered your senses to serve our needs. The ageless one had the respectful demeanour of a holy man, but a murderer's piercing eyes. His blue gaze lowered the temperature of the room. *We manipulated your thoughts. Your eyes stayed closed, yet you believed they were open, seeing only darkness. We blunted your tactile sensitivity, so that you felt nothing but smooth stone beneath your fingers. You were a prisoner in your own mind. The door was never even locked. You were simply unable to feel its existence.*

He had to hand it to them, they made for some ingenious, twisted prison wardens.

'Who am I?' He hadn't even meant to ask it, but it slipped out after dangling too long on the tip of his tongue.

You are Twenty-six.

'No,' he shook his head, and regretted it immediately.

Nausea swept back over him. 'No, I mean before. Before I came here.'

Irrelevant, said three voices at once.

Your past is gone, cast aside in the name of necessity. From the moment you came to us, you were reborn.

You will be addressed by your number until you earn your true name. What you were called is meaningless.

All that matters is what you will become.

He drew in another breath, suspecting he knew the answer before he even asked the question.

'And what will I become?'

You will become one of us, the first voice intoned. *Or you will die trying.*

PART ONE

HYPERION

So begins **[DATA RESTRICTED]** *testimony of*
[DATA RESTRICTED] *Hyperion of Castian.*
Transcribed by the hand of Scrivener Elrek
[DATA RESTRICTED] *under oath,*
In the Year **[DATA RESTRICTED]** *of His*
Imperial Majesty's Eternal Reign.

ONE
EXECUTION

IMPERIAL DATE: 444.M41

I

They say Fenris breeds cold souls.

I wasn't certain how much of the sentiment was poetic license, but the frozen world definitely left something cold in the blood of its sons and daughters. For better or worse, we are all the children of our home worlds.

Annika wielded her authority with curious ease. I was never a wordsmith to match my brothers, so I found her presence difficult to describe. Galeo would say it best: that she commanded authority with an economy of effort, as if she expected her merest words to be obeyed at all times.

The night we set foot on Cheth I heard him thinking it again, even as I watched Annika work. Galeo read my mind, a passive perception, gently leeching my senses for residual information on what I was witnessing. It left him close enough for me to feel his own surface thoughts in return.

Galeo, of all my brothers, was always the least intrusive. I let him remain in my mind to see what I saw.

Annika was tall, but not unusually so. Her world bred its children tall and strong, and she was no exception. The dark flow of her mane was rare for a Fenrisian: long hair, the sable of clean black silk, was braided into obedience, streaming down one shoulder. Her skin was a healthy pale, the white of winter cliffs rather than the pallid bleach of a consumptive.

The blue of her eyes was rich enough to make others uncomfortable. I had only seen that shade matched by one sight before, in the storm seasons of my own home world. The cryovolcanoes of Titan breathe liquid ammonia and nitrogen into the sky, and in the low gravity, their exhalations freeze into crystals that hang high in the air. Those that do not rain back down to the rocks will drift into the atmosphere and beyond. The irises of her eyes could have been cut from those crystals – they were the same clear glass turned cerulean blue by the night sky.

They were artificial, of course. Despite the exquisite craftsmanship used to shape them in absolute mimicry of human eyes, I could hear the softest clicks when she would use her bio-optics to take a pict. I often wondered if she had chosen the colour for its inhuman hue.

We did not talk often, so the chance to ask had never arisen.

She no longer dressed as a warrior-maiden of her birth world, preferring to go clad in the bodysuits and jackets worn by so many ranking Imperial agents. Still, some trace of her origins remained: at her hip was a throwing axe of white wood and poor-quality bronze, its blade drenched in green patina stains. I sensed a theatrical edge in why she bore the antiquated weapon, but she claimed she'd used it the line of duty several times before. I'd never tried to read beyond her words to seek the truth.

On her back was a bolter, and this gave me pause each time

I saw it. She carried no scaled-down weapon to fit well with human hands. Hers was a mass-calibre Adeptus Astartes bolt-gun, Mk Vb Godwyn pattern, hefted like a cannon when she held it in her gloved hands. Evidence of its craftsmanship was in every contour along the weapon's body: an artisan of rare skill had wrought the black iron alloy with jagged Cretacian runes of dirty gold.

That only raised more questions. I could speak three dialects of Cretacian Gothic, for it was one of the six hundred mongrel threads of the Imperium's root tongue I studied in the course of my training. The weapon had been crafted for her, that much was undeniable. The scripture along the bolter's side proved it, though what deeds she had performed alongside the Flesh Tearers Chapter that claimed Cretacia as their home world, I could not guess.

The weapon, so monstrous in delicate human hands, was rendered usable by a streak of thumbnail-sized suspensors attached to the stock. The rare antigravitic coins – three tiny thimbles of bronze – buoyed the weapon by countering its weight.

She carried the bolter slung over her back, on a thick leather strap.

'My lord regent,' she said, not bothering to smile. 'We must speak.'

The Imperial Regent of Cheth nodded. His expression showed indulgence, as if he had any right to refuse her demand. 'Yes, inquisitor. Indeed we must.'

He was fat to the point of being grotesque. By my estimate, he had fewer than thirty seconds to live.

II

Cheth was a world like ten thousand others.

Populated, clad in a clanking grey covering of industrial

cities, yet claiming neither a forge world's honour, nor a hive world's flesh resources. It paid its Imperial tithes in coin and trade to the subsector capital, which in turn shipped them to the sector hub, and theoretically on to the coffers of Holy Terra. The last Imperial Guard founding was eleven years ago, and raised almost two hundred thousand fresh Guardsmen, known under the collective regimental name 'Cheth Sixteenth Rifles'.

The regiment's nickname for themselves was less official, and obscenely biological. I see no need for its inclusion in this archive.

Cheth supported its own colonies on two nearby mining moons, and maintained a standing defence garrison of one million souls. The Cheth defence force was the usual mixture of veteran ex-Guardsmen and career soldiers, unified with a minor percentage of volunteers who possessed little more training than how to load and shoot straight. A million bodies between invasion and conquest, though. No small figure. Sheer weight of numbers counted where expertise did not.

Even the heavens were well-defended. Thirty-seven weapons platforms orbited the world, and Cheth was a frequent resupply point for Imperial Navy patrols.

Any invader coming to Cheth faced a long, grinding struggle to overthrow a well-defended and entrenched government, making it an unenviable task for the Imperial Guard, should they ever be summoned there.

Even for a contingent of Space Marines, there was no guarantee of an easy victory, or a fast one.

Cheth's delicate infrastructure was ruled by the office of the Imperial regent. Unlike many Imperial worlds answering to a lord governor or governor militant, the seat of the Imperial regent was a spiritual post as much as a temporal one, named in honour of the man who would rule the world in lieu of the absent God-Emperor of Mankind.

How very quaint.

But Cheth differed in one crucial way to ten thousand other Imperial worlds. Those worlds were loyal. Cheth was not.

While deviancy, dissidence and apostasy were hardly rare in the great kingdom humanity had carved across the stars, it was rare for a world in the Imperium's heartlands – with no evidence of former corruption – to fall into sedition. Cheth turned sour, rotting at the core of its government, with the taint threatening to spread to the rest of society's ruling tiers. From there, the spread would never be contained. I knew all of this after studying the Inquisition's briefing data en route to the world. It made for bleak reading.

The wider Imperium had two choices. The first was to wait for public evidence of rebellion, and thus declare a crusade of reclamation; the second was to cut out the cancer at the world's core before it could infect planetary society.

Inquisitor Annika Jarlsdottyr of the Ordo Malleus had chosen on the Emperor's behalf, as was her invested right. She'd kept us at her side for a third consecutive operation, citing that ancient truth: the best way to win a war is to strike before the enemy can fire the first shot.

III

The Imperial regent smiled at Annika.

He grinned, confidence emanating from him in an aura that was almost palpable. I'd seen it before, of course. It was always this way when they had no idea we were there. All he could see opposing him was Annika and her team, and they were plainly not arrayed to do battle.

They stood behind her, not approaching the raised dais as she had. Darford was first, in his dark dress uniform – complete with silver aiguillette ropes from collar to shoulder

– with his moustache and beard neatly trimmed close to his tanned features. He looked curiously incomplete without his weapons, though they would be useless in such confined quarters. I wondered where they were, and if he felt as incomplete as he looked. A simple brush over his thoughts would have provided an answer, but it was hardly the time to bother with such things.

The Khatan was next to him. Her auburn eyes were narrowed, displeasure writ clearly in their depths, and she was clad in her animal furs with the ever-present spear over her shoulder. She had the look of a dreadlocked beast finding itself cornered, as she always did when standing beneath a roof. I didn't need to read her mind to know she felt irritation rather than fear – the Khatan always pined for open sky. She never spoke of it, but her nightmares on long void journeys were loud and unpleasant. In her dreams, she was always trapped, always choking for air that wouldn't come.

Vasilla, robed in black, hadn't come to make war. A lily flower was tattooed beneath her left eye, like some red-inked tear. Short hair the colour of mahogany framed her features. She could be no older than seventeen, and I doubted she was even that. I have never been skilled at judging human age, but Vasilla still walked the border between girl-child and the woman she would soon become.

Like Darford, she lacked weapons. Unlike the elegant Mordian, she did not seem diminished for that fact. With no sloshing tanks of promethium fuel on her back, and no flamer unit in her small fists, her hands were empty, clasped together with fingers linked over her stomach as if in prayer.

Garven Merrick carried his bulky shotgun slung over his back. Asking him to disarm was an exercise in futility, even when it was his mistress giving the order. He wore his scratched, sloping enforcer armour – all evidence of

rank torn off, leaving only the beaten copper aquila on his
chestplate. If Darford sought to display his former affiliation
loud and proud with his dress uniform, Merrick was the
unprepossessing opposite. He wore his armour because it was
reliable, comfortable, and familiar. All traces of his former
life as a lawbringer were absent from the bare carapace gear.
At his side, tall enough to reach his hip, a cyber-mastiff stood
at motionless attention. The enforcer's gloved fingers reached
down to scratch behind the ridged sensor node clusters that
served as the cybernetic hound's ears.

The wretch came last. Clovon, his face a mess of old scarring overlaid by aquila tattoos, was forever deadlier in a game
of cards than with the pistol at his hip or the throwing knives
across his chest. Not for the first time, I wondered how the
inquisitor tolerated his presence. Foul creature.

Annika tossed her head back, perhaps not realising how
she resembled a spirited horse in that moment. Her crystal-
cut eyes were cold reinforcements for her scowl. In truth,
Inquisitor Annika Jarlsdottyr gave very imperious scowls, as
an effective indicator of her temper. I'd been on the receiving
end of several of them.

The regent still smiled. 'We welcome you to our court,' he
said, offering his signet ring to be kissed.

Annika remained where she was, tall and proud, a daughter
of Fenris and an agent of the Emperor's Inquisition. I could
feel her rising ire as she met his eyes. He was taking the wrong
approach with her; not that it would matter for much longer.

'And the last inquisitor.' Annika's voice was a displeased
purr. 'Did you welcome him?'

Several of the courtiers laughed, as if she'd uttered some
great witticism. Her displeasure grated hotter, higher. I could
feel just how keenly she wished to reach for her bolter and
end the charade, but the odds weren't in her favour just yet.

Even for a planetary governor's palace, the royal chamber was ostentatious to the point of caricature. Psyber-cherubs flitted in the throne room's rafters, carrying white silk banners proclaiming the regent's holiness and the many wars won by Cheth's distant Imperial Guard regiments. The vat-grown cloned infants flew on anti-gravitic angel wings of white iron, giggling and communicating in monotone buzzes of information to one another when they weren't singing in choir. They had their uses to those enamoured of vile decoration, I'm sure. I still found the spawning of such things to be an abhorrent and blasphemous waste of resources. Was it mankind's place to breed a soulless imitation of true life? Surely not.

An honour guard of marble statues lined the central red carpet, each one an armed and armoured rendition of a past ruler that had never raised a finger, let alone a blade, in the defence of their world. A dynasty etched in stone, looking down upon the gathered courtiers with expressions of dignified pride.

The regent's seat of rulership rivalled paintings I'd seen of the Emperor's own Golden Throne. Ornate armrests led to a curved back, while the entire thing squatted heftily on twelve thick stumps. For a moment, I wondered what kind of mind could find such a thing beautiful. To my eyes, it resembled something flawed and half-digested. No amount of gold could save its grotesque architecture, though in ages past some maddened craftsman had certainly tried. The throne was a lesser planet's annual wealth incarnated into something grotesque, flanked by royal guards and rising before an ocean of courtiers in forty shades of red.

'My dear,' the regent began. His silks strained to contain the fatty meat beneath. I'd always struggled to respect any soul that could allow the temple of its body to wither into corpulence. Perhaps you couldn't fight age without money and the contacts for rejuvenat surgery – but one can fight sloth alone. A corrupt body is the result of a weak mind.

'You will address me as Inquisitor Jarlsdottyr,' Annika told him. More laughter from the lackeys.

'Inquisitor Jarlsdottyr,' the regent acquiesced with another smile. He wasn't blind to how his smirk aggravated her. Even without touching his mind, I could see the perceptive gleam in his eyes. 'We were overjoyed to learn of your arrival. I trust you have enjoyed your time on our world thus far? The harvest season is a time of great praise to the Emperor. Tell me, inquisitor, have you heard the chants rising from the temple district? Is it not a sound to soothe the very soul?'

'I received Inquisitor Kelman's final astropathic message.' Annika slowly, purposefully, turned to take in the entire throne room. 'I am here by the authority of His Holy Majesty, to do the work of His blessed Inquisition.'

More laughter. Even the regent's chins quivered as he heaved with suppressed chuckles. Without reading his mind, I couldn't tell if it was a facade of feigned confidence, or if he genuinely believed things were going well.

'We have welcomed you to our court, have we not?' For a moment, his honeyed voice pushed my thoughts forwards, leading me to imagine the great speeches he gave at gatherings of the populace. Despite his appearance, his bio-record listed him as a powerful public speaker. I saw the first inklings of it in that moment.

'Enough, regent.' Annika still made no move to go for her weapon. She merely turned back to him. 'I will not allow you to drag this world into sedition with you. Confess, and your execution will be swift. The people of your court will be imprisoned, to be released if they reveal no trace of heresy during interrogation.'

The regent was no longer smiling. His courtiers still

whispered and snorted, but the laughter had faded.

'And if I resist?'

Annika gave a Fenrisian smile, breathing through her bared teeth. 'Resist, and no one leaves this room alive. Either way, the office of Imperial regent on Cheth will no longer exist come the hour of sunfall.'

Sunfall. Another Fenrisian term. Annika always slipped back into instinctive habits when she was losing her temper. She'd probably be snarling soon.

'You presume a great deal, girl,' he told her. Something black moved behind his teeth.

'A governor militant will be appointed to guide Cheth through the turbulent months ahead. Your little coven–' she fairly spat the word, '–won't even make it into the history scrolls.'

The regent stood taller. And taller. And taller. I saw the veins in his face writhe under the skin like whips cracking against a barrier. The thing wearing his body was making itself known at last.

Annika backed away, and a single thought lanced into my mind. My name. She silently said my name.

'Hyperion.'

IV

A thousand kilometres above, I opened my eyes.

'Now,' I said to my brothers.

The chamber's lights fell to deep red as an engagement siren began to whine. Robed adepts worked clanking machines by the chamber's edges.

'Fifteen seconds,' one of the tech-priests called in a blurt of tinny vox-voice.

Each of my brothers was clad as I was. Each of us raised our weapons in unison.

+Are you ready?+ Galeo asked in our minds. The white mist began to rise, clouding the air between us.

'Ten seconds.'

Dumenidon replied for all of us, as he always did. 'For the Sigillite and the Emperor.'

'Five seconds,' called the tech-adept. 'The machine-spirits sing. Initiating telep–'

A blur of pain and fire. A storm of noise and cancerous colour. Liquid nothingness, yet with a spiteful sentience in its tides. It manifested enough solidity to grip at your arms and legs as you fell through it.

Before I could focus my concentration enough to repel the sensation back, we–

–appeared in perfect arrangement, all five of us ringing the regent's throne. Our weapons were still raised: five wrist-mounted storm bolters aiming ten barrels at the convulsing ruler of Cheth. His robes rippled at the tidal mercies of the fleshcrafting beneath.

The sonic boom of our arrival shattered almost all thirty of the great stained-glass windows, letting even more sunlight spill into the throne room. The white mist of teleportation, now poisoned to arterial crimson, lingered in coiling tendrils. Even as it dispersed, it stroked at our armour, dulling the polish.

The regent actually managed to gasp at our appearance. He was flushed and mutable in his spasms, bleeding pus from his tear ducts, but stupefaction and fear halted his change.

Galeo spoke without speaking. The weight of his psychic proclamation was enough to grind my teeth together.

+In the name of the Emperor of Mankind, we do judge thee *diabolus traitoris*. The sentence is death.+

We closed our hands into fists, and five storm bolters boomed in the harmony of absolute rhythmic unity.

The regent's physical form burst across the five of us, painting silver armour with vascular, stringy viscera. Bones shattered and crumbled, blasting apart, cracking off our helms and breastplates. A partially articulated ribcage crashed back onto the throne.

+Peace.+

On the justicar's order, we ceased delivering sentence, but did not lower our weapons. Smoke rose from ten barrels, adding a powdery chemical scent to the surgical reek tainting the raised dais.

Only the regent's shadow remained. It twisted in the centre of the circle we had formed, writhing and clawing at nothing, straining to build a physical form from the air.

+Dumenidon,+ pulsed the justicar.

The named warrior drew his blade in a sharp pull. Each of us added our emotions – our disgust, our revulsion, our hatred – to his own, layering our surface thoughts around his clear, clean rage. The touch of our minds spurred his anger deeper, blacker, into a wrath intense enough to cause him physical pain.

But he was strong. He let his own body and brain become the focus for our psychic force, channelling it along the length of his blade. Psychic lightning danced down the sacred steel, raining fragile hoarfrost to the marble floor.

All of this, from our arrival to the focus of killing energy, happened in the span it took Annika's heart to beat five times. I know that because I heard it. It formed a strangely calming drumbeat to the execution.

Despite barely being able to see it, Dumenidon impaled the crippled shadow with a deep thrust. His blade instantly caught fire. This time, the burst of gore was ectoplasmic and ethereal in nature. Slime hissed against our warded aegis armour plating, failing to eat into the blessed ceramite. The creature's shriek rang in our ears, shattering the few windows our teleportation arrival hadn't.

Thus ended the reign of Regent Kezidha the Eleventh.

I turned to Inquisitor Jarlsdottyr, finding her in a canine crouch halfway down the steps leading up to the throne. A hundred silk-robed courtiers stared at us. Fifty armed palace guards did the same. None of them moved. Most of them didn't even blink. This was not quite the gala ballroom event they had been expecting.

'And them?' I asked her. My voice was a rasp-edged growl from my helm's vox-grille.

'*Skitnah*,' she said, her lips forming a Fenrisian snarl. Skitnah. I knew the word from her home world's tongue. Dirty. Foul. Tainted.

We raised our weapons again. That sent them running.

'I will cage the vermin,' said Malchadiel. He raised his arms as if pushing at the chamber's great double doors, even from this distance. The rest of us opened fire, scything down those fleeing slowest, or who dared raised arms against us. Insignificant las-fire scorched my armour, too sporadic and panicked to be worthy of concern. A crosshaired targeting reticule leapt from robe to robe, flickering white with screeds of biological data.

None of it mattered. These were vermin. I blanked my retinal display with a thought, preferring to fire free.

The nobles of Cheth hammered on the throne room doors, crushing each other in their attempts to escape. Fists beat against the solid bronze, forming a revolting cacophony in their fear. As they wept and screamed, they burst like bloated sacks of blood under explosive bolter shells.

I spared a glance for my brother Malchadiel. He stood rigid

by the throne, facing the double doors, hands taloned by his efforts. Psy-frost rimed his splayed fingers, crackling into ice dust with each fractional movement. The doors held fast as the dying nobles surged against them, and I wondered if he was smiling behind his mask.

Less than a minute later, all guns fell silent and blades slid back into sheaths. Malchadiel lowered his hands at last. The immense bronze doors creaked as they settled back onto their hinges, at the mercy of gravity and architecture once more, rather than my brother's will.

Stinking, opened bodies lay in ruptured repose along the carpet, and a world's worth of aristocratic blood ran across the floor. Annika was toe-deep in a spreading lake of it, clutching her bolter in her hands. Red stains flecked her face in a careless impression of tribal tattoos.

'It's the smell I hate most,' she said.

They do say Fenris breeds cold souls.

Darford's uniform was drenched. There was no way of knowing where one stain ended and another began. His trimmed moustache was fairly trembling with irritation.

'They always do this when you summon them,' he said to Annika. 'Every bloody time.'

Vasilla was on her knees, pressing bloodied palms to her face as part of some pious ritual. She whispered voicelessly through lips that dripped with warm gore, praying to the distant Emperor.

Merrick was distractedly reloading his shotgun, with the percussive *snick, snick, snick* of shells sliding home. The cyber-mastiff stalked around at the other side of the chamber, dipping its bloody iron jaws into the dead.

'Get back here,' Merrick called to it. It obeyed, red eye lenses gleaming.

The Khatan poked a fat corpse with her spear, lifting a gold medallion from its throat. Her grin formed a marble crescent in her tan features. This was her favourite part: after justice came the looting.

+We are returning to orbit,+ Galeo sent to the inquisitor.

Annika inclined her head in gratitude. 'My thanks. We will handle the rest.'

But I turned away. I could hear a heart beating.

'Hyperion?' Annika called.

+Hyperion?+ Galeo echoed inside my mind.

I ignored them, scanning the bodies, letting my eyes follow my ears. The heartbeat was little more than a dull, wet pound, weak with arrhythmia.

There. One of the palace guards – his burst body spread across the carpet – no longer existing from the stomach down. Somehow, he still lived. Loyal to the last, his rifle was in his shaking hands, aimed at the source of all this destruction.

Darford saw the danger in the very same moment. He managed to say half of Annika's name before the guard fired. The lasrifle cracked as it discharged. I lifted my left hand towards the inquisitor as the weapon spat.

She had only half-turned when the energy beam whined aside at the last moment, deflecting to carve a groove in the gilded wall.

A second later, I released my anger as flame. The violet fire ignited him, body and soul. He shrieked as he burned, dissolving to powdery bones in a lake of his own boiling blood. The smell would have been something formidable, but my helm's olfaction filter negated much of its strength.

Annika cleared her throat when nothing but a blackened skeleton leered up at us. Her eyes were fixed upon the burn slash in the white wall.

'Which one of you should I thank for that?' she asked.

I lowered my hand, letting the shield of protective force fade from around her.

'I live to serve, inquisitor.'

TWO

INSTINCT

I

She came to me just over thirteen hours later. The door chimed once before rising on grinding hydraulics. Curiously, she didn't enter right away. She stood in the open doorway, her hands on the steel frame.

'*Mijagge kovness an?*'

'Yes, inquisitor, you may come in.'

'Ah.' She gave a knowing smile. 'No Fenrisian today. You are angry with me.'

Did I seem so? Strange to consider it. I wasn't angry, exactly. She'd been careless in the palace, but no harm had come of it.

'Not quite, inquisitor. I am eager to make speed from the system. That's all.'

Stripped of her wargear and symbols of authority, she was clad in high boots and a black bodyglove undersuit. It clung to her figure with a tension that approached tenacity. My training had torn away the capacity to feel biological desire,

45

but it was still pleasant to watch the ruthlessly feminine grace in the play of her muscles. She was a healthy animal in her prime – a huntress clad in black, her long hair now loose about her shoulders.

Alas, Fenrisians seldom pay heed to such notions as manners. Annika walked into my modest chamber, immediately letting her fingertips glide across the parchment scrolls hanging on the walls.

'Please do not touch those,' I said.

'What are they?'

They were my own writings: parchments detailing the deeds my brothers and I had achieved in the short year since I'd been appointed with honour to serve Justicar Galeo. The reason she couldn't read them was because of the runic language used. I wrote everything of import to our Chapter in Trecenti, one of Titan's encrypted tongues. It used three hundred separate letters in its core alphabet, and had no spoken equivalent.

'They are a private archive,' I told her.

'The paper is beautiful. The texture...' She hesitated, her fingers just shy of touching it again.

'It is papyrus.'

Annika raised an eyebrow. 'Terran?'

I tried not to laugh at the idea of trees on Terra. 'Very amusing, Inquisitor Jarlsdottyr. Is there something I can help you with?'

Annika sighed through her teeth, wolfish even when she didn't mean to be. 'I returned from Cheth not twenty minutes ago. A thorough investigation of the remaining Administratum tiers is now under way, but we have purged the hoggorm nest.'

I said nothing. She looked at my raised eyebrow.

'You do not have hoggorm on Titan, do you?' she asked.

Again, I didn't answer. We had nothing on Titan; the surface of the world was hardly welcoming to life, indigenous or otherwise. She knew that as well as I.

Annika smiled. 'Then what of before Titan? Did you not have reptiles on your birth world?'

This time, I couldn't help but smile. 'You should know better than to ask a Grey Knight about his past, inquisitor.'

Her smile became a grin, all white teeth and bright eyes. 'Perhaps I do know better. Perhaps I like this game, anyway. A hoggorm is a writhing serpent. Very venomous.'

'A snake. I'd guessed, thank you.'

She chose to be oblivious to my dry tone. 'When a new lord militant arrives, he will have to rebuild the infrastructure of planetary governance.'

There was nothing unusual in that. Deep purges often required nothing less, and I didn't understand why she was choosing to tell me all this. There were three inquisitors and their retinues on the surface, of which Annika was merely one. More than enough to deal with such matters. Darford would have called that overkill, in one of his dramatic turns of phrase.

'Inquisitor, the particulars of your bureaucratic restructuring hold no interest for me. I presume you are here for a relevant reason?'

Reading her mind took no effort at all. Irritation was turning each of her thoughts jagged, and her words were mired in hesitation. She knew what she wanted to say, but wasn't sure how to phrase it.

She also expected I would refuse her request once she'd made it. That had me curious.

I withdrew the psychic caress, guiltless about the intrusion. Passionate souls were always the easiest to read. It actually took effort not to hear their thoughts much of the time, and

Annika was a prime example of why. I'd conversed with relatively few humans outside the monastery's walls, but Annika's mind was distinctly among the loudest.

'I have already received a summons to deal with another matter of great urgency. I must leave Cheth at once to deal with it.' An informal sense of dignity buoyed her words. Whatever she had been called to do was something that granted her secret pride. Few tasks would be considered more important than retaining the loyalty of an entire world.

'And?' I prompted.

'And I'm making a formal request to the Titan fortress-monastery to secure your presence for the upcoming operation.'

I finally put down the helm I'd been cleaning. The sacred oils, thrice-blessed by the Purifiers, clinked in their glass jars as I set them aside. She was young. Perhaps she didn't understand what she was asking.

'That is not possible,' I said. 'With our duty on Cheth complete, we are oathbound to serve Inquisitor Harul in the Cybele Reaches.'

'I know it's not customary,' she confessed. 'I also know he has seniority.'

'You have your own team for your purges. We are the final weapon, brought to bear in times of absolute need. What is this duty, that it requires us at your side?'

'I cannot say.'

I laughed at the idea. Nothing was so secret that the Inquisition couldn't reveal it to us. 'That's a lie,' I told her, 'and I do not need to read your thoughts to know it.'

'A slip of the tongue,' she amended with an arch air. 'I could say, but I won't. Not until I'm more certain of the operation's exact details.'

And just like that, I was suddenly curious. 'What code is this undertaking?'

'Code Regalia.' Again, the glimmer of pride in her words. She was honoured and pleased to be summoned for such a vital matter. 'So you cannot, in good conscience, refuse me.'

Maybe so, but conscience had nothing to do with it. In our duty, it rarely did. 'Where is this operation?' I asked.

'Valdasca.'

'Given the empyrean's tides, Valdasca could be as much as two months away under conventional warp flight. Inquisitor Harul's summons still takes precedence. You can summon others of our order to meet you there.'

She scowled, and looked surprisingly regal in doing so. In that moment, she looked very much the warchief's daughter she would have become, had the Inquisition not reached down and plucked her away from Fenris, to serve a finer fate.

'It is less than three weeks for the *Karabela*,' she pointed out, as if I needed telling.

'The *Karabela* is our vessel, inquisitor, not yours. And we are already overdue to serve Harul at Cybele.'

Her thoughts curled, sharpened, growing edges. 'This is not going the way I wished. I have this feeling... On my world, we call it *anellsa*. Do you know this word?'

'I know its meaning. Nevertheless, we cannot remain with you simply because you have a sense of foreboding.'

'Foreboding.' She tasted the word. 'Yes, that's it. And I was right about Cheth, was I not?'

'You also had a great deal of evidence supporting your prosecution of the Cheth aristocracy, not least the last missive of Inquisitor Kelman, three weeks of investigation on the planet's surface, access to the planetary Administratum archives, and the auguries of our own Prognosticars.'

Indeed, the last of those was the reason my brothers and I had been sent with her in the first place. The Prognosticars' vision had been one of rare clarity, heralding a world going dark within the year if the source of the corruption was not ended before it could bloom.

She gave me a look that showed just how little attention she paid to my assurances. 'I trust you,' she said. 'I trust your pack. I want you with me for this.'

I inclined my head in respect, hoping to remove the bite from my words. 'I am honoured by your regard, inquisitor. All of Castian is honoured by the faith you have in us, and I hope we serve you again in the future. But to be blunt, the daemon spoken of in prophecy is banished. We have other duties, closer to other stars. You will come to trust and respect the other Grey Knights that attend you on your next undertaking.'

She narrowed her eyes at me, as if I'd said something intentionally offensive.

'Hyperion, are you always so formal?'

She asked the strangest things, sometimes. 'Yes, mistress. Always.'

'It's very aggravating, you know.'

'I can only apologise.'

I didn't understand why she was being so obstinate. Anellsa? A sense of foreboding? Surely she was far above feeling any lingering acknowledgement of some infantile Fenrisian superstition.

'I wish to journey with the five of you. I need a pack I can trust implicitly, and one I have worked with before. I feel it in my bones.' She jabbed her finger at me accusingly. 'I stood in that chamber with you, surrounded by the bodies of heretics slain with your sacred shells. I've shed blood alongside you many times in these last ten months. Before Cheth, it was Melaxis, and Julland before that. We work well together.'

I decided to stop arguing. We weren't getting anywhere.

'If you are so desperate for our presence, why did you not

go to Galeo? He leads us. I am the youngest of my brothers, and my word carries the least weight.'

She bared her teeth in another smile. 'As hard as it is to believe, you are actually the easiest to talk to.'

I hadn't considered that, nor did I see how it could possibly be true. Thankfully, she denied me the need to reply.

'Will you come with me to speak with the others?' she asked.

I nodded and rose to my feet. 'If you intend to ask them the same question you have asked me, you will receive the same answer. We are sworn to attend Harul immediately.'

Annika's eyes glinted. 'We shall see.'

II

Malchadiel was first.

He stood in the starboard docking bay, unhelmed, with his eyes closed. The air literally tremored with his concentration – a faint shiver of resistance met us, as if we waded through the thinnest liquid.

The air was also populated by debris. It hung above the ground, orbiting Malchadiel with stellar serenity, making him the star at the heart of a system of scrap. Metal tubing turned in the slow aerial dance, along with focusing lenses, rivets, screws, bolts and slats of matt-black armour plating.

Whatever he was working on, its component parts floated around him in conflicting directions without ever colliding. Annika weaved out of the way as a gun barrel drifted past her head.

'What the...' Her sentence ended in hushed Fenrisian invective.

'I was not expecting a distraction.' Malchadiel's tone was dense and tight, showing just how much he was focusing. 'Please give me a moment.'

The servitors and loader crews gave him a wide berth. They

laboured at the far end of the hangar, a population existing at our sufferance and in our service. In their red robes,
adepts of the Palladium Kataphrakt went about their worship, soothing the machine-spirits of the cradled tanks and
gunships. Even from this distance, I could smell the sanguine
tang of their incense.

The mess Malchadiel had made began to condense and
twist together in the air, with only the faintest whisperings
of metal against metal as each chunk of debris met. Screws
rolled unerringly into place, turning of their own accord to
spiral down and lock tight. I watched a series of focusing
lenses drift into a piecemeal gun barrel, while unseen hands
screwed each section together with patient care.

Annika caught on at last, and the realisation narrowed her
eyes. In less than a minute, a fully assembled, many-barrelled
multilaser turret hovered in the air before Malchadiel. He
lowered it to the decking with a gesture.

'Practice goes well?' I asked.

'I am getting faster, but the greatest progress is in how
much control I can exert over each piece in my grip. Yes,
brother, it goes well. Thank you for asking.'

Annika was still looking at the armoured turret with its gun
barrels resting on the deck.

'You took that from my tank,' she said.

'Yes.' Malchadiel gave a small smile. 'I did. And I will return
it before you require the use of it. I needed a construct of suf-
ficient complexity to remain challenging.'

She exhaled something like a growl, seeming to dwell
on just how best to reply. The two of them could argue for
hours. I'd seen it happen several times, and decided to abort
this argument before it could begin.

'The inquisitor comes to us with a request,' I said to
Malchadiel.

'Does she now?' His pale eyes turned to Annika again. 'Strange then, that she comes to us, not the justicar. How may we be of service, inquisitor?'

'I wish to appeal to the Titan monastery to secure your presence at my side for another undertaking. My demand takes equal precedence to your next duty with Inquisitor Harul in the Cybele Reaches.'

Malchadiel turned to me. 'Brother, please explain this performance of Fenrisian humour. If this is some witticism, it is beyond my grasp.'

Annika snuffed a lock of hair from her face. 'I'm quite serious.'

'She's quite serious,' I said, scratching my cheek to hide my smile.

'I see.' Malchadiel gestured for two of the Palladium Kataphrakt adepts to come forwards.

'Sire?' they said in unison. I couldn't see their faces beneath the hoods, but one voice was human, the other warbled through a vocabulator.

Malchadiel gestured to the gun turret. 'Please restore this to its rightful place. You have my thanks.'

His manners set him apart from any other soul I knew. No one ever addressed a Machine Cult menial adept with quite the same needless politeness as Malchadiel. He even said please and my thanks to servitors, though the lobotomised cyborg slaves never acknowledged it.

The two tech-priests set to their task, deploying several additional servo-arms from their robes in order to lift the turret. Malchadiel moved aside to let them work, and turned his eyes back to the inquisitor.

'May I ask why you have not taken this unorthodox request to Justicar Galeo?'

Annika shrugged. 'This way felt right. To ask you all first, before going to the *jarl*. I'd hoped to enlist your agreement.'

Malchadiel's unscarred face showed none of his surprise. He was, as always, consummate at shielding his emotions.

'And why would we agree to remain at your side, when such an act would require breaking an oath to another inquisitor? The Prognosticars' vision has been averted with absolute finality. Cheth is cleansed. Castian is pledged to answer another lord's summons.'

'I knew you would say that.' Annika gave her Fenrisian grin again. 'I wish to speak with Sothis next. He will agree with me.'

III

Neither Sothis nor Malchadiel had served for much longer than I. They'd passed their trials and earned their armour only six years before I'd taken my final oaths and earned my own place in the Chapter.

To me, they were already veterans. I felt as though an eternity separated us, for six years in sworn service was six years of harrowing, gruelling frontline purges I could scarcely imagine.

Yet the two of them were still considered fresh blood by the Chapter. More than that, in an order that held no faith in notions of fortune and luck, these two represented the absolute pinnacle of improbability. Sothis and Malchadiel were a mathematical miracle, manifest in skin and bone.

Our training scours the mind beyond simple lobotomy. All memory is flensed away, stripped and removed as a surgeon cuts cancer from healthy flesh. Sothis and Malchadiel were no different to any of us in that regard. They remembered nothing of their lives before coming to Titan as children.

But one had only to look at them to see that they were twins, true twins, brothers by blood as well as by the bond of sworn oaths.

I can't accurately record the sheer number of infants harvested from the Imperium who fail in their training on Titan, to die forgotten and alone in the bowels of our fortress-monastery. I've seen archival evidence that for every million children stolen by our agents, a single one survives to become a Grey Knight. The rest are fated to end their lives as servitors, Chapter serfs, or more likely as names in the Archives of Failure.

And yet, within our ranks were two sons of the same ovum. The odds against such an occurrence were beyond astronomical, deep into the realm of being laughable.

Malchadiel bore little evidence of his half-decade as a knight of the fortress-monastery. The same couldn't be said for Sothis. He wore his battles plainly, each of them written upon the re-stitched mask of his face. The structure of his visage still resembled his brother's, but his face was a discoloured mesh of bare bionics, regrown flesh and synthetic skin. Most of his teeth were replacement metal pegs set into his gums, and the left side of his lips was pulled by overtight flesh into a permanent, crooked sneer.

We found him in reverent meditation. His patchwork features softened as he ceased his chanting, but he didn't rise from his knees at the centre of his small chamber.

'Is something amiss?' he asked.

I gestured to Annika.

'I wish to speak with you all,' she said. 'I have been issued a Regalia-code summons, and I require the presence of hunters from your order.'

'Knights,' all three of us said at once. 'Not "hunters",' I amended.

She breathed slowly, and again it was almost a growl. 'You know what I meant.'

Sothis never smiled, for his wounds denied the expression.

However, his amusement reached his eyes. 'I am intrigued. What is this undertaking?'

Annika grunted in dismissal. 'I will not speak of it until your agreement is secured.'

'Is this a joke that I have failed to comprehend?' Sothis glanced to me. Both of his eyes were still natural – practically the only part of his face that had escaped his grievous injuries.

'Evidently not,' I told him. 'She hopes we might help her convince Galeo to remain at her side.'

Sothis rose to his feet in a chorus of low snarls from his armour joints. 'Inquisitor?' he asked her.

She nodded, just once. 'Your brother Hyperion speaks the truth.'

Sothis's abused cheeks tightened again, hardening the ugly smear of his lips into a rictus. 'Very well. Let us first find Dumenidon.'

IV

He was training, which was a surprise to none of us. He hadn't even removed his helm.

The blade in his hands was a blur of deactivated cerulean, moving fast enough to sing in sharp chimes as it sliced the unresisting air. I confess, it was always a pleasure to watch Dumenidon move. He had no equal among us with a sword, executing each cut and thrust to seamless perfection. Few warriors, even among our order, could claim such flawless control over a blade. He personally mentored Sothis, but even the mutilated twin scarcely came close to Dumenidon's skill.

In a great deal of human literature, it is a cliché to state that a fighter's weapon is an extension of their body. Such a sentiment, thought trite, at least comes close to describing the reality. His mastery over the blade's movements was more than post-human, it was consummate. I'd never once seen him make a mistake. Not one.

I'd beaten him a handful of times in our sparring over the last year, though I had an advantage few of our order could claim. I didn't use a blade.

Dumenidon ended his whirling display before us, sheathing the sword as part of the final motion. Even coming to rest, he was an exemplar of grace. To my shame, I envied him his prowess.

'Kindred,' he greeted us. His helm regarded each of us with eye lenses of emotionless blue. 'Inquisitor?'

Annika stepped forwards. 'I have something to ask of you.'

The ceramite mask tilted slightly. 'I am listening.'

V

We stood before Galeo soon after.

The *Karabela*'s strategium was an orderly chamber, resembling a prayer room as much as a traditional warship bridge. Coal-burning braziers stood by command consoles, their rich, smoky fumes inhaled by the air filtration systems to be cleansed and recycled. Scrolls were draped across the walls, some penned in my hand, others written in the script of those who had come before me. Nine banners hung from the fresco-painted ceiling: each of them a great victory worthy of inclusion in the monastery's own Hall of Valour, achieved since Justicar Castian founded the squad ten thousand years before.

The most recent, depicting a lone knight, haloed in vibrant gold thread, was woven by the Chapter serfs in memory of the Ajanta Insurrection. This last knight stood in a circle of nine fallen brothers, his blade deep in the skull of a slain daemon. The creature itself was a stylised representation of something drawn from human legend – I recognised many of its features from the devils and false gods of Hinduvian mythology. The serfs had never borne witness to the great beast itself, and thus could be forgiven for their embellishment.

The scrollwork at the banner's base reeled the names of the fallen, and the sole survivor. The latter was a single name in flowing Gothic script: *Galeo*.

The warrior himself, now six years past the battle that killed his brothers and elevated him to leadership, stood unhelmed before the oculus screen. He watched the planet turn below, bearing witness to its infinitely slow dance in the void. His thoughts were unquiet, rumbling things that almost melted into the thrum of the idling drive engines. He was dwelling on something – the thoughts had the sepia quality of distant memories.

Galeo turned at our approach, while the nearby serfs all bowed in a whisper of robes. The servitors ignored us, continuing their murmuring attention to their duties. Bionic limbs thudded on the deck as the mono-tasked cyborgs went about their business.

Captain Talwyn Castor lounged in the command throne, reading a data-slate in his gloved hands. He offered us a faint nod upon entering, but it was clear he was busy. He wore his experience like a uniform – a man unashamed by the burn scarring that speckled and pockmarked his throat and the left side of his face. Rather than receive an augmetic implant, he kept his ruined eye masked behind an archaic patch of black cloth.

Galeo greeted us with a bow.

+Brothers,+ he pulsed into our minds. +Inquisitor. What brings you to the strategium?+

Annika never bowed, not to anyone. Instead, as always, she tilted her head back slightly, baring her throat for a moment.

I sensed from her thoughts just how she viewed the gesture of respect, performing it exactly the same way she would offer greeting to a tribal jarl on her home world.

'Justicar Galeo. My astropath has received word of an immediate summons. With the principal purge of Cheth complete, I must make speed to the Valdasca Caul.'

Galeo was another man who wore his wounds well. Except for the scar tissue ringing his neck like a torc, he was unbroken by a century and a half in service to the order. He scratched at his throat, an unconscious habit that always drew attention to the choker of lumpy, pale flesh.

+Valdasca.+ His dark eyes never left her face.

Annika met him eye for eye. Despite her Fenrisian height, she still had to crane her neck to look up at him.

'I understand that you are oathbound to attend Inquisitor Harul on his ongoing operation. Nevertheless, I ask you to remain with me while I journey to the Caul. Harul can summon another force from the monastery. I want you for this duty. I want the *Karabela*, and I want Squad Castian.'

Galeo smiled at the praise. Relations between the Inquisition and its Chamber Militant were always ruthlessly efficient, but they were rarely warm. Galeo considered Annika's demeanour as something of a pleasant rarity.

+Harul's need is as urgent as yours. He possesses our oath of service, and his duty is closer. If you wish to retain our blades, I will need to know why.+

For the first time, Annika looked uncertain. I'd never seen her hesitate in doubt before, and I found it a strangely compelling sight. She looked very human in that moment – so vulnerable, young and ultimately mortal.

Humans. Sometimes it's easy to forget how fragile they are.

+I sense your caution, my lady,+ Galeo sent. +Commune with me.+

He locked us out of the communion. As simple as that; as easy as a moment's thought, he shielded his thoughts from all of us, speaking to Annika in psychic secrecy.

Their communion lasted no more than three heartbeats. It ended when she closed her eyes and nodded.

Galeo's words returned to our minds. +I see. And why did you bring my kindred here, inquisitor?+

Her honesty was admirably blunt. 'I hoped they would trust me enough to lend their support, even if I could not reveal the mission's details.'

Galeo regarded us in turn. +She asks us to break an oath of service. Should we serve her and forsake one duty for another? The decision is mine to make as Justicar of Castian, but I would hear your thoughts first. What say you, brothers?+

Sothis answered first. 'I trust the inquisitor's judgement. I would travel with her. Necessity or not, we are with her already.'

'Let Harul summon others from the monastery,' Malchadiel agreed. 'The *Karabela* will allow her to reach her objective in a fraction of the time. A Regalia-code assignment requires nothing less.'

Dumenidon shook his head. 'I abstain from the decision. I have no desire to break an oath, nor turn my back on one duty to fulfil another. I will follow the judgement of my justicar.'

Galeo nodded at each answer. +And you, Hyperion?+

'I find it intriguing that she even asked us, rather than demanding our presence. I would travel at her side, if it came down to a choice.'

+Then we will journey with Inquisitor Jarlsdottyr.+

A tide of questioning thought rippled from each of us. Galeo moulded a reply.

+The warship *Frostborn* lies dead in the void at the heart of the Valdasca Caul.+

I could feel the tight, narrow focus of his silent voice. If a standard psychic emanation was akin to a shining a light upon a mind, this was a thin, sharp blade of communication, jabbing directly at each of us. The justicar was taking great care to ensure no nearby minds overheard his words. Each of us shifted our own speech to the same unspoken communion.

+I know that name.+ Dumenidon leeched a touch of Galeo's strength to respond with the same focus. The justicar offered it readily, for Dumenidon always struggled with the subtlest use of his powers. Some of us were born to be blunter instruments than others.

We all knew the name. Annika had served aboard the *Frostborn*, albeit briefly. She always told those tales with a smile.

Galeo nodded, sensing our understanding. +According to the inquisitor's summons, an Imperial Navy patrol found a Hunter-class destroyer powered down and cold in the void, deep within the Valdasca Caul. It has been confirmed as the *Frostborn*. The jarl's daughter is the closest agent of the ordos with the clearance to investigate, thus the responsibility falls to her.+

+And to us,+ I added. Proximity to the others using their powers always strengthened my own. It was no effort at all to embrace Galeo's psychic pulse, reform it, and push it back with my own words within. +Where was the *Frostborn* assigned before it met this fate?+

It was Annika who answered, still bound to our silent speech. *'When I left, they were bound for the Jopal and Ruis systems,'* her voice drifted through our minds.

Jopal. Ruis. I knew those stars from my study of stellar cartography. They were close to Tisra, the star that warmed the

manufactory-dense hive world of Armageddon, but there
was little else of interest nearby.

+My thanks, inquisitor. The Valdasca Caul is a far cry from
Jopal and Ruis.+

Galeo's agreement came with a moment's hesitation.
+They were almost certainly warp-lost.+

I was smiling behind my faceplate, and I suspect each of
them knew it. +At the very least, it will be interesting.+

'You sound eager,' Malchadiel said with his true voice.

'I am,' I admitted, then added in silent speech: +I have
never met a Wolf before.+

'Yes.' Annika bared her teeth in a particularly feral smile.
'You have.'

THREE

DUST

I

The Valdasca Caul is named for the streak of ionised sulphur and hydrogen gases forming a pale, ashen nebula through the subsector's coreward edge. The Caul blankets several suns and their respective worlds, bleaching them clean of life and drowning entire solar systems in lethal gases. Mankind has never settled here, and to my knowledge, neither have any of the xenos breeds. Few regions of the galaxy are anathema to all life, but the Caul is one of them.

The first thing I sensed upon arrival was the raining of dust against the hull, as the clanging rattles woke me from my meditations. For a murky moment, I recalled a similar clattering: the sound of hard rain beating down on tin roofs and metal window frames. Instinct forced me to reach for the memory, but it fled as soon as I focused upon it, sifting from my mind the way sand falls through open fingers.

It happens from time to time, these flashes of insight into

a denied life. Childhood memories can tease the senses when accidentally dredged up by meditation. Such things are stripped from our psyches in the very first stages of our training, yet there are always echoes. We were born human, and despite the proximity to perfection offered by the Emperor's Gift, we still carry a few of the flaws that plague our birth-species.

I opened my eyes as the ship shook around me. More particulate clattered against the hull with a gritty, rattling lack of tempo. The nearby minds on other decks were wild and emboldened, fired by our arrival.

I fastened my helm into place, gathered my weapons, and left the broken solace of my arming chamber behind.

II

The Khatan and Vasilla waited outside the strategium's eastern doors, speaking in low voices. For Vasilla, this was as natural as breathing. The girl had a mouse's voice, barely more than a whisper. By contrast, the Khatan's voice could cut cold iron – for her to speak quietly meant the sharing of secrets.

'Mistresses,' I acknowledged them.

'Master Hyperion.' The girl pressed her palms together and offered a bow.

The Khatan grinned, white teeth in a face the colour of burnt honey. Her dreadlocks hung down in their usual mess of dark tangles. She was the only Attilan I had ever met, but I'd studied the archives on their society. Their clans took great pride in being an unwashed people. The Khatan exemplified this cultural tendency, though it gave her an earthy, natural scent of sweat, rather than one of sloth.

'Two-Guns,' she said. 'How do you fare, my handsome killer?'

Her flirtation didn't make me uncomfortable, but nor was I sure of how to respond to it. I always struggled to understand the point of her humour. Perhaps that was the point of it. I was none the wiser, and had no desire to be illuminated.

'Why do you remain outside?' I asked.

Vasilla's youthful face was the picture of serenity. 'We await the inquisitor,' she said. 'Your kindred are already within.'

I turned to face an empty side corridor, sensing the approach of two more minds. Darford and Clovon rounded the corner together; the former clad in his impeccable dress uniform, the latter in his jacket and loose clothes. Darford smelled of clean skin and the artificial musk of his aftershave. Clovon smelled of lies and polished knives.

'Which one are you?' Darford asked me. 'Actually, don't tell me. I'll get it right this time.'

This was a game I'd grown bored of some time ago. I leaned, just slightly, to show the name etched in burnished gold lettering upon my shoulder guard.

'Ah, of course,' he said. 'Hello, Hyperion.'

Clovon didn't greet me. He lingered at the edge of their group, his lacerated face turned away from me. Unlike Sothis, who bore the ruin of his visage as a legacy of honourable battle, Clovon's wounds were the neatly arranged, symbolic marks of ritual desecration. To stand in the presence of one who had been a heretic... I felt a foul taste in my mouth from even looking at him.

Darford ran his thumbs down the sides of his close-trimmed beard. 'I loathe boarding actions, you know. Have I mentioned that?'

'Once or twice,' Clovon said softly.

'A thousand times,' said the Khatan with mock gravity.

'No place for a sniper,' said the uniformed soldier. 'That's all I'm saying. If Annika doesn't start choosing her missions more carefully, I may just go back to Mordian and take that promotion they offered me. I'd be a colonel by now, you know. Colonel Frederic Darford of the Iron Guard. That's got quite a ring, now I think about it.'

The Khatan spat onto the decking. 'Always the same whining. Enough. Spare my ears for one week.'

The sniper's smile was amusingly rehearsed. From prying into his mind on more than one occasion, I knew he practised in front of the mirror a great deal, seeking a smile that made him look the most handsome. He liked to think he wielded it as a weapon.

'Can you even hear me, my filthy darling? Can you hear anything with all that dirt in your ears?'

'Perhaps I read your babbling lips, *nai-mori*.' The Khatan grinned as she used the Attilan insult for a warrior who went into battle on foot, rather than mounted on a horse. I'd read that honour duels were fought on her world over the use of that slur. As grave cultural insults went, it seemed a curious one: the equivalent to naming a man incapable of hunting for himself and his tribe, or being too weak to fight in a clan war.

I listened to their banter, watching in silence, unsure of what to say. Any words I spoke would jar the flow of their conversation, so I opted to say nothing at all. I rarely had the chance to witness humans interacting like this.

Clovon was watching me. His thoughts betrayed him – he had no capacity to mask his deeper thinking. The facade of disinterest was brittle, the way drying lava forms a crackable crust over the fusion of ooze beneath. He was afraid of me, and he was the kind of man to hate what he feared. You couldn't hide emotion like that.

Annika's timely arrival spared anything more on the matter. Her black hair was arranged in long twin braids hanging over her shoulders, in some Fenrisian arrangement that I suspected was supposed to be either feminine or regal. Perhaps both. To me, it seemed neither.

'Hyperion,' she greeted me.

'My lady.'

'Were you waiting for me?'

I had no desire for her to know I'd lingered here, captivated by the casual way humans spoke to one another. Still, I would speak no lies. Not to her.

'No, my lady.'

Her smile told me that she knew why I'd waited. She was a keen one.

'Come, then.' She gestured to the doors. 'Let's see what there is to see.'

III

The hololith flickered above the projector table in grainy, distorted mimicry of the image on the oculus screen. The *Frostborn* was a standard Adeptus Astartes destroyer, meaning it bristled with weaponry, statuary, jagged battlements, and was close in size and bulk to the *Karabela*. Our own vessel was a modified Nova-class frigate, better armed and much faster than its counterparts in the Imperial Navy or the lesser Chapters. We were the only Grey Knights on board.

The *Frostborn*, an escort vessel of the Space Wolves Chapter, looked both familiar and unknown, all at once. I recognised the standard patterns of its battlements and gun batteries, yet the icons of wolves' heads rendered it different enough to be unfamiliar.

'I see no signs of battle damage.' Malchadiel reached for the hololith, rotating it with the sensor pads in his gauntlets' fingertips. He turned it slowly, his expression rapt. For some reason, he reminded me of a child delicately holding a family heirloom.

'Definitely no battle damage,' he confirmed.

The strategium had its usual muted hum of activity as the serfs and servitors went about their duties. The five of us stood with the inquisitor's team, close to the central table.

Galeo's voice flowed through our minds. +What of the damage along the battlements and central spine?+

'Damage, yes. But it isn't battle damage. If you look at the superficial bleaching...' Malchadiel turned the image towards Galeo, '...there. The ship should be blue-grey, in the colours of the Chapter. But the armour plating is bleached and melted into this colourless nothingness. That's the surest sign of how she took so much damage.'

Galeo nodded, unsurprised. +I had an unpleasant feeling you would say that, brother.+

'I don't follow,' the Khatan admitted.

Malchadiel rotated the image again, baring the ship's slender, skeletal back as he continued. 'The malformations along the superstructure are almost definitely the result of aetheric scarring. The spinal concourse is torn in enough places to depressurise the entire vessel, even without the rest of this...' he ran a fingertip along the ship's side, '...this extensive damage. But none of it was inflicted by weapons used in void warfare.'

'Wait.' Darford cleared his throat. 'Aetheric scarring?'

Malchadiel was still cradling the ruined destroyer. 'Damage from the warp's tides. She was running through the warp without a Geller field.'

'For how long?' asked Annika.

'Seconds. Hours. Years.' Malchadiel shook his head. 'There is no way of telling without plundering the onboard archives. And even that presumes the vessel's animus machinae is still sane, and remains alive. If it's dead, we will be unable to recover the archived information without a great deal of effort.'

'Uh.' Darford cleared his throat again. He didn't speak High Gothic. 'The animus machinae?'

'He means the machine-spirit,' I explained. 'The ship's soul. Have we detected any life signs?'

'Unquantifiable,' Malchadiel admitted. 'There is a trace sign, but the Caul is ruinous to auspex sweeps.'

I turned from the hololith to watch the ship itself, hanging in the void. 'She is powerless and open to the void, and she's survived an unshielded run through the warp. But there are trace signs of life?'

Malchadiel wouldn't abandon the holo-image. Its flickering green light bathed his face. 'The mystery deepens, brothers. Do you see the damage along the second and fourth quadrants?'

The warriors of Castian nodded, but the Khatan leaned over the table to see. Malchadiel moved the hololith away from her – a child unwilling to share a toy.

'The holes?' she asked. 'Aren't they the same warp wounds?'

'Aetheric scarring,' Malchadiel corrected. 'And no, they are not. Look at the way the ablative armour is wrenched outwards, like the petals of a flower in bloom. These hull ruptures are all from internal sources. Something inside broke its way out. Many things, judging by the number of ruptures.'

The Khatan sniffed. 'Your eyes are better than mine, Ironmonger.' Malchadiel couldn't quite resist a smile at the tribeswoman's nickname for him.

Darford's sniper-eyes were a touch keener. 'I count thirty-three hull breaks on the port side.'

I'd counted the same. Some were large enough to drive a tank through. 'What of the Navy vessels that found the *Frostborn*?' I asked.

Annika consulted a data-slate. 'It was a patrol of Viper-class destroyers, led by the *Indefatigable Heart*. Their long-range sensors found the *Frostborn*, but their mandate was to ghost the edges of the Caul. The patrol captain requested – and was explicitly denied – permission to sail into the dust from the Holy Ordos.'

'The Viper patrol, were they mere pirate-hunters?' Dumenidon asked. 'I am not familiar with the Naval vessel classes of this subsector, but I know this nebula is a haven for reavers.'

The inquisitor nodded. 'The Vipers were ill-equipped to deal with a threat like this,' she confirmed. 'It was brave of them to even ask permission to investigate.'

'There's a fine line between bravery and ignorance,' I ventured. 'Has there been any vox-contact with the destroyer since we arrived?'

'Nothing, brother.' Malchadiel finally released the hololithic image. Freed of his grip, it drifted into the slow roll being performed by the actual warship in the dust cloud.

Annika wrinkled her nose. 'Not even a distress beacon?'

'No, mistress.'

I looked at the others as they stood in silence. 'But what of the psychic cry?' I asked. 'Have we managed to source it?'

'The… what?' Annika turned to me.

Everyone turned to me.

'Can't you hear it?' I asked, growing unsure myself now. After a moment, my gaze found Galeo. I sensed him quest out, linking with my sixth sense the way a hunting hound would snuff after a scent.

+I hear it now,+ he said. +An indistinct whine into the warp. Human, or close enough to feign humanity with ruthless accuracy.+

I nodded, for I'd heard it the same way. 'I don't understand how the astropaths could have missed it.'

The justicar watched me for a long moment. Judgement rode in that gaze, even hidden behind his eye lenses.

+They missed it because it is so weak,+ he said at last. From the focus of the message, I knew it was designed only for my mind to hear. +You are growing strong, Hyperion.+

+Thank you, justicar.+

Annika tapped her knuckles on the table – another of her habits when concentrating. 'The saga twists,' she said with an annoyed sigh. 'Very well. Go aboard. Make preparations for my team to join you as soon as it is deemed an acceptable risk.'

She glared at the oculus where the powerless vessel turned in the void, enslaved to gentle, unfading momentum. 'I want to see inside that ship,' she said at last.

We saluted as one.

+Gunship insertion into the port docking bay.+ Galeo gestured to the sealed bay doors. +Dumenidon will lead us in the preparatory rituals. We will be aboard the *Frostborn* within the hour.+

FOUR

FROSTBORN

I

A Space Wolves warship. At least, the remains of one.

In a way, it had come full circle. From birth in the frost of Fenris, it now drifted dead in the deep void, lost to ice and far from any sun. The ship's oceans of coolant and internal oils were likely hard as diamond, blocking the internal systems beyond hope of thaw.

My first step onto the hangar deck sent a gentle hum through my armour. With the power out and the ship open to the void, the bay was a hive of silence and zero gravity. Beyond my slow breathing, sighing through my helm's respiratory feed, the only sound was Sothis's murmurs as he locked his own boots to the deck behind me.

A pair of human eyeglasses, almost certainly the former property of a Chapter serf, tapped against my shin. I glanced down at them as they drifted away. Blood flecked the corrective lenses.

'The chamber is riddled with debris,' Dumenidon voxed. 'Personal items. Drifting rockets and ammunition crates. Several lifter/loaders. The Wolves' one gunship and Rhino troop carrier are both secured to the deck. The ship has taken on dust and grit from the nebula. Visibility in human spectrums is poor. Eye lenses compensating.'

'Bodies?' came the inquisitor's crackling reply. We could barely hear her. The dust was murder to vox cohesion.

'None. No bodies.' I disengaged my magnetic seals and drifted ahead of the others, rising to the chamber's girder-thick roof. To move, I dragged myself gently across the ceiling. A loose, unfired bolter shell *clacked* off my shoulder guard, slowly spinning away. 'There's nothing here, inquisitor. Nothing alive.'

Her reply was stolen by static distortion.

'Repeat, please,' I said. 'Interference.'

Again, her words were abused by the struggling vox.

'Justicar, I am losing contact with the *Karabela*.'

+I've lost her, as well.+ I felt Galeo inside my head, a soft presence without the solidity to be intrusive. +It was to be expected.+

+Inquisitor,+ I reached out to her.

'*I hear you.*' She sounded close enough to be standing next to me. Close enough to be sharing my suit of armour. With a momentary lurch of perception, I twisted in the air, locking my boots onto the ceiling. '*Show me what you see,*' she said.

Sharing my senses was one of our gifts that had always come easily to me. It took a fragment of concentration to open myself to what I was seeing – past the flickering target locks and scrolling runes of my retinal display. The angle of the chamber as I stood upon its ceiling; the revolving stars beyond the open bay doors; the debris drifting through the air, like the wreckage in a drowned city.

Our Stormraven gunship was a bloated silver tick latched onto the hangar deck, its tongue unrolled into a gangramp. Malchadiel, the last of us, was descending it now. Sothis had drifted over to the Predator tanks in their ordered rows, and was brushing his hands over their bleached, deformed armour plating. Galeo stood by the open docking bay doors, staring out into space. Dumenidon had stomped across the platform towards a deactivated control panel, and was clearing floating crates aside to reach it.

'I see,' came Annika's response. For a split second, I reached too far into the bond between us, and my vision doubled as I saw through her senses. She stood in the *Karabela's* strategium, facing the oculus. Darford and Clovon were with her. The heretic was muttering something.

My surge of irritation strained the psychic union, leaving my vision watery and indistinct. It took a moment to claw it back to stability, little different from staring into darkness and waiting for your eyes to adjust.

'What happened?' she asked.

+Nothing.+

'Now I can hear you whispering something.'

I was reciting the ninety-second litany of absolute focus. Rather than answer her, I turned to the reason I'd drifted up to the ceiling. Manoeuvring through the girders was no trial at all; no incidental contact would breach my armour. The inquisitor's presence receded, leaving her a passive observer through my senses.

Blood had frozen into a crystal crust along several of the dark iron beams. It flaked away under my touch, turning to red powder in the dusty air.

+Kindred,+ Galeo sent. +Be ready to move on. Hyperion, what of the psychic distress call?+

'It ceased the moment we set foot aboard,' I voxed. 'This

feels like a very crude trap, justicar.'

+Almost certainly. Stay alert.+

I unlocked my boots and kicked off the ceiling, drifting through the debris. At the last moment, I turned and landed on the hangar deck, relocking my stabilisers.

'No bodies.' Malchadiel echoed what we all knew, and what we were all still thinking. 'They have a gunship here, and never managed to reach it.'

Through my psychic link to Annika, I heard Darford's distant grumble. *'This just gets better.'*

II

An Adeptus Astartes warship is a bastion in the void, designed to break blockade fleets, rain bombardment upon the surface of a world, and face down warships many times its size. Many of the secrets in our fleet vessels' exact design are lost to us, predating the Imperium, with their roots back in the Dark Age of Technology. Suffice to say, any Imperial Space Marine warship is a fortress in space, and its insides are a labyrinth of ornate architecture and grand chambers.

We made our way from the modest hangar bay, consulting retinal schematics as we moved to the primary armoury. While a Hunter-class destroyer lacked the scale of its larger cousins, it wasn't entirely devoid of majesty. Wolf-headed gargoyles leered from the walls, watching us with frosted faces and unblinking eyes. Door arches showed carvings of elaborate bronzeworking, which would be considered masterpieces on many worlds. Gold-leaf runes ran the lengths of whole corridor walls, while many of the chambers boasted entire floors encrusted with mosaic tiles. In the gothic bowels of these warships, ostentation met practicality like nowhere else in mankind's galaxy.

We didn't split up. We were Grey Knights, not a pack of

idiotic salvagers. Each of us had been raised and trained to act as his brother's shield, and we kept our minds faintly linked, ready to see through each other's senses at a moment's notice.

The artificial pulse of Malchadiel's auspex scanner was a clockwork heartbeat we couldn't ignore. It *tick, tick, ticked* in contemplative rhythm, seeing nothing, hearing nothing, sensing nothing.

We moved with our weapons high. As always, Galeo and Dumenidon led the way. I walked as rearguard, my storm bolter raised and my pistol in my other hand.

The ship had suffered, there was no doubt. A serf or servitor team navigating through the wreckage would have required a great deal of doubling back on themselves to seek other passages. Any blockages we found, where wreckage barricaded the way, were cleared by Malchadiel and Galeo working in telekinetic unity. They hauled the mangled iron aside with pulls and bursts of kinetic force.

Malchadiel was breathing in low grunts over the vox by the time he wrenched aside the thirtieth pile of twisted iron. His primary gift was as a telekine, but the human body has limits, even one implanted with the Emperor's Gift. Psychic ice hoarfrosted his armour, flaking away when he flexed his muscles to refocus.

We found the first bodies in the primary armoury chamber. Servitors and Chapter serfs decorated the room in murdered profusion, hanging silent in the weightless air. Each corpse told of a foul death: the bodies were burst open, pulled apart, or cleaved clean in twain.

The first corpse of note sat slumped against the wall, a ceramite-clad hand on its armoured stomach. He'd died while failing to restore the ropes of his intestines to his belly. Like us, he'd locked his boots to the deck. Unlike us, he was unarmed. A rune-inscribed bolter drifted just out of his reach.

'*Sova gudt, hell'ten,*' Annika murmured in my mind – a Fenrisian benediction for a hero to rest in peace. Unfamiliar with the Chapter's inner workings, I didn't recognise the company markings on his war plate: a riveted iron wolf staring from his shoulder, with wolf-tail talismans hanging from his belt. A pool of frozen blood spread in all directions from his corpse at its epicentre. Not all of the discoloured fluid was human.

+Hyperion,+ Galeo prompted. I knew what he wished.

'Aye, justicar.'

I walked to the corpse, letting my fingers rest on his helm. The warrior's hanging head left him staring down at what was left of his torso.

+What do you see?+

I saw as if through a veil of mist – the view from another's eyes. This chamber, alive with running serfs and servitors armed with industrial tools... Lithe, daemonic figures ran between them, cleaving about them with serrated blades that looked to be forged of brass or bronze. The mist veil thickened, clearing again to show the warrior's very last sight. One of the creatures – a thing of swollen, molten veins beneath cracked black skin – sprayed bile into my vision as it lanced its blade into my stomach. I heard nothing, felt nothing, but the sight left little to the imagination.

I lifted my hand from his helm.

'Children of the Sanguinary Unholiness, justicar. Dozens of them.'

+Spread out,+ he ordered. +I want answers.+

The primary armoury lay undefended but for the bodies of the slain, its great doors open to resemble toothless maws. The walls were barren racks, holding no sign of blades or bolters. Every weapon had been claimed. Since the death of gravity, crates of ammunition and spare chainsword teeth-tracks had spilled their contents into the air, punctuating the spaces between the floating corpses.

The only light came from our weapons, blades softly gleaming with low-tuned power fields, occasionally sending shadows dancing along the walls as a crackle of electrical force rasped down a sword's edge. The flickering play of silhouettes turned the broken, frozen faces into the trembling visages of daemons.

'They depleted this place,' Sothis said. 'Not a weapon left.'

I gestured to the ceiling, pitted and cracked to absolute ruination with bolter fire, as well as the impacts of smaller calibre weapons. 'Something was above them in this chamber. They sought to bring it down.'

Even our enhanced vision suffered in the dusty near-dark. My armour sensed my straining sight and switched my eye lenses to a different frequency, piercing some of the ashen distortion. Still nothing there.

+We're deep enough now. Hyperion, commence a sending.+

I holstered my bolt pistol. 'At once, justicar.'

III

There is a saying, drawn from the ages of Old Earth and written by a council of Ancient Merican kings, that all men were created equal. I'd often wondered if the words sounded as false and idealistic to those men's ears as they did to mine. Truly, humanity has an infinite capacity for self-deception.

Deceit is a sin against purity, as recorded in the fifteenth decree of piety. To lie is to stain the soul, and he who deceives himself is thrice-blackened by the falsehood.

All men are not created equal. The proof is there for any eye to see.

While we are no longer men in the human sense, we carry our origins within us, so no Knight is exactly equal, either.

Sothis had no affinity to carry out a sending, nor did Dumenidon. Malchadiel's abilities were primarily those of a telekine, while I was classified in the strictest terms as a pyrokine. But of the five souls in Castian, the responsibility for a sending always fell to Galeo or myself. They were almost always undertaken alone.

How to describe a sending? How does one describe a storm to an underhive child who can't imagine wind and weather? You can explain that rain is water against the face, and that the black clouds above are like a bank of pollutant fog, but the picture will always be incomplete. The child has never seen the sky. The only wind he has ever felt is the asthmatic breathing of ventilator exchangers.

In my earliest nights, I'd needed to kneel to commit a sending – to chant scripture and focus on ignoring the sensations of my body. Thankfully, my training had brought me far from those first halting trials, and the bond with my brothers amplified my talents. On the *Frostborn*, I merely had to close my eyes.

The ship resisted me. I could feel the taint in its bones, the spoiled iron and sour steel repelling my questing touch. Hall by hall, chamber by chamber, I unfolded my senses and drifted through the dead ship.

To see without sight, to perceive without any physical sense, is disconcerting even for a prepared mind. I'd once performed a sending in a habitation block, and the assaulting feedback had been a siege against my senses: a hundred minds hammering their needs and thoughts back into my brain, all in one toxic flood. Beneath that maelstrom of sentience lingered the simple, sharp hind-brain instincts of the vermin breeding behind every wall, and the contours of the building itself – its angles, the porous holes in its materials, the way its weight leaned on its foundations...

Sending my senses through the destroyer was poisonously kin to that experience. The baroque walls and narrow conduits pulsed with a secret heartbeat, alive in a way that no scanner would ever detect.

Nowhere at all did I feel any closer to reaching the source of the psychic whine. Whatever had been weeping into the warp now shielded itself with tenacity and strength.

'I sense no living souls on the ship,' I told them.

+Bodies?+

I could feel them, and their spirits lingering nearby. Every time I passed a corpse, I'd catch a half-sentence of whispered last words, or a flash of fanged maws and jagged blades.

'Hundreds, justicar. All cold. All dead. The hull is rotten through with taint. It occludes my sight, but there are no survivors. At least, none awake. Hibernation remains a possibility.'

'Speak of the taint in the walls,' said Dumenidon. 'I feel no such presence. Is it possession?'

I ghosted through the corridors, feeling the walls ripple in my wake, though the structure never shifted. They recoiled on a psychic level, as if by instinct.

'Not possession. Just taint. Nothing more than the dullest malice, from lingering corruption in the ship's bones.'

+Engines?+ Galeo asked.

I narrowed my senses, focusing the sending through the grand chambers of the enginarium deck. The arcane fusion reactor machinery that had once been the warship's burning heart lay silent and still, decorated in frozen blood and drifting debris. The plasma in its pipes and core was similarly motionless, thick in its frozen state.

'Cold, justicar. As cold and dead as the crew.'

+Deactivated?+ he quested towards me, +or powered down through abandonment?+

'Difficult for me to tell, justicar. Mal?'

'I'll go with him,' Malchadiel replied.

I drew his essence with me as I drifted back to the enginarium decks. Back in the chamber with our brothers, I
heard his body stagger. He went to his knees, unable to focus
on his physical form with his mind divided. But he knew his
task, letting his senses roll over the control consoles and the
reactor's surface.

He spoke out loud, his voice distant and distracted. 'The
drive core in the primary enginarium chamber was manually
terminated.'

I could sense his movements as if I could see them, as his
invisible reach trailed over rank upon rank of inert command consoles, visualising the network of machinery within
each one.

'All nine ignition ciphers have been removed.' He hesitated
then, and I listened to him breathe over the vox. 'There's
carbon scoring in the sockets, and damage to the subdermal
cables linking the consoles to the animus machinae. The
ignition cipher keys were extracted while the ship was still
in flight.'

Sothis adjusted his weight. The murmur of his armour was
a sudden distraction I had to compensate for. 'They tried to
kill the engines to drop from the warp,' he said. 'I do not
understand. Why did they not eject their warp core? Was
there no other way to return to real space?'

Malchadiel fell forwards to his hands and knees, his senses
still with me in the enginarium chambers. I was sweating
now. Maintaining this level of focus forced my muscles to
lock tight, and my temples ached from teeth that wouldn't
unclench.

'Their Navigator,' Malchadiel breathed. 'It was their
Navigator.'

I felt his essence thinning, dispersing through the cob-web of cables and conduits that reached out from the drive rooms. His breathing grew ragged, and like a wolf scruffing a rival in its jaws, I pulled him back into himself.

'That was unpleasant,' he muttered, and managed to rise to his feet on the third attempt.

'You were drifting,' I told him.

'My thanks for recalling me,' he said.

+What of their Navigator?+ Galeo prompted.

'It was him,' Malchadiel confirmed. My brother checked his weapons, as if to reassure himself they were still there. 'They couldn't break from the warp. They couldn't even cripple the ship to stop it, by hurling their warp core into space. The Navigator wouldn't let them. There's a network of labyrin-thine cables beneath the deck still aching to touch, stinging with the resonance from the Navigator's spite. He wouldn't even let them slow down.'

I tried to visualise what he was saying. Surely that amount of control over a warship's journey was unprecedented. A Navigator was a guide, a pilot through the warp, not an overseer of every single system. He couldn't have been acting alone in the vessel's damnation.

+Your skills will be missed when the Grand Master sends you to Mars.+

Malchadiel nodded to the justicar's compliment. His desire to train under the guidance of the Martian Mechanicus was no secret to any of us. Had Castian been able to spare him, he'd already be gone – a handful of years into his shrouded training as a Techmarine.

'The machine-spirit is dead,' he said. 'Wholly dead. The core cannot be reawakened to full function, short of recon-secration in a soul forge. This ship wasn't simply shut down.' Malchadiel shook his head. 'They sought to kill it, to rip the life from every system.'

'The enginarium chambers are playing host to a warzone's worth of bloodstains and solid round impacts,' I added. 'Whatever battles raged through the ship's bowels, the crew preferred to break back into material space aboard a slain hulk, rather than remain in the warp. When we leave, we need to scuttle the ship. There can be no purification. Its ashes must be consigned to the void.'

+And no systems can be restored while we're aboard? Not even artificial gravity?+

Malchadiel hesitated. I could sense him remembering the damage in the enginarium. Images of the devastation skittered across his mind's eye, fleeting and cold.

'I can resurrect several minor systems, justicar. They will be slaved to temperamental auxiliary cogitators, though. Without a machine-spirit to control them, it's a temporary rebirth at best. The ship is slain,' he finished. 'She was cut to her core.'

+And the warp-cry?+

I shook my head. 'It seems sourceless, justicar.'

'Echoes, perhaps,' Dumenidon suggested. 'The lingering resonance of great emotional trauma. The archives are full of such tidings. I have felt it myself on many missions.'

'That seems likely,' I said. 'Still, there may be something hiding on board. I can't be sure, either way.'

Galeo nodded. +We will move to the enginarium and restore what we can, then press towards the ship's prow and the Navigator's occlusiam. Hyperion?+

'Yes, justicar.'

+Inform the inquisitor her presence will be not be possible for several hours at least.+

'At once, justicar.'

I did as he asked. The response I received was the one I'd

expected. Inquisitor Annika Jarlsdottyr knew a great many curse words, and in that moment, she spat many of them freely into my mind.

I tuned her out, returning my attention to the sending, drifting along the warship's central spinal concourse.

The walls still resisted me, affronted by the intrusion. Saturated by the dullest intelligence, the ship was poisoned through. It wanted to be left alone to grow ripe and corrupt, isolated in the void.

I saw bodies hanging in the air, surrounded by the frozen organic displays of their own innards. I saw bodies stuck fast to the deck or the walls by bloodstains turned to thick ice. I saw bodies torn apart so that it became impossible to tell where one ended and another began, or which pieces had belonged to each corpse.

More and more whispers snaked their way into my head. Each body I passed added to the sibilant sound, layering a fresh hiss upon the chanting melody.

No no please the final concourse reload no God-Emperor no out of ammunition no no please for the Emperor failed the trials one more shot for myself the ship is screaming I can't see mother mother I can't breathe I'm blind where is it I can't see no please no not me I can't do it help me no no no help me my arm my arm no no

+Return now, Hyperion. You've seen all there is to see.+

I could taste bile in the back of my mouth. Perhaps Galeo was right. I started to say 'As you command,' but never finished the second word.

He sensed it in the same moment I did. They all did. Each of them turned to me, alerted by our bond, sensing what I felt.

'The enemy,' Dumenidon growled. Weapons sparked into brighter life, charged by rising emotions.

'No.'

At that word, they all turned back to me. I blinked as my senses snapped back into the cradle of my skull, swaying but not falling as Malchadiel had done. The sending was complete at last. 'Someone still lives, but they are not the enemy.'

The threads of their life were thin enough to be masked the first time I sought them – and even the second time, I'd almost ghosted right past. The soul was nothing more than a candle in the cold.

+Where?+ The question needled into me, as bladed as any weapon. Sometimes Galeo would forget his own psychic strength.

I opened my eyes at last. 'The starboard arming deck.'

IV

We moved quicker than before, drifting through the powerless decks, pulling ourselves along the ceiling and walls of the central spinal. Galeo led us with a sense of urgency we'd lacked since first boarding.

At one point, the vox enjoyed a brief resurgence. The inquisitor made the most of it.

'Hyperion, I command this mission,' she was saying.

'I know, inquisitor.'

'I want pictographic evidence of all you witness, please. You cannot destroy an Imperial warship with nothing more than a sensor sweep to file in the evidence archives.'

'Maybe so,' I allowed, 'but the testimonies of five Grey Knights will make for compelling authority, will they not?'

She muttered something away from the vox-mic. Something about 'overzealous bastards'.

'Inquisitor?'

Her grumbling tirade ended with the kind of sigh that suggested she was being as patient as could reasonably be expected.

'I am not objecting to the cruiser's destruction,' she said. 'I am saying I need to bring back more than your assurances that it had to be done. The ordo demands archivable evidence for an operation of this magnitude. As much as possible, especially when dealing with a warship wearing the Wolves' colours.'

She was breaking up again, stuttering as the vox grew choppy. I confess I found that to be a relief, but my training took precedence over comfort. As I dived through the nothingness, I reached back for her. It was no effort at all to make the connection, feeling her behind my eyes, letting her see what I saw.

Blessedly, she chose to remain silent this time.

We came to the end of a long corridor. I twisted in the air, shouldering aside a crate that immediately released a twinkling cloud of frozen autogun rounds, and kicked off from the wall. It put me ahead of the others as we glided down the adjacent hallway. Doors sliced past on either side, each bulkhead open, revealing brief glances of ruined serf dormitories, lesser armouries, storerooms, meditation chambers.

'What did you sense?' Malchadiel voxed to me. I felt him reaching for my mind, as if it were a puzzle to be unlocked, layer by layer. My surge of irritation battered his clumsy questing aside.

'A soul,' I told him, 'bloodied and broken. The presence was indistinct, almost too weak to sense, or seeking to remain unfound.'

'One of the crew?'

'I believe so.'

'Untainted?'

I was less certain of that.

+Weapons,+ Galeo ordered. +Be ready.+

I reached for a bulky doorframe on the left side of the

corridor, using my momentum to turn and swing through the open bay doors.

The first thing I saw, by the light of my own eye lenses and the gleam from my weapon, was the arming chamber stretching out before me. Great cradles of blackened iron held the immense turrets of a weapons battery, facing out into the open void.

On any other warship, this would have been a place of great industry and tremendous solemnity, as servitors and serfs made ready to wage war in the Emperor's name. Here, it was a tomb.

I felt the crawling sensation begin. A sick creep up the backbone; an itch behind the eyes. Taint. Filth. The enemy.

At last, we'd found the Wolves.

FIVE
LONE WOLF

I

'*Skitnah,*' she said behind my eyes.

+No,+ I sent back. +He is untainted.+

'*I did not mean the survivor, Hyperion. I meant the dead.*'

My targeting reticule flashed across them all, body after body hanging in the air. Each one was a twisted marionette: limbs loose, war plate ruptured, backs broken.

To arrest my headlong drift, I reactivated my mag-lock boots, thudding to the deck. Red diamonds shattered against my armour, breaking against my eye lenses. It took me a moment to realise that it was their blood. An ocean of blood, crystallised in the air.

One of the Wolves, disturbed by my arrival, turned slowly as he drifted away. Oceanic grey ceramite marked with bronze runes reflected the glow of my weapon. When the warrior's face rolled into view, I saw the damage to his helm – something had drilled its way through his eye lenses and into the skull beneath. His gauntlets were frozen at his throat, fingers locked into cold claws. He'd died trying to tear his helmet free. Seven of them floated there. A third of the ship's Wolf population; traditionally, vessels this size were assigned to single squads.

The deck vibrated as my brothers landed alongside me.

'Blood of the Sigillite,' Dumenidon breathed over the vox. The others looked at the desolation, waving blood-crystals away from their faceplates.

I reached for another drifting Wolf to examine his injuries. The scream struck us the second my fingers connected with his armour.

I'd been expecting something – the psychic echo of any soul expiring always left a trace – but this struck like a storm's wind, hard enough to send me reeling. I saw Galeo in the corner of my vision, stumbling as I did. Several of the crew on board the *Karabela* cried out as a lesser echo grazed their receptive minds, travelling through my link to Annika.

It was all I could do not to flee my body. Fire licked from my fingers, summoned without intent, burning without air. I could feel the same flames flaring in my eyes.

+What… is… that…?+ Dumenidon's strained voice reached me.

And then it came. The words, a name, pealing in a voice of silent, psychic thunder.

+DEVOURER+
+OF+
+STARS.+

+Devourer of Stars!+ Dumenidon and Sothis cried out in sympathetic unity, as the sixth sense blastwave overpowered them both. It took all of my strength to resist shouting it aloud, as well.

+A mortis-cry,+ confirmed Galeo. His voice was still

shaken. +The last words of someone very powerful.+

I said nothing at all. My senses ached in the mortis-cry's wake. A weak telekinetic shove sent the ruptured body drifting away.

+A psyker,+ I managed to send a few moments later, gesturing at the corpse. +One of their shamans.+

Galeo nodded. I could hear him catching his breath in the scream's wake. My ears rang; all sound was muted, as my mind echoed with prickling aftershocks.

+Go with caution, Hyperion.+

+Aye, justicar.+

The survivor was the only body on the deck, while all others hovered in the silent airlessness.

+He should be dead,+ sent Galeo as we drew near.

+He almost is,+ I sent back. +And he will be soon.+

He was a Wolf, armoured in the Chapter's distinctive blue-grey ceramite, with a white wolf's cloak draped over one shoulder. Blood marked his armour in visceral dappling. It marked his cloak. It marked his helm. It marked the decking all around him, glazed over into ice, and it marked the floor where both of his legs ended in hewn stumps at the knees. Ice had frosted him to the deck in a pool of his own blood. Through the shattered portholes, the Caul's dust stretched on far beyond mortal sight.

To look at him with human senses, I'd never have known he still lived. Even my retinal display read nothing of life within him. Only the infinitesimal thread of warmth from his psychic presence told a different tale.

I approached first, kneeling down by him. Activated by proximity, runes cycled across my eye lenses as my armour sought to tune into his vox-channel. There was a click, and a pulse, and a long, ragged breath.

I rolled him over, looking down into the cracked helm.

Superficial damage, nothing a servitor would struggle to repair. But he didn't acknowledge me. His bio-readings were barely above a flatline. Hibernation, then. It made sense. We'd need the correct balance of chemicals to revive him, back on the *Karabela*.

'I sense no taint on him,' Dumenidon said behind me.

'There is none,' I replied. 'And he has triggered his sus-an membrane.' +Inquisitor?+

'Yes?'

+We require the chemical compound Somnambulist, found in the south store racks in the *Karabela*'s apothecarion. Use a servitor in an environment suit to send it to us.+

'No. I'm coming over myself.' Somehow, I'd known she was going to say that.

+It is not safe. We haven't scouted the entire ship.+

'Shut up, Hyperion.'

+Hyperion is correct, inquisitor...+

'Shut up, Malchadiel.'

+Inquisitor...+

'I am an inquisitor of the Ordo Malleus. Don't argue with me. You will not win if I make it a contest of rank. I don't need your permission for this. Can you move the wounded Wolf?'

I looked over the body again. +Yes. Suspended animation will keep his wounds from worsening.+

'Bring him to me. That's an order.'

II

We met her in the hangar. Her own shuttle was a sleek counterpoint to the blunt aggression of our gunship, and I suspect none of us were surprised when she didn't descend the gangramp alone, but with several other figures in full matt-black void-suits, each one marked with talismans of the Inquisition. A cyber-mastiff lingered close to one of them, utterly untroubled by the lack of gravity, its iron paws locked to the deck.

'Two-Guns.' One of the faceless black glass helms nodded over at me.

'Hello, Hyperion,' said the shortest, in a softly feminine voice.

'We were bored,' said another, the tallest. Even vox-crackle couldn't hide Darford's amused snort. He was a man easily amused by his own wit. I often wondered why.

Inquisitor Jarlsdottyr walked over to us, somehow making a zero-gravity stomp seem graceful. She was clad in an environment suit, with her Cretacian bolter slung over her back. Her pale face stared out at us from the armoured helmet's reinforced visor. Occasionally, the glass misted with her exhalations.

Galeo was drawing breath to speak, but Annika lifted a finger in warning, silencing the justicar with her scowl. Behind her, the Khatan and Darford carried a crate of medical supplies.

Annika crouched by the fallen Wolf we'd carried back with us.

'Awaken him. He has a dirge to sing.'

III

The warrior's first action upon waking was to grip my wrist with sudden and surprising strength. He said nothing – or rather, anything he did say was lost as his armour's systems came back to life and sought to retune him into his squad's uplink. With the automatic connection displaced, I made the gestures for seven numerals in succession: our communication frequency.

A moment later, the vox crackled with a new link. His voice was a wet, burbling snarl, forced through clenched teeth.

'Now I remember,' he growled. 'Bastards took my legs.' He lifted his head, his eye lenses meeting mine. 'Name yourself kindred or name yourself my foe, for I don't recognise your armour.'

It wasn't an uncommon reaction, even among the Adeptus Astartes. Most Chapters believed our order to be a myth, if they'd heard of us at all. Few souls were allowed to remain aware of our existence.

+Hyperion,+ Galeo pulsed. I nodded in understanding.

'We are Castian, of the Grey Knights,' I told the wounded warrior.

For a wonder, he made his bloody right gauntlet into a fist, and pounded it on his breastplate.

'Grauvr, of Haken Ironchewer's Great Company.' He barked a laugh that carried nothing of mirth. 'Though Ironchewer is as dead as I am. A new Wolf Lord will mean new markings. Hnngh. I'm glad to be dying. Too old to repaint my shoulder guard yet again.'

I could hear the unwelcome wetness of blood in his breathing as he continued. 'The Great Wolf, High Jarl Grimnar, told us of you. He sent us to find you. To Titan, he said. Sail to Saturn's mightiest moon. Ha! I almost swore he lied to us. But you're real, eh?'

Each time he opened his mouth, I heard the wet thunder of his body's organs struggling to push on.

'You are far from Titan,' I told him. 'Fortune brought us here.'

'Fortune? I piss on fortune. The Allfather brought you to me.'

'The...?'

'He means the Emperor,' said Annika. She stepped ahead of us, crouching by the dying Wolf. 'I am Annika Jarlsdottyr, now of the Inquisition and once of Fenris. My tribe was the Broken Tusk. My father was Ranil the Skinner, Jarl of Maulma. The warpaint we wore when we sailed to make murder was–'

'The red of blood,' wheezed the warrior, 'painted from the mouth's edges, down to the throat. Well do I know the Broken Tusk, girl. I have three centuries to my name within the Chapter, but I knew the Broken Tusk in the time before I was taken.' He broke off, coughing wetly into his helm. 'I was old when your grandsire sucked milk at your great-grandmare's teats. You hear me, girl? I made murder on the cold seas and the shifting lands ten generations before you were even born.'

She… She was actually smiling. Although I couldn't see her face, I could feel her amusement; her warmth for this warrior. From her surface thoughts, I gleaned the Fenrisian tradition of good-natured boasting when fighters from different tribes crossed paths.

A curious custom.

'Tell us what happened,' Annika pressed him, gripping his huge fist in both of hers. Her fingers didn't even wrap his palm. 'What brought you here?'

'Where… Where is here?'

'The Valdasca Caul.'

'The warning,' he snarled again. 'The warning. Did you hear Angriff Blightbreaker? Tell me you heard Blightbreaker's final howl.'

Devourer of Stars. The words drifted back behind my eyes.

'We heard it,' I said. 'Explain its meaning.'

'We had to run here. Do you understand that, Grey One? Our Rune Priest, Blightbreaker – and our Wolf Lord, Ironchewer. It was their wish that we run.'

Some of our order possessed the psychic might to reshape the emotions of others. One of them might have been able to do so now, undetected, but I didn't dare take the risk. He was already close enough to death.

'Slow down,' I said. 'Focus.'

'I am focused. Listen to me. Casting the runes no longer worked. The shaman-speech reached no other ears. They came in a red tide from the bleeding sky, and strangled our voices when they first kissed the cursed earth.'

'Who?' Annika whispered. 'Who did these things?'

I didn't need to ask. I was already sensing echoes of his thoughts, but what I saw made no sense. Oceans of ash. Cities aflame. The hallways of this very ship, overrun by the burning Neverborn.

'The enemy,' Grauvr snapped. 'The thrice-damned enemy. Are you deaf, all of you? We ran from them. Jarl Grimnar sent as many ships as he could spare. No other way to get the word out. The storm eats all sound. We had to run, to escape, to find a place of silence where we could howl for help.'

The Wolf laughed his bitter laugh again. 'But they followed us. They came with us, and made murder upon the crew. They stepped from the darkness, blades in hands, casting horned shadows against the iron walls.'

+The Neverborn,+ Galeo pulsed to us. +Wherever they ran from, the daemons followed. It seems the Archenemy is viciously keen to keep the Wolves silent.+

Annika was the one to speak next. 'Where did you come from?' she asked. 'Where is this storm that swallows all sound?'

'Armageddon,' he said. 'The manufactory world. The hives and the ash wastes and the toxic skies. Above it all, like a cancer in the night heavens, the storm itself. The Devourer of Stars.'

+We're killing him,+ Sothis pulsed to the rest of us. +His mind is wracked and lost; his hearts are beating to the point of bursting. He's too weak for this.+

+Then he'll die,+ Galeo replied. +The storm he speaks of...+

'It's not a storm,' I said with my human voice. 'Not a storm at all.'

I saw it as clearly as if it hung in the heavens above me. A macro-agglomeration of vessels – human, alien, Imperial, Traitor – moulded into a brutish hulk large enough to eclipse the sun. The thing stank of the warp; of steel and alien metals melted together, of the Neverborn and the infected mortals infesting its black bowels.

The image was gone as abruptly as it'd come. Grauvr released my wrist at last, nodding to himself.

'Yes,' he said. 'Yes, now you see. The Great Wolf calls for the Grey Knights. He knows you exist, in the shadows. He howls for you to step into the light.' Coherence was deserting him. He reached around with his one remaining hand.

'My bolter,' he said. Despite his wounds, he was reaching for a weapon that wasn't there. It was impossible not to admire that.

'Armageddon endures siege,' I told my brothers, sharing what I'd seen. 'I've never seen a hulk of that size. I've never even read of one to match it.'

+There has never been one,+ Galeo replied. +The monastery must be warned at once. We leave, we scuttle the ship, and we make ready for war.+

Something in his words set my blood running cold. Malchadiel felt the same, and commented upon it.

'You said war, justicar. Not battle.'

Galeo nodded. +I know.+

'My bolter,' Grauvr said again.

'Later,' Annika told him. 'Rest, warrior.'

He made the sign of aquila as best he could with one hand – and a bedraggled, one-winged Imperial eagle was just as unimpressive as it sounds – but he had little choice when his other arm hung limp at his side.

Grauvr coughed into the vox. 'One of my hearts has stopped. I feel it wedged in my chest, dense and still. And I cannot breathe well. My lungs are ripe with filth.'

'You will die without our aid.' Even the crude sensors in my helm's auto-senses could tell me that. I didn't need an Apothecary's skills to know it was true. 'We will tend to you on board our ship.'

'First, tell us what happened here,' Annika pressed. 'We must know the whole truth.'

+He can tell us on board the *Karabela*.+ Galeo's silent voice held a rare edge. +We are leaving, inquisitor.+

Annika looked over her shoulder back at him, at all of us. 'This is a Fenrisian ship, and I am not leaving until I know every detail of its death.'

+Your allegiance is to the ordos, not the Wolves of Fenris. We have a greater duty than this, inquisitor,+ he said, with less-than-subtle emphasis on her title.

'I am not leaving until I've seen what killed this ship. Do you understand me, knight?'

I felt Galeo suppressing his anger. It fairly rippled from him in a tide. +As you wish, inquisitor.+

She turned back to the wounded Wolf. 'Speak,' she bade him. 'Speak of the *Frostborn*.'

And he did. Grauvr spoke in strained detail, though few details were necessary. The story of the *Frostborn*'s demise was a straight one, cutting right to the quick. A tale of possession, corruption, and the Emperor's warriors over-whelmed by the blasphemy of their weak, human crew. At the end, only a few of the mortals had escaped unscathed. Those that resisted corruption were hurled from the air-locks, or eaten by their sickened kin. And all of this, all this madness, began with one soul. One weak man, trusted with the ultimate responsibility when he should have been purged from the annals of the Imperium.

'The Navigator.' Grauvr breathed the words in a wet growl. 'Our accursed Navigator. The enemy came through him.'

'We've seen the damage he caused,' said Malchadiel. 'How long did it take for the ship to fall?'

'Minutes at most. No time to organise a defence. The Geller field died, and the crew died with it.'

'No fouler foe than a Navigator fallen from the Emperor's light,' Sothis interrupted. 'No sadder lament.'

When Grauvr came to the Wolves' last stand, Vasilla made a warding gesture against evil over her chest.

'Your brothers died with all honour,' she said in her eternally soft voice.

'I know that.' Grauvr's reply was understandably graceless. 'I saw it with my own eyes.'

Annika turned her visored face to us as Grauvr finished speaking. Her blue eyes pressed into me.

'You know what must be done,' she said. 'I will meet you back aboard the *Karabela*.'

Darford cleared his throat over the vox. 'We've no idea if the source is even still aboard. Even if he is, the justicar is right – just scuttle the damn ship, Nika.'

'No,' she replied. 'We have to be sure. If the creature still walks, it must be banished.'

'This isn't about being sure,' I said. 'This is about vengeance for your Fenrisian fallen.'

'Perhaps it is,' she allowed.

'Then you are compromised by human emotion.'

'Perhaps I am.' Never had I seen her so passionless. 'You will still obey me, Hyperion.'

I looked at Galeo, but none of my brothers said a word. At last, the justicar surrendered with a nod.

* * *

IV

We moved through the silent decks again, drifting to the prow, weaving around corners as we made our way to the occlusiam.

The vox made several abortive clicks as one of my brothers kept almost saying something, and choosing to keep quiet at the last moment. I let my mind coast through theirs, skimming their surface thoughts. Sothis was focused on one of the chants of incorruptibility, repeating it in the melodic tone of his inner voice. Dumenidon's guard was up, preventing any casual brush against his thoughts – his mind was even less emotive than the cold walls around us. Galeo was an open book to Dumenidon's sealed tome, and his thoughts were purely of our immediate surroundings. That left Malchadiel, and in fairness, I could have guessed it would be him.

My retinal display responded to my irritated instinct, opening a vox-link to Malchadiel.

'Just say it,' I told him. 'Just say whatever it is you wish to say.'

'The inquisitor.' Like his twin, Malchadiel's voice was soft, but coloured by a contemplative edge Sothis usually lacked. 'The justicar should have refused her.'

'We are the Chamber Militant of the Holy Inquisition, brother. One does not refuse an inquisitor.'

'Galeo should have, this time. You said it yourself: Annika is compromised by the weakness of human emotion.'

I hadn't called it a 'weakness', though when my brother stated it so plainly, it was hard to see it in any other light.

'She may even be censured for this,' Malchadiel added. 'Inquisitors make mistakes. We've all seen it in the archives.'

We moved from the central concourse, drifting along a subsidiary corridor. The only light came from the glare of our active weapons, blending an undersea ripple of bluish light along the walls. Like all gothic architecture, its elegance was in its stark, skeletal angles. Each arch and hull-hallway seemed almost armoured by reinforced bone-like beams of black iron.

I sensed a deeper, truer thought behind the words he spoke. I pulsed a slight stab of irritation through the link between our minds, letting him know I sensed he was holding back from saying something else.

'This madness with the *Devourer of Stars*...' he said. 'If Grauvr truly saw it...'

'Grauvr did see it.'

'Are you certain? He's been on a corrupted warship, ripe with taint, for an unknowable amount of time.'

I knew because I'd been sifting through the Wolf's mind the entire time he spoke, dredging for signs of deceit or the jagged edges of altered memory.

'You can guess how I know,' I replied. 'And before you ask, I found nothing untoward inside his skull. Merely flashes of pain, and a life dripped night after night into unending duty.' I smiled then, despite our circumstances. 'It was almost familiar.'

Malchadiel's thoughts darkened. 'I have no idea why you are so entertained by all this, brother. I've read the archives as often as you, and I recall precious few incidents where destroying a possessed Navigator was anything less than a savage trial.'

That rather stole the smile from my face.

+Focus.+ Galeo's demand broke through the conversation. +And be ready for what is on the other side of this door.+

We locked our boots to the decking, readying weapons. The door itself was an armoured oval, clad in a crust of sparkling frost. It was easily wide enough to walk through five abreast, even in Terminator plate.

I felt nothing until I physically rested a hand against the door. My gauntlet was no barricade to the sudden feeling – a sense of something greasily venomous slipping into my body. My lip curled in disgust, with a growl I couldn't control. How could I have failed to sense this? I foresaw punishment in my future.

'There is taint behind this portal,' I grunted. My anger was already getting the better of me. 'Something that bleeds rage. I feel it reaching out to me.'

'Why didn't you sense it before?' asked Dumenidon.

+Do not blame Hyperion. This presence masked itself to perfection. Remove your hand from the door, brother.+

For a moment, I didn't want to. The anger humming through me rode my blood in a saccharine rush. Rage had never felt so pleasantly bleak, so righteous, so absolutely vindicating. I should have stood my ground before Annika and her idiotic posturing. She was only human. What right did she have to order us to her whims, as though we were no more valuable than servitors?

I pulled my hand back with a jerk, surprised to find it trembling. The anger's urgent heat faded, but its aftertaste did not. No matter what the justicar said, I still felt I should have sensed this, even from such a distant sending.

'Whatever is on the other side of this door,' I voxed to the others, 'it knows we are here.'

+We will cut our way in to greet it.+

Dumenidon and Galeo hefted their long blades, raising them high and casting the darkness back. Our shadows jerked in a spastic dance across the arching walls, their twisting movements rendering them daemonic.

Some of the Imperium's more backward worlds are said to believe a shadow is an outer reflection of the soul. Our shadows cavorted as the blades fell, and perhaps to some feral world shaman, it might have meant something more than the simple play of illumination.

V

I had never seen a Navigator's inner sanctum before.

It was said that no two were the same, each one turned into a private haven by the near-human creature destined to spend its life within its confines. When one lives a whole life in a prison, even a willing captive will shape a cell to enhance its comfort. On the *Karabela*, our Navigator Orolissa was a woman I'd never met, dwelling in a chamber no Grey Knight was allowed to enter. All I knew of her was that her mind was a loud one: she dreamed often of black seas, and the beasts that swam within them.

The Navigator of the *Frostborn* claimed a large chamber of surpassing beauty, laid out with typical Imperial ostentation magnified many times over. Walls were decorated in great friezes of stained glass, depicting scenes of purity in the Imperium's past. There, the founding of the Temple of the Emperor Messiah, on the world of Cadia; there, the Second Siege of the Eternity Gate; there, the end of the Reign of Blood, with a Custodian in royal gold receiving the peace offering from the First Bride of the Emperor.

A dozen other images from a dozen other worlds, depicting events of great, holy import – most of them displayed the deeds of the Wolves, which was no surprise at all. I didn't know those battles, nor did I recognise the heroes that fought in them.

We stood within a monastery in miniature, condensed into one perfect room. A central dais faced a dozen oculus screens depicting the stars outside, faint in their blanket of infinite dust. Every single screen was cradled in the arms of two sculpted basalt angels, reaching from the wall with their great wings spread. The craftsmanship was exquisite – they looked real enough to move, to speak, to sing if anyone would dare to ask. Even the unusual choice of stone had to mean something; perhaps they'd quarried it from the Wolves home world, or hauled the pitted, grey rock from a mine on a holy world deep within the Chapter's protectorate.

Everything seemed untouched, pristine. I saw nothing of the desecration our order had long come to expect of our tainted enemies. I couldn't even see our prey.

And yet, the stinking taste of taint was thick in the air.

'This is a lie,' I voxed to the others. 'Beware treachery.'

+Hyperion is right. See with your true eyes.+

A moment's focus tore the shroud from my sight, revealing the chamber as it was, not as we'd seen it. The angelic statuary had fallen from their aeries to break upon the deck. Whenever the gravity finally died, the corpses had taken flight once more, drifting in the air as rubble. Ungripped, the oculus screens drifted alongside their shattered bearers. Several were still leashed to the wall on their optic cables.

I turned from the smashed stained-glass windows, no longer seeing the artistry that had once existed in their panes. The sanctity of this haven was no more.

Someone stood at the chamber's heart, a lone caretaker of this airless mausoleum. He was barefoot on the decking, clad only in stained rags, with his flesh blackened by frostbite and void exposure. What little of his body had escaped discolouration was split in frozen crevices lacerated across his form. Blood haloed him in floating crystals, each one a frozen gem of liquid life on the wrong side of his skin.

He could not be alive in this void vacuum. No human could survive it. Grauvr's story bore truth, as I'd known it would: this was no human. As the ragged man turned to face us, I heard the distinct hiss of Annika swearing in my mind.

I'd not even realised she was still there.

'Skitnah!' she spat. 'Fyenden sijaga skitnah!'

The man had three eyes. The third, in the centre of his forehead, opened to reveal a bloody black orb. I didn't meet its gaze. None of us did. To do so was death, even through the dubious protection of our retinal displays. Ceramite and devotion were no armour against a Navigator's third eye. Some deaths cut right to the soul.

I threw Annika from my mind, banishing her back into her body even as she cursed at me, severing the link before she could be harmed. I'd deal with her anger later. I couldn't risk her here.

+Why have you come?+ The voice buzzed into our minds, resonating with a waspish duality. Strange, how so many of the Archenemy asked such things, as if they genuinely believed we owed them an answer.

+In the name of the Emperor's Inquisition, you will kneel before the judgement of the Throne.+ Galeo's decree echoed through our minds as we advanced. All the while, I kept my eyes on the man's mutilated chest.

+I will not kneel.+

'This has to die quickly,' Dumenidon voxed. 'Its power is immense.'

He wasn't wrong. Corruption lapped at me with keen fingers, and the Navigator's questing tendrils of thought caressed my armour, seeking entrance to my mind. Even without gravity, it was like wading forwards through warm tar.

Galeo's chanting almost drowned out every other sense. His reverent words unified us, forming a conduit to pour our power into him. In this moment of execution, he became Castian, the manifestation of all five of us, wielding our strength as his own. This was our brotherhood brought to life, focused into a killing weapon.

+The Anathema's sons.+ The thing in the Navigator's flesh was recoiling now. I was close enough to see its bone-webbed fingers, the way its fused hands twitched. More blood left its maw in a crystallised spray as the creature's insides haemorrhaged and burst. With a marionette's absolute absence of grace, the thing jerked and twitched, enslaved to its own snapping bones. Torment wrenched its voice into a desperate squeal. +All was peace before you came... All was silent... Now anger returns in a flood of black bile.+

I'd seen daemons wither in the aura of our united anger. This was something else, something worse.

'Go...' I voxed the word through teeth I couldn't unclench. Galeo, siphoning our energies for the execution, was the only one walking forwards untroubled. He broke into a run, kicking off from the decking to launch at the possessed husk. The blade in his hands rippled with energy, the strength of our souls in fiery form.

The blade descended, falling like a star from the night sky, all retinal purple and screaming white flame – and ceased dead in the air, caught in the man's skinless hands.

'No.'

Movement, over my shoulder. I turned, even as my brothers turned, and faced the trap we'd known we were walking into.

SIX

THE NEVERBORN

I

Gashes in reality heralded their arrival, roaring and screaming as they made themselves known. The Neverborn melted out from the shadows, from the broken stained-glass friezes and from the airless air itself.

Each one was angelic in form, possessing spectral radiance in place of wings, yet each was debased by flayed wounds, weeping blood from the carvings across their pale skin. Unarmed they came, silent in the airlessness, with lashes of bleached light reaching from their shoulders. Their eyes bled the deepest, richest red.

We needed no warning, as we reacted at once, but not as one. Dumenidon's great blade, the twin to Galeo's, slashed out in a blazing arc, cleaving the closest creature in two. Bisected, the angel tumbled away through the chamber, beautiful hands still reaching for us. Those pale fists opened and closed like the mouth of an asphyxiating fish.

'Wraith Angels.' Dumenidon's voice was brittle over the vox. 'Don't let them attach their mouths to your armour.'

Sothis and Malchadiel were exemplars of unity, shadowing one another's movements, cutting and carving with their shorter falchions. I blocked a toothed lash of light with my wrist guard, letting it skid across the ceramite vambrace before thundering a boot into the thing's chest. The impact shattered its ribs, if the crunching sensation was anything to judge by. A second kick had the effect I'd hoped for; my attacker, a shrieking thing with the swollen yellow eyes of a drowned man, crashed back into his floating kindred.

All around us, they drifted closer with no regard for physics, ghosting through the vacuum on unseen forces. I counted fifty in a single scan, though their limbs and bodies melded together, overlapping as they neared.

A glance spared towards the justicar showed that his two-handed blade still hadn't fallen clean. Galeo heaved down with its weight, head turned from the Navigator's glare, while the ragged mutant trapped the blade between its hands.

+I know you, Anathema's son.+ The Navigator's words carried through all our minds. +I smell your soul. You are the Tongueless One, forever silenced by R'vanha of the Venomous Lash.+

I sensed Galeo's anger as a physical force, spilling from him like infection from a sour wound. His focus was slipping, though his grip on the blade was not. +She still laughs about it, even as she rides the warp's winds. You remember her, do you not? You remember how she burst your brothers' hearts, and stole your voice with a crack of her whip...+

'Get in the fight, Hyperion,' Dumenidon hissed.

The poisoned celestials moved with a will, interlacing their corona-flare wings to form a silent host between us and our embattled justicar. The barricade of unhealthy light blazed from floor to ceiling. Whatever animated them was growing stronger. I could hear the psychic chorus as they murmured, though what such things had to say to each other was beyond me.

Malchadiel and Sothis slammed back to back, their blades carving out in each other's defence. Dumenidon cut around them, joining with me. He cleaved the head from one of the creatures above us, and I hurled the body away with a burst of kinetic force, sending it spinning and crashing through its grim choir-kin. Fire sprayed from my open hand in a sorcerous torrent, igniting those foes closest to us. Even burning, they fought on until the white fire immolated them beyond hope of movement.

'The justicar,' I voxed. 'I can reach him.'

'No.' Dumenidon backed against me. 'Stay with us. Galeo is holding.'

'Guard me, Dumenidon.'

'Don't. Don't do it.'

I couldn't run, so I crouched. A moment's thought set a rune on my retinal display flashing white.

'Fool,' Dumenidon breathed. Another bisected celestial fell past me, twisting in two directions.

My armour's internal hum became an angry whine in sympathy with the vibration of accumulating power between my shoulder blades. A coil of witch-lightning danced down my arm. Others arced from my power pack, keenly serpentine, leaping and crackling.

I focused on Galeo, on the ground by his boots as he was being forced back.

'Emperor guide you,' Dumenidon said.

I couldn't reply. I couldn't break my murmured Chant of Repulsion.

'...the strength to repel the corruption that lies unseen–'

* * *

II

Entering the warp unprotected is nothing less than madness. We're taught this from the first night we leave our holding cells in the monastery.

There was a brutal crack of discharging power, and the occlusiam shattered before me, flensed from my sight as surely as if the scene had been skinned from the surface of my eyes.

I ran thirty steps, only it wasn't running. I swam it without swimming, and leapt without jumping. The distance meant nothing, and in truth neither did the direction. Such things, even in the vaguest terms, were byproducts of the strained, human need to codify what the five senses tell the brain.

For a breath's span, I stared into a sea of searing plasma, comprised of colours that couldn't exist, formed from a billion faces mouthing my name. The tides shrieked their many voices into my head, crying their lies, their weakness, and their pain.

Some say the Emperor's Gift makes us immune to corruption. This may be so, or it may be that our resistance requires a simple explanation for our Inquisitorial masters' minds. Sometimes I believe our lords and mistresses within the ordos fail to understand this about us. As sons of Titan, we are incorruptible through devotion, attaining purity only through tireless effort. No soul is born perfect, but a warrior can be bred to become it.

I moved the moment I fell into the ocean between worlds, plunging through the screaming tides, and focused on the last sight I'd seen: the decking next to Galeo. This, I held in my mind to the exclusion of all else.

Ignoring the press of Hell's tides against my armour, I projected myself forwards, running thirty paces without moving a muscle. On the last step, I killed the power surging into my backpack, and tumbled out of the storm.

III

'–behind the veil of blessed ignorance.'

The prayer finished, leaving my lips by rote as reality reasserted itself with a sonic boom. I was already spinning my stave in a fan-blade's revolution to build speed, and as the Navigator turned to face me, the silver-shod haft cracked against his temple. He rocked to the side as his spine gave way with a crackling crunch I shouldn't have been able to hear in the vacuum. Such a blow would have torn the head from a mortal man.

On a flopping neck, he brought his tilted face around again. My second strike blinded him in the only way that mattered, lancing into the juicy socket where his third eye nested. The orb split with a cracking wrongness – a pebble smashed underfoot rather than the jellied pop I expected. My hands were itching in their gauntlets as I pulled my stave free. Above his human eyes, his head now barely existed.

I saw myself – the reflection I cast in his two remaining eyes. My helm angled down in threat; the ornate stave effortlessly turning in armoured grey hands; my armour still alive with snake-cracks of lightning, arcing out from the conductive nodes on my power pack.

Galeo's blade ended the image. The Navigator flew apart, not only cleaved in half but blasted into viscera by the justicar's anger. Strength flooded me, flooded through each of us, as our leader returned our borrowed energy.

+That was foolish, Hyperion. Focus.+

I didn't reply. My spinning stave crashed out at the Neverborn closest to us, punching through throats and crunching through their bleeding eyes. Each strike hissed when I drew the haft free. Runes carved into the sacred silver steamed at every contact.

But the Navigator's destruction rang cold. I'd felt no cry of thwarted rage so common to the Neverborn in their final moments before banishment. Galeo's words threatened to make unpleasant sense; if my interruption had allowed the daemon to flee its host before the body had been executed...

In that battle, time lost its hold on my senses. Even an eidetic mind cannot process a thousand actions undertaken through instinct when you move faster than perception can follow. My stave spun and cracked, stabbed and crushed. Each strike was a killing blow, as lethally sure as any rending sword or pounding hammer.

They tore at us, grabbed at us, weighing us down with sheer numbers. One of them clawed at my throat from behind, its desperate fingers disengaging one of the seals at my collar. Warning runes flashed across my eye lenses, warning of venting air – as if I couldn't feel it sucked from my lungs in a dragging heave.

The weight was blessedly gone a second later, and I heard the tolling bell of Galeo's blade striking daemonic skin.

+I told you to focus,+ he said, his silent voice coloured by effort.

A fist thump resealed the collar lock. I breathed again. 'You could show some gratitude,' I voxed, and in my agitation I sent the words psychically in the same moment. It was the most disrespect I'd ever shown to my justicar, and the fact shamed me.

A second psychic pulse triggered the generators within my stave, and blurry iridescence hummed from between my gauntlets.

* * *

IV

Of the many weapons forged in our monastery's subterranean foundries, few required the same complexity and care in their crafting as a nemesis warding stave. Like any nemesis-breed weapon, its inbuilt matrix was a shielded, inert core awaiting psychic activation, and just like the more traditional blades, its functions could only be activated by the thoughts of the warrior it had been built for. And there the similarities ended.

Every stave bore a headpiece of punishingly rare purity. I'd seen a small handful topped by the armoured skulls of Imperial saints, or psykers of great majesty. My own was rarer still.

Atop the stave, haloed by consecrated gold, was the skull of Justicar Castian, veined by mercury-threaded circuitry. Ceramite plating had preserved the relic for these last one hundred centuries.

I am no scribe, and certainly no poet. Words have failed me often enough in my life, but I doubt anyone could do justice to the sense of honour I felt when Galeo presented me with the weapon upon accepting me into his squad. I'd trained with staves, just as I'd trained with every weapon available in our armoury, but I'd never expected to be given one to wield upon passing my knighthood trials.

A warding stave's haft was an adamantite sheath encrusted with hexagrammic banishment runes, constructed to house several linked, amplified refractor field generators. Psychic activation awakened them, priming the stave for its defensive use as more than a daemon-slaying weapon.

If I had to estimate for the sake of archival completion, I would say that I activated my stave between sixteen and eighteen seconds after completing my teleport jump.

* * *

V

It flared in my hands, banishing the darkness in staccato flashes as each impact I blocked displaced its kinetic energy as spreading light. A fist, a leering mouth, a lashing wing – all of them burst in pale brilliance as they met the refractor field's resistance. Likewise, every blow I hammered into the enemy sent illuminated detonations playing across the chamber, the way sheet lightning turned night to day on its own intermittent whim.

I wasn't a swordsman. I couldn't stand back to back with one of my brothers; I needed the room to spin and swing the power stave. In an atmosphere, the jagged discharges were accompanied by the active stave's baritone growl, and the wheel-skidding shrieks of the refraction aura deflecting incoming kinetics. In the vacuum, only silence reigned.

I no longer fought to injure the implacable bodies pressing against us. Every blow was a block, every whirling twist made to buy a moment's freedom from the raining tendrils. The few short seconds I could spare from wielding the stave were spent forcing the creatures back with focused thrusts of concentration. On the third repel, a host of daemons flew back on a tide of invisible force, buying us another few seconds to breathe before they could attack once more.

I made the mistake of letting my thoughts graze their consciousness. A tidal flow of anger, black and bleak and cold, flooded through me. Banishing that cost me another moment's concentration.

+Focus!+ The justicar's voice was ripe and urgent. +You are throwing away your energy without a care.+

There was no arguing there. I knew he spoke the truth.

One of my more vicious blows cracked shards of frozen flesh clean from one creature's head, ripping a streak of glassy skin free. The flayed skull that met my gaze bore a rune engraved into its forehead. A second blow rammed a metre of silver stave through the thing's face. Crystallised black vomit sparkled into the air from its shattered jaws, and instead of coming for me a third time, the silver of my weapon set the creature's flesh aflame. It surged backwards, writhing in a blanket of white fire that needed no air to burn. Faith was its fuel.

'The heads,' I voxed to the others. 'Runes mimic a third eye.'

Instantly, my brothers' blows changed, abandoning dismemberment and heart-strikes in favour of splitting skulls. Bodies spilled back from us, wreathed in holy flame as they dissolved. Ash rattled against our armour, scoring the surface like grit.

The five of us fought our way together, though not without cost. By the time we stood in a united ring, Sothis was limping, the back of his knee joint venting a soft hiss of air. Dumenidon, the only one of us always so dedicated to fighting in absolute silence, was whispering a benediction against pain.

I was tiring fast. We all were; I sensed my brothers' efforts as clearly as I felt my own, and unleashing this much psychic force was taking its toll on each of us. There was a reason we usually channelled our might through the justicar. He had the training to measure it as a precious commodity, and spend it most carefully.

Physical weariness was less of a worry. Our genetic enhancements would allow us to fight until the system's star went cold; I had once duelled Malchadiel for a hundred and twenty-two hours before finally landing the winning strike, and even then, he failed due to misjudging his footwork rather than exhaustion.

'This is like holding back an ocean,' Malchadiel voxed, 'by standing on the shore and shouting "Stop".' His complaint was cut off by something striking his helm. I couldn't risk turning to see what.

'We're winning,' Sothis countered. 'That's all that matters.'

A silently shrieking face crashed against my shoulder guard, the pliant lips pressing to the frosty ceramite and sticking fast. Insidious tension locked my arm into spasms, the muscles no longer obeying at all. I couldn't bring my stave to bear.

With my free hand, I clutched the daemon's face, fingers gripping the grotesquely beautiful flesh. Its skull hummed, then cracked, then came apart completely. Fluids bubbled from the mess, forming a flow of perfect spheres. A psychic shove blasted it away the same moment another attached itself to my forearm. This one clung with a lamprey's tenacity, stealing heat from my armour with its sucking kiss. I released a burst of psychic fire to throw it free.

Nothing happened. My eyes grew heavy, my hearts cold, my reflexes sluggish. I mustered the concentration for another psy-thrust, but focus eluded me. I could think of nothing beyond my weakening limbs.

The weakness, the helplessness, was achingly familiar. This – or something so very like it – had happened before. Why couldn't I recall it with any clarity? Was it from my life before coming to Titan? A shadow from my days and nights before waking in that cold cell?

Yes. I could almost see it before me: the cold, cold hallways of an abandoned ship. A name that eluded me – the name of a king seated upon a black throne.

I…

+Brother.+

I opened my eyes, only then realising they'd been closed. As vision cleared, target locks and bio-data streamed back in flickering urgency. 'Brother,' Sothis said, with his voice this time. 'You're drifting.'

He gripped a fistful of the angel's silver-thread hair and

tore the creature free, wrenching its head back, baring its sleek throat. Where its mouth had been on my armour, a discoloured bruise warped the ceramite, while it stared at me with depthless, malicious sentience. A hacking chop slit the celestial's throat, and Sothis carved his sword through the neck, back and forth like a bone-saw.

Two more crashed into him from behind; he whirled to deal with them, blades in hand. The released angel reached for me again, leaping into a single stave thrust against its half-severed head. As the cracking impact finished Sothis's work, I repelled the burning angel away with a pulse of psychic force. It drifted in immolating serenity.

'This is too easy,' I breathed over the vox. 'Something is wrong.'

'Easy?' Sothis laughed. I shared his senses for a moment, drawn into his skull by the ferocity of his emotions. The venting of his air supply from the crack by his knee was causing him more concern than he wished to admit. He yanked both falchions from the chest of his enemy, and decapitated the body with a backhanded cleave. Glittering red gems dribbled from the severance as the seraph burst into smokeless flame. A kick to the sternum sent the corpse drifting away, spinning and tumbling.

'We are still alive, aren't we?' I voxed back.

'You almost weren't,' Malchadiel pointed out.

I sent Sothis my thanks in silence – a psychic sense of admiration and gratitude.

+Hyperion is right.+ Galeo's thoughts were calmer now the foe's numbers were diminished. His movements had cooled to something clinical. +We face the lesser corruption. These are no more than spiteful dregs pulled from the warp by a desperate enemy.+

Sothis wasn't convinced. 'But you banished the–'

+It fled.+ Galeo's reproaching aura prickled at my skin, for I was its target. +It fled before the final blow.+

'Fled to where?' Dumenidon voxed. My brother's words died as the deck rumbled beneath our feet. I knew that motion. Anyone that had ever set foot on a spaceship knew it. A drive pulse. The *Frostborn* was breathing again.

'That's not possible,' Malchadiel whispered. 'The ship is dead. This isn't possible.'

Weak light flooded the ruined chamber, and brought power to everything else with it. Industrial warning sirens flashed amber along the ceiling, their wails still lost in the vacuum. Elsewhere on board, machines were awakening to their abandoned duties. I sensed cranes grinding to life, sending shivers through the deck as they turned slowly in their sockets, loading huge warheads into their turret feeds. The ship was readying itself for a battle that would never be fought, preparing to fire on an enemy that didn't exist.

The angels were mist-thin and weak now, so few in number as to offer no threat at all.

'Guard me,' I said again.

'You always say that,' Sothis voxed, 'when you are about to undertake someth–'

I never heard the rest of his sentence.

I fled my body.

The sending was an inelegant, fevered thing, formed from rage and need. While my physical presence remained a chanting, motionless weight in the Navigator's chamber, my senses roared down the labyrinthine corridors, leaving the brittle touch of hoarfrost on the walls in my wake. The whole ship was alive, even if only barely lit by flickering lume-globes. Several shattered as I cut past them.

I screamed through the ship's core, senses peeled raw to the merest sight, sound or scent of life.

+You are reaching too far, too fast. Return, brother.+

I raced on. This was my fault. The flaw lay with me. My error had led to the daemon fleeing the Navigator's form, and it fell to me to redeem the tarnish done in the name of duty.

+Hyperion,+ Galeo warned me. +Return to us.+ As if I'd not spent decades enduring soul-breaking trials to earn the armour I wore. As if I had no ability to spend my strength according to my own judgement.

+I know the limits of my own power, justicar.+

+Do not mistake an order as a request, Hyperion.+

I was close to the answer. The enginarium was bathed in the same illumination as the rest of the ship, and here the evidence of activity was undeniable. My senses crashed across consoles, sucking up the taste of any lingering sentience in the chamber in the hunt for psychic spoor. Something, something…

+Return now.+ Galeo buffeted me with the demand, and I almost obeyed the psychic compulsion laced behind the words. He'd trained us well.

+Wait, justicar. I see it.+ And there it was, as obvious and sourceless as the taste of blood in the back of the throat.

I focused. Breathed. Turned. The sensation stroked over me in a bitter caress, born from a cluster of secondary power generators latched with parasitic glee to the still-cold plasma drive. While all other power stations remained cold, this lone generator was shuddering as it resurrected itself.

The drive core's turgid, grey plasma gave a liquid heave. I saw a hand, or something like one, press against the glass from within the fusion ooze. As it dissolved into the dense muck, leering features – the side of a human face – pressed one eye to the glass. It vanished within a moment, absorbed back into the engine slime.

Other secondary generators started shivering.

+The daemon is here, justicar. It swims within the drive core, inside the machine-spirit's bones, resurrecting the ship.+

I snapped back to my body for long enough to tear Malchadiel from his. So deprived, his armoured form would have collapsed but for the lack of gravity. Instead, it stood swaying, bolted down by its boots. Both of his swords drifted out of slack grips. His head rolled loose on his neck.

+Wh–+ he tried to send to me.

+Wait. Look.+ I hurled his consciousness into the enginarium. +That,+ I demanded. +What is that?+

The generators were bleeding. Blood the colour of oil ran in a sheet down the transparent tube beneath it, obfuscating the cooled plasma solidified in the main core. The rippling blood didn't freeze. It obeyed no physics beyond its own.

Malchadiel needed a moment to focus himself. +It's...+

And then he was drifting. I'd torn his senses free without warning or ritual, and I could feel his essence spreading thin across the chamber. The psychic equivalent of a slap thankfully forced him to come together. After the battle, I lacked the strength to reassemble him if he'd truly drifted apart.

+That is the...+ He hesitated. His presence grew cold.

+Mal?+

No answer. He was gone in an instant, clawing his way back to his body. I was faster. I surged back, and dragged him with me.

We opened our eyes in the same moment, and both said 'Justicar' at once.

Galeo was wrenching his blade from the last burning body. +Speak.+

Faster by far to send the images into his mind: the daemon within the plasma ooze; the creature spreading itself through the drive core; the secondary brain-cogitators once belonging to the machine-spirit, now housing a panicking daemonic intelligence.

+The bleeding generators. What do they control?+

Malchadiel recovered his blades from the air, sheathing them at his hips. 'The magnetic ignition for the warp drive.'

Dumenidon ceased his reverent chanting, sheathing his own blade. 'Our prey seeks to jump the ship back into the warp with no guidance? No crew? With only us on board?'

Malchadiel shook his head. 'No, brother. It is cycling up the generators necessary to eject the core into the void.'

'That makes no—' Sothis started.

'The detonation will not be contained by a localised Geller field.' Irritation coupled with desperation, leaving his voice sharp. 'There is no failsafe, no contingency. A daemon pulls these strings. The core will blow cold, right in the void.'

'A beacon to those behind the veil,' I finished.

+Move,+ Galeo sent. +Move.+

SEVEN

RIFT

I

Annika's first reaction when I reconnected with her was to curse at me. It was a theme in my dealings with the inquisitor thus far, and in the past I'd found it amusing. Not so, this time.

+Be silent,+ I told her. For a wonder, she actually was. +Inquisitor, you must get the *Karabela* to a minimum safe distance immediately. The *Frostborn* is ejecting its warp core.+

'Why?' she sent back. '*Destroy the Navigator and end the corruption at the source, with visual confirmation.*'

We were moving as fast as we could, kicking off walls and shooting down hallways, guiding our flight through the arched corridors by boot and palm against the dark walls. Anaemic lighting flickered as the ship's temperamental power core objected to its false reawakening.

+We aren't voiding the warp core – the ship itself is doing it. The daemon is stronger, subtler, than we believed. It fled

123

the Navigator's body, to dwell inside the ship's heart. There it pulls at the machine-spirit's strings. We are unlikely to be able to stop it in time.+

'But the detonation will–'

+Get the *Karabela* to a safe distance.+ I felt her wince at the strength of my sending, but I was far beyond caring. Why was she trying to tell me things I already knew? Did she believe now was the best time for such redundancies? +Do it now, human.+

'As you wish.' A pause. I could feel her breathing, so far away. *'We're under way. You know I cannot teleport you back from this distance.'*

+I know.+ I was touched she'd even consider it. Many inquisitors wouldn't. +We all know. If we don't survive, be ready to run for Titan with word of Armageddon. The monastery must be warned.+

'So be it.' She faded into silence. I could feel what she wanted to say. She wished to apologise for letting her anger get the better of her, and for sending us here to die, but the word 'sorry' was too alien to an inquisitor's tongue. *'Hyperion?'*

+Mistress?+

'Hiljah kah uhtganjen mev tarvahettan.'

My laughter carried over the vox. *Greet the end with courage.* Fenrisian poetry at its blunt best.

'What is it?' Malchadiel asked. 'What's so amusing?'

'Nothing, brother,' I replied. +Inquisitor?+

'Yes?'

+We have a similar valediction in the Terran System. We say 'Die well'.+

I felt her faint amusement, through our bond. *'I prefer the Fenrisian term.'*

'The *Karabela* is moving,' I voxed to my kindred. Sirens

flashed in the soundless air around us. Ahead of me, Malchadiel kicked off from a slanting wall and surged down a side corridor.

'I'm not going to die here,' he said. 'I will not die before seeing Mars.'

The deck shook beneath us, a lurching heave as the warship disgorged its intestines into the void. I heard Malchadiel murmuring to himself, speaking of Geller fields and the madness of a daemon infecting a machine-spirit. He sounded both disgusted and amazed.

'The *Frostborn* has jettisoned its power cores,' Annika sent to me.

+I know. We felt it. Are you clear?+

'We're clear. I've never seen an active warp core breached in the void. Not without its failsafes and containment fields.'

Nor had I, and archival description was a rather dry substitute. +Tell me what you're seeing.+

She was silent for some time. 'Witch-lightning. The plasma drive tubes are covered in it. They're going to... Hyperion? Did you feel that?'

How could I not? Wetness at my mouth's edge let me know I was drooling, as every muscle in my body contracted and flexed to their own desires. Unable to focus, I felt myself crash into a wall.

'It's gone,' she said. 'It's destroyed.'

Galeo, suffering as I suffered, pulled me back to face the corridor's end. +Warp breach,+ he sent, his silent voice tight with pain. +A painful one.+

'Hyperion?'

I couldn't separate the voices in my mind – not the justicar's, not the inquisitor's, nor the hundreds of new voices that screamed and shrieked, demanding to be heard. Whatever foulness lay on the other side of the breach, it promised to be numerous.

In that moment, the blast wave struck. The *Frostborn*, what was left of its magnificent bulk, juddered in an invisible grip. Each of us slammed to the floor, locking our boots to the decking and crouching to ride out the storm.

'I'm beginning to wish,' Sothis voxed, 'that we'd never come with Annika after Cheth.'

II

The warp core chamber no longer existed. The entirety of its rear half was open to the void, offering a mist-wreathed view of the shrouded stars. All the walls and machinery I'd seen in my sending – all gone, spat out to tumble through space. Where power generators and fusion cores had rested, bound in immense sockets, empty tracks and scorched metal marked the systems' absence. The *Frostborn* would never move again. She'd jettisoned every vital generator across a dozen decks, breaking her own back purely to make her last shriek that little bit louder.

It had worked well enough. That last shriek had torn a wound in reality. Had the *Karabela* been closer, our own vessel would have been caught in the detonation, and its own sensitive warp core could easily have died in sympathy with the *Frostborn*'s.

We watched the bulk of broken black-iron machinery twisting away through the nebula, drowning in dust. No more than three thousand metres away, where the principal drive engines had been, a slice in the galaxy was bleeding filth into the void. Voices lashed at me from that rift – human, alien and otherwise – all screaming in languages I came tantalisingly close to understanding. A word here, a meaning there. I knew I'd be able to comprehend them if I concentrated.

+Don't.+

I glanced at Galeo. He was shaking his head. +Don't,+ he said again. +Do not even try.+

The gash of sliced space stared back at us, a slitted violet snake-eye with a writhing white iris. I felt the malignancy of an inhuman intelligence staring right back.

Dumenidon was the first to tense. 'I see them,' he said softly.

They came on wings the colour of tormented flesh, their skin the same aggrieved red. Even as they spat across the void, streaming towards us from such a distance, I could see their reaching claws. Hundreds of them. Hundreds. Some weak. Some strong. Some I recognised from the archives or their inscriptions upon the Arcus Daemonica; many more perhaps no one had ever borne witness to.

+Focus on the Aegis,+ Galeo ordered. +Maintain it with all available strength. They will break against us like a tide against the rocks. Many, many of them are weak and spineless things, emboldened only by their first taste of the material realm. We will banish them with no effort at all. Stand ready, brothers.+

We raised our weapons as one. Galeo and Dumenidon clutched theirs in two-handed warding grips. Malachadiel stood absolutely motionless, falchions crossed at the hilts. Sothis stroked his blades together, sending sparks of force spitting from the edges as their protesting energy fields over-lapped. My stave whirled slowly, a propeller of blurring force. It flared with light as larger chunks of grit burst in its refractor aura.

+One last matter. Twins?+

'Yes, justicar,' they said in perfect harmony.

+Castian will not end this way, nor on this night. Sothis, I did not survive the massacre at Ajanta just to let the squad's legacy end here. And Malchadiel, you will see Mars. On my life, I swear it.+

'I never doubted it, justicar,' Malchadiel replied. I could sense his smile, even if I couldn't see it.

I was still watching the nascent rift, and the sickness spilling forth. A great shape, something more mythological devil than man, screamed its way through a horrendous birth. The thing clawed its way from the burning warp-womb to fall, hissing and smoking, into the cold vacuum. It streaked towards us, slaying its weaker kindred in its vicious haste.

'I never believed I would see one of those,' Sothis said quietly. I could scarcely believe my eyes, either.

+We will see it slain, Castian. Faith is our shield.+

It took me several heartbeats to realise I'd been the one to send those words, not Galeo.

III

They broke against us, just as Galeo had promised. The Aegis slowed them, withering the strength in their limbs, but our collective aura was never going to do more than weaken a horde of such size. In union, my four brothers began chopping, cleaving, carving. Viscera burst across our armour, sizzling in the void as it evaporated in our reality. Temperature gauges flashed and chimed as the daemons' burning blood washed against my ceramite in short-lived splashes. The cold void did nothing to freeze netherworldly blood.

Each crack of my stave broke a ridged skull or pounded through an open mouth, cracking fangs and impaling the throat beyond. In banishment, the creatures had little binding them together: some ruptured in the weightless air, others writhed as they were immolated. Horns and malformed skulls crashed against my war plate in a melody made from blunt clanks; I spared my stave to block each incoming blade, ignoring these lesser threats. Every deflection was a star in the gloom, refractor flares lighting up the remains of the chamber with the intensity of a stuttering star.

'Up,' Malchadiel voxed. He crashed his swords together once, forcing the energy fields to burn any trace matter away from the blades, and kicked off the decking without another word.

Two creatures barred my way, their too-long tongues lashing across my armour in a scraping caress. The first beast died to a surge of psychic force, blasting it back against a wall to dissolve against the hull. The second staggered, its head cracked open by my return blow, barbed tongue thrashing with blind anguish. I reached for the staggering creature with my sixth sense, caught it with a telekine's grip around its throat, and dragged it closer. Its worthless struggles ended as I butted my helm into its choking face, breaking whatever passed for bone in its hideous head. With an outstretched arm, I cast it back into the void. Let it bleed its sick fire into space.

+Maintain the Aegis,+ Galeo sent, his thoughts bladed in their urgency. +Cease whoring away your power, Hyperion.+

I was already up, soaring higher, joining my brother on the curving ceiling. We locked our boots to the roof, weapons spinning, falling back into a killing rhythm as we stood back to back.

From then on, to my shame, it was impossible to follow my brothers' battles. Every shred of my focus bled into spinning the stave, crashing against black sword blades and cracking into unprotected bodies.

I killed something with seven faces. I killed something that knew my name, and something else that addressed me by names I'd never heard, or only read about in the monastery's archives. I killed and killed and killed, saving my strength as best as I was able, for what we knew was soon to come. Angels and daemons alike fell back from us in a broken tide of shrieks and searing blood.

The chamber fell dark as the nebula's gritty, gaseous brightness was eclipsed at last. Unable to turn and face the new threat, I leeched from Malchadiel's senses. His thoughts had never felt so cold.

'War given form,' he said beneath his breath.

EIGHT

GAMBITS

I

Our salvation lay in the Archenemy's innate corruption. Even as it descended upon us, it was killing its kin more decisively than even we could.

In the bluntest terms, the Daemon of Wrath butchered its lesser spirit brethren in its bid to reach us, but its presence alone was enough to diminish them. Such a beast's very life force is a bane to its lesser kindred. Away from the warp, creatures of raw Chaos suffer in the physicality of the material realm, and the greater daemon's dominance sucked at those weaker bodies, siphoning from them in order to continue manifesting in our reality.

Around us, the lesser things withered and crumbled in the shadow of their sire. In their maddened spite, several even struck at their colossal overlord, hating it for the affront, despising their master for its theft of their incarnated lives.

It roared, somehow bellowing air and boiling spittle

131

through the vacuum. But for the dubious security of our mag-locks, we'd have been hurled back against the hull and pulped against the dark iron.

The creature would reach the ship's wreckage in moments, and be on us a heartbeat later.

A second, even weaker tide of lesser devilry made its last bid to bring us down. A spindly thing of bladed limbs and leathery flesh scrabbled onto my back, and its knuckly stabs dug into the joints where my armour plating overlapped. Queasy recollections of burrowing parasites came to me, digging between the scales of a reptile's encrusted skin. I'd seen such insectile things in the monastery's archives, populating great underground hives on distant death worlds.

Another of them attached itself to my stave arm, dragging at my hand even as its flesh blackened in the weapon's aura. Warning runes flashed across my eye lenses, agitated by my labouring life signs. In a strangely cold, distracted sense, I felt knives of black bone puncturing my armour joints, digging into my body. They brought pain with each push, mostly focused behind one knee and in the base of my spine. Something scraped against my backbone, setting my nerves aflame. It wasn't such a distant feeling then.

'Mal,' I voxed through clenched teeth.

My brother was no help to me – he'd lost his magnetic grip on the ceiling. I saw him through the boiling melee, as embattled and buried in these wretched leathery scavengers as I was. His swords rammed over his shoulders to impale the horned things on his back.

Pounding a fist into the creature reaching around my shoulder did nothing of any use, beyond feeding it my fist. My hand stuck fast in the thing's jaws, adding a nasty scraping from its teeth breaking on the ceramite. It took all my strength to turn, to see the daemon trying to eat my arm.

Its distended maw wrapped my hand to the wrist, tongue coiling all the way to my elbow. It even wrapped the storm bolter mounted on my forearm, little realising it would need to eat a holy weapon if it ever intended to swallow the limb.

Idiotic creature. I closed my fingers, a bloom in reverse, and as my fingertips touched the trigger-plate in my palm, the daemon's head blew apart.

II

Bolters in the void.

A vacuum blunts the teeth of our sacred shells, but they are far from worthless. The biggest change isn't in what they do, but in how their rendering judgement appears.

In an airless void, the explosion of live shells against armour and flesh is the briefest flicker of light, gone in the shadow of a second. The explosion's dispersing force encounters no other forces to oppose – not air, not heat, simply nothing at all. Unaugmented eyes cannot grasp the subtle beauty of a void explosion, for despite the perfection of the human form, the physics at play occur too fast for the eye to follow.

Our eye lenses were a different matter. Each bursting shell bred a spherical afterimage of expanding light from their impact points, a visual echo on our reactive visors to show the impact points of gunfire. My brothers deactivated the feedback from registering on their retinas, finding it a worthless distraction. I kept it active, though I was never certain why. In a way, it always reminded me how far I'd come, from whoever I'd been before this.

I still recall the first time I trained in the void, wearing a featureless, honourless suit of thin ceramite only barely approximating a knight's true armour. To look down was to see the nickel-dull skin of the strike cruiser *Unforsaken*; to look up was to stare into the far reaches of absolute space, where distant stars winked in reply to my silent stare. I hadn't been human in some time – the Emperor's Gift wrought too many changes in me even then – but such a sight couldn't fail to move me. Nothing prepared me for it. And how could I be ready? I'd seen little beyond my cell within the monastery and our fortress's great stone chambers, forever ringing with the sound of crashing weapons even when all voices fell to whispers.

I looked into the dark for a long time, hearing nothing but the slow, uneven rhythm of my own two hearts. Never had I felt so alone, so unsure of my worth in the endless, hostile expanse of mankind's galaxy.

Saturn was a tilted orb to my left, oppressively vast despite its distance, its curdled skies making my stomach coil. I remember how I raised my hand to it, as if it were a bauble to be drawn from the night sky. From so far away, it looked no larger than my palm.

Deep below the cruiser's hull, I could make out the curvature of Titan itself: milky with poisonous cloud cover, yet the only home I knew. To fall from my footing would be to plunge through its rancid atmosphere, ending my training as ashen particles caught by the nitrogen winds.

I looked away again, out into space. Far, far beyond Saturn lay the sun itself, and even with its corona crown it was no more than a remote, pulsing speck.

Just one star among millions.

In that moment, I felt what ancient generations must have felt when they first sailed into the sky. Should we ever have come here, so far from humanity's cradle? Was this manifest destiny, to reach out into the black and carve an empire upon the rocky bones of conquered worlds?

Our masters tell us that to consider every perspective is a dangerous virtue. On that night, I learned why. Blessed is the mind too small for doubt. Humanity's champions should never question mankind's right to own the stars.

I carried that lesson with me when I first swore to serve the Inquisition. I carry it with me now, as a knight in the war our species must never see.

III

Against my better instincts, I released the warding stave. Surrendered to the airless void, it floated untouched, anathema to the beings dragging us down.

I drew my pistol the moment my hand was free, opening up at intimate range with the storm bolter on my left arm and the bolt pistol in my right fist. Firing with two weapons was no easy feat if accuracy was a concern, and when every shell you carried had been ritually forged, consecrated and blessed by the Imperium's holiest hands, it was a grave sin to miss the foe.

Of the many martial disciplines all knights must learn, there were few in which I excelled above my brothers. I was worthless with twin blades compared to Sothis, and a failed long-blade duellist by Dumenidon's standards. But marksmanship was one aspect of our secret war I'd long-since mastered. My retinal display bisected, offering me the separate views of both weapons. My senses melted into the familiar cadence of glance-aim-fire, glance-aim-fire, firing both weapons at once, never slowing, never ceasing.

The storm bolter bucked on my arm, bellowing twin bolts at the skittering creatures furthest away. The pistol shots were saved for the clutching, crawling things scratching at my armour. Within a handful of seconds, my retinal display was bleached by the calculated pyrotechnics of shell impacts.

Everything I struck burst apart into sizzling viscera, dissolving from the material universe in acidic spurts. Around us, the air thickened with black mist.

The daemon-sire was almost upon us, and still we struggled with lesser vermin. I couldn't shoot them off Malchadiel; the risk to his armour's integrity was too great. Instead, I sent him reeling with a compacted, kinetic wave of force. Daemons fell and scattered as he tumbled through the chamber. Several left scratches on his unpainted ceramite. To arrest his drift, he plunged both falchions into the roof, and relocked his boots to the metal.

Through ragged breaths, he voxed two words. 'Behind you.'

Both guns rose to follow his warning. All three barrels spat out in the same moment, pounding three shells into the chest and wings of a leaping, scarlet-skinned creature resembling a cathedral gargoyle granted poisoned life. I had the briefest glimpse of bronze bone in the rare-steak pink of its internal meat before it lost all grip on our reality. Dissolving blood stained my armour, but the creature was gone.

Twin runes, the Trecenti script for *hollow*, flashed on my eye lenses, warning me to reload. I holstered the pistol and summoned my stave, pulling it through the air to land in my palm.

To pull itself into the severed chamber, the daemon was forced to furl its immense wings against its back. Metal corroded at its very presence. I watched the walls rust in the wake of its rippling pinions, and steel rotting in the shadowed mist rising from them.

Our justicar faced it first, and he faced it alone. Galeo made his wrath a weapon, distilling it into a blade of psychic sound and hurling it from his throat as a spear leaves a fist. When he shouted at the daemon-sire, teeth broke in the daemon's mulish maw, and its right eye ceased to exist in a black blood rupture.

+I will deal with this,+ Galeo pulsed to us. Already, he was charging. The remaining daemons parted before him, stagger-ing, thrown away in a burst of force. In the lack of gravity, his charge ended with a leap. The force sword in his hands was a crescent of burning white light.

'Focus,' Malchadiel voxed. I turned in time to catch one of the weakening daemons' blades with my stave. As Mal impaled it from behind, I broke its neck with a backhanded blow.

I never saw Galeo's first strike land, but I most definitely felt it. The blade meeting daemonic armour bred a feverish buzz in all our minds, thickening my tongue and itching my gums. The sudden, severest need for a chemical purification shower overtook me, to cleanse this mission from my body.

'We have to help him,' said Sothis. 'These wretches are finished.'

'Go,' came Dumenidon's reply. 'Together now.'

Malchadiel turned to follow them. I kicked my last attacker away, incinerating him in a second of uncontrolled anger. The contrails of fire lashed over the daemon, melting its wings from its shoulders even as it burned.

Mal called my name, yelling for me to hurry. I killed the flame stream with a whipcrack of effort, and followed my brothers into madness.

IV

A battle with a greater daemon occurs in two realms. There's the physical aspect: the world of numbing blows, sweating hatred, and the breathless release of energy that lesser minds would call sorcery. And then there's the spiritual side: a duel of prickling wills and jagged thoughts, where even standing in the enemy's presence causes a spiritual sickening.

A greater daemon of Sanguinary Unholiness is, quite lit-erally, the negative emotion of war given form. Take the emotion of every human ever to pick up a sword and rifle, blended together in the poisonous realm behind reality's veil: every agony suffered by a gutshot soldier crying for his comrades; every dehumanising flush of hate felt in that grotesque intimacy of stealing another man's life; each and every nightmare suffered by a crusade's survivor; or the crippling fear of facing down an outnumbering horde when there's nowhere to run...

All of this, and more, radiated from the creature in a seething wave. Truly, mankind's sins returned to plague us.

It was said that upon their vulgar warp-worlds, each of these avataric warlords reigned over legions of the lost and the damned. Even the Inquisition's archives were vague about such things. Few could stare into hell and retain presence of mind enough to meticulously record what one saw within its tides.

The daemon drew back from our Aegis, but it knew nothing of retreat. Pain only drove it to frustrated anger. As we drew near, my first instincts faded. Revulsion gave way to realisation.

'I know this creature.' I had no idea if I spoke the words with my mouth or my mind. 'Justicar...'

+Speak.+ Galeo stood before it, his long blade shedding sparks as it ground against the beast's axe. I was glad I couldn't hear the strained thrum in the vacuum – the sound of blade on blade always set my teeth on edge. Strange, the things that we can never quite get used to.

But the image from my memory was as clear as if I had the book in my hands. On the fourth row of the Aventinus Juncture of the Librarium Daemonica, contained within the texts detailing the Juruga Uprising almost three thousand years before, a stylised etching showed the daemon that now stood before us.

Malchadiel, always the closest of my brothers, knew my

thoughts as easily as he felt his own.

'I am so glad you study these things,' he whispered over the vox.

+I know its name.+

As we ran, I reloaded my storm bolter. We were close, but the daemon gave no ground. Its wings, cobwebbed by juicy veins along the leathery membranes, rattled and flapped in the haze of smoke. Rather than a chest protected in a breastplate of bronze, its bones had pushed through the bristled skin to form overlapping plates of mouldering yellow armour. The beast's body still bore a dozen spears and swords impaled deep in its flesh, the legacy of failed executions in generations past.

And then we were upon it, with no time to do anything but fight. The link to my brothers gave me insight into their movements. Galeo stood facing the daemon like a champion of old, sword raised as he duelled a creature ten times his size. Each impact of axe against blade seemed to slow time, as even enhanced human senses struggled to process what we were seeing. Sothis and Dumenidon joined the justicar, adding their blows and blocks to his. Without even communing, Malchadiel and I shared another idea.

We disengaged from the ceiling, kicking off to launch onto the daemon's back. To grip the thing's wings was no different from clutching at the billowing sails of some primitive oceangoing ship, thrashing in the wind. Malchadiel struck first, carving cuts of stinking meat from the creature's flesh. I felt a burst of emotion from him, of vicious eagerness as he sought to cut one of the wings from the beast's back.

I landed higher, my boots thudding into the creature's shoulder and clutching at the thing's greasy, battish ear for something to hold onto. The storm bolter clicked on my arm. The two shells hammered into the beast's temple, blasting a hole in the bestial skull, making a flapping ruin of the leathery flesh that remained.

As it reached for me, writhing to throw me off, I sent a focused pulse right into its mind, aiming for the quivering ridges of brain-meat visible through the skull's breakage.

It wasn't a word – it wasn't even language – I forced an amalgamation of sounds and concepts into its bared brain. Imagine a hundred bronze bells ringing out over a deserted city; the scream of falling timber in a burning church; the prolonged agony of an untreated amputation; and a man breathing through lungs that bubbled with blood.

I shouted that into the daemon's mind.

And nothing happened.

The fist hit me with the force of being trapped beneath a tank's treads. Before I could react, the daemon-sire threw me from its back. I saw motion blurs, but nothing more. My armour's auto-senses sang out in alarm.

Even post-human reflexes have their limits. Before my hearts could beat twice, I struck the chamber wall at an angle bad enough to wrench my spine into a crackling twist. The metal was too smooth for a grip, and my velocity stole any chance at punching a handhold. After that single impact, I skidded along the wall, shedding sparks in my wake.

I clawed at the metal with a single scrape, all I had time for. It didn't even slow me down.

A moment later, I was out in the void.

The runes scrolling down my faceplate flashed warnings I evidently needed to know. Yes, I was aware my armour's integrity was breached in several places. Yes, I knew I was venting air in a hissing slash of uncontrolled gas from a rent in my chestplate. Yes, I was aware the stabilisers and power conduits in my left leg were in need of immediate attendance. A thought cancelled the information feed, leaving me looking around as I fell for anything to catch my bearings.

I was drifting fast, falling through the dusty void, deeper out into space. Grit rattled against my armour as I tumbled through the directionless expanse. I could barely even see the ship's hull through the dust, shrinking every second.

This was going to be a humiliating way to die.

+That... was extremely... foolish,+ Galeo sent to me. He sounded strained, almost to the point of collapse.

Runes flickered in response to my thoughts. I watched my armour's power displays struggling against the damage. The warp alignment nodes jutting from my power pack started their bass rumble. I had to confess, even to myself, that this probably wasn't going to work.

+Hyperion?+ Malchadiel's voice was weak. It always cost him to speak telepathically, for his own talents were so different from mine.

+I'm jumping back,+ I replied.

+It will come for you. It will come for the warp pulse.+

+Only one chance. Watch for me.+

+I ca– +

V

I held my breath this time.

The warp embraced me, squeezing at my armour in the hope of cracking it apart. I felt hands, or something close to them, scrabbling at the joints of my warplate. I couldn't run, though I gave it my all. Charging forwards was no different from pushing through tar.

Power gauges drained with malicious speed, and more runes flashed warnings I couldn't heed. I had one chance at this, one chance to teleport back to the ship before my armour's jump-systems failed. If I missed it, I was as good as dead. The *Karabela* could cut through this dust for an eternity and never get a teleport lock on my armour.

Something wrapped my throat. I felt it seeping into my armour with all the insidious, wet chill of a melting icicle held to my neck. Blind-firing achieved nothing: the storm bolter belched its payload into the thick muck, and the shells immediately froze in the tidal winds, all momentum stolen.

It didn't matter if I'd made it or not. I shut the warp nodes down, because to do anything else would be to die.

+Mal,+ I sent out into the nothingness. +Mal.+

VI

'I've got you,' he voxed.

Vision took a few seconds to return, as my eye lenses re-tuned into reality's spectrum. Malchadiel clutched my forearm, hauling me back onto the deck.

No. It wasn't Mal. Sothis moved back three steps, pulling me with him, back from the edge. My retinal display was still a mess of hazy silhouettes and scrambled runes, but I could faintly see the daemon's immense shadow, dark against a greater darkness, and the flashes of repellent energy as my brothers struck at it. It was coming, looming above us. My warp arrival had drawn it upon me, as I'd known it would. It sensed the breach in the universe, a power so similar to its own.

+Sothis.+ I pulsed his name laced with a warning, hard enough to send watery ripples through the iron floor, distending reality in its wake. My brother dragged me another step, still gripping my wrist, and was already turning when the black talons burst through his chest.

Three of them, a trident's tines, fingernail claws the thickness of a man's thighs. I heard the worst sound of my life in that moment – the choking gurgle as Sothis vomited blood into his helm. It carried over the vox with hateful clarity.

Both of my boots thudded and locked onto the decking as I rose to my feet. Sothis twisted in the impaling clutch, too defiant to even realise he was dead. He reached for me, voxing sticky, gargling nonsense, as if I could ever pull him from that monstrous claw.

It began to lift him, and he reached for weapons that weren't in his hands. I was already firing at the daemon over his shoulder. Blood crystals decorated the air in a disgustingly festive spray, spilling from his annihilated body.

Malchadiel screamed across the vox and into my mind, a union of sound and pain, as his twin brother came apart in the daemon's claws.

I felt Sothis slipping away, and my mind made an instinctive reach, as if I could somehow pull him back into the bond we shared. For the ghost of a moment, I followed him as his thoughts and presence dispersed, feverish in a futile need to reassemble the fragments of his thinning essence.

There was his pain, burning hot enough to bisect me. I felt his regret, his furious shame at dying with his duty unfinished. And I felt, without knowing such a thing was possible, his fear. The natural fear of a fallible, killable creature at last succumbing to death. I couldn't think less of him for it. No amount of post-human manipulation could change what it meant to be alive, and the gravity of finally surrendering that gift.

At the very last second, I saw a young boy in ragged clothing, his face turned to the polluted sky. With the image came the whispery murmur of half-remembered words.

'They'll take us up to the stars,' the boy said. Tears ran down his dirty face. 'Won't they?'

'Don't worry, Mal,' a fading voice replied. 'It'll be fine.'

And then it was gone. The image, and the soul fuelling it, vanished. A hole yawned open in my mind, hungry and cold.

I'd never realised how much my Castian brothers relied on one another – how we were always present to some degree in each other's minds. With Sothis's sudden absence, my senses gave a queasy jolt, seeking something, anything, to bind themselves to.

All of this happened in the time it took me to draw a single breath.

'Hyperion?' The inquisitor's voice was frantic. The strength of my emotion restored our bond. I felt her seep back into my mind as I instinctively reached out, clawing for any familiar soul. *'What was that? What's happening?'*

+Sothis… Sothis is dead.+

With those words spoken, I never heard her reply. I snapped back into my body with a brutal lurch. Something had kicked me back into my own consciousness. The justicar's anger licked at the edges of my thoughts.

+Get back in the fight, you useless bastard.+ Galeo's words were knives of ice. +Or I'll kill you myself.+

I opened my eyes, without realising they'd been closed, and raised my weapons again.

VII

Malchadiel dealt the final blow.

As executions went, it was an ugly, graceless deliverance. We took the beast to pieces, blending spell and steel, eviscerating it with the edge of blades and the raw contours of killing lightning. Rage loaned strength to weary muscles and ripened our psychic sorcery. Alchemical blood torrented in arcs that wouldn't freeze. I'd never fought with such disarray before. Each discharge of power was a long exhalation ending in breathlessness, needing a moment of recovery in the dizzying serenity that followed.

The daemon's greatest mistake was in seeking to eat

Sothis's remains. It opened the way for several heartbeats' worth of uninterrupted assault, even as the daemon mocked us with laughter. We savaged the thing as it sought to back away, and when the deathblow finally came minutes later, the tide hadn't once turned back in the beast's favour.

We stood in the wake of its dissipating corpse, black with unholy blood from boots to silver helms. Silence reached out then: a tainted, pregnant silence between the four of us still standing. No one said a word. There seemed to be nothing to say.

A nudge of concentration killed the power to my stave. In the noiseless chamber, I wondered how loud my swallow translated over the vox.

+Hyperion,+ Galeo sent at last.

Malchadiel came up behind me. I turned just in time for his fist to meet my faceplate.

'You said you knew its name.' His hands were at my throat before I'd even righted myself. 'You said you could banish it. You said you knew its name. What happened? You killed my brother. He died bringing you back.'

Dumenidon dragged him away from me, though he kept thrashing, sending weak waves of exhausted force against me. I shielded myself against them easily enough.

'I thought I knew its true name. I recognised it from the archives.'

'A grievous error,' Dumenidon said quietly.

+He died saving you.+ Mal spat a vicious pulse at me. It cracked against my helm with a bolter shell's thud. Without thinking, I almost lashed back in kind, but kept my hand clenched, resisting the temptation.

+Enough.+ Galeo's single word was enough to calm Mal's hate, and I sensed more than a touch of manipulation in his psychic contact. +Calm, Malchadiel. We will speak of this back aboard the *Karabela*.+

NINE
AFTERMATH

I

I watched it burn.

The *Frostborn* bared her belly, rolling in the momentum of her destruction. Our weapon batteries ripped through the defenceless vessel's armour with ease, but the ship still took a long time to die. With so few of its systems active, there was little combustive effect. And with nothing to explode, our guns had to take the ship apart in a series of patient strafing runs. It took almost an hour, such was the destroyer's cold tenacity. It didn't want to die.

I stood in the observatorium along the *Karabela*'s spine, staring through the dust at the gradual ruination taking place. My brothers lingered below decks, though I wasn't sure where. That was strange enough – our bond had grown cold since Sothis's death, and I resisted the urge to reach out to them. All I knew was that they held counsel together. I could feel their closeness as clearly as I could sense my exclusion from it.

So I watched the ship burn alone. The assault was reaching its end when I sensed another presence approaching nearby. The observatorium took the form of a domed chamber, usually shielded by retractable armour plating. Now, its sides and roof were open to the void, the walls bare, transparent plastek. I felt his presence coming from some distance away, and felt no need to turn when his footsteps began to echo across the chamber.

I couldn't conceive of anyone I'd rather see less.

'Hyperion,' he said.

'What do you want, heretic?'

'The same thing I always want. Just to talk.'

I looked at him, uncaring if my face reflected the disgust I felt inside. 'I can think of no words worth sharing with you, Clovon.'

He inclined his tattooed head, as if I'd scored a victory of sorts. An aquila was inked over the worst of his burn scars, with its black wings spread like a dappled shadow over his face. This close, he smelled of ritual oils, the pistols at his hips, and the inquisitor he served.

'It's beautiful, isn't it?' He gestured to the dying *Frostborn*.

'In a way.' Standing this close to him made me want to spit. I could taste the acid on my tongue. 'Speak, if you wish.'

He chuckled then. 'How gracious of you.'

My armour was a cracked and discoloured wreck, but I still towered above him. I looked down, letting my irritation show plainly.

'I am trying to be polite to you,' I pointed out. 'You are not making it easy.'

He zipped the front of his beaten leather jacket. 'It's cold in here.'

I hadn't noticed. I rarely noticed the little details like that.

'What do you want, Clovon? I am in no mood to suffer irritants with any grace.'

'The mistress is meeting with your brothers. Despite the loss of Sothis, this ranks as a significant achievement for the Inquisition.'

'I do not see how.'

The heretic held up a hand, a finger rising with each point he made. 'You obtained evidence of a Navigator possessed by the Archenemy, and that's a rare thing to see. You recovered a survivor, and we both know that eyewitness accounts are the ordos' bread and butter. The survivor was also one of the Wolves, which makes him doubly valuable to Inquisitor Jarlsdottyr, doesn't it? Considering the vessel's crew was largely purged into the void, even a single living soul is a triumph. You also banished a threat of – to use Annika's colourful Fenrisian term – "greater maleficarum".'

I watched the ship crumbling, and said nothing.

'She said it was a blessing any of you survived.'

'She sent us into that fight.'

'That's probably why she considers it a blessing. She'd never admit to a mistake, of course. You know how she is.'

'Her decision has its merits, though. If she blames herself for Sothis, she speaks from ignorance. It had nothing to do with her.'

How to explain dæmonic choirs to someone so blind to the truths behind the veil?

'There are degrees of power in the Neverborn, as in mortals. This was a relatively weak fragment, albeit of the greatest choir. With care, we would have lost no one. Like the crew of the *Frostborn*, we were undone by the enemy's cunning and our own foolishness, not the foe's strength.'

'I see. So you made a mistake. That's what you're saying.'

I didn't like how he was looking at me.

'Yes,' I said.

'It happens, Hyperion. It happens across the galaxy, in every walk of life. People make the wrong decisions. They choose poorly.'

'I am not people. I am a Grey Knight. We are the Imperium's flawless blade, mankind's faultless heart. We are the Emperor's Gift.' I broke off before it could go any further. 'Why does she tolerate you, heretic?'

'A good question.' His expression twisted the eagle wings across his face. 'She tolerates me because I am one of her many triumphs. She saved my soul. She redeemed me.'

I shook my head. 'You whored your soul away to the gods behind the veil. No matter what salvation came later, some sins cannot be forgiven.'

'That's your view, Hyperion. Not an inviolate truth.'

'And there speaks the voice of corruption.'

'Think of your Inquisition's pet Adeptus Astartes mongrels – the Exorcists. Their training is spoken of in the ordos' archives, you know. They've housed daemons within their bodies, and endured exorcism under the Inquisition's watchful eyes. They are forgiven. Why not a human like me? Where does your hypocrisy come from?'

'They are as corrupt as any other.'

He smiled at that. 'Such a puritan.'

His mockery curled my fingers. Even the subtle movement of muscles tensing made my armour growl. I doubted he knew how much effort it took not to kill him.

'Leave.' I breathed the word.

He refused. That was a surprise in itself – he'd always seemed so meek. Perhaps his past distance was a form of respect, rather than evidence of fear. I'd need to muse on that.

'Will you tell me what happened?' he asked.

The laugh I forced was bitter even to my ears. 'There is little to say. Mistakes were made. My brother died because of them.'

'Will you tell me what happened?' he asked again.

What was there to lose? He had Annika's clearance, anyway. So I told him. I relayed every detail from the moment we boarded the *Frostborn* to the moment we left again, with Sothis's remains in the troop bay of our gunship.

Clovon said nothing at first. He watched the destroyer coming apart among the dusty stars. After a time, he finally spoke.

'It was unwise to attack the creature from above without securing yourself as Malchadiel did. You know that. But Sothis chose to risk helping you back aboard.' Clovon drew one of the throwing knives from the baldric over his chest, and proceeded to clean his nails with the tip. That was his judgement, delivered as casually as anything else in life.

'That is your appraisal? That's all?'

Clovon nodded. 'Sothis is dead because he chose to help you. You were half-blinded by retinal re-tuning. He was not. He knew what was happening, and still risked bringing you back.'

'I...'

I hesitated, unsure of what to say. My thoughts turned thick and slow.

'He didn't just risk his life for you, Hyperion. He gave it. Willingly.'

It didn't matter. Throne, the only thing worse than Clovon's presence was actually speaking to him. 'I have no wish to discuss this further. And it is still a mystery to me why the inquisitor keeps you at her heels.'

He sheathed the knife and offered a polite bow. 'I was only a minor recidivist, in truth. But my mistress is a firm believer in redemption. Mistakes will always be made. What matters is how we deal with them, and what we can bring forth from their aftermath.'

I looked at him for several moments. 'Subtle.'

Clovon merely grinned, and the aquila tattooed across his face spread its wings.

II

Soon enough, I stood before my brothers. Annika had refused to leave, and the five of us met in the war room, around the central table. Sothis's meagre remains were in the care of the Palladium Kataphrakt, sealed in cryo-storage.

The inquisitor greeted me with a weak smile. Dumenidon inclined his head. Galeo and Malchadiel stared at me; the former without expression, the latter with dull fire in his eyes. Anger's embers had become an unclean resentment. I hardly blamed him. Their thoughts were unreadable, shielded behind iron resolves. With time, I suspected I could force my way into their minds, though I wondered where that temptation had even come from.

Cut off from our familiar psychic union, it was all I could do not to shiver. They looked almost like strangers to me, with something missing – the way a blind man would have to guess his friends' positions, expressions and emotions by the sound of their voices.

'I was summoned,' I said.

+You have failed Castian,+ Galeo said. +From the moment we boarded the wreck, you were too headstrong, too incautious, and too overconfident. This is not the first operation flawed by your arrogance, Hyperion. You stand on the edge of censure. I cannot tolerate a warrior who will not obey orders.+

I said nothing, for there was nothing to say. Dumenidon spoke next, his sterner features set closer to resignation than anything else.

'You are the most gifted of us in some ways,' he said, 'and also the least capable of controlling the power. Together, we are Castian. United, we are Grey Knights. Divided, we are little more than men, Hyperion. We bleed, we fall, we die. We've all seen this within you for months now – you fight for yourself, defending yourself rather than the brother at your back. It is not simple selfishness. Selfishness could be easily punished.'

He sighed, and for the first time I truly felt the depth of his disappointment. My failure was a pain to him. I knew it, for he allowed me to sense it. Dumenidon at least lowered the resistance to our empathic bond. I felt his reassuring presence return the way a shivering man feels the touch of sunlight. But he wasn't finished.

'It is worse,' he continued, 'because ignorance fuels your actions. You should know better, yet you do not. You have been trained to blend with us, yet you fail to do so. In all the millennia of Castian's history, you are the only one not to have bonded with his brothers. When you manage to focus, you are a powerful force in the Aegis. But more often, you hinder us. We defend you when you act alone, and we struggle to align our powers when yours flare up with instability.'

My blood ran cold. 'You cannot excommunicate me from Castian,' I said, hating the tremor in my voice.

'Can't we?' Malchadiel grunted.

+We could,+ Galeo sent.

'But we will not.' Dumenidon spared a glance at the others. 'We have spoken of this.'

Galeo nodded. +You carry one of the few remaining artefacts from Castian's founding. Perhaps the most precious. It is time to prove you deserve that stave, Hyperion. Heed my orders. Fight with your brothers, joining your movements to theirs. Lone wolves die alone, brother. The pack is a hunter's strength.+

Galeo opened to me again, just as Dumenidon had done moments before. To feel the background sense of his mind linked to mine was blessed relief, even as it made me more keenly aware of Sothis's absence.

He shook his head as he responded to my thoughts. +We do not blame you for Sothis,+ he sent. +Purge the guilt from your heart. We were with you, even if you could scarcely feel us. We know you were blinded by retinal realignment. The grudge Castian brings against you is for the mistakes you made in those hours, Hyperion. Not for Sothis's choice to tempt death by saving your life. The daemon was coming for you with all fury, and you were next to helpless. Our fallen brother knew what he was risking, and he was almost fast enough.+

'Almost,' I said. 'You can command me to purge the guilt I feel, justicar, but not the shame.'

+Perhaps that is as it should be.+

'Sothis made a mistake, as well,' Dumenidon allowed. 'Once I'd seen you could not be defended, I would have let you die.'

I searched his face for any sign he was joking. I found none.

+Malchadiel,+ prompted Galeo.

Malchadiel looked at me, but there was no hint of deeper emotion behind the glare. He wouldn't lower his walls.

'Mal,' I started.

'The others are right,' he interrupted. 'Sothis was a fool to disengage and reach for you. He should have let you die.' Malchadiel gestured to my broken armour. 'You nearly died countless times this night. Every mission, you charge ahead, again and again. Now, we've all paid for your careless soul. What trust I had in you died with my brother. Remember that, the next time you believe you can win this war alone.'

I nodded, almost a shallow bow. 'I hear you,' I told them.

'I hear and obey.'

At last, Malchadiel's mind meshed back with mine. He was in such pain, I almost bled with him. It throbbed within him, a blunt pounding so fresh that it defied easy description. Deeper than pain; this was grief. He was in mourning. I'd never felt it before, neither in my mind, nor inheriting it from my brothers.

I sent a drift of emotion towards him – a gentle thing shaped from regret and shame. At first he recoiled, and I feared he'd raise his walls to me again. After a moment, he accepted the pulsed emotion. He returned a faint, so very faint, nod. It wasn't a healing of the wound between us, but it was a start.

'May I ring the Bell for Sothis?' I asked.

Dumenidon exhaled softly as he looked to Galeo. The justicar, in turn, glanced to Malchadiel. Mal was paralysed in hesitation. I saw him swallow with some difficulty.

+It is tradition for a justicar to ring the Bell,+ Galeo ventured, +but it would be appropriate in this case.+

'I would like…' Malchadiel trailed off. 'Yes. I have no objection.'

'Thank you, Mal,' I said. Silently, I sent to him, and him alone, +They will hear the Bell toll across the Throneworld. I promise you that.+

He gave another barely perceptible nod.

As my brothers left the chamber, Galeo met my eyes for a moment. +No more mistakes, brother.+

I saluted, making the sign of the aquila over my chestplate.

Only Annika remained afterwards. She leaned back against the wall, her arms crossed over her chest.

'A dark day, but a fine victory.'

'That is one way of looking at it,' I agreed.

She smiled. 'Brother Grauvr is stable, not that you asked.

He may not die, after all.' Her crystal-blue eyes glinted in the reflected light. Before I could reply, she offered a melancholy smile. 'I am sorry for what happened to Sothis. Was Clovon any comfort to you?'

'You sent him to me?'

'Not exactly. Vasilla and the Khatan both wished to speak to you, as did Clovon. I decided if only one was to be granted permission, it should be the one with a lesson to impart.'

I mused over that for a moment. Vasilla would have wanted to pray and discuss the state of my soul. The Khatan would have told bleak jokes and teased me for not joining in with her.

'Thank you for not sending the others,' I said.

'To Titan, then. We must relay what happened here, and spread the word of Armageddon falling under siege.' She paused, as if weighing her next words. 'I know who Sothis was, Hyperion. I know who you all were.'

I looked at her for several seconds. 'I don't understand.'

'Before the Inquisition took you, I mean. The Ordo Malleus keeps the most meticulous archives. I know who you all were as children.'

I wasn't sure where she was leading with this. 'Such lore is irrelevant.'

'It may be irrelevant to you, but I'm a curious woman. Sothis and Malchadiel were born into poverty on a miserable industrial world called Tereth. When the Black Ships came to take them, they were eleven standard years old, and already three years into indentured servitude as menials within a munitions manufactorum. They were fated to spend their lives working to build shell casings for Tereth's defence militia.'

'Why are you telling me this?'

'Because it matters. Without the Inquisition, Sothis would

be a wasted old manufactorum worker, or more likely dead decades ago in an industrial accident. The Grey Knights turned him into a weapon, and he served mankind with honour. Even if his service was brief, it was a life lived with more honour than most humans can ever imagine.'

She made the sign of the aquila, her hands pale against her bodyglove. 'Remember that, Hyperion, when you ring the Bell of Lost Souls for your fallen brother.'

'I will, inquisitor. Thank you.'

Her ice-crystal eyes flashed again. 'Do you ever wonder who you were? Who you might have been?'

I didn't even have to think about that. 'No. I know I was close to rejecting the Emperor's Gift because of my age. I believe I was halfway through my teenage years, and several implants almost failed to take. Sometimes I have weak dreams of what came before. Images. Feelings.'

'Like what?' She raised an eyebrow. 'Go on.'

'The sound of rain on cheap metal rooftops. A sense of staring through windows, but seeing nothing beyond. A black throne. I recall that more than anything else: a black throne, cold and dark.' I shrugged a shoulder. 'Nothing is ever clear, but it doesn't matter. As I said, it is irrelevant to me.'

She was smiling again. 'I didn't ask if it was relevant. I asked if you were ever curious about it.'

'No.'

'You're an awful liar, Hyperion. It's one of the things I like best about you.'

III

The voyage took eleven days. For a conventional ship, it would have taken several months.

The *Karabela* bolted through the turbulent void, warded against the unholy caress of the warp's denizens. The journey of a Grey Knights vessel may be rapid, but it is also spiritually tectonic. Hexagrammic shielding and consecrated armour plating protects our warships beyond anything else humanity can create, but the Sea of Souls burns in response to such invasion. The endless, tireless shrieking of daemons dying against the hull is an unceasing erosion against patience.

In flight, the *Karabela*'s machine-spirit was as bright and alive as any member of the crew. She gained presence, almost a personality, in those hours. Her voice was the song of overcharged engines blaring into the void, and her face was haloed by the radiant burst of daemons immolated by her prow. I could feel her, a living soul, singing her tremulous rumble through the decks as well as within my mind. Her song was a hymn, and she sang it beautifully.

At random intervals, the deck would give a violent heave, signaling another diversion as we turned aside from the Astronomican. The ship would shake with greater force as we dived deeper into the aetheric ocean, slicing days from our journey as our Navigator trusted the ship's resilience to hold while he guided us through darker seas.

To push one of our vessels so hard was hardly a rare occurrence, but we all knew the *Karabela* was earning herself a great deal of time in orbital dock for this. The damage inflicted upon the Grey Knights fleet from such travelling meant many of our ships lived housed in repair docks as often as they sailed out of them. Given the advantages, it was a price willingly paid.

On the seventh hour of the last day, we dropped from the warp at the edge of the Throne System. I'd been training alone for the entire journey, having made it clear I did not wish to be disturbed. Only when I felt the lurch of transition back into real space did I finally lower my stave in the middle of the sparring chamber.

I felt the overtaxed muscles in my arms and legs cramping

taut, but it was nothing I couldn't ignore. Sweat dusted my exposed skin in a fine sheen.

'Hyperion,' the inquisitor voxed over the wall-mounted speakers. 'We're home.'

TEN

LAST WORDS

I

Wounded by her headlong rush through poisoned tides, the *Karabela* limped in-system. On the bridge around us, servitors and robed menials worked to interpret the influx of lore as the monastery fed the freshest stellar charts to our cogitators. Docking at Titan was never a fast process. Orbital charts depicted the gas giant's moons and their current locations in the heavens as they drifted on their sedate journeys around the immense world, and catalogued the rapidly shifting data on all Imperial traffic nearby.

We drifted in from the far reaches, sailing along the Enceladus Strait. The *Karabela* came close enough to feel the moon's pull, and I couldn't help but watch the world's jagged luminescence filling the command deck's viewports.

I'd walked on Enceladus once, witnessing the geyser icebursts through the rune-thick red bleaching of a retinal display. Even years later, it was a memory I treasured. While the spraying plumes lacked the majesty of the cryovolcanoes on Titan, it was still a fine sight to see the ice particles blasting high into the void, merging with the outermost, haziest rings of Saturn. A moon's breath, crystallising in the void, becoming one of its sire-world's rings... The galaxy hated us, there was no doubt, but it still offered wonders to those strong enough to bear witness.

Vasilla came to the railing, standing next to me. 'You smile,' she said.

'It is good to be home,' I admitted. The sight of Saturn and its moons always did this to me: that great, ringed world, so monstrous in size, its skies forever rancid, concealing the poisonous nothingness beneath. I was a weapon, not a man, but moments like this always reminded me that I was a weapon born with a soul. It made all the difference.

We watched Enceladus turning away as the ship powered past. We'd reach Titan within the hour.

Vasilla watched the receding moon for several minutes, and turned to look up at me again. Her modest height left her reaching my waist. Just.

'I have never set foot on Titan,' she said. Something in her gentle voice almost made me hesitant to answer. Despite the lily tattoo on her cheek, never before had she seemed so young. 'I would like to go down to the world this time.'

'It is rare for any but my order to set foot on the world itself.'

She nodded, for she'd stayed on our orbiting void station before. 'It may be uncommon, but we live in an uncommon age, Sir Knight.'

'What do you mean?'

The girl stared out at the stars. In the far, far distance, the dull, grey eye of the moon Tethys stared back, showing its shadowed side.

'We live in the Last Age of Man,' Vasilla said softly. 'This millennium hasn't yet reached half its span, and it's already the darkest ever faced by humanity. It will be the last one, Hyperion. The last, before everything finally falls black.'

And with those words, suddenly she'd never seemed older. I would never understand her. In a way, she was akin to one of Saturn's moons – half-light; half-dark; cold in the deep void, with a buried core of warmth.

'Mankind will never fall,' I said. The words were instinctive, spoken by rote in place of passion.

Vasilla tilted her head, the mahogany bob of hair perfectly framing her youthful expression of curiosity.

'From whence do those words come?' she asked. 'Your head, or your heart?'

'A million worlds turn within the Emperor's Light. Countless billions offer their lives for the Throne, while endless trillions live by His grace.' I looked down at her, her dark robe another contrast against my armour. 'Mankind will never fall,' I said again.

She smiled with genuine affection, and touched her hand to my arm. 'You truly believe that, don't you?'

A sense of Galeo's amusement reached me from across the chamber, a gentle wave of humour at what he was seeing: one of the Emperor's sons – a warrior trained to wage war against daemons – being lectured by a child.

Before I could answer, Darford joined us at the railing. He wore a dress uniform, as he always did. In fact, he seemed to possess an inexhaustible supply of them. This one was a rich red with gold epaulettes, braids and lanyards. Knee-high black leather boots met the crisp white trousers, and the pompous effect was completed by three medals showing on his chest. They depicted whatever acts of valour he'd achieved in the regimental forces of his home world, before coming into Annika's service. I wasn't familiar with the trophies and awards given by the Imperial Guard institutions of Mordian, but the medals were almost certain to be for acts of marksmanship.

'Looks cold,' he nodded at the diminishing sphere of Enceladus.

I knew he was making a joke, but it was difficult to see the point of it. His humour often seemed to slip beneath my comprehension.

'It is cold,' I said. 'The surface of Enceladus is–'

'Throne aflame, don't start that.' Darford smoothed his trimmed moustache and beard with a thumb and forefinger. 'You're as bad as Malchadiel. It's like talking to a bloody cogitator, sometimes.'

I looked down at him for several seconds. He slapped my armour in what I assumed was supposed to be a good-natured way. Vasilla gave a small shake of her head, no doubt knowing what was coming.

'Happy to be home?' Darford asked.

'I have told you before about touching my armour,' I replied.

He chuckled. 'You're as charming as always. I see eleven days of training alone didn't help turn you into decent company.'

The rise of irritation was a petty response. I knew it, and I tried to swallow it back down. I was not entirely successful.

'You didn't miss much,' he continued. 'Clovon, the swine, cheating at cards. Our beloved mistress stalking the decks like a hungry wolf.' He put an arm around Vasilla. 'This little saint praying her heart out, because she didn't trust the Geller field to keep us safe.'

The young Sororitas girl met my eyes. A human's face is a palette of expression, and nothing says as much as a smile.

That expressiveness is definitely something we lose when we accept the Emperor's Gift. I think we internalise so much of ourselves in learning our new powers that even the effortless display of emotion becomes muted and unnatural.

For all its rarity, Vasilla's smile was more expressive than most. It conveyed her sense of weariness at Darford's insistence on treating her like a child – a little sister to be teased at her elder brother's will.

Admittedly, I wasn't gifted at reading facial expressions, but I could skim her surface thoughts to compensate. I often wondered how the warriors of other Adeptus Astartes Chapters managed without the same psychic gift. Understanding humans was difficult enough for me, even with the ability to read their minds.

'If you touch my armour again,' I said to Darford, 'I shall kill you.'

'Of course you will. Just like all the other times you've threatened that, hmm?'

'You.' I gestured to a nearby servitor. 'Attend me.'

The augmented slave trudged over. One of its legs was a grinding limb of dark iron and false-muscle cables. Its skull was largely augmetic, as was the left side of its face, lost in a polished coating of ridged bronze. Emotionless eyes stared at me, past me, through me. Touching its mind betrayed only the dullest edge of sentience. It lacked enough awareness for me to make the most rudimentary connection; I couldn't even see through its senses.

'Your order, benevolent master?' it asked, with a voice rendered harsh by cyborging. Spittle ran from the corner of its slack mouth, and I caught a glance of darkening teeth behind its lips. In a sense, lobotomy was a mercy: mind-scraping allowed it to live in ignorance of the pain from its teeth rotting in its gums.

I turned to Darford. He was regarding the lobotomised slave with a slight curl to his lip. The servitor stared on, drooling, saying nothing.

'I say,' Darford muttered, 'have we found your conversational equal, Hyperion?'

I shook my head. 'No. This is the last man that kept slapping my armour the way you do. He was modified to serve humanity in a less irritating way.'

Darford blinked twice, and softened his voice to a conspiratorial whisper.

'Blood of the Emperor, did you just make a joke? Is there actually a living, breathing man with a sense of humour inside all that silver?' He touched my armour again, this time tapping it with his fingertips, as if testing to see if it was hollow.

It took no more than a moment's concentration to let my senses slip free, drifting through his mind. A pinched blood vessel here, a flicker of tissue massage there...

Darford winced, holding the bridge of his nose. 'Bitch of a headache,' he muttered. Blood dripped from one nostril onto his lip. He sniffed slightly, then reached for a handkerchief, worried about getting stains on his immaculate uniform.

'I know that was you,' he said, still holding his nose.

Vasilla hid her smile by turning away.

'I have no idea what you mean,' I said.

'Very childish,' Darford's murmuring continued. 'Very childish indeed. Good one, though.'

II

Titan. Saturn's largest moon.

Not my birth world, but still the only home I'd ever known. We drew nearer to the great glowing orb with its thick, sour skies. Here we would re-arm, restore our kinship with the warriors in our Eighth Brotherhood, and put Sothis to rest in the Dead Fields below the world's surface. Here we would tell our brothers that Armageddon, a world of factories and industrial misery, was under Archenemy siege. The Wolves were already embattled there, and they needed us.

Perhaps our masters would send us in the crusade force. I hoped for such an order.

As I watched the cloudy orange sphere swell before us, Dumenidon's strained voice brushed against my mind.

+I apologise for intruding upon your thoughts, brother.+

+No apology is necessary.+ I tuned out of the conversation between Darford and the Khatan. They were arguing about a gambling game with modestly variant rules on both of their home worlds. Each believed their version to be superior, and came armed with a host of reasons why. +Is something wrong, Dumenidon?+

+Not at all. I sensed you cataloguing our duties for when we reach the monastery, and felt it worth mentioning that you've forgotten one last thing. We are down to four souls now. Castian will need to accept an initiate before we leave the monastery again.+

Ah. He was right, I'd not considered that. Still, it was rare for him to touch minds with me directly, without using the squad's shared bond. His powers were almost fully focused along more lethal lines.

+I wished to ensure Malchadiel could not hear,+ he confessed. +The wounds of loss are still fresh for him.+

+Forgive me for saying so, but that is unusually considerate of you, brother.+

+I have my moments.+ Dumenidon's tone vibrated with amusement before fading away.

A new initiate. A new soul to join with ours, blending his blade and gifts with our own. No two squads operated quite the same way, nor did they channel their powers along the same paths. To be accepted into a squad was to harmonise one's entire life with those who would be your brothers, learning anew how to focus your powers alongside your kindred. Even after decades of rigorous training, failure to meld with a squad was hardly uncommon. I was in danger of it myself.

'Approach vector received,' one of the helmsmen called.

'All-ahead, standard,' replied Captain Castor. 'Prime docking thrusters.'

+Nothing foolish this time, Talwyn,+ Galeo sent, from his place by the command throne.

'Perish the thought, sire.' The captain's burn scars twisted as he suppressed the smile making a race for his lips. Tonight, Castor wore a tricorne hat of beaten red velvet. It was quite the most foolish thing I'd seen him wear, and in the past year he'd given me plenty of examples for comparison.

+I mean it, captain,+ Galeo added. +This is a solemn return.+

'As you say, sire.' Castor remained seated on his ornate bronze throne, and made the sign of the aquila across his jacketed breast. The man was bizarrely foppish in his attire, but we were fortunate to have him. Few of our order's life-bonded servants came willingly. Talwyn Castor, formerly master of the Battlefleet Obscurus warship *Evangelica*, was one of those rare souls that swore away from a life of traditional service without needing to be mind-scraped into secrecy for the good of mankind.

Still, it was pleasant to know he wouldn't be irritating the dockmasters this time with his casual disregard for docking instructions. We were returning to bury our dead and bring warning of war, after all.

'Come about three degrees to these coordinates,' he called,

tapping a code into his throne's arm-console.

'Coordinates received. Three degrees, aye.'

Titan filled the viewports, its soft orange gleam the perfect backdrop to show our fleet in orbit above. Huge, battle-mented cruisers and interceptor frigates alike glided through the void, stationed in defensive formations, ever vigilant over inbound vessels and forcing them into narrow docking runs.

In all of mankind's galaxy, only Mars, Terra and distant Cadia could claim such defences. We sailed through the heart of the most advanced fleet in humanity's arsenal, well aware that ten thousand guns tracked our passage.

The *Karabela* was far from alone in the ocean of patrolling vessels – dozens of other ships drew close to dock or made ready to leave Titan's orbit. Our world was an Inquisitorial nexus, receiving a constant stream of the ordos' Black Ships, their sterile holds packed with children to be tested, trained, and most likely to die on the surface of Titan. By far the largest flow of stellar traffic came in the form of bulk-hulled Adeptus Mechanicus cruisers, laden with supplies. Our own immense forges on Titan were still unable to provide the amount of ammunition and weaponry our crusade required, such was the scale of war we waged. Freighters and cruisers from Deimos, the forge-moon gifted to us by ancient decree, ferried material back and forth in an unceasing convoy.

In the rarest cases, a red-armoured cruiser from Mars herself would arrive within our space, heralding the return or depar-ture of a Techmarine, and the secrets he carried with him.

As we came past one immense grey battleship, its ridged gunports filled the windows. I couldn't help a small smile as the name *Unforsaken* passed by, in massive silver script along the dark hull. A grand old vessel; it was good to see her again.

Once we passed her vast, ornamented prow, our true desti-nation finally hove into view. It wasn't a mere space station, it was *the* space station, and it played home to thousands of souls, dozens of ships, and the greatest secrets in the Imperium of Man. I could think of no other void-citadel in the Imperium – including the *Phalanx* of the Imperial Fists – that would match the Apex Cronus Bastion in firepower. The size of a small moon in its own right, our navigational charts tended to refer to it by its more militant title: Broadsword Station.

'Ahead one-third,' called Castor. 'Make for the northern sector, sixteenth umbilicus.'

The engines quieted, but didn't die. We crawled forwards, heading to our docking port. I could already feel Galeo in communion with our brothers on the surface – his presence was a wavering burr, relaying all we'd learned and the warning we brought.

'Sir?' called one of the few uniformed ratings on the command deck.

'Speak,' said Captain Castor.

'The *Unforsaken* has ordered us to cease all forward momentum immediately.'

'Delightful.' Castor faked a smile. 'Would you mind asking them why?'

'Proximity warning!' one of the robed menials called from his console deck at the strategium's edge.

Castor sat straighter. I felt him grow sharper, more focused, as he shook off the lingering, muffling echoes of a hangover.

'I see nothing. We're on course.'

'Proximity threat: blue,' intoned another robed figure. I turned to him, one of the Palladium Kataphrakt, seeing him working at his station with four arms – two of which were slender mechadendrites reaching over his shoulders from a ticking power pack surgically attached to his spine. 'Proximity threat: blue,' he said again, his voice carrying no more passion than an automaton's.

I'd never heard that warning before. I had no idea what it meant.

'Track it, damn you,' Castor demanded. The captain rose from the throne, straightening his ludicrously archaic hat. At his hips were a brace of slender las-weapons crafted to resemble antique black powder pistols from his home world, Cirasha. He couldn't take his eyes from the central oculus screen as it exploded with hateful colour.

'Oh, shit me,' Darford whispered, seeing the same thing.

'Warp rift,' a dozen of the crew called at once. 'There's no room to–'

'Aetheric dissilience,' came the dead-calm voice of a nearby servitor. 'Aetheric dissilience, at coordinates–'

'Crash dive!' Castor gripped a nearby railing, screaming across the deck. *'Crash dive!'*

III

The deck lurched beneath us as the *Karabela*'s prow sank. Our surroundings gave another kick as the engines flared into brightest life, leeching power from every other system on the ship. Lights dimmed around us, gravity lessened, and the hull gave a chilling groan along the spinal structure. I heard it echo through the whole ship.

Hardwired servitors automatically declared their console readings, though their mumbling voices went ignored in the aural melee. Although the oculus remained fixed upon the warp rift forming dangerously close by, the windows offered a sickening view of Titan swelling before us.

'Report,' Captain Castor demanded.

'Maximum sustainable negative pitch,' called the primary helmsman. 'The fleet is scattering, but… There are too many for an orderly break. The manifesting ship may still strike us if it comes through without changing course. Shields, captain?'

'No shields,' Castor ordered. 'They'll leech from the engines. Run.'

'Engines at full burn,' stated one of the Palladium Kataphrakt priests from across the chamber, where his cowled coven of tech-adepts worked at the enginarium console. 'We will reach Titan's gravitational hard deck in thirteen seconds. Eleven. Ten.'

'If we turn, they clip us. If we slow down, they hit us. In the Emperor's holy name, tell me what ship is coming through that jump point.'

'Five seconds until gravitational hard deck, captain.'

'I don't care. Auspex! Answer me.'

I clutched at the railing, the ship shaking all around me. Annika looked across at me as the strategium lights faded to an ominous red. She'd strapped herself into a restraint throne by the captain's command seat.

+We're diving below the gravitational hard deck,+ I answered the look in her eyes. +We're below the safe altitude for lowest orbit, suffering Titan's gravity and the resistance of its atmosphere. And we're still diving.+

'I know, but… the *Karabela's* enhancements…'

Gravity started to exert its inevitable force in that moment. Several of the crew started slipping forwards. A reflexive thought activated my magnetic seals, pinning my boots to the deck. I caught Vasilla's wrist as her feet went out from under her.

She mouthed 'thank you', though the rattling stole her words.

'Will we crash?' Annika sent.

+Almost definitely.+ Wind-streaks ripped against the windows as we ploughed through Titan's upper atmosphere.

'Sir!' the mistress of auspex called out as she secured herself in her restraint throne. 'The ship jumping in-system reads as the Adeptus Astartes destroyer *Veregelt*.'

Not one of ours. None of our ships bore that title.

'It's a Fenrisian ship!' Annika shouted silently. *'One of the others Grauvr spoke of... It's reached Titan.'*

The vox rasped into life, as the beleaguered destroyer blared for all to hear: 'This is the *Veregelt*, iron-sworn to the Wolves of Fenris. The world Armageddon suffers in the grip of rebellion and heresy, on a scale never before seen. This is the *Veregelt*, iron-sworn to the Wolves of Fenris. The world Armageddon–'

The recorded voice died in static, as abruptly as it'd been born from it.

+Give me the view from the stern,+ I pulsed into the mind of every human on the command deck. The oculus tuned to the new angle immediately, showing the massive strike cruiser above us, bursting from its warp-rift as it re-emerged into real space.

I watched it through the turbulence taking hold, slashing from the wound in reality with its engines flaring hot, cutting right through the *Karabela*'s docking path. Even if we'd heeded the *Unforsaken*'s demand to cut engines, the *Veregelt* would still have ploughed right through us.

Of course, we'd likely just exchanged one death for another.

'We're clear,' two of the helmsmen said at once. 'The *Veregelt* has missed us.'

'Engines to one-third, fire all cessation thrusters,' Castor yelled. The captain hadn't strapped himself down. Instead he gripped the handrail, his whole body slanted as he held fast. 'Let's slow this beauty down, if you please.'

'Engines, one-third, aye.' One of the enginarium adepts counted down. 'Cessation thrusters in five, four, three...'

'Brace!' Castor called out.

I pulled Vasilla closer, embracing her against me, though it was difficult to gauge how much strength would keep her in my grip without crushing her. I caught a glance of her wide eyes staring up at me. Human fear had a scent like nothing else – a coppery sourness that instinctively repulsed me. It was the smell of duty; of blades raised to defend the innocent; of priceless immortal souls in fragile mortal shells. And yet it stank.

I realised I'd never seen her afraid before. It was so easy to forget she was little more than a child.

When the cessation thrusters fired, the entire ship kicked backwards. Several servitors and crewmen were thrown from their stations, crashing against the deck and walls. Blood burst from most of them, spraying against the walls in angled smears from broken skulls or snapped limbs. Loose debris, data-slates, weapons and tools sliced through the air in a tumbling blizzard.

We were still falling. Castor spat blood onto the deck. He had a gash along his head that I hadn't seen him earn. 'Helm, I'm losing my patience. Get us out of this dive. Fire the docking jets, for the Throne's sake. Every little will help.'

'Docking jets, aye.'

'And shut that bloody siren up!' the captain shouted.

'*At least the crash will dig our graves for us,*' Annika said inside my mind.

In that moment, we burst through the clouds. Titan's surface in all its frozen and sepia glory spread out beneath us. Lakes of frozen methane reflected the rich cloud cover, while plateaux of orange rock stretched out as far as the eye could see.

Slowly, so painfully slowly, the horizon began to rise. The ship still didn't stop shaking. The *Karabela* wasn't designed for atmospheric flight, and the engines protested each second it was forced upon her.

Castor was an avatar of bemusing calm. He returned to his throne at the eye of the rattling, shaking storm, and steepled his fingers under his chin, looking out of the view windows. Following his gaze showed what captured his attention, but revealed nothing of why he was so tranquil. Despite climbing, we'd only managed to lift the *Karabela*'s prow enough to be diving right for the base of a mountain range.

I shared a moment of that same calm. Those are the Rachnov Mountains, I thought.

'Maintain climb,' Castor ordered, 'but bleed all starboard engines by forty per cent, and veer hard to port as we rise. I would rather not drill my way through that mountain; it will do no favours to our lady's paintwork.'

The *Karabela* groaned from prow to stern, protesting at the sensation of a thick atmosphere against her cold bones.

'Up, girl.' Castor was laughing. 'Up you go, my fat-arsed duchess of the stars.'

'Sir–'

'I'm not blind, helmsman. All crew, all crew: Brace for impact.'

We clipped the tallest mountain. The barest clip, yet enough to pound the edge of our hull into the peak and breed a colossal avalanche in our wake. If the cessation thrusters had been a kick, this was a hammer blow that rang my bones like a bell. Deafening thunder broke out around us as the deck gave a monumental heave, and more of the crew went flying – even several who'd been restrained. Darford was one of them. I reached for him with my free hand as he fell from the handrail, but momentum threw him too fast.

He halted in the air as I clenched my teeth. Other crew

members crashed against the hull and deck, but Darford remained suspended in the air.

+Got you.+

Bridge debris rained all around him. He covered his head as a data-slate slashed past. Like Annika, he possessed no telepathy himself, but he could ride the psychic link if I left it open.

'*Bloody hell,*' he sent back. Even his psychic voice was breathless. '*Think I owe you a drink.*'

I pulled him back slowly and lowered him as the deck returned to its slightly less violent shuddering. We were climbing now. The *Karabela* was raising her prow, cutting the sky as she lifted back up.

'Well now.' Captain Castor regarded the devastated bridge around him, and deliberately adjusted his hat back to its usual rakish angle. 'That was a dash of unwanted excitement. Medicae staff to the command deck at once. Someone tell me the orbital status, if you please.'

Crew members picked themselves up and returned to duty. The dead lay where they'd died, while the wounded moaned nearby. The humans still at their stations checked their consoles.

'Sir,' the master of vox called. 'The *Veregelt* has fired escape pods. She…' The robed serf paused as he listened to his earpiece. 'She struck the *Unforsaken* on the way down, and is burning up in the atmosphere.'

'On screen.'

The oculus resolved into a new view of the horizon behind us. A burning streak of smoke, flame and dark metal billowed down through the clouds, losing chunks of itself in the poisonous winds.

'Damage report from the *Unforsaken*,' ordered Castor.

'She's gone, sir.' The master of vox shook his head. 'The

Veregelt ended her. Minor collisions are being reported across the fleet, sustained in the rush to scatter.'

'They should have crash dived, eh? Bloody cowards. It worked for us.'

On the oculus, we watched the massive hulk spear into the orange desert, tearing its way across the ground and forming its own grave canyon. Dust and smoke hid most of the view, but the odds of any survivors walking from the *Veregelt* weren't high. I released Vasilla, barely hearing her soft words of gratitude.

I said nothing at all. We reached low orbit less than a minute later. As normality reasserted its grip, our fleet and the stars they guarded drifted back into sight.

+Sacred Throne.+ Galeo's curse was a whisper.

The *Unforsaken* was a cleaved hulk, spilling escape pods the way a body in the void spilled drops of crystallised blood. For a grim second, the sight put me in mind of Sothis dying upon the creature's claws.

Both of the warship's ruined halves were iron carrion, reduced to wrecks by the amidships ramming she'd taken. Rescue shuttles and cargo haulers were pulling close, launched from the orbital defence platforms. Even so, dozens of life-pods were already streaming down to the planet's surface. I hoped they landed undamaged and were fitted with on-board respirators, else the crews would be dead long before rescuers from the monastery reached them.

We sailed past the *Unforsaken*'s wreckage, close enough to read the inscriptions upon her hull.

'Request docking permission with the Apex Cronus Bastion,' Captain Castor said quietly.

'Docking permission received.'

In silence, we watched the ruination at the heart of our fleet, and limped into port at last.

'Welcome home, *Karabela*,' came the dockmaster's crackling vox-voice.

No one replied.

ELEVEN
BURIAL

I

Tradition demanded that my brothers and I leave the *Karabela* together. I knew they waited for me, so perhaps I didn't entirely hide my impatience as I delivered the final requisition lists for the tech-priests of the Palladium Kataphrakt.

Seven of them gathered around me in the gunship hangar, each shrouded in their scarlet robes. I could smell the consecrated oil beating through their bodies in place of blood, and the misty chlorine sprays they used to moisten their eye lenses. Seeing beneath their hoods and body cloaks was difficult, but I doubted there was much of their birth-flesh left to any of them. Like many tech-priests, the cultists of the Palladium Kataphrakt modified themselves extensively over the years. Unlike most, they used only certain metals in their enhancements, as a sign of devotion and purity. What few augmetics were visible gleamed with silver polish, almost entirely formed from iron-reinforced palladium and platinum.

They covered themselves not out of awkwardness or shame, but to hide their precious metals from the dirt of their duties. I found it a curious vanity.

Axium processed the list and handed it back to me. 'You are forgetting one thing,' he said. His voice was human in every way. That never ceased to amaze me. I could hear almost nothing of the machinery within him, not in his movements, not in his voice, not even in his breathing.

'I doubt that. I have thoroughly checked and rechecked this requisition.'

'Nevertheless,' he smiled, 'you are forgetting something crucial.' He had an odd smile – I knew it was a simulation of human expression, yet its engineering was so flawless that all sense of artifice was stolen away.

'Enlighten me,' I said.

Axium was the only one of the Palladium Kataphrakt not wearing his hood, perhaps because covering his features would be a crime against human ingenuity. He resembled a handsome, healthily muscled male in peak physical fitness, not a day over thirty. His physique was sculpted to exacting standards, almost always draped in an elegant scarlet toga, rather than the shapeless and overbearing robes worn by his lesser kindred. Axium's lips moved as a human mouth moved. His eyes betrayed the same emotions. He was the embodied perfection of the human male form, in all ways but one: his body was formed entirely from silver.

In their dealing with the wider Imperium, the Adeptus Mechanicus occasionally mandated the modification and use of specialist ambassadors for the comfort and ease of unmodified humans. These executors and famuli were often reshaped with the human norm in mind, their augmetics kept entirely internal or externally subtle, and communicated via traditional speech rather than the emission of binary cant screeds.

Axium had only served us as executor primaris for ten months. When the Palladium Kataphrakt had presented him to us, the first question Galeo had asked was a simple, abrupt, +Why?+

His inquiry had nothing to do with poor manners, and everything to do with the fact that Axium's surgineering reconstruction had clearly taken intense degrees of both time and effort. We needed no executor in our dealings with the Adeptus Mechanicus, especially not on a modest vessel like the *Karabela*. Communications had never broken down between Castian and the Kataphrakt even once in the ten millennia both factions had served mankind together.

Axium had answered for his brethren with a smile, and the words: 'Simply to see if it could be done. We are artisans as well as engineers, and all artistic labours please the Machine God.'

He'd been with us ever since.

I'd heard it said that several other ships envied Axium's presence aboard the *Karabela*. He certainly displayed more personality and efficiency than many of his tech-priest brethren, but that seemed irrelevant to the rumours. If the talk was to be believed, many other Adeptus Mechanicus cults aboard our fleet vessels considered him something of an icon, forged in glorious worship of the Omnissiah.

When standing before him, it took a long time to drink in every detail of his construction. His face was far from smooth – to mimic the nuances of human expression, even his silver lips and eye sockets were formed from hundreds of minute servos – but his body's musculature was shaped from interlocking plates of burnished silver, concealing much of the metalworking and circuitry beneath.

Sophisticated sound suppressors the size of common tin coins were fused to his joints, muting his movements.

Instead of the gentle purr of servos and the heavy tread of silver feet, Axium sounded perfectly human: his heartbeat was the natural rhythm of the human organ within his chest, and his breath came from biological lungs. His voice was so perfectly coded to match human frequencies that it sounded more natural than any of my brothers', with their gene-modified biology.

Silver was a soft metal by comparison to the materials used elsewhere in the *Karabela's* forges. I suspected that was why Axium did so little artificer work himself, except for the finest engravings upon our weapons and armour.

I'd once asked him how much coin and time had been spent in his construction. 'A great deal of both,' was his thoughtful answer.

In the hangar, he took the data-slate back from me, scrolling past the primary requisition supplies and into the personal allowances.

'Here.' He showed me the same information I'd entered into the slate during the long voyage. I saw what he meant.

'Ah.'

'Ah,' he mirrored me. 'This is materiel for only four knights. I was given to understand Castian would recruit before we left.'

'We will. My thanks for pointing out the discrepancy.' Twice now in the last hour, it had been pointed out to me. I'd made the list before Dumenidon mentioned it, however.

Axium tilted his head as he regarded me. 'And your armour is a disgrace. The healing we were able to administer in the last eleven days is hardly suitable for a return to battle.'

I had the strangest feeling of being lectured by an elder, something even Galeo had never managed to inspire in me.

'I know.'

'You will surrender it to the Kataphrakt's care for at least three weeks before we journey back into the void?' Despite the subtle note of inquiry, his tone made it almost an order.

'I will.' If, I thought, we aren't going to Armageddon.

'Good, good.' Axium returned the data-slate. The tiny gears and servos in his knuckles gave only the faintest, softest whirs. 'What news of the *Veregelt*?'

'We will know once we make it down to the monastery. I will ensure you have a full report.' It occurred to me that this was only the third time since his augmetic reconstruction that Axium had docked at Titan. 'Will you be travelling to the forge moon more than once?'

He performed an amusingly courtly bow. 'Deimos does indeed call to us. The Kataphrakt has resupply needs of its own.'

'Ensure you log all transfer times with the strategium.' I was already half-turned, trying to leave. Annika had surely taken the Wolf to the surface by now, and my brothers were still waiting. Time was a most precious resource.

'Sir Hyperion,' he chuckled, 'have I ever given you the impression that I and my kindred are anything less than perfectly efficient?'

'Not in the least. But this is the first time I am taking responsibility for our resupply. I wish it to go flawlessly.'

He nodded to that. 'Did the captain and the justicar ask this of you?'

'No. I volunteered.'

'I see.' Axium's eyes weren't human either, but they were perfect simulacra, right down to the moisture in the sockets that made them shine. They glinted with amusement as he spoke. 'Taking the initiative.'

'Something like that.'

'Seeking a justicar position for yourself, one night, perhaps?'

'Axium... I really must attend to my other duties.'

'Ah. Of course. Go with the Machine God's graces.'

Instead of replying, I made the sign of the aquila. Axium returned a salute in absolute unity with his six brethren – each of them making the knuckle-linked sign of the cog.

II

I joined my brothers at the thoroughfare umbilicus, ready to leave the ship. Most of the crew, those with permission to disembark, had already gone over to the station through other passages. This tunnel was for us, and us alone.

I was the last of Castian to gather. None of them complained at my delay.

+Ready?+ Galeo sent.

'Yes, justicar,' Dumenidon answered. I merely nodded, as did Malchadiel.

+Lift.+

Each of us held a corner of the coffin. Formed from silver-threaded iron, the casket was hardly light, but what would be impossible for unenhanced humans was merely a minor burden for us.

We moved through the airlock, marching in unison, boots thudding on the deck grille with each step as we crossed the umbilicus.

The crossing to Broadsword Station took no more than thirty seconds, and rather than pass into the main sections of the spaceport, we carried the coffin through darkened hallways to a secluded hangar bay. The walls were bas-relief carvings of silent, staring warriors standing in ranks. Not once did we pass another living being.

I knew what awaited us from my years committing the order's rituals to memory, but this one was scarcely detailed in the monastery's librariums. I found I wasn't sure what to expect, though my brothers showed no hesitation at all. I brushed against their minds, feeling nothing more than their solemn reverence and, in the case of Malchadiel, a bleary, cold sorrow.

The hangar looked out upon Titan, filling its open bay doors with an orange, creamy light. Only the waspish throb of an energy field separated us from the void outside.

A lone shuttle was the hangar's only occupant. It resembled nothing of Adeptus Astartes design, but nor did it show the blocky, armoured efficiency preferred by the Adeptus Mechanicus. But it was old, no question about it. Its sleek, backswept wings were a throwback to an ancient age, before the homogenisation of safe, accepted vehicle templates.

+I cannot speak to the Ferryman,+ Galeo sent. +Hyperion, the responsibility is yours.+

Up until that moment, I'd never realised just how reliant upon my powers I'd become. My sixth sense so often became my first sense, as I passively reached out to brush my mind against everything nearby, sensing other living beings long before I saw or heard them. When I saw the robed figure by the shuttle's wing, I almost fell out of step with my brothers. No wonder Galeo couldn't speak to the figure. It didn't exist to my psychic sense beyond a shadow in the warp. Here was a man without a soul.

We lowered our brother's coffin onto the hangar deck. Traditional words filtered back into my mind, recalled through the discomfort of standing before the soulless figure. Looking at him made my lips peel back from my teeth, and my sixth sense closed in a snap of loss, as if I'd suddenly been struck blind.

The Inquisition made use of psychic nulls, mortals casting no soul-echo in the warp, as anathema to all psychic activity in their proximity. Such creatures were useful as weapons, in their own servile, incorruptible ways, but it took effort just to stand near the hollow man. I wondered how he was even alive, and what genetic aberration allowed him to be born.

Outwardly, he was one of us – his bulky physique was unarguably the result of Adeptus Astartes genetic enhancement – yet he stood unarmed and unarmoured, clad only in a patchwork grey robe that had clearly seen better years. Eyes of unremarkable blue watched each of us in turn before resting on the coffin we'd carried, until he lowered his shaved head in a nod of greeting.

'Who speaks for the fallen?'

My revulsion got the better of me. 'What are you?' I asked.

'Focus,' Dumenidon hissed.

I cleared my throat, forcing myself to look at the figure. 'Hyperion of Castian speaks for the fallen. Who bears our slain to the Dead Fields?'

'Phlegyras of Titan will bear your slain to the Dead Fields. Present the Sigillite's symbol.'

We raised our left hands, showing the black symbol acid-etched into the silver of our gauntlets' palms. We each bore the same tattoo inked into the flesh of our hands beneath.

'We present the Sigil of Malcador,' I said.

The Ferryman nodded a second time. 'Speak the name of the fallen, and the words to be engraved in memoriam.'

I considered trying to reach Mal, but Phlegyras's presence stole all hope of that. I couldn't sense anything outside my own skull. I'd been chosen to speak; the responsibility of answering fell to me.

'Sothis of Castian,' I said, feeling my primary heart beating harder. 'Knight of the Eighth Brotherhood. Valiant to the last. Revered by his brothers in life. Remembered for the lessons taught by his death.'

'It will be so.'

Galeo bowed, and began to walk away. I wondered just

how many times he'd surrendered his brothers to one of the Ferrymen to be interred in the Dead Fields below our monastery.

'Brother,' Dumenidon voxed. 'Come.'

I couldn't explain my sudden reluctance to leave Sothis in this aberration's care. When one of our order died, we surrendered the remains to the Ferrymen to cleanse and bury. It had been this way for generations, since the Chapter's founding at the hands of the Sigillite. As slaves, they were trained for this duty, purified and sworn into service. What right did I have to resist tradition?

And yet...

'Who are you?'

The Ferryman turned towards me. His eyes seemed glassy and hollow, but I knew that was a lie born of my deprived psychic sense. I couldn't sense life within him, so my lesser perceptions struggled to see it, as well.

'I am Phlegyras of Titan,' he said calmly.

'One of the Ferrymen,' I said.

'One of the Ferrymen,' he repeated. I wasn't sure if he was answering, or simply speaking my own words back to me in dull-witted imitation.

'You serve the Sepulcars, do you not? You are a seneschal to those who tend the Dead Fields?'

I ignored Galeo's hand on my shoulder. His voice was as banished as my sixth sense.

'I serve the Sepulcars.' Phlegyras nodded. If such a creature could be said to be amiable, he seemed to be trying to be polite. Even meeting his eyes made me want to spit, knowing there was no soul beyond them. Knowledge of my hatred's irrationality was no salve against its heat.

I looked at the enigmatic figure for another long moment. This time, he spoke to me.

'You are reluctant to let the fallen be buried.' He smiled, and I suspected he was trying to be kind. 'May I ask why?'

'Who are you?' I asked again, feeling my voice growl through my teeth. 'You were one of us once, weren't you?'

Phlegyras smiled and said nothing.

'Come, brother,' Dumenidon voxed. 'He has a duty, as we have ours.'

I left with my kindred, though not without a lingering glance at the Ferryman loading the coffin aboard his shuttle.

He lifted it with no trouble at all.

III

As soon as we left his presence, my psychic sense flared back into life. And as soon as it did, I heard our names being called. Not my name, in the sense of individual appellations. This was a call from the surface of Titan, resonating through all our minds, ripe with images of Castian's proud banner and the alkaline taste of teleportation mist on the tongue.

+We're being summoned,+ Malchadiel pulsed.

Galeo lifted a hand to stop our march. +No. We're… This is an order, not a summons.+

Relaxing my mind was all it took. I let the psychic touch wash through me, achieving communion almost at once. I saw the surface of another world, the earth itself black with rot, while a city burned at the horizon's edge. I'd seen that sight once before, when I rifled through the mind of the Wolf, Grauvr.

+Our lords wish to speak to us,+ I sent to the others. +I've never felt such a call.+

+You are young,+ Galeo sent. +What you sense now is something you may never feel again. I've only felt it once in the past.+ His aquiline features, so plainly lined by the trials of service, were further darkened by the surrounding disquiet.

+I sense the unease of many minds,+ sent Malchadiel. +Nothing more.+

+This is tied to the *Veregelt*'s arrival, and the communion I shared with the Third Captain as we came into dock. But more than that, Inquisitor Jarlsdottyr's survivor has revealed all to the Chapter lords. And so we are ordered to heel. All of us.+

+A Chapter-wide summons+ I ventured. +That can't be. The threat to Armageddon cannot be so dire.+

+I don't understand,+ Malchadiel admitted. +No threat could ever demand the entire Chapter.+

+So very young,+ Galeo pulsed to all of us, with the slightest smile. +Hyperion, I have a favour to ask of you before the gathering takes place tonight. Castian requires a fifth knight. You will be the one to ask him.+

TWELVE

FORTRESS-MONASTERY

I

I'd not seen him in almost a year, since Castian had claimed me and we'd sailed for our first mission with Inquisitor Jarlsdottyr.

I found him in the Dead Fields, tending the monuments of the lost. A ripple of psychic force left his outstretched hand, brushing over a statue and shedding a layer of dust from its granite shoulders.

He wore his armour, as was his right. No ceramite girded his left arm from the elbow, or his right arm from the bicep, or either leg from the thighs down. Polished augmetic limbs clicked and whirred in place of his true arms and legs – the legacies of old, old injuries sustained before I'd been born.

Whenever that was.

'Enceladus.'

He turned at the sound of my voice, though he'd surely been able to sense my approach the moment I'd set foot in the catacombs. The right side of his face was clean, shining chrome, sculpted in mimicry of his former features. Both eyes were red lenses in sockets of dark iron.

'My boy,' he said. 'It gladdens me to see you.'

Traditionally, it's considered an honour – and a prophetic sign of great deeds in one's future – to be given a name matching one of Saturn's moons. Such nomenclature was accordingly rare; as far as I was aware, beside myself and Enceladus, only Tethys stood among the knighthood's current generation. As a matter of interest, the last knight to bear the name Hyperion died four thousand, three hundred and eighty-one years before I swore my oaths of service to the Golden Throne. He was killed with all honours, in battle with the Archenemy. His brothers recovered his remains. I'd visited his grave several times.

Enceladus's voice was strong despite his age. As he was so fond of reminding me, he'd been crusading when the millennium was still newborn.

We didn't salute one another, we embraced without shame. 'Sothis,' he said, not quite a question.

'I would like to see him,' I said. 'But that's not why I came here.'

'Speak as we walk. I will take you to him.' And he did.

We walked the Dead Fields, boots echoing around the catacombs, moving between the statues and plaques. Each chamber contained the interred dead of an entire century – the sarcophagi numbering in dozens to hundreds, room by room, depending on the number of brothers fallen in those particular decades. You could walk for hours in the Dead Fields, and never read the same inscription twice. I'd done it myself, many times.

We passed beneath the watchful stone eyes of a granite army, walking side by side along the black stone floor.

'You've heard the call to war?'

He nodded. I could hear the soft purr of the mechanics in his augmetic spine. 'I have. Armageddon is a bleak and unwelcoming industrial globe, but when has the value of dirt and iron mattered when the knighthood calls a crusade? The abomination must be banished. I may come to the gathering tonight, I may not. Either way, there will be war. The sins of Armageddon will not go unanswered.'

'Enceladus,' I said. 'Master...'

'It has been a long time since you trained under my guidance, Hyperion. I think we can put the "master" aside now, don't you?'

I gave him a look. 'You greeted me with "boy".'

He didn't chuckle. He never did. A smile was all I'd ever gotten from him. 'Forgive an old knight his habits. Do as I say, not as I do.'

We passed more graves, walking down the centuries, closer to the present day. The smell in the Dead Fields is a mix of dust flavoured by endless journeys through ventilation exchangers, coupled with mouldering bones and mildewing parchment. Spicy, in a way. Difficult to imagine, for no tomb ever smells quite alike. Memories never smell the same.

'You're building up to say something. I sense it in your mind.'

I glanced at my former mentor. 'Galeo sent me.'

That stopped him in his tracks. 'Did he now?'

Rather than explain in words, I let the offer settle in his mind. A gentle nudge was all it took to get it there.

We resumed walking. Enceladus seemed more annoyed than confused. The lines of age cracking his face seemed deeper, less kindly. 'I can't,' he said. 'How can Justicar Galeo ask this of me?'

'There is no other to ask, master. Castian cannot go to war under strength.'

'Ah. Foolish of me not to see at once. We can't risk one of the new initiates on a crusade none of us are likely to survive, can we?'

I tried not to laugh. 'The noble justicar didn't phrase it in quite those terms. And how do you know we are destined to die?'

'A guess, from the Wolves' desperation in contacting us.' He met my eyes for a moment. 'Galeo has guessed the same. That's why he's asking me to join Castian. As I said, we can't waste young lives.'

'Castian needs a fifth knight, master. You are a proven warrior.'

'I am old, Hyperion. There is a reason they appointed me to the Sepulcar's role.' He gestured at the statues as we passed them. 'I like it here. I like the peace, the serenity. I fought my wars, boy. I fought them for centuries, crusading when the millennium–'

'When the millennium was newborn. I know, master.'

'I have no desire to do this.' He met my eyes with the lenses that replaced his own.

'Is that a refusal?'

The ancient knight shook his head. 'Of course not. Only in death does duty end. I fear I may slow my brothers down, that's all. I have no wish for my nameplate in the Dead Fields to read that I died an old and useless warrior, unable to keep pace with his kindred.'

'Would you rather it read that you died down here, alone in the dark?'

Enceladus's lips quirked in the suggestion of a smile. 'Perhaps. I've seen things you can't imagine, Hyperion. I hope you never have to.'

Silence reigned between us the rest of the way. When we reached Sothis's grave, Enceladus stepped back to give me room.

My first thought upon seeing the statue was that Malchadiel stood cast in the grey-black stone, rather than Sothis. Gone were the scars that made a patchwork of his face; here he was cast in his perfect prime, as Malchadiel still remained. Beyond that discrepancy, the statue was so lifelike I almost drew breath to speak to it. The cast of his eyes, tilted slightly down, matched his patient attention so perfectly. He neither smiled nor scowled, but regarded his surroundings with a thoughtful stare.

At his boots, the plaque read in gold on black:

Sothis of Castian
Knight of the Eighth Brotherhood

Valiant to the last. Revered by his brothers in life.
Remembered for the lessons taught by his death.

'Your servitors and serfs work fast,' I said.

'They do. Most are psychic, in the least and most basic sense. They lay their hands on the fallen, perceiving his life through echoes, and sculpt the image from there. I've seen them create a statue from a block of untouched granite in less than an hour.'

He paused then. 'It looks so much like him,' Enceladus added at last. 'I will always be proud of you, Hyperion, for you are the strongest of all the knights I ever trained. But Sothis was by far the noblest. Everything he did – every deed, every word – filled me with pride. He had more heart than Malchadiel, and more loyalty than you. Given time, he would have rivalled Dumenidon with a blade.'

What could I say to that? There was no answer but to nod, for he spoke the truth.

'He died for me, master. I will never forget it.'

'It wasn't your fault,' Enceladus replied. 'I know that. No

one blames you, except perhaps Malchadiel. You're right to
remember his sacrifice. Sothis believed your life was worth
more than his. Make sure he died being right about that.'
The old knight turned away. I didn't think less of him for his
silent tears.

My gauntlet rested on Sothis's breastplate, as if I could feel
a heartbeat within the cold granite.

+Thank you,+ I sent into the stone, into the plaque with its
gold letters, into the body interred beneath.

'I sense your guilt, Hyperion,' my master said behind me.

I thought of the moment again: of Sothis coming apart in
the daemon's claws, of a blood-storm spilling into the air as
a shower of red diamonds.

Finally, I lifted my hand away from my brother's chest.

'I'm making no effort to hide it, master.'

II

Before we left the Dead Fields, I paid my respects at the Tomb
of the Eight. Here, immortalised in blood jade, the first eight
Grand Masters of the Brotherhoods stood at the catacombs'
entrance. Seven of them claimed a plinth of silver, depicting
their names and the brotherhoods they'd commanded. The
central display, on a plinth of gold, was the statue of the first
Supreme Grand Master – Lord Janus himself – his helmeted
head tilted up in watchful reverence, looking towards the
stars he was destined to save. Time had toyed with the jade
statues, but erosion's fingers hadn't yet managed to wipe all
detail from their forms. Perhaps in another ten thousand
years, knights of my order would come to pay their respects
to featureless figures down here in the dark.

Or perhaps Vasilla was right, and this millennium would
be our last. My skin crawled afresh at the thought.

The statue on the eighth plinth showed a warrior in the

same armour of blood jade as his brothers, one boot lifted to rest on a sculpted boulder. He carried a nemesis halberd, the spearpoint thrust into the plinth itself, letting him lean upon it with casual indifference. Whatever features he possessed in life were hidden beneath his helm, which in turn was weathered to near smoothness by time's touch.

Khyron
Grand Master of the Eighth Brotherhood

'Already, you exalt me for my triumphs,
When I ask only that you remember me for my
treacheries.

Victory is nothing more than survival.
It carries no weight of honour or worth beyond
what we ascribe to it.
If you wish to grow wise, learn why brothers
betray brothers.'

I'd never understood the words, though they'd always fascinated me. Was the truth behind the inscription locked in the inner sanctum's archives, secreted away only for the eyes of our leaders? Who could say? We had as many legends of our brotherhood's founding lord as there were stars in the night sky. The champions he'd slain, the wars he'd won, the daemons he'd banished – who knew how much had been twisted through the centuries? Even our records, meticulous as we liked to believe them, still suffered from human error when inscribed, and a great deal of our records were sequestered by knight-lords and our Inquisitorial masters.

I rose from my reverence, and looked back at Enceladus. 'Who will serve as Sepulcar in your absence?'

'The servitors can abide, for a time. The serfs will manage them.'

'And the Ferrymen?'

He said nothing. Even his mind retreated from mine, growing colder, tighter. Some secrets were not to be probed, even between close kindred.

'Forget I asked,' I said.

+Hyperion.+

+Coming, justicar.+

'Enceladus, I am summoned.'

The old knight acceded with a nod. 'Go, my boy. Tell Galeo he has my blade, for what it's worth. I have preparations to make down here before we leave for Armageddon.'

III

The Hall of Champions could seat one thousand warriors in neat order, with room for a legion of serving menials.

That night, it housed scarcely more than a hundred of us. Even this was a gathering of rare significance; like all Chapters of the Adeptus Astartes, we rarely came together outside of the largest crusades. A handful of squads was considered a force worthy enough to purge an entire world – what gathered there in the hall then would have conquered nothing short of an entire subsector.

Every squad gathered bore the heraldry of their own brotherhoods, with the tilt plates affixed to each justicar's shoulder guards declaring their own squad's prowess and history. I saw the names and deeds of knights I'd only read about in the archives, just as I saw a spread of titles and squads I'd never heard of at all.

How many of them saw the Seven Blade insignia of Castian on Galeo's shoulder guard and felt stirred by the presence of such a squad? I couldn't guess. He received more than his fair share of nods and salutes, however. My justicar's heroism had been told in countless tales across two hundred years. I was proud to stand at his side, and prouder still to have Justicar Castian's skull on the weapon over my shoulder.

Lining the Hall of Champions on either side were the statues that gave the immense chamber its name: A marble army – the Stone Legion, we'd named them during our decades as squires and acolytes – stood in silent vigil. Nine and a half thousand years of war is an eternity for heroes to rise from the ranks and fall in battle. Every one of the knights enshrined here in white stone had entire litanies written in honour of their deeds. Our greatest heroes, immortalised in marble, still standing among us. Galeo would surely stand with them one night, when his blade no longer defended mankind among the stars. It was difficult to imagine his graven image rendered in cold stone, watching from the walls.

He smiled as he sensed my thoughts.

+Perhaps,+ he allowed. +Nothing is certain.+

Castian himself was here – one of the few knights beneath the rank of paladin or captain to be placed in such exalted company. He stood with his head bowed in solemn reverence, eyes sculpted closed, both hands resting on the nemesis warding stave he'd favoured in life. The haft of my weapon had been forged for my hands and tuned for my consciousness, but the similarities were there for all to see. Not for the first time, I felt unworthy in the eyes of my brothers.

Rather than sit at the feasting tables, we stood in loose ranks, squad by squad, facing the highest table.

Tradition dictated that one of the Grand Masters of the Eight Brotherhoods must always remain on Titan, guarding it in his brothers' absence. Lord Karas Vaurmand, Grand Master of the Third Brotherhood, stood by the table. His posture spoke of his grave frustration, with his fisted gauntlets pressed to the table's surface, supporting him as he leaned forwards to address us. His face betrayed his advanced age

– he was a warrior that would never see four hundred again
– while his burnished armour dictated victory upon victory
in gold-leaf script.

Four paladins, armoured in colossal suits of Terminator
warplate, stood at his side. Unhelmed, they watched the
gathering with naked eyes, their own faces lined by the trials
of several centuries' service. I'd never met any of them face to
face, but I knew all four of them by name, by deed, and by
the destruction they'd brought to mankind's enemies.

Vaurmand took a breath before continuing. His voice was
low enough to carry with ease.

'The Space Wolves vessel *Veregelt* lies dead on the surface
of our world. It carried naught but fragments of a message
Logan Grimnar would have us hear. Now she lies at the heart
of her own tomb-canyon, broken by her final fall to the surface and split open to the poisonous air. More than that, she
caused lamentable loss of life among our fleet. This, you all
know. We know the Wolves of Fenris fight on Armageddon.
We know they believe the situation dire enough that the
Great Wolf has broken his vow of secrecy and told his warriors that we exist. If we are to believe what we've seen, no
other way existed for him to reach us.'

Vaurmand paused, letting his words sink in. If the Space
Wolves survived Armageddon, the Chapter would need to
endure telepathic scouring. Only Adeptus Astartes Chapter
Masters could know we walked in the Imperium's shadows.
So stated the tradition, and so had it always been since our
Founding. Most Imperial Guard regiments we fought beside
were simply executed. Mere men armed with cheap lasrifles
were an inexhaustible commodity all too easily replaced in
humanity's empire.

'The *Veregelt*'s wreckage was wretched with taint, with no
pure survivors. The downed escape pods held nothing more

than the slavering dregs of an infected crew, seeking to preserve their worthless lives for another handful of hours. Each
of them has been tracked, codified, and purged.'

Rare was the enemy that managed to set a defiling foot
upon Titan's surface. Several of the knights beat their fists
against their chestplates in applause, while others shared
whispered words.

'We also have the warning brought by the noble Galeo of
Castian, and his knights of the Eighth Brotherhood. Another
Space Wolves ship, this one cast off-course, also soured by
the foulest taint. And with them comes something more: a
survivor. Inquisitor Annika Jarlsdottyr of the Ordo Malleus
has questioned this Wolf. He speaks of a world lost to war,
of entire continents overrun by the Archenemy.

'Our own augurs and Prognosticars have spoken with the
survivor, as I speak with you. They have studied the testament
of Justicar Galeo, and listened to the words of Inquisitor Jarlsdottyr. They quest now, piercing the Sea of Souls, to see with
their own eyes the poison that threatens Armageddon.'

The gathering of so many powerful minds generated
a muted background hum, underlying everything Lord
Vaurmand said. But as he reached those last words, when
he spoke of our own prophets and seers heeding the Wolf's
warning, I felt the presence of every knight grow sharper. To
look upon the gathered warriors, nothing was different – but
to hear their minds, every consciousness was suddenly as
keen as a sword's edge.

'Brothers,' Lord Vaurmand continued. 'Before this, our Prognosticars sensed no greater unrest in the Sea of Souls, else
the call to crusade would have come down from the monastery's spire-tops long before now. Whatever madness the
Archenemy has brought to Armageddon, the Ruinous Powers
masked it well. I bid you sit, and feast in the sanctity of this

great hall. The truth will be ours before the night's end.'

We saluted in unity, all one hundred and twenty-three of us. As we turned to take our places at the feasting tables, a voice drifted through my mind, as subtle as my own thoughts.

+Castian,+ it said. +Come with me.+

IV

Few souls, even among our order, ever set foot in the monastery's Augurium. At the height of the tallest tower, high enough that its spire pierces the toxic Titan skies, sits the aerie of the knights we name Prognosticars.

Lord Vaurmand led us from the teleportation platform, after sparing us the sixteen thousand steps – or a slow lifter ride up the tower's side. We emerged in a preparation chamber, the marble floor patterned in pink veins, with two paladins standing watch before a great gate of blackened bronze. Each of them wore Terminator plate with personal heraldry: the former bore a crow clutching a blade in its talons; the latter, two crossed halberds above a red skull.

Even the floor fascinated me. +This marble is from Holy Terra,+ I pulsed to my brothers.

+How do you know?+ Mal sent back.

+The pink veins in the stone. That kind of marble doesn't form anywhere else in the Sol System.+

Our boots thumped across the sacred stone as we approached the paladins. Lord Vaurmand inclined his head. The rest of us gave more distinct bows.

I felt them trying to read me, the way one knows when someone is watching in secret from nearby. That same sense of gentle discomfort, an elusive invasion, prickled the hair on the back of my neck.

I resisted it. Partly from instinct, partly to see if I was

capable – I reinforced my thoughts behind a wall of concentrated pressure. One of the paladins grunted, and both turned their helmed heads towards me.

+Hyperion…+ Galeo warned.

I lowered my resistance. Both of them raked through my mind, less gentle than they would have been had I not resisted in the first place. I felt them dredging through my recent recollections, pulling up what happened to Sothis, and seeing my shame in the aftermath.

+That's enough,+ I sent, and repelled them with a focused shove. The one who'd grunted before took a step back.

+Hyperion,+ Galeo pulsed again. +Control yourself.+

I could have argued. I could have cited that they were being needlessly invasive. Would it have sounded as foolish as it felt in my own mind? Far better to stay quiet and say nothing.

'You may enter.' The paladins spoke as one. They were still watching me as we walked between them. Lord Vaurmand didn't come with us, nor did he acknowledge us as we left him there.

+I felt you force them back,+ Malchadiel sent. +Your strength is admirable, Hyperion, but the Librarius will come for you if you're not careful.+

I had no answer for that, either. To be pulled from service within a squad and isolated from the rest of the knighthood… It was said to be an honour, of course. Such a position carried rank and responsibility, but it came with its share of sacrifice. No one wished to stand alone on the fringes of an order founded on the strength of brotherhood.

The bronze gateway opened in stages, rattles and clanks accompanying the withdrawal of the sliding bars keeping the portal sealed shut. When it rumbled open at last, I watched both doors grind back on heavy tracks, close to three metres wide.

The warm gloom of candlelight greeted us.

+Enter,+ said another voice – one laced with weariness. +I bid you welcome, Castian.+

V

Even looking in his direction caused me pain. Behind the corona of psychic strength, his features had an agelessness that defied easy explanation. I caught the sense of someone young, idealistic, but ferociously strong and so very, very tired.

+Forgive me,+ he pulsed, though his sending was an insistent pressure behind the eyes, rather than a whisper.

The strength of his presence faded – not diminished, but consciously dampened, with the sense of the figure holding it inside the way someone might hold their breath.

'It is rare that I receive other psychic visitors in person.' His mortal voice differed only in how weary it sounded. If anything, he seemed even more exhausted. 'I forget how consciousnesses can clash, sometimes.'

With the corona gone, we stood before a knight out of his battle plate, wearing a style of formal attire I didn't recognise: a polished chainmail hauberk with a grey cloak draped over one shoulder. He was surely no older than I or Malchadiel, and he carried little evidence of life beyond the monastery's walls. Even his hands looked soft and unmarked by calluses or scarring.

'I am Torcrith,' he said.

+Galeo,+ the justicar replied. We followed suit, saying our names in turn. He smiled at that.

'I know who you are. I knew even before I spoke with Inquisitor Jarlsdottyr.'

'Where is she?'

He looked at me. 'The spire has a hundred chambers,

Hyperion. She is above us, in one of them. Her wounded ward, Grauvr, is in another. I will take you to her soon, but some of what we say is not for human ears to hear.'

'We've not been told why we were summoned,' Malchadiel admitted. 'Are we to be questioned by the Prognosticars?'

Torcrith's tired smile returned. 'Brother Malchadiel, I am the only Prognosticar here.'

'The only one present on Titan?' I asked.

'No.' He shook his head. 'The only one still alive.'

THIRTEEN

LORD OF THE TWELFTH LEGION

I

Torcrith led us through into a larger, circular chamber. This one offered the same cold atmosphere of austerity and emptiness, even though hundreds of candles lined the walls in neat alcoves. A meditation mat lay at the room's heart, surrounded by silver hexagrammic wards. Some were ringed in turn by concentric circles of white dust.

Torcrith lowered himself to the mat. Despite his physiology, no different from ours, the Emperor's Gift wasn't enough to sustain him. He was weary, that much was obvious, but the lines cracking his face and the halting movements spoke of a deeper flaw. I'd seen the effects of psychic overexertion in humans, but never before in one of the knighthood.

'Do I look so weak to your eyes?' he asked. Once he knelt on the mat, he looked over at me.

'No, my lord. Just weary beyond measure.'

'I am no "lord", Hyperion. I am your brother and you are

mine. Nothing more, nothing less.' He brushed his closed eyes with a thumb and fingertip. 'I have failed the order most grievously. The Wolf told the truth, you know. The Armageddon War has been raging for weeks now, and their world has fallen silent. Is it not a Prognosticar's duty to hunt through the Sea of Souls, seeking the ripples caused by our Archenemy's greatest intrusions? And yet... at no point have I sensed a whisper of this in the warp's winds.'

He looked at us again, each in turn. 'What does that suggest to you?'

'That the enemy masked its approach to Armageddon,' stated Dumenidon.

+And the threat is powerful enough to conceal its own existence,+ Galeo added.

Torcrith nodded to both answers. 'Both are true, but not the truth entire. You have something to say, Hyperion?'

Had he been reading my mind? 'No. I have nothing to say.'

'But you are holding something back. Speak your thoughts, if you would.'

'It suggests to me,' I ventured, 'that one Prognosticar is not enough to serve the Grey Knights Order.'

He nodded. 'Coldest truth, from the tongue of the youngest among us. It doesn't exonerate me from blame, but yes, the order is poorly served when I alone reside at the apex of the Silver Tower. The galaxy is vast, and I am but one man, with one mind. Still...'

Torcrith trailed off, slowing his breathing as he closed his eyes. I could feel him reaching beyond his body, his consciousness drifting into the aether.

+Come with me, Castian. I will show you the world we call Armageddon.+

II

I have, in my life, witnessed many acts of supreme psychic power, on both sides of the Eternal War. I've seen a lone man

– admirable for his deluded courage if nothing else – sacrifice his soul to render his body an open gateway for daemons to enter our reality. I've seen one of my brothers reassemble an entire battle tank over the course of an hour, without physically touching a single piece of the wreckage. I've travelled across the surface of a world, from one continent to the next, city by city, drifting from mind to mind in search of a single secret.

I believe nothing will ever match what Torcrith was capable of at the top of the Silver Tower.

He gathered us up the way a tired beggar collects his coins at the day's end, with no more than a sigh of effort. For a moment, I felt part of him – an observer within his consciousness – feeling the same strain he laboured through every hour of his life.

+Forgive me,+ he pulsed. The stress that threatened to crack open my skull vanished as his attention grazed over us. +It wasn't my intention to share that torment.+

We moved without moving. The way he pulled us from our bodies was kin to a psychic reaching only in the way human breath is kin to a storm's wind. One moment we existed in the candlelit chamber, the next we sailed among the stars.

Few of us project our psyches the same way, and no knight but a Prognosticar had the same strength Torcritch displayed. We didn't move through the heavens; no stellar dance of planets passing by. He pulled us from our bodies, up into the black sky above Titan's curdled atmosphere, and plunged right into the warp.

Undefended by a warship's Geller field – even unprepared to muster my own psychic strength – instinct forced me to resist his control. I thrashed in his invisible grip, throwing silent force against his consciousness even as it shrouded us. Too little, too late. We slid through the oily seas, ripping through an infinity of screaming souls.

For the first time, I couldn't make out individual faces in the boiling colours.

+That is because we are moving too fast for them to manifest, let alone reach out to us.+

+Even the *Karabela* cannot move at this speed.+

+In warp flight, the *Karabela* is a physical construct in a realm without physics. She is real in an unreal place. So she struggles and suffers, labouring against the tides.+

But he suffered, too. I could feel the echoes of his pain. He couldn't mask it entirely.

+How powerful are you?+

I felt Torcrith's weary amusement. +Not powerful enough, else Armageddon would never have been a surprise to the order.+

Even as we tore through the shrieking ocean, I felt his focus spreading and shifting, casting about in every direction.

+I am reading the tides,+ he answered my unasked question. +Seeking any sense of invasion into the material universe. They flow as the ocean becomes rivers, and rivers become the ocean. Thousands and thousands and thousands every second; on worlds, on deep space outposts, on ships lost in the warp…+

Is this what he did? Was his life reduced to night after night of projecting his soul into the empyrean, tracking the flow of every single thread into humanity's empire?

+Yes. But I am only one hunter, Hyperion. I cannot stalk my way down every thread. Only the largest incursions matter to me. The most infected. The most dangerous. The most laden with ripening prophecy.+

I felt Torcrith mustering his strength for something, but he gave us no time to brace. We tore back through the veil, lashing back into the true void in a sudden burst of absolute silence.

Somehow, that was more disquieting than the shrieking.

+How... How could we be here so quickly...?+ one of my brothers asked. I wasn't sure which one, for Torcrith's consciousness overpowered ours. +It will take the *Karabela* weeks to reach this world.+

Torcrith didn't answer. He merely bade us look.

Armageddon was a world much as Terra had been, in the heathen ages of Old Earth. Jungles belted its equatorial regions, lush and green from the serenity of orbit. Wastelands bleached across much of the world's face – tundra at the poles, and ash waste deserts across the larger continental bodies. Deep seas covered much of the globe, which marked it apart from Terra more than any other distinction. Terra's oceans had burned away into dust and nothingness millennia before my birth.

I turned from the world to seek the Imperial ships in orbit. With the world besieged and its cities flooded by the Archenemy, I expected an armada of Naval battleships and Imperial Guard troop transports – to say nothing of the Space Wolves cruisers.

Beyond the satellite network and orbital docking stations above each of the hive cities, I saw little evidence of activity. The Space Wolves ships numbered three in total: a battle-barge of ancient and grand heritage, drifting alongside two smaller destroyers.

+Where is the reclamation fleet?+

+Do you see those hive cities burning? The war is only a handful of weeks old. While that's an eternity to the people suffering in those cities, it's not long enough for Imperial reinforcement. The Wolves sent their lesser ships out to cry for aid – messages in bottles – but to no avail. The Archenemy followed them, overran them, and rendered them silent.+

+But the *Frostborn*,+ I pulsed, +and the *Veregelt*.+

+They reached us eventually, though at great cost in priceless blood and loyal iron. I've quested through the tides, Hyperion. No other help is coming. By the time the rest of the Imperium learns of this war's true depths, the world will be broken.+

+I don't understand. Your strength brought us here. Project yourself into the minds of governors and generals on nearby worlds. Rally them. Bring them here.+

+I am a seer, not a speaker.+ For the first time, I sensed Torcrith's frustration. He struggled to see things as we did, so different were our perceptions of the universe. +Think of astropathy, brother. It isn't a clear bridge from one mind to another. Even contact between the strongest minds is an exchange of dreams and flickering memories that may or may not be understood, or heeded. Look to our own speech, when the knights of our order speak mind to mind. How much stronger are we by comparison to mortal men? Our minds make words from the connection between one consciousness and another, but are we speaking these words to one another? Of course not. We share emotions, intentions, meanings… and our perceptions twist that contact into something we can process with ease.+

No. That wasn't good enough. +You should still try.+

+Should I? Perhaps I have. Perhaps I've already done so, and these mighty reinforcements will still not arrive in time. What vessels cut through the warp with the same speed as ours? None. And even if these legions of reinforcements arrive, will they be able to defeat the Principal Evil? Never.+

+A shame,+ one of my brothers pulsed. +Their lives could be spent delaying the enemy's advance before our arrival.+

Dumenidon, then. I knew him well. Torcrith's reply rippled with cold sincerity.

+You speak as many of our order might speak, but the

choice becomes one of morality against pragmatism. Every soul that witnesses the Archenemy on that world will be put to death for the sin of knowing daemons are real. Should I summon great hosts of Imperial soldiers, merely to doom them to the same fate? Armageddon lives and dies by its human defenders, brother. The Wolves stand with them. And, soon, so shall we. That will be enough death, I fear, without dragging more into the slaughter.+

+I still don't understand,+ Galeo confessed. His silent voice, so familiar to my mind, was undeniable. +I sense no greater corruption from this world than any one of a hundred other missions.+

+I felt the same,+ Torcrith confessed. +First, look to the world's skies. Do you see the debris burning up during its descent? Here a flare of flame, there a spark of fire. That is all that remains of the *Devourer of Stars*, dead to Space Wolves guns and consigned now to become ash. It was, in its foul prime, a twisted hulk large enough to sustain thousands of warriors and Neverborn aboard its warped decks. It drifted here upon the Sea of Souls, guided by the hands of black gods. I sensed nothing of its voyage, or its arrival. And at last I know why.+

+Show us,+ sent Galeo.

We fell towards the world, soaring above a city lost to char and ruin. Smoke choked the air, veiling our sight until we sank below the morbid cloud cover.

In the city's heart, ragged warriors armoured in ceramite of scarlet and bronze chanted and screamed to the blackening sky. They gripped axes forged in the Imperium's infancy, chain-teeth roaring out of time with the warriors' maddened chanting – which itself owed little to rhythm. Many of them were hunched and howling things, desecrating the human dead; eating the flesh of the slain or taking trophies. Others

were screaming, laughing while piling the defenders' head-
less remains into great corpse pits.

And yet, there was something else here. Something vast
and molten, giving off a sense of threatening size and devas-
tating heat, without truly revealing itself.

+You can't see it,+ Torcrith pulsed, +can you?+

I looked over the devastation, reaching out with my senses
no differently from a blind man reaching with his hands. I
sought the same resistance he'd feel when his fingers finally
brushed a wall.

And there it was. Behind the diseased humidity and stench
of fresh blood: a shadow that stained the horde's core. It rose
from the wreckage of a temple, spreading monstrous wings
to the sky.

One of my brothers breathed the words +Throne of the
Emperor.+ It may have even been me.

Bone and ceramite armoured its sweating flesh in equal
measure, while its skin was a scorched and cracked display of
inhuman red meat, strained by pulsing veins of black iron. A
thrashing mane of dreadlocked cables rose from the back of
its malformed head in a daemonic crest. Some became brass
chains ending in bound skulls. Others were connected to the
creature's ornate bronze-scale armour.

+I... I...+ Malchadiel pulsed. +What am I seeing...?+

+Rage.+ Torcrith sounded almost saddened by the thing
in the ruins, wreathed in black smoke. +You are seeing rage
incarnate. The serenity of depthless wrath.+

+The smoke is bleeding,+ sent Dumenidon. And it was
true. The way rain formed in thunderheads, so too did blood
fall from the smoke rising in thick coils from the creature's
scarred flesh.

With our senses shared, I realised we all saw something
different. Dumenidon saw little more than the smoke. Galeo

witnessed a thing of cracking bones and scaled armour, haloed not by flame and smoke but by a crescent of spiked gold. Once I became aware of our divided perceptions, the creature shifted between them all.

Dumenidon had been wrong, though.

+That isn't smoke,+ I sent. Faces contorted in the mist, twisting and drowning in the foulness. +Those are souls.+

It turned its eyes to us. The skeletal landscape of its face turned with a slowness I could only describe as bestial, but it most definitely saw us. The coal pits of its eyes steamed as blood bubbled and boiled in the thing's swollen tear ducts. Slowly – still so very slowly – its jaws opened to reveal a quivering tongue the colour of spoiled meat, with pinkish saliva roping and stretching between rows of sharkish teeth. The thing's tongue flopped in its jaws, slapping against the fangs – a fish trapped out of water.

+How can it see us?+

Torcrith didn't answer me.

It roared without warning, without even needing to drag back a breath. The sound shamed thunder – shamed even the storms of Titan – as the creature bellowed out a sonic boom.

The last thing I saw was its claw, armoured in bone and brass, curling as it reached for us.

III

I was the first to rise. The purr of my armour joints was a reassuring touch of familiarity after Torcrith's enforced dis-embodiment. Blood flowed back into my fingers, setting them stinging.

Torcrith had no need to rise, for he hadn't collapsed as we had. He remained sitting on the contemplation mat, watch-ing us in meditative silence. When I met his dark eyes, he answered with a nod.

'You saw it,' he said.

I helped Malchadiel rise, hauling him to his feet as I answered. 'We all saw it, though we each saw something different.'

'That's not unusual, when confronted by an entity of such strength. Just as reality warps around its presence, its form is so bound to the realm behind the veil that it remains in flux. In the truest sense, it is whatever it wishes to be, having ascended past the limitations of a physical form.'

'How did it see us?'

This time, he deigned to reply. 'It smelled our souls.'

'Could it have killed us?' Malchadiel asked.

'Of course. It intended to. That's why I pulled you back.'

Dumenidon waved me aside as I moved to help him rise. Galeo rose on his own as well.

+It masked its own existence.+

'Indeed so,' Torcrith agreed.

'I've never heard of such a thing,' I admitted. 'Never once, in all my time amidst the archives.'

I looked to Galeo for enlightenment, but it was Dumenidon who replied. 'The Conclave Diabolus.'

Galeo nodded. +I concur.+

The Conclave Diabolus was as close to legend as our archives could come: a record of the most reviled, most ardently pursued Neverborn our order had encountered in its ten-thousand-year history.

Even an eidetic memory has its flaws. Having never expected to confront any of the Conclave Diabolus in my lifetime, I'd paid little heed to their existence beyond the barest mentions in historical texts.

'Even so,' I said, 'there are fewer than ten among the Conclave Diabolus capable of such mastery over reality. It cannot be one of them.'

Torcrith smiled, though I wasn't sure why. 'It cannot be one of them, Hyperion? Right now, the Imperium suffers through countless worlds enduring daemonic incursion across the vastness of space. In the last few days alone, I have sensed the portents and written prophecies on many of them myself. I have sensed an inhuman voice whispering words into the mind of a three-year-old girl almost three-quarters of the galaxy away from where we sit at the moment. Yet I sensed nothing of Armageddon – not the winds of the warp that brought the *Devourer of Souls* to the world, nor the horde of abominations that are butchering their way across it.'

He ended with a tired shake of his head. 'So tell me, brother, how it cannot be one of them. It can be nothing else. Nothing else has the strength to mask its presence. The Dark Gods themselves hid this invasion from us. They would never act for a lesser being.'

Galeo made the sign of the aquila over his chestplate. +You were right to call the Chapter to war, Torcrith. We must commit to a crusade.+

'But the order is spread thin across the Imperium,' I said. 'What can we bring to Armageddon? Ninety knights? A hundred?'

Torcrith's eyes never left mine. 'We will form a ragged brotherhood from the squads still within the fortress-monastery, and sail for Armageddon before the solar week is out. Hyperion, I understand your caution, but you haven't seen all I've seen. Armageddon is a world on the edge of falling to the Archenemy. Already, the Wolves stand with the human defenders on the final untainted continent, falling back to defend the very last cities still standing.'

'But there are scarcely one hundred of us,' Malchadiel joined in. 'That isn't enough.'

Galeo looked over to him. +Will it be enough to annihilate

the enemy hordes with overwhelming force? No. But it will be enough to banish him, brother. The Wolves and the Steel Legions can handle the rest.+

'Suicide,' Malchadiel said, but amended it with a smile. 'And duty. I fear no death in the Emperor's name. I fear only to waste his Gift.'

+This will be no waste.+

Dumenidon nodded. 'Aye, justicar. A last charge to be remembered.'

I made the sign of the aquila myself, my fists banging on my breastplate. 'One last matter, Brother Torcrith.'

'Be swift. I must speak with each squad in turn. They must see what you've been shown.'

I gestured to the hall in which we stood. 'You spoke of being alone here – the last Prognosticar.'

He inclined his head to that. 'Individuals blessed with my psychic strength are rare, and my calling is no less dangerous than yours. Each death is a loss the Prognosticars feel most keenly. You were almost one of us, Hyperion. Did you know that?'

My silence answered for me.

'It is true,' he continued. 'Your powers drew notice, even before you were lingering in the trials of assessment. But your lack of self-control was considered a terminal flaw for Prognostication. You were deemed unfit for entry into the Augurium.'

'Who deemed me unfit?'

'I did. It was I, and my brother Sorren, before his recent death. Now I am the last, and as you can see, such a weakness is a hole at the heart of our order. I pray more will rise to dwell within the Silver Tower soon.'

'My self-control is still a flaw,' I confessed, 'but I thank you for your honesty.'

He smiled his subtle, sad smile again. 'Go in honour, Castian. Ready yourselves to shed a primarch's blood. The Lord of the Twelfth Legion awaits you on Armageddon.'

PART TWO

WAR WITH THE WOLVES

FOURTEEN
THE JARL

I

My legs wouldn't move, but they didn't really hurt. That was the problem; that was what made it frightening. I'd expected pain. Not being able to feel my legs at all might mean I'd never walk again. I didn't want to ask anyone else in case they agreed.

Everything looked the same with the city gone to rubble. Were we in the wreckage of a temple? A commercia? Too hard to tell. Grey stone dust covered everything, clouding around us since the building's last wall fell.

'Feeling's coming back,' I said. 'Give me a minute.'

My friends were looking at me with expressions that said what their mouths wouldn't: they knew I was lying.

'Hey,' one of them started to say.

+Hyperion.+

* * *

II

I sheltered in the shadow of a Chimera troop transport, trying and failing to ignore the rain still falling.

It was cold. Cold, cold, cold enough that it should have numbed me, but didn't. It just hurt – hurt like an ice-burn.

The archives never described war like this. They never described the shit you actually went through, did they? It was all about the fear and the courage, the funerals and the parades afterwards, the warmth of brotherhood and the friends you made for life.

It never mentioned the weariness. That's what war was – true war, not some little series of skirmishes between squads in the streets. Hell, no – in true war, when armies crashed together for hours and hours and hours on end, you had nowhere to run. You couldn't just fall back to a safe haven and wait for another patrol to start.

Before a battle, you'd stand there holding back the need to piss, while forcing out bad jokes with a tongue as dry as boot leather. And after it, you'd be tired to the bone, with your arms and legs trembling with strain. After the last charge, I'd collapsed with hundreds of my regiment, just crouching or sitting where we'd been standing and fighting only moments before. Too tired to puke, too sore to voice a complaint. War stank, too. The sweat, the blood, the breath – and that was just to begin with. In the last months, I'd seen men and women soil themselves just for a few precious moments of warmth at night, and after every battle half of us would realise we'd pissed ourselves without noticing; not from fear, but just biological necessity. We'd pissed like animals in the wild, no matter what we were doing at the time.

Jaesa pulled her rebreather mask off her swollen face, and three of her teeth came out with it, stringy with pink spit. Tym sagged to the earth with insane slowness, lying down in the wet soil with his head on a rock. I knew even as he was going down that he'd never get up again. Shalwen and Kal the Easterner were both laughing – or trying to, at least. They brayed a strengthless, breathy wheeze, thrashing in the mud, amazed to still be alive. Others kneeled in groups, thanking the distant God-Emperor, while their brothers and sisters went about the business of dying in their hundreds across the battlefield, still screaming, still crying out as they lay there in the rain.

A hand rested on my shoulder. I could smell the hot blood on those fingers before I turned to see it smearing over my uniform.

'How bad is it?' Cion asked. His face was as bloody as his hand. And his arm. And his chest.

'It's…'

Holy Throne, he'd lost an eye along with half of his face. Half of his head, even. What was I supposed to say?

'It hurts,' he said.

Yeah, I bet it did. How was he still alive?

'Cion…' I tried to say.

+Hyperion.+

III

At first, I'd tried to explain what I was seeing, but I didn't know the right words. No, wait, that's not quite right.

I didn't know enough words. I couldn't remember them, any more. Nothing I said made any sense, so I stopped saying much at all.

After that, I'd tried drawing. The patterns I drew never meant anything to the others, though. I sketched them on the walls of the command centre with a Guard-issue stylus, then on the hulls of our tanks with my boot knife, and at last, on the walls of my cell. They didn't let me keep the knife, though. I had to use my fingers. Blood made good ink.

'The war's broken him,' they kept saying. They looked at me when they said it, as if that made them right. The war hadn't broken me. What did that even mean? I just couldn't make them understand what I'd seen.

The last time I'd spoken to another person had been when they dragged me in here. 'If I can just make you see,' I'd said. They locked the door, leaving me with a bucket for waste and the walls as my parchment.

Then the attack had happened. I'd beaten on the door, shouting for a gun, swearing that I could help, and that I wanted to stand with the others.

Only I hadn't. I hadn't done those things. I'd stayed in the corner of my cell, silent as a secret, waiting for the sounds to go away.

The gunfire faded first. Then the screams had stopped. The base had fallen quiet soon after.

The door was still locked.

'Thirsty,' I said. I didn't even realise I was talking to myself, as I drew runic symbols in a language I didn't know, and sketched soulless creatures that had never been born.

'Thirsty.'

'Thirsty.'

'Thirsty.'

+Hyperion.+

IV

I huddled in the dark, listening to the children cry. It didn't matter any more. They'd find us even if we hid. They found everyone.

The knife in my hand was a sliver of glass from a broken window.

'Girls,' I said. 'Come here.'

+Hyperion.+

* * *

V

I opened my eyes to the cold comfort of my meditation chamber aboard the *Karabela*.

Galeo's presence was a ghost at the edge of my mind, insistent as a haunting. +Brother,+ he sent from elsewhere on the ship. +That's enough. I have warned you to stay out of their minds.+

+Forgive me,+ I pulsed back. +It strengthens me to reach out.+

While true, that wasn't the entire truth. Reaching out to the minds of humans on the world below took supreme focus and continual effort, but I hungered to see the world through the eyes of those caught in the chaos. It could be considered a vicarious pleasure of living through another being's senses, but my curiosity was nothing so base. I wanted to know this world. I wanted to feel it the way I never would once I set foot upon it. I wanted to sense everything I could about this one world that had somehow drawn the foulest of foes to defile its surface.

Galeo's voice came laced with patience. +I understand that, and I understand the temptation to see the world through mortal eyes. But you are needed. The brotherhood gathers.+

I rose to my feet, armour joints purring. +The Great Wolf comes?+

+He comes. And he's not coming alone. We are to greet him aboard the flagship.+

I reached for my weapons, and left the chamber.

VI

Few souls in the Imperium command as much respect as the Master of an Adeptus Astartes Chapter. Their majesty isn't the result of respect offered up by the masses – though many Chapter Masters earned the devotion of entire worlds, when they chose to make themselves known.

No, their respect was earned in the eyes of their brothers, and to stand at the forefront of one thousand of humanity's finest warriors, proclaimed by the other nine hundred and ninety-nine as the one soul worthiest of leading them... What souls were worthy of such reverence and respect?

We waited for him in the main hangar of our fleet's flagship, the Third Brotherhood battle-barge *Ruler of the Black Skies*. For organisation, we presented no pretence of rank and order, aligned only by the unity of squads. Justicars stood before their brothers, and ahead of us all, waiting to receive the Great Wolf, was Captain Taremar Aurellian – called Taremar the Gold for his maddeningly long list of noble deeds – Warden of the Third Brotherhood and master of the flagship.

He'd been chosen to lead us with no hint of opposition. Grand Master Vaurmand, as overall Lord of the Third Brotherhood, was bound to remain in the fortress-monastery. Tradition dictated his fate, no matter how he'd raged against it: Titan must always have one of the eight Grand Masters present to oversee the order's operations. With Vaurmand, only a skeleton presence remained to walk our ancient castle's cold halls.

One hundred and nine knights stood upon the deck here. A mere eighteen remained on Titan. The rest of the Chapter, may the Emperor bless them, fought their own battles spread across the stars.

A cadre of inquisitors stood with us, arrayed in their finery and battle armour respectively, depending on their personal preferences. Annika was one of thirty inquisitors to journey with us; she noticed my attention and returned it with a nod. At her side, Darford, the Khatan, Merrick, Vasilla and Clovon lingered in something approaching formality. For once, Darford wasn't the only one standing with his back straight. A brief drift over their surface thoughts betrayed their focus, which to my shame was tighter than my own.

Armageddon rolled below us in stellar slowness, visible through the open hangar bay doors. Its visage was a patchwork of blue, green and yellow, marred only by the scabrous black pockmarks of burning cities. The merest flicker of psychic sense was all it took to feel the tension emanating from the gathered knights. We had no desire to be standing up here, safe in orbit, while the world below suffered violation after violation.

We'd arrived almost twelve hours ago, and the first message received from the surface had been from the Great Wolf himself.

'Bide,' he demanded. That, and nothing more.

Talk spread through our makeshift brotherhood soon enough, even though we journeyed here on different ships. Taremar was said to be enraged at being ordered into docility, like some bladeless serf. The justicars reacted variously with anger of their own, or reluctantly ceding to the Great Wolf's greater understanding of the war below.

Galeo had been one of the latter. +We are a weapon best used once,+ he'd said to us, hours after our arrival when we were beginning to pace. +The Great Wolf will draw us as a blade and ram us through the Archenemy's heart in one swift thrust. We will serve no one if we reveal ourselves too early, and commit to uncoordinated strikes.+

Dumenidon hadn't been so sanguine. 'Are you not offended? The Wolves speak to us as if they hold a leash around our throats.'

+The Wolves are down there, and have been for months. I trust their eyes for now. If you cannot survive a touch of bruised pride, then you still have as much to learn about self-control as Hyperion.+

While I couldn't argue it was undeserved, I didn't appreciate the comparison. It still rankled hours later as we stood on
the hangar deck waiting for the Great Wolf's gunship.

'Why don't they just teleport up to us?' I voxed to the
others.

+Fenrisian superstition,+ Galeo replied. I couldn't miss
the taste of derision in his silent voice. +I do not know the
details, so I try not to judge them too harshly for it.+

The gunship came in slow, though its landing gear had
scarce touched the reinforced steel of the deck before the
gangramp began to descend on whining hydraulics. A group
of figures stood in the red gloom of the Thunderhawk's crew
bay – thirteen by my count – before walking down in a loose
pack.

We didn't stand at attention, no more than they did. We
watched in our vague ranks, conceding no dominance and
offering no submission, facing them as equals. Perhaps they
considered that their right, though in truth we did them
a great honour. They were genetic thinbloods; their gene-
seed formed from the flesh and blood of the Emperor's son,
Leman Russ. Our gene-seed came from a more direct, purer
source. We didn't call it the Emperor's Gift as a jest.

Talismans rattled against their armour as they walked:
trinkets and fetishes of string, amber, ivory and stone. Their
armour was grey – not the unpainted purity of burnished
ceramite, but the unsubtle grey of winter skies given over
to storms. Wolfskin cloaks and loincloths overlaid their
armour, the hues ranging all the way from as black as coal to
a dirty, spattered white that reminded me of blood against
snow.

Logan Grimnar led his pack directly towards the waiting
figure of Captain Taremar, who wore a cloak of his own,
in regal white trimmed by traditional grey. The Great Wolf

was unhelmed, his scarred features bared without shame, his shaggy mane of hair entwined with knucklebones and the fangs of beasts, filthy enough to form accidental dreadlocks. Perhaps once it had been a darker, oakier brown, but winter had salted it with the first signs of silvering. Grimnar had led the Wolves for over a century; he'd earned the right to his scars. His steps thundered with dull echoes, as the joints of his Terminator warplate gave dry snarls in uneven accompaniment.

When he grinned, which he did without any humour, he showed bestial canine teeth that spoke of his Chapter's brazen genetic deviation. The Inquisition had never looked kindly on the Wolves, and his smile was merely one of the reasons why.

I took in all of these details with the briefest glance, but something else eclipsed them all, impossible to ignore. Every single one of the thirteen Wolves was stained in unequal parts red and black – their armour marred with dried blood or scorched black in flamer wash. The reek of their battle plate was the stench of charnel houses, of abattoirs, of battlefields newly given over to crows. As these rattling, burned warriors approached, I felt shamed by my pristine suit of armour. They'd been fighting a war for weeks, while we'd been locked in transit, readying for our eventual arrival.

A strange moment of insecurity. I had nothing to be ashamed of, but there it was.

Grimnar's greeting was as gruff as everything else about him. He looked at Captain Taremar – both of them matched in size in their Terminator plating – and sniffed once, wetly, before spitting bloody saliva onto our deck. I'd been expecting a formal acknowledgement of our presence, but three words were all he said.

'And you are?'

No disrespect. No impatience or suggestion of anger. He spoke the words as one would address a harmless stranger entering one's domain. The voice itself was as rough as tank treads grinding over gravel.

Brother-Captain Taremar inclined his head in acknowledgement of a superior, given the divide between their ranks. 'I am Taremar Aurellian, Captain of the Third Brotherhood, master of the *Ruler of the Black Skies* and a Knight of Titan.'

One of the Wolves snorted. 'Sounds very mighty,' he chuckled. Several of the others joined in.

Taremar's eyes were the colour of clean iron, that same warm blue that edges into grey. They fixed on the Wolf for a moment, long enough to mark the man's features, before snapping back to Grimnar.

'Did I say something to amuse your kinsman?' he asked.

The Great Wolf growled – literally growled – in that moment. It left his parted lips in a wet rumble. 'Forgive my men. They're short on good humour.' He looked back, casting a glance over his shoulder. 'Rawthroat. Watch your words.'

The one addressed as Rawthroat chuckled again. 'Aye, jarl. As you say.'

Grimnar's eyes were the earthy brown of soft loam, but their glare was as wicked as a blade's edge. 'Rawthroat speaks the Wolves' way,' Grimnar explained. 'Rare is the Wolf to put titles in a greeting before his deeds.' As Taremar drew breath to speak, Grimnar lifted a hand in warning. 'I don't call your deeds into question, captain, nor do I care what they are. I called. You answered, and you wear that armour. What I see is enough for me.'

He sidestepped our traditions without disrespecting them, without forcing his own upon us, while still praising our arrival. Galeo clearly sensed my thoughts.

+He is easy to admire, this Wolf Lord.+

I nodded in reply.

The gathered inquisitors took the moment as a cue to begin their own introductions. The presence of the Wolves had an effect on Annika that hadn't been too hard to predict: she looked as wide-eyed as a lost girl, yet as proud as a new mother. Still, it would be some time before the introductions reached her. She stood in the middle of the group, not quite as hungry for attention as some of the others.

Grimnar silenced the first of them by raising his hand again. 'These... niceties... can wait.'

Taremar nodded. 'I concur. We have a war to win.'

Grimnar gave the Inquisitorial warbands the briefest of glances. I didn't know under what circumstance that could ever pass as a greeting.

'I am Jarl Grimnar and these are my Wolf Guard. There. Now we are all brothers.' He gestured to one of his men. 'Rawthroat.'

The named Wolf activated a handheld hololithic projector. It beamed a wide image onto the hangar deck, showing the landscape of the continent called Armageddon Prime. Entire swathes of the image were bleached in an unhealthy, flickering red, while hive cities were marked out as streams of angular Fenrisian runes. Grimnar stalked around the map, speaking as he moved.

'You made fine speed to reach us so swiftly, but you have missed much. Blood was first shed months ago, when this war began with a rebellion. Cults rose. Seditionists preached. Entire sectors of the cities spat on the Allfather's name.'

'The rebellion was a significant, but pathetic, heresy.' Grimnar circled the map again. He reminded me of a hound seeking somewhere to sit down. 'The planet soon suffered through the warp's turmoil. Astropathy died in the minds of those who sought to send messages. The world fell silent. The Enemy of All masked its approach. Then came the *Devourer of Stars*.'

As he spoke, more of the map bleached with red. 'The Steel Legions and Armageddon's own defenders fell back from Armageddon Prime. The entire continent is a wasteland. Any human still drawing breath in the fallen cities no doubt wishes they weren't.'

More and more of the map fell to the spreading stain, as inexorable as a tide. 'We joined the fight after Hives Volcanus, Death Mire and Tempestora had already fallen.'

I watched the red spreading from the cities he named. 'They are lost, though we've slowed the enemy's advance time and again since those nights. Much of their populations were already in the Archenemy's service even before we made planetfall.'

The hololithic changed to the other continent, Armageddon Secundus. Grimnar gestured next to the swathe of darkness marring the image's edges. 'This is the equatorial jungle. Our forces fell back ahead of the enemy, expecting to fight every step of the way.' He spat again, marking our deck a second time with bloody spit. 'That fight never came. The enemy delayed their advance. My scouts all told the same tale, no matter where I sent them: our foe halted his army's advance to reign with pride over the rubble he'd created from the bones of the lost cities. Cairns of skulls rise where homes and manufactories once stood. Retaking the continent will be a war of rebuilding, not reconquest.'

Grimnar looked up from the hololith to spear Taremar with his gaze. 'But now, the enemy comes. Look to the Styx, the river threading life through Armageddon Secundus. They will ford it within the week, and break through to the remaining hives.'

'We will end him.' Taremar's voice was just as deep as the Wolf Lord's, but much less ragged. Only one of them had been shouting orders every hour of every day for weeks on end.

'Yes, you will.' Grimnar's face was sunburned leather, split by a white-fanged grin. 'And if that were all we had to speak of, I'd leave you in peace to make your preparations. But there's more.' As he turned, taking in the entire hangar deck and all of us present, his mirthless grin left no doubt as to his authority. 'Hives Helsreach and Infernus have seen nothing of the true threat. Their citizens have remained behind high, safe walls, far from the war.' He turned his eyes back to our captain. 'Do I make myself clear?'

'I believe so.' Taremar's half-smile spoke more of suspicion than amusement. 'Humour me, nevertheless.'

'Sedition was weak and spineless in the cities of Secundus. What little rebellion rose was quickly quenched, even without our presence.' Grimnar banged a fist on his breastplate, sharp and loud as a tolling temple bell. The sudden sound made several of the inquisitors flinch. 'They are innocent, and more than that, they are good people guarded by faith and fine soldiers – far from the front lines. With the cities untouched and the people free from taint, they will not be "processed" by the Inquisition after the last day has dawned. Am I being clearer?'

Taremar's eyes flicked to the gathered inquisitors. The glance lasted less than a second, but it was enough for Grimnar to release a low, dry growl in the back of his throat.

'Look at *me*, damn you. Not them. Do you understand what I'm saying?'

'High King–' began Taremar.

'Jarl is enough of a title for me.' Grimnar looked back to the hololith. 'The situation is grave enough. I have no wish to let

your… associates… in the Inquisition take a heavier hand
than necessary. Do you understand?'

Taremar conceded with a nod. 'I do. But the mistrust that
plagues you is not my burden to bear.'

'Be that as it may, you'll remain in orbit until you're summoned. I will summon you for the final strike, and the
people of this planet will never know you existed.'

Taremar was no lesser lordling to be commanded like this.
To his credit, he did nothing more than nod in respect of
the Wolf Lord's wishes, when a battle of wills and authority
would serve no one.

'I am a Grey Knight of Titan, and I have a duty to do. A
warning, however: do not presume to order me as you would
a servitor. We will do as we must, and no word or action you
take will sway that truth, Wolf Lord.'

Grimnar laughed for the first time – a dry bark of a sound.
The Wolf Guard at his side relaxed with his laughter.

'I know how your Inquisition works, captain. I know
how those wheels turn, with regiments of Imperial Guard
butchered for the sin of seeing into the ordos' dirty secrets,
or entire ship crews given over to void-graves because they
chanced to catch a Grey Knights vessel out of the corner of
their eyes. Let me speak clearly, son of Titan. These people
have seen nothing, and suffered no taint. My brothers and
I fight for their lives, watering this world's earth with our
blood so they might breathe another day in the Allfather's
empire. So you will do more than nod and agree, you will
give me your word not to appear before them. I will not have
your presence damn them into early graves. Now nod or
swear an oath or do whatever you need to do. But I will have
your agreement, Captain Taremar.'

Taremar nodded. It looked as if even the negligible motion
cost him dearly.

'Good,' said Grimnar. 'It's more than a matter of morals, of course. You and your warriors are the final weapon, captain. We can't let the enemy know you're coming.'

One of the inquisitors cleared her throat. 'What of the *Devourer of Stars?*'

I noticed Jarl Grimnar never stood with his back facing the Inquisitorial representatives. His mistrust ran deep – as deep as an old wound, perhaps. I wondered at the history there, and whether Annika had access to those archives.

'What of it?' he asked the sharp-faced woman who'd interrupted. In her robes of red velvet, she seemed more ecclesiarch than inquisitor.

She sighed, as if already weary of dealing with the Wolves and their lord. 'Where is it?'

Grimnar stared at her for several heartbeats. Several of the Wolf Guard followed his gaze. One even removed his helmet to stare with his kindred.

'We destroyed it.' Grimnar spoke slowly, as if explaining something painfully obvious to a lackwit. 'We blew it up. What, in the Allfather's name, did you expect?'

Again, the sigh. 'Where,' she said with exaggerated patience, 'is its wreckage?'

Grimnar turned to face her fully. The growl of his armour joints matched the growl from his throat.

'We–' he snarled the words in low-tenor mimicry of her tone.

'–destroyed that, too.'

'It had critical value as an object of study, and the–'

'Hush, witch. Don't make me kill you.' Grimnar turned away from her, ignoring her completely. 'Captain.'

'Jarl,' Taremar replied.

The Wolf gestured back to the hololithic display. 'I am gathering the world's forces – the armies of this last continent – to hold back the enemy's advance at the River Styx.'

Taremar followed the lord's sweeping hand wave. Any irritation he'd felt vanished in that moment, replaced by his gaunt, cadaverous calm. He's an ugly hero, Darford had said of Captain Aurellian on the journey here. I couldn't argue with that, though I couldn't imagine why he thought it mattered.

'Casualties will be catastrophic,' Taremar replied.

'I'm not blind to that, Knight.'

'Defending the cities would offer a far greater advantage.' The two leaders shared another glance. 'But the people will witness the enemy,' Taremar finished. 'Why save a world if all its people are put to death for knowledge of the Principal Evil?'

Grimnar gave a breathy snuff of air. I wasn't sure if it was a chuckle or a snort. 'A fast learner. Look to the Styx, Captain Taremar. That will be where I need you. I'll send the signal, and your men must strike with every breath in their bodies.'

'It will be done.'

'We have a day. Two at most. The outriders of their red horde are already dogging at our lines. You know what you face, do you not? You know what I'm asking of you, and what you'll be teleporting into?'

In answer, Taremar merely gestured to the hundred Grey Knights standing alongside him. A suggestive impulse flashed through our minds, a nudge from our captain, and we saluted in perfect unity, hands to breastplates in the sign of the aquila.

'We know,' said Taremar.

Grimnar returned the salute, as did his Wolf Guard. A lesser leader might have addressed his final words to our commander, but Grimnar took the time to meet each of our eyes before speaking.

'Watch from the skies, brothers. Come running when we howl.'

FIFTEEN

NAMES

I

In the hours after the Wolves departed, most of our ragged brotherhood retired to their own final preparations. My bond with Castian allowed me to reach out and find them with no effort at all, but I had no wish to stand with them for now. Malchadiel, Enceladus and Galeo were joined in psychic communion, meditating to be ready for what we faced on the world below. Dumenidon, like myself, had retreated to be alone. I sensed his exertions, the burn of his utter focus, as he trained with a blade in his arming chamber.

I had no desire to train, nor did I wish to waste the time in meditation. I'd given all time to those pursuits during the journey to Armageddon. Something else dragged at my attention now.

I stood before the entrance to her private suite, and rapped my knuckles on the bulkhead. The wall-speaker came on with a click.

'Who comes?' asked a soft female voice.

+Hyperion,+ I sent through the door. The speaker clicked off, and the doors rolled open on oiled mechanics.

'Hello, Hyperion,' Vasilla said with a smile. She had the gunmetal-grey promethium tanks strapped to her back.

They were in the middle of their own preparations. Darford stood by a workbench, poring over his disassembled rifle, cleaning the spare barrels with a cloth. The Khatan was wrapping the grips of her spear, while Merrick had taken a screwdriver to his cyber-mastiff's jaws. Annika and Clovon attended to their own weapons. They were sitting on opposite sides of the room, which only spread the scent they shared. He smelled of her skin; she of his. It wasn't the first time they'd reeked of last-minute intimacy before a mission.

I would never understand humans.

'Are you well?' Vasilla asked.

'Well enough.' I wasn't sure I liked how the girl was looking at me. For want of anything sensible to say, I asked if she was well herself.

'Glad to be here,' she said. The saddest thing was that she meant it, at no older than sixteen. Her devotion to duty was admirable, but our order was supposed to carry these burdens so humanity didn't have to. I felt guilty every time I looked at her.

'You are a scrivener,' I said to her. 'I don't understand why you gird yourself for war.'

'Even a scribe can fire a weapon, Hyperion.'

I neither agreed nor disagreed. Annika either sensed my awkwardness or my attention, for she rested her bolter down and raised an eyebrow.

'What is it?'

'May we speak?' I asked. +Alone.+

'Of course,' she said, and added *'Here?'* silently.

+Here will be fine.+

She cleared her throat, drawing her companions' eyes. 'Give me a few minutes,' she said to them. They filed past me. Only Clovon tried to meet my eyes on the way out. I ignored him.

Once they were gone, Annika moved to sit up on the edge of Darford's workbench. Her black hair was still loose; I knew she'd tie it up before she went into battle.

'What's wrong?' she asked.

'Nothing is wrong. I have a question, that's all.'

'I know what you're going to ask.' The tribal tattoos on her cheeks curved as she smiled. I couldn't tell if her expression was one of amusement or sympathy – it wasn't easy for me to discern the minor differences in such things.

I had to take a breath and gird myself to the words before I spoke them.

'Who was I?'

Annika reached across the table, picking up a data-slate. She tapped the screen, cycling through readouts.

'Are you sure you want to know this?' From the tone of her voice, she seemed to be teasing, or amused in some way. 'This isn't like you, Hyperion. Disregarding the traditions like this.'

That was true enough. 'I die tomorrow, Annika.'

Her smile faded, no different from the sun going behind a cloud. She had the sense and grace not to argue with me, or offer a worthless denial. We looked into each other's eyes for long enough that I began to grow uncomfortable. I wasn't sure why.

'I have the information already, but it's behind several cipher locks.' When she spoke, her voice was quieter, softer. 'I'll need a few minutes to enter all the passcodes.'

'I will wait.'

I walked around her chambers, as she'd walked around mine so often in the past. The principal difference was that

I didn't touch anything, thereby annoying her. Room by room, I walked through the suite of chambers. Darford's room was a mess of weapons and clothing, which I found odd for such an immaculately attired man. Vasilla's chamber was almost devoid of furniture, but for a writing desk and a small shrine. The Khatan's smelled of her – that is to say, of sweat, dreadlocks, and long nights.

'Hyperion.'

I moved back to her, feeling a tightness in my chest that I couldn't quite place.

'You look... worried,' she said.

'I feel unusual.' I had to swallow, and to make fists of my hands to prevent her noticing the tremble in them. My throat was inexplicably dry, making it difficult to speak.

'You're... are you nervous?' she asked, her voice dangerously soft. Her eyes were wide.

'That's a physiological impossibility.'

+What... What is that feeling?+ Malchadiel sent in a rush. +What is happening?+ I felt Galeo, Enceladus and Dumenidon similarly questing for me, reaching out for the source of the insane sensation.

+All is well.+ I contained myself in absolution, internalising everything, letting nothing slip free. My hearts began to slow.

'Hyperion...' Annika said, still with her soft voice.

'Just tell me,' I said, sharper than I'd intended. 'Please.'

She didn't hand me the data-slate. Instead, she slid from the table and walked to the communal chamber's main oculus screen, mounted on the starboard wall. As Annika slid the data-slate into the receptacle, the screen flared into glowing life.

She showed me a boy. A rough pict of a boy in his middle teens, though the image was grainy with distortion. He was thin, undernourished, unhealthy. His eyes were dark, cocky, suspicious.

More than anything else, he looked tired.

No. That is a lie. More than anything else, he looked like me.

I felt myself stepping closer, closer, until my hand rested on the screen. Annika leaned on the wall nearby, watching me watch myself. Even without looking, I could sense her gentle smile as well as her melancholy.

'Is there more?' I asked. 'More than the picture?'

Her answer was to key in a second code. I stepped back from the grainy visage in order to read the text that scrolled into view.

By Order of His Holy Majesty the God-Emperor of Terra
Authorised Souls Only
Case File – SAB-Tertius AQ901:SS:GX1345L:88:XHD
Secondary Relevance: SIGIL – SIGIL – SIGIL
Tertiary Relevance: 77-EP:513T:X:3a:ASP:8183659

Imperial Representative Responsible – [Inquisitor Lilith Abfequarn, Ordo Hereticus]
Imperial Heavenly Solar Reckoning: XXX.XXX.406.M41 [Empyrean Variance Allowance Noted; See Subsidiary Documentation (HERE) And (HERE) And (HERE) And (HERE).]

SUBJECT borne in stasis from Eustis Majoris to Titan. Stasis integrity absolute upon arrival: confirmed absolute by Inquisitor Lilith Abfequarn (Representative), confirmed absolute by Apex Cronus Bastion (Destination).

SUBJECT before and after reanimation presented as Human Male, chronological age 15-Fifteen-XV, physical age lower – all variances attributed to biological stunting. Physically underdeveloped, significant signs of Malnutrition, Carpopedal Spasm, Muscle Atrophy and Related Halt of Growth, Abuse of Detrimental Substance, Scurvy, Iron Deficiency, Iodine

Deficiency, Onset of Mania, Delusional Perceptive Sense, and
Reflective Psychic Ability.

Inquisitor Lilith Abfequarn presented SUBJECT to Chapter
VI-VI-VI on basis of the latter anomaly. SUBJECT has recorded
involvement with the actions of INQUISITOR GIDEON
RAVENOR, ORDO XENOS.

Initial testing confirms SUBJECT'S heightened Reflective
Psychic Ability, cross-reference: 'Mirror Psyker'.
Clarification – SUBJECT has no capacity to access his own
innate psychic strength. SUBJECT leeches from nearby sources
of psychic power. SUBJECT then displays ability to mimic any
and all psychic ability he has leeched from others.

Principal Refraction to the Anomalous Condition: SUBJECT
shows signs of potential to be Unlocked. In the process of
Unlocking, SUBJECT will be broken of parasitic instinct and
reshaped accordingly. Immense potential for psychic mastery.
As noted, SUBJECT'S chronological age at variance with
physical development. Implantation of gene-seed at
chronological age cogitated at eighty-nine per cent (89%)
chance of rejection-failure. Implantation of gene-seed at
physical age cogitated at seventy-seven per cent (77%) chance
of rejection-failure.

Post-initial testing, SUBJECT transferred to Titan Fortress-
Monastery. SUBJECT consigned to INTROSPECTION CELL
D-3111-ENC-AX44-JA.
SUBJECT rendered ready to begin Time of Trial. All memory
banished.

SUBJECT'S identity to be purged from all UNPROTECTED
Imperial Records, in the Emperor's name, and for His Glorious
Imperium.

I read it in silence, every word. Once I reached the end,
I read it all again. Twice. Only then did I turn back to the

inquisitor. Annika was still smiling, but as before, without being able to read her facial muscles, I wasn't sure what it meant.

'There's no name,' I said.

'Actually, yes, there is.' She keyed in another code, bringing up a secondary screen. It showed a report filed on the investigative trial of Inquisitor Gideon Ravenor, detailing access to several of his testimonies.

Annika gestured to the first one. 'There,' she said.

I followed where she pointed.

EFFERNETI, ZAEL

It meant nothing to me. I looked back at her. 'Zael Efferneti. That was my name?'

'It was.' She blanked the screen and withdrew the data-slate. 'And you caused quite a stir all those decades ago. You were present at the side of one of the ordos' most respected inquisitors, during some of his darkest hours.'

Inquisitor Ravenor. I knew of him. Who, within the Inquisition of Segmentums Solar and Obscurus, hadn't heard that name? Such was his renown, his writings were considered required reading for Inquisitorial candidates in several subsectors.

'I don't remember.'

'Did you expect anything else?'

I didn't know the answer to that myself. 'I'm not sure.'

Annika shook her head. 'You've remembered flashes, Hyperion. Try to focus.'

Discomfort ran through me, as sudden as a sharp wind. I didn't want to do this any more.

'No. I think I'll leave. Thank you, inqui…'

'Hyperion?'

'The black throne.' I knuckled my closed eyes, irritated

by the memory. 'I told you I've always dreamed of a black throne. A black chair. Of course.'

She nodded. 'Inquisitor Ravenor's life support throne. See? You remember more than you realise.'

'How difficult is this information to find? You know who I was, who Malchadiel and Sothis were... How common is such lore?'

'It doesn't exist outside the Inquisition. I doubt it even exists on Titan.'

'That much is obvious, inquisitor.'

'Even in the Inquisition, this data is rarely accessed. I went looking because I was cursed with a curious soul, and called in old oaths for favours. In truth, this kind of lore is often archived and forgotten, rather than consciously buried in the Throne System's annals. Even among the Inquisition, who but the most curious souls would care for such knowledge? It's worthless beyond its value as a harmless curiosity. It offers no advantage over an enemy. The Grey Knights are trained and bound and scourged to rarely care about their former lives, and inquisitors gain no special influence over them by having it. Few souls are curious enough to look. A handful every decade. No more than that.'

'I appreciate you sharing it with me.'

'Curiosity is no sin, Hyperion. I like picking through the bones of old archives. The things you learn.' She gave me another smile. 'I'm glad I could show it to you.'

I looked at her – a thought occurring now for the first time. 'Is there some punishment for what you've shown me? Would the ordos take punitive action against you?'

Annika shrugged. 'Hyperion, the Inquisition isn't... organised... in that way. It's not one cult on one world ruled by one council. A lot of outsiders don't see that clearly. Every world, system, subsector and segmentum has its own organisation, rituals, archives and politics... Do you see?'

'Not really.' I had the order, and nothing outside it. I struggled to envisage something that spanned the galaxy, made up of millions of conflicting souls united only by the loosest interest. Such disunity made my skin crawl.

'One inquisitor's sin is another's salvation. It's like the Imperial Creed. On one world, they worship the Emperor as a god enthroned on solid gold. On the next, He's a metaphor for eternal life through acts of self-sacrifice. On another, He's a sun deity, responsible for the daylight and the growth of crops – they pray to Him for ripe harvests. And yet, on other worlds, He will be venerated as a prophet whose words are lost to time, and lesser men conjure up apt phrases in His name, that make sense to the local populace. On yet another world, He's the supreme being that welcomes and protects the spirits of people's ancestors after they die. And on another? He's the Guiding Light: the source of the Astronomican, the living, mortal man with the powers of a god, whose machines project the beacons for our ships to follow in the endless night.'

'I understand.'

I'd never seen such cultures – I possessed precious little first-hand knowledge of any culture beyond my monastery's walls. Even when I trawled the archives for lore on the worlds we purged, I focused on what was relevant to the operation.

Annika took it a step further. 'All of those religions are a tolerable variance on the Imperial Creed. They are the Imperial Creed. The galaxy is vast, and the Ecclesiarchy cares nothing for what any of these worlds and nations do – so long as it's the Emperor to whom they pray. The Imperium is not a unified whole, Hyperion. It's humanity in its infinite, lost, separated variety. The Inquisition is the same. Tell me, how many inquisitors in your experience are no different to me?'

Perhaps she was forgetting I'd met a total of four inquisitors in my life, thus far. How was I supposed to know such things? They were rarely recorded, assumed as fact only by those who dealt with it in their daily lives. I'd spent four decades within the monastery, and the year since my ascension to knighthood had been spent largely in warp transit, punctuated by rare flashes of battle.

'I have almost no experience with the Inquisition outside my dealings with you.'

'Of course. Forgive me, I forget how young you are.'

I looked at her, and said nothing.

'I mean… relatively speaking,' she qualified.

'I see.'

'I've met many others,' Annika said. 'Inquisitors who use primitive talismans, and others that swear by alien technology: shamans and progressive heretics all fighting for the same cause. Yes, some of us hold authority over others, but ultimately we're alone, every single one of us, only as powerful as our own reach and those we ally with. We fight with one another as much as we fight the Great Enemy. The Inquisition – as imagined by the populace in its guise as a monolithic, ultimate entity – just doesn't exist. It's a… *valdelnagh*. A misunderstanding. A convenient deception.'

I realised what she was doing. It had almost worked.

'You are avoiding the question, inquisitor. Would you be punished for this?'

She laughed, a gentle sound. 'It depends who found out. Most inquisitors wouldn't care, knowing most Grey Knights would be similarly uninterested. Others might wish to kill me for it. Others would consider it a novel manipulation. None of that matters.'

I looked down at my hands, sheathed in silver ceramite. 'It

said I had no psychic ability. They had to unlock my talent for me to function.'

'Only the Grey Knights could do it. It's why Lilith brought you to Titan.'

'Was it her idea?'

'The report doesn't say, but I doubt it. More likely, she was issued a *sammekull* by the Prognosticars.'

Sammekull. Another Fenrisian word, meaning a summoning. It did seem likely. And what had Torcrith said of me? 'Your powers drew notice, even before you were lingering in the trials of assessment.'

Intriguing. Perhaps he'd been the one to send for me.

'At least it explains why my powers function so much better in the presence of my brothers.' I'd always wondered about that, and why it seemed unique to me. The fact it concerned none of my kindred even the slightest had been firm reassurance, leading me to think it was merely a matter of familiarity and confidence. The truth was that my psychic capabilities had had to be nurtured late in life, while I was naturally more… vampiric with my talents.

I couldn't help but ask myself if I still leeched from them, as I leeched from others in my youth.

A much colder realisation was that this explained why my masters had been so hesitant during my initial training. I'd probably come closer to destruction than I'd ever known.

I recalled the first words I shared with others of my order, when Enceladus and two others freed me from my cell.

'These symbols,' I'd asked them. 'What are they?'

'Wards. Hexagrammic wards. We had to be sure you were free from taint. We also had to be certain you recalled nothing of your former life.'

The second voice was no warmer. 'You have remained here for the mandated ninety-nine nights, as we scryed into your soul.'

'The ritual is complete.' The third voice, who I'd come to know as Enceladus, spoke at last. 'We are satisfied with your purity.'

But the armoured knight's joints growled as he inclined his head. 'Though some doubts yet remain.'

Blinking pulled me free of the reverie.

'I should leave.'

Annika didn't offer objection. 'As you wish. Will I see you before... before we make planetfall?'

I know why she hesitated. She nearly asked 'Will I see you before you die?' It's almost amusing that she thought to shield such a sentiment from me. I was born to fight, born to die. Neither fate held any mystery or fear for me.

Courageous words indeed, from one who'd trembled at the thought of seeing his youth. That, at last, made me smile.

'Unlikely,' I said. 'If you are going down to Armageddon to stand with the Wolves, then this will be our last meeting. Farewell, Inquisitor Jarlsdottyr.'

She placed her palm against my breastplate – against the icon of the *Liber Daemonicum* there.

'This book is the closest thing you have to a holy text, isn't it?'

I nodded. 'It contains our rites and traditions, and–'

She shushed me. She actually shushed me. She had to reach up to do it, to press a tiny, frail human finger against my lips. The madness of the moment almost reduced me to laughter.

'Hush,' she said. 'Have faith, Hyperion. You were made to win wars like this. All of you were.'

I couldn't think of an adequate reply. Lacking the right words, I inclined my head and left her alone.

The call to war came nine hours later.

* * *

II

I stood with Castian on the *Karabela*'s bridge. Captain Talwyn sat straight in his command throne, wearing his official grey tunic, further darkened by the addition of a black jacket with gold buttons. For Talwyn Castor, the attire was almost funereal, which was fitting enough.

His officers were at their stations, and a quiet dignity had come over the bridge since we entered. Every human wore their uniforms, showing exacting standards of neatness. Even the servitors had been muted to speak in low murmurs for now. The ship itself maintained perfect position in the fleet – Talwyn had seen to that.

The oculus gave an aerial view of the land around one of Armageddon's final hive cities. The River Styx – named, as everything on this world was named, from the various underworlds of Terran mythology – was a fork of rich, blue lightning splitting the earth itself. What had the first settlers seen in this globe, to give its landmarks such rancid names? I'd never know.

On the oculus, we watched armies grinding together on a scale I'd never even imagined possible. Entire battalions of Imperial Guard and militia charged and fled, rose from trenches or held the line, all to the whims of their own hearts and the orders shouted by their officers. Tank divisions, hundreds and hundreds of war machines, churned up a storm of dust as they crashed through the enemy's ranks or drew back in ragged, broken formations.

The horde they faced was an agglomeration of men, mutants, and much worse besides. The fact any man or woman stood their ground against such a host spoke with crystal clarity of the immeasurable courage within the human heart. Before my very eyes, I was seeing just why mankind deserved to inherit this galaxy. No other species twinned such virtue with such intellect.

I confess, as I thought such things, I could almost imagine Annika telling me I was being naive. Even Vasilla would have smiled to hear such thoughts, and reminded me how little I really knew of the species that gave birth to me.

We watched the greatest battle of the war raging on both sides of the Styx. From our aerie, it was a black stain across the land, spreading minute by minute from a murderous epicentre. From this altitude, and with the smoke rising from the engaged armies, almost all detail was obscured.

Vox-traffic crackled above the sedate quiet, bringing voices from the surface. We kept communication bonds open to three souls: the first, Jarl Grimnar, embattled at the river. The second, Annika, her exhausted breathing eclipsed by the heavy crash of her bolter. The third, Captain Taremar, as we listened to him relaying, squad by squad, those among our brotherhood who stood ready for the final strike.

'Status, Castian?' his voiced rasped over the speakers, filling the bridge.

Galeo nodded to Dumenidon, to answer in his place.

'We await the last blessings upon our teleportation platform. A matter of minutes at most, Third Captain.'

'Understood.' Taremar's voiced crackled away, returning the sounds of Jarl Grimnar bellowing at his brothers, and Annika swearing in the most obscene Fenrisian I'd ever heard.

+Something amuses you, Hyperion?+

I turned to Galeo, unable to keep the smile from my face. 'I find it oddly comforting that the last voice we'll hear is destined to be Inquisitor Jarlsdottyr, calling the foe's parentage into question. I never thought I'd die like this.'

Galeo's lips never moved, but I saw the same humour reflected in his eyes. +The moment does rather lack a certain solemnity, doesn't it?+

Even Dumenidon gave a grunt that passed for laughter.

We wore our Tactical Dreadnought plate, adding significant weight and mass to our armoured bulks. Castian rarely went into battle wearing our most precious heirloom wargear, and I already missed the reassurance offered by the warp-jump generator mounted on my power armour's backpack. Terminator plate had an internalised power source – one of many reasons it was infinitely more durable than our standard warplate – but I'd have gladly traded the extra protection for familiarity and freedom.

I felt slow, sluggish, despite the additional strength humming in the fibre-bundle machinery muscles insulating my body. When Captain Taremar had first ordered us into the suits, even Galeo objected.

+My brothers and I would prefer to enter this battle in our traditional armour, captain.+

Taremar had been unmoved. 'We are descending into the jaws of hell, Galeo. Every second we remain alive down there is another second with which to banish this thing. Don your finest armour, Justicar of the Eighth. That is an order.'

So we obeyed.

On the bridge, I lifted my helm into place, sealing it with a clicking crunch, and a hiss of air pressure.

In the same moment, the strategium doors rumbled open. Axium stood in the doorway, his resplendent silver form flanked by several robed tech-priests.

'It is time.'

III

The machines' clanking made it hard to hear anything else. Mist was already curling around our boots as we made our way onto the teleportation platform. None of us said a word. There was nothing to say. We'd gone over the details, such as they were, a hundred times and more. Every squad on every

ship knew what it was teleporting down into. Last-minute
footage from the surface – choppy, tearing and static-laden
as it was from the helms of the Wolves still fighting – showed
the merest slices of what we'd be facing.

Our forces were in a fighting withdrawal to their defensive
bastions two kilometres back from the river's edge. I watched
the feed from one Wolf's eye lenses as he held up the stump
of his left arm, and heard his disbelieving curses.

The first waves of Archenemy forces to crash against the
Imperial lines had been outriders, scouts, and the rabble
hosts in the foe's vanguard. Even the advance elements of
the horde fought hard enough to mire Armageddon's armies
in a deadlock.

With the true threat making itself known at last, after hours
of pitched battle, the Wolves ordered hundreds of thousands
of men and women back, back, back. I'd paid little heed
to the tactics at play. Few of us had; our role was to be the
blade's thrust to the heart. We were the hammer, not the
hand that wielded it.

It wasn't the weapon's place to question the general, nor to
know the placement of every regiment in a war. It was the
weapon's place to fit the fist, and to taste the enemy's blood.

I suspected a colder, more pragmatic reason lay behind our
distance from the overall battle plan, as well. We wouldn't
be surviving the next hour, so the ebb and flow of the entire
campaign meant little to any of us. I knew the raw basics,
the position and commanding officers of most regiments
making up the Imperial force, yet couldn't imagine what circumstances would give me cause to speak with any of them.
Merely seeing me would mean a death sentence for them in
most conditions. Admittedly, they were doomed to execution anyway, after having borne witness to the Lord of the
Twelfth Legion and his armies.

Such a reward, for unfailing valour. I found myself wondering for the first time if it were truly necessary to–

Galeo sent a telekinetic nudge against my shoulder, to catch my attention. +Do not think such things,+ he warned. +Do not question our masters. That way lies heresy.+

Axium inputted the codes and coordinates from his raised balcony overlooking the platform. Adepts began their chanting.

+Castian stands ready,+ Galeo pulsed to Captain Taremar on his flagship.

+Acknowledged, Castian.+

+Remember,+ Galeo sent to us. +Remember what we must do.+

'For the Emperor,' the four of us replied as one.

The others waited in silence for the final summons, watching the juddering helm image-feeds. On a whim, I lifted my hand as I watched Axium working.

'Goodbye, Axium.'

He looked up, his silver features perfectly composed in an expression of warmth. 'Die well, Hyperion.'

'I plan to.'

The order, when it came, was a moment of absolutely perfect communion. One hundred and nine minds aligned in intent, in unity of purpose, and the bonds of brotherhood. Never in my life had I ever felt so secure, so vindicated, so righteous.

Taremar's voice rode the communion, ghosting along the invisible threads linking each of our consciousnesses.

+Grey Knights of the Ragged Brotherhood...+

I would never understand how Taremar managed it with such clarity, but the next sound we heard was Jarl Grimnar's howl on the world below. Taremar pulled it from the Wolf's mind, spreading the summons to all of us.

My blood boiled at that sound. The mists closed in, the engines whined louder, and I roared my squad's name into the cobweb of connected minds. I wasn't alone in doing so. Every knight silently screamed into the communion, unifying us one last time before the world burst apart into madness.

SIXTEEN

THE SWORD FALLS

I

I do not wish to speak of Armageddon.

I understand that for the purposes of this record, it's my duty to illuminate others. However, not all duties can be approached with equal relish. That day on Armageddon stands as one of the darkest moments in the history of the Grey Knights Order, even before the following months became a blight on our code of honour. I didn't know that then. I couldn't have known. It changes nothing. It doesn't diminish the sorrow that lingers, nor the shame that followed.

You cannot imagine what Armageddon cost me. You cannot imagine what we saw, what we faced, and what we did. I can describe it, but what are one warrior's words against the true picture?

I was warned that the accounting would not be complete without it, so I will speak of Armageddon. I will speak of what we did that day, and frame the unimaginable truth into the limits of language, so mortal minds may comprehend what I saw.

The last thing I saw aboard the *Karabela* was the gathering of misty light, obscuring all sight of Axium. The last thing I heard with my ears was the thunderclap of generators discharging their sacred duties. My mind was open to the brotherhood's final defiant cry.

Then came the warp. A controlled descent – we burst through it in a heartbeat. It was nothing. I scarcely even recall it.

My boots kissed earth with a grinding smack. I could hear screaming. Nothing but screaming: outside my helmet, inside my mind, even leaving my own lips. My senses couldn't interpret anything else.

The Neverborn were screaming. Not because the warp flux drew their attention, though it would have done that as surely as it will have blinded any Imperial mortals looking at our arrival point. Neither was it because air displacement sent a peal of thunder across both sides of the river.

No. They screamed even before we unleashed our powers.

II

I couldn't accurately judge just how far the effect spread. Suffice to say, in the brief seconds I had to perceive my surroundings, the Aegis broke every single one of the Neverborn as far as I could see.

The Emperor's Gift makes us anathema to the daemons of the worlds behind the veil. That much is no secret. Many times in my first year of service, I'd seen Neverborn crumble before our presence, recoiling from the sheer fact our souls were girded in gene-coded divinity. Castian's presence – the Aegis of five knights wielding their psychic aura as a weapon – weakened daemonkind, sickened them, purified them against their will by sapping their ability to remain manifest in our reality.

Five knights.

The world burst back into existence. The shouting. The screaming. I've said these things happened. I've not said why.

We appeared at the heart of the enemy's forward ranks. All of us. I learned later that the bang of air displacement shattered the reinforced windows in hundreds of Guard troop transports on the far side of the Styx.

The Aegis of one hundred and nine Grey Knights tore from our hearts in a tidal flood, hurling creatures of bronze, bone and bloody flesh from their cloven feet. Ivory horns cracked and limbs snapped in their sockets as the Neverborn were hurled back, physically and psychically, from our arrival in their midst.

I had mere seconds to take this in. The poisoned smoke faded, leaving us standing tall among thousands of fallen Neverborn. I saw things with brass skin and diseased oil for blood; I saw spindly, spined things clutching blades that dripped broken souls; I saw daemon-breeds of the lesser and greater choirs, winged or unwinged, clawed or possessing hands that were grotesquely simian, unarmoured or clad in plate of bone, gold, brass and bronze.

It would be a lie to claim every single daemon was blasted aside. The strongest of them, those of the greater choirs, stood strong against the Aegis even as their skin blistered and burned to be so near to us. We'd appeared as planned, in the formation Captain Taremar had arranged for maximum chance of success.

We had him surrounded. The Lord of the Twelfth Legion, heart of the pack among his colossal praetorian-creatures, was contained within a ring of silver ceramite.

I saw all of this in the time it would take to blink. We stood, knee-deep in thrashing daemonkind, weapons in hands and facing something that had no place in reality.

First came its bodyguards, as if such a thing could ever require huscarls. Each of them was devilry incarnate, rivalling a gunship in height, drawn from the pages of human myth and given these most hateful, bloody forms. Wings of black smoke and bleeding leather beat the gore-stench of split bodies across the battlefield. Whips lashed with the feral intelligence of beast-tails, while tongues cracked from mulish, bullish, malformed visages with the same curling intent.

One of these – one of them, the basest weakling among its choir – had killed Sothis and almost killed me.

That day, we faced twelve. The Cruor Praetoria, the twelve strongest; the twelve daemons whose lives and deeds most pleased their wretched Blood God over forty thousand years of warfare. They came on, despite the Aegis. They came *because* of it. It was nothing to them, less than a joke – a mere irritant that pulled at their attention. Every one of them had thousands of heresies etched under its name in the great libraries of our monastery. We were looking at the history of warfare in physical form.

These beasts spearheaded the main host, at their foul sire's side.

Angron. To think such a creature had ever borne a human name. Was this truly one of the Emperor's own sons, infected by unholiness at the Imperium's dawn? The passing of enough time will make all things myth. No one, even among our order, knew which ancient secrets were once fact, and which were misguided fiction.

It rivalled a Warhound-class walker in size, standing even above the beast-lords that served as its bodyguards. Chains and cables dreadlocked from its saurian skull, and from the clawed tips of its dripping wings to the ridged, stinking red iron that served as its skin, it had long since surrendered any claims to humanity. When it roared, which it did the moment its army began to crumble and tumble about its booted feet, it made the strained, throaty whine of an enraged mammoth. The sound carried across the sky, curdling the clouds above.

Lightning split the heavens. The storm began a second later. It was raining blood, making a ruin of the parchments and scrolls fixed to our armour; stealing the polished shine of our holy ceramite.

The rain buzzed and fizzed along the powered edges of our weapons. Justicar Castian's skull, enshrined in gold, seemed almost to chatter as my stave's energy field superheated the red rain into steam.

Six seconds had passed since our arrival. Just six seconds. We were already running, already closing the circle with a garrotte's intent. One hundred and nine knights charged in perfect unity and in perfect silence. The sensation of our powers rising before release was no different from the way air turns cold and dense with ozone in the seconds before a storm.

If the Wolves were obeying their own battle plan, they would be leading the human armies back into battle now. The sword had fallen, and the Archenemy's princes were distracted by the threat in the midst.

And surely enough, shells began to hammer down around us, throwing up avalanche sprays of sandy soil along with the bodies of dying daemons.

Eight seconds. Nine. Ten. We still ran.

The Lord of the Twelfth Legion roared again. It lowered itself, stared dead at us, and bellowed with all its strength, hard enough to make its wings rattle.

+Force shield,+ came a voice across the Great Communion. I obeyed, just as I felt every brother nearby obey. It took no effort at all to bind our power together into a repelling wall of force. The wave of bestial sound crashed against us, rolled over us, and hurled hundreds of the beast's own warriors into the air.

Fifteen seconds. Sixteen. Seventeen.

We were prepared for this. We'd meditated on our fate, and death held no mystery, no fear, no shame for any of us. Years of indoctrination and cognitive conditioning by the lords of our order meant we could be no other way.

Yet I wasn't prepared for the reality of war. This wasn't some urban engagement in city ruins – a firefight between soldiers exchanging gunfire from the security of cover, where perhaps one side boasted greater weaponry than the other. That took bravery, patience, concentration... But this was open war, a pitched battle, demanding greater savagery, greater strength, greater courage, and calling upon greater depths of feeling. One couldn't enter into such a battle between clashing armies without being certain of one's death.

Past experiences meant nothing that day. The conditioning broke. The indoctrinations were forgotten, left far behind. Brotherhood meant everything. I ran because my brothers were running, and they ran because I did. We were one. I'd sooner die than let them down. I felt the same appalling, addictive devotion emanating from Galeo, Dumenidon, Enceladus and Malchadiel in waves.

It unlocked something primal within me, something unarguably human in my core. This was how humanity's ancestors had fought, blade to blade on open battlefields, in the heathen centuries of Ancient Terra. To think unaugmented, frail mortal men and women battled like this was almost too much to bear. That was courage, and perhaps futility, on a scale my imagination couldn't encompass.

We were butchering the weakened daemons as they rose

again. Every step meant another murder. I was already sweating; it ran into my eyes and made stinging tears. I couldn't look away from the towering black form and its winged slave-generals. I couldn't focus on anything else, neither could any of my kindred – we were slaughtering through muscle memory alone, sending bolts into the ocean of heaving flesh around us.

And then... a lessening. A voice in the communion fell silent, and the song was irredeemably diminished.

Harwen of the Second Brotherhood was the first to die. I'd learn that later, when the skies no longer wept blood onto a world gone mad. He was killed by a daemon ramming a brass runeblade through his belly, slowing him enough for other chittering, howling creatures to drag him down. At the time, I knew only that one of the voices in our perfect psychic chorus had fallen quiet.

We had our orders. Those who fell behind were already dead.

I felt a brief jab of painful curiosity – were that knight's closest brothers wracked by his loss? Was he just a voice lost in the furious song, or was it as sharp a loss as I'd felt when Sothis died?

My bolter kicked and my stave crunched into meat. We were barely moving now, but that didn't matter. The Neverborn of the Greater Choir were almost upon us. Their stinking wings cast great shadows, as if a sky turned black with blood-swollen clouds could be any darker. My automatic night-sight activated. It made no difference. I couldn't see with the blood splashed across my eye lenses. Curses and psychic irritation told me my brothers were suffering the same.

From nearby, I heard the crack of a whip, sharp as a snapping bone. The song quietened further; it's difficult to describe how that felt, how it sounded, with the blood thundering in my ears. I mean no insult when I say it, but some sensations require six senses to understand.

No time to think. Skill meant nothing, any more. That was the fiercest difference between this and the battles of the past. Skill with a blade and a dead-eye with a bolter no longer meant anything. This was warfare stripped to its bluntest purity, closer to wearying labour than a duel between equals. We killed and killed and killed without conception of time, knowing nothing beyond the ache of shaking limbs and the savage anger saturating the Great Communion.

That anger was the greatest shock of all, how wrath in symbiosis overtook each of us. We were Grey Knights. We were born to go into battle with cold blood and cold hearts, protected from passion by our own sanctity. Yet my blood was aflame – both my hearts boiled it in their thundering chambers and pushed it back into my body for nourishment.

Each of my brothers felt the same. Their anger crashed against me, just as I felt mine pressing against them. We felt it, reflected it, channelled it back into the cobweb of consciousness linking us all.

The ground shook as one of the Cruor Praetoria landed among our advancing ranks. I didn't care. I didn't turn to see which of our brother-squads was engaging it, nor did I care what happened to them at the battle's outcome. We pushed on, butchering our way step by step.

Another voice fell silent. And another. And another. And another.

Unholy blood hissed and steamed against my armour. I was killing by sound and psychic sense now – wherever I heard a noise no human could create, my storm bolter barked in that direction; wherever I sensed sentience without a soul, I crashed the weaponised head of my stave against it.

+Hyperion,+ Malchadiel's voice echoed through the threads

of linked minds. He sounded weak. +Hyperion, I can't see.+

I risked it. I risked turning to him. A momentary pulse of focus into my stave overcharged it, forcing the power cells to shout out a sonic charge of repelling energy. The Neverborn shrieked and fell back, and with the precious seconds it bought me, I turned my helm on dense Terminator neckservos to face my brother. I couldn't see much myself. I wasn't sure what he hoped from me.

He was down. I could see that much through the streaming gore. He was down and we were leaving him behind.

Galeo must have sensed something. +Hyperion,+ he sent, quick and cuttingly sharp. +Stay with us.+

My refusal was wordless, but no less obvious. I threw my stave as a spear, sinking it into the ground by Malchadiel as he struggled to rise with the creatures digging their spines into back and shoulders. A second's concentration duplicated the flare of overcharged power cells, blasting Mal with a wave of kinetic force. A surreal wave of reeking red fluid splashed aside in the same moment. Blood. I hadn't realised until then: we were wading ankle-deep in blood too thick for the ground to drink with any speed. Between the slashing rainfall and the foulness leaking from the enemy, we were flooding the craters across the plain.

He reached for the stave, using it for support as he hauled himself to his feet. The second greatest surprise of the day hit me then, a bolt from nowhere. Galeo didn't bleed disappointment at my disobedience. Castian stood right with me. Dumenidon slammed back to back with me, warding me with his blade while I summoned my stave. Galeo and Enceladus killed the creatures making a second surge for Malchadiel.

+What about our orders?+ I sent, already too tired to speak.

Galeo responded by opening his mind. Beneath his weariness

was the truth: he'd not known Malchadiel had fallen, he was too focused on advancing. He thought my lapse had been nothing more than a flicker of wandering attention.

+Well done,+ he sent as we regrouped. +And to the warp with our orders. We're dead anyway. Fight. Kill. Let's get this done.+

Everywhere around us was the clash of blades, the crash of bolters. I saw Atrayon of the First Brotherhood disembowelled by something made of claws and bone and hate. I sensed Furus of the Eighth snap out of the communion, as a Neverborn with bronze blades for arms cleaved his head from his shoulders. I saw Dymus of the Seventh Brotherhood fall with an ivory horn through his throat. His voice didn't fade from the furious chorus – it only grew louder, harsher, as he gargled across the vox in vocal disunity. One of the Neverborn ended him before he could rise again.

Throne, we were so close now. The Great Beast screamed in the vascular downpour, charging faster than anything of such size could possibly move. In a fist large enough to curl around a Rhino tank, it gripped a long blade of blackened bronze that seethed in the storm. Runes I couldn't read writhed along the tainted metal, changing with every fall of the sword – perhaps with each life it ate.

And each time it fell, it shook the ground and stole more voices from the communion. How many of us remained alive, only a minute after manifesting here? How many of the Cruor Praetoria remained alive to stalk through our ranks?

I couldn't say. I had no idea. None of us did.

Another aspect of open warfare is the dust. Two armies throw up a blizzard of filth from the ground that must be seen to be believed, all born of marching boots, scuffing feet and grinding tank treads. The dust becomes another enemy to be faced; acting as a thief of calm, robbing a force of all cohesion and leaving individuals scattered, separated from their kindred. I'd read about it so many times in the archives, but experiencing it myself defied all former imagining. Without my psychic gift, sensing what shape in the murk was a brother and what was a soulless husk, I'd have been as blind and lost as any mortal. Perhaps even as panicked. I say that with no shame.

As we drew nearer to the Lord of the Twelfth Legion, even sparing a second to cleanse the gore from my eye lenses made no difference. We were as good as blind, fighting shadows and marching to face a silhouette. Eye lenses cycled through vision modes to compensate, corrupted by intermittent static.

I saw the first squad reach the Great Beast at last. They reached its knees, even in Terminator plate. I saw them raise their weapons, each blade and stave wrapped in layers of lethal lightning.

I heard the sky tearing itself apart. I heard the screams of men going mad, kilometres away. I saw the black-and-bronze blade fall.

III

Their names were Korolos, Taymul, Jesric, Nyramar and Justicar Gauris. Sagas and legends alike fall back on classic imagery; they will often describe certain deaths with the simple analogy of foes despatched with the same ease of a man crushing an insect.

But a man must take aim at an insect – he must exert at least a modicum of effort to see it dead. I saw no such effort, here. Those five knights were wiped from life with the ease of a man wiping sweat from his brow. The Lord of the Twelfth Legion scarcely even seemed to pay attention to them – when the immense, keening blade swung, the beast was already turning to face other foes. Chain and cable tendrils thrashed as the daemon moved – a dirty simulation of a mane of hair. The thing never even saw my five kinsmen die.

But I did. The beat of the Great Beast's wings made it possible, gusting the dust cloud aside for that briefest of moments. I saw the knights of Squad Hargrian take flight, spinning and soaring into the air above the embattled horde, three of them bisected and all five of them suddenly silent in the communion's song.

The dust swirled back before the bodies fell. I never saw where their rag doll remains landed.

Malchadiel's storm bolter burst one of the last creatures remaining in front of us. +They never even had the chance to unleash their power,+ he sent.

+I know.+ Some of the Neverborn's acidic blood was digesting the soft-armour joints of my ceramite, making it even harder to focus. When the beast turned again, its fire-eyed gaze raking over us, I realised that I had mere seconds left to live.

This was how I would die. Here. Now.

I felt nothing at all. At least, nothing beyond a sudden urge to laugh.

Shells were bursting against the behemoth, striking it from every angle. Sacred bolt shells, inscribed with holy writ and blessed against the foulness of the warp. Strings of viscera arced from its exploding flesh.

Galeo lifted his storm bolter. Ours rose alongside his in perfect unity, and Castian added its fire to our brothers'.

It was the last thing we ever did together.

IV

+Now.+

Every knight still standing unleashed their power at Captain Taremar's silent cry.

The enemy host was forgotten. The devil-lords of the Cruor Praetoria – if any still walked among us – were ignored. They were lesser threats, relatively speaking, that lesser warriors could deal with.

Angron. Lord of the Twelfth Legion. This was why we'd come.

With blessed shells already bursting threads of wet gore from his body, the fallen primarch withered beneath our unified assault. I was shouting as I raised my weapons; we were all shouting, out loud and in each other's minds.

The most common manifestation of psychic power is the phenomenon often referred to as witch-lightning. Coruscating arcs of the crackling, jagged energy washed over the Great Beast's red flesh, ripping like razors and shedding splashing gouts of stinking, searing blood. Atop this base expression of rage, we fed our own energies into the weaving of sixth-sense sorcery hurled up at the colossus.

No Grey Knight displays the exact same gifts as his brothers. Try to conceive of the actual manifestation of a species' wrath and defiance. That's what we threw against the Blood God's chosen champion. Slices in reality cleaved open in the sky and across the ground, vortex-strong, sucking in the nearest Neverborn and even pulling at the Great Beast itself. Smoke and blood from its wings and armour were drawn away in a sucking rush, pulled back behind the veil where all of the creature's foulness belonged.

Other knights, lacking the gifts of such mastery, attacked with gleaming blades, their psychic strength fed into the sacred steel to burn with the divine light of banishment. Nemesis-creed weaponry was anathema to daemonkind, as surely as our own souls were, and every sword and hammer meeting Angron's flesh elicited fresh agony in the enraged godling. They scarred it, bruised it, shredded flesh from broken bones – yet seemed to have no effect at all.

Telekines in our ranks – of which Malchadiel was merely one – protected the rest of us with shimmering domes of repellent force, resisting the beast-lord's great blade. Such manifestations of holy protection still burst like bubbles after the second or third strike. Angron's screams shook the entire sky, redoubling the blood-rain in a scything downpour, burning at the kine-shields our brothers held above us.

The beast itself was a savage, hideous blur. Its blade moved faster than the eye could follow, cracking down to blast light-flares across force domes or carve without pause through entire squads. Nothing pure remained in our communion, now. Too few voices rose in defiance, and each of them was coloured only by concentrated rage.

My own gift manifested in the way that had always been easiest for me to express. Fire. It streamed from my fists, blanketing the primarch's wings with the clinging tenacity of naphtha, sticking and dissolving all it touched like an acidic second skin. Other pyrokines unleashed the same corrosive spillage – we were melting the thing alive.

More than that. We were carving it to pieces, breaking it apart, incinerating it and dissolving it, all at once.

It laughed.

It laughed, and kept killing us.

V

Dumenidon was the first of Castian to fall.

One moment he was with us. The next he was gone. I think, when it happened, I actually felt him reach for me. I can't be sure.

The beast was laying about with its blade, its edge crashing aside from the straining, flickering domes of kinetic force. It burst through another, reaved through the knights beneath it, and immediately turned to another threat.

Us.

Eyes of black fire bored into the five of us, and the blade descended less than a heartbeat later. The crack of it striking Mal's kine-shield was the same thunder of a warship entering the warp between worlds. A second blow, a third, a fourth...

Mal was on his knees, shouting wordlessly across the vox.

+KILL IT KILL IT KILL IT+ he pulsed in an agonised flow.

On the fifth blow, the kine-shield shattered with another thunderclap. Malchadiel collapsed. Dumenidon fell with him, crushed into unrecognisable ruin by the blade. Just like that, he was gone, leaving a hole in my mind.

The blade rose and fell again.

+HYPERION+ came Galeo's voice.

I caught the blade.

Not with my hands. With my mind. I locked that grievous, immense sword immobile with a surge of desperate focus, keeping it trembling in the air above us. Waves of psychic force turned the air into a heat mirage around my armour.

+*Do... something...*+ I managed to send.

Enceladus and Galeo threw their swords as spears. Both sank deep into the beast's wrist, and both immediately caught flame, igniting the creature's unholy blood. It still didn't release its hold on the blade.

Angron roared. Without a force barrier, the sound blasted across us with dreadful physicality, tearing parchments and tabards from our armour and sliding us all back in the sloshing, blood-drowned mud.

I gave everything I had left. Absolutely everything. With my hands raised, I slowly curled them into fists, pouring body and soul into my sixth sense clutching that blade. They wouldn't close completely. They just wouldn't.

My vision blurred. I felt saliva trickling from the edge of my mouth. My muscles went into cramp, and my hearts started to beat ragged.

I was killing myself with this. The focused depletion of life force, channelled into psychic energy. But I was already dead, so what did it matter?

In the air above us, the black blade cracked.

And everyone froze.

The sound was as stark and alien as a laugh in the middle of a funeral march. Even the Lord of the Twelfth Legion hesitated, huffing a stinking breath in disbelief.

I swear, the loudest sound on that battlefield was me screaming into the vox. I felt psychic hoarfrost riming my armour, densest on my outstretched hands. My eyes lit with ghost-flame, painless but still blindingly bright, purely as an overspill of psychic energies.

+Hyperion...+ I heard Galeo whisper. He may have said more. If he did, I didn't hear it.

I closed my hands, made them fists.

Above me, the blade shattered. Cursed black bronze blasted across the field of battle, raining on the just and unjust alike. Several shards tore gashes across the daemon's skin, or lodged into his flesh. There came a roar, the likes of which defied reality. It had no place outside a nightmare.

And I was on my knees without knowing when I'd fallen low.

+Mal,+ I sent to his prone body, not knowing whether he was alive or dead. +Mal. Mal. Mal...+

Galeo and Enceladus drew closer. I didn't know why. I didn't know anything any more – I couldn't see, I couldn't focus, I couldn't speak.

The last thing I remember of the battle was Captain

Taremar's voice, cutting right to my core.

+Angron,+ he called. +Justice comes. Turn, beast, and face me.+

SEVENTEEN
BLADEBREAKER

I

'This one's still alive.'

The voice was what woke me. It was too deep to be human.

Something jerked my head, pulling at my helmet. I opened my eyes in time for my retinal display to fall dark, unpowered as my helm was dragged clear.

The sky above was a bruised grey. Gone was the sanguinary richness that had covered the heavens above the battle. The air smelled of burned hair and dirty coal fires. It tasted just as sour.

I was alive.

Cold, but alive.

'Easy, brother,' said the same voice. It sounded familiar this time, though still too low to be fully human. 'Can you stand?'

The figure moved where I could see him, offering me an armoured hand. I took it – we gripped wrist to wrist. Every movement of my joints sent dull, weary throbs through my bones, not quite sharp enough to be called pain.

The leaping silver wolf on his breastplate might be something worn by many warriors in his Chapter, and the wolfskin cloak was lost to incineration, but I recognised the Fenrisian runes on his helm and the axe slung over his back.

'Brand,' I tried to say. I had to swallow and try again, my tongue was so parched. 'Brand Rawthroat.'

'Aye,' he said. 'The one and only.'

Standing was a trial in itself. My legs shook with unfamiliar weakness. I kept blinking, trying to clear my eyes and make them focus. It wasn't working.

'Bladebreaker,' another voice said nearby. I turned to see another Wolf picking through the bodies. He grinned at me. 'Good to see you still breathing, Bladebreaker.'

Brand chuckled, as low as an avalanche and no friendlier, either. 'Now there's a name worthy of a saga or two. Will you live long enough to hear them, knight? You look like a kraken chewed you up and shit you back out.'

I felt like it, too. I gestured to his scorched, bloodstained armour. 'You look little better.'

'That's the truth,' Rawthroat agreed.

My eyes were clearing, though they revealed a vista devoid of any joy. The Neverborn had dissolved away, leaving little trace beyond grotesque stains on the ground. Silver-clad bodies lay everywhere else.

'No,' I said. 'Please, no.'

Galeo was the first one I recognised. He lay twenty metres from me, missing one arm and both legs beneath mid-thigh. Hs breastplate displayed the killing wound – it was cracked and split around what looked like a spear thrust.

I couldn't run to him. My armour's damaged servos wouldn't allow it. Instead, I limped closer, dragging a leg that wouldn't bend. Gunships flew overhead, some from the

Wolves, others from the Imperial Guard. I ignored them all.

+Galeo,+ I sent, knowing it was futile even as I said it. I couldn't sense anything from him, and that's when I realised why I felt so strangely cold and hollow. I couldn't sense any of my brothers. Malchadiel, Galeo, Dumenidon, Enceladus... all had fallen as silent as Sothis, unreachable no matter how I focused.

My fingers rested on my justicar's bare throat.

His storm bolter wouldn't reload. He shouldn't have thrown his sword. He needed it now. Accursed gun. Accursed–

The spear lanced into him from behind, a heavy, scraping pressure that bored its way into him. He bit back the scream, even as the things drove him to his knees. When it snapped through his breastplate, amazingly, he felt a sigh leave his lips, akin to the relief after a ripe boil is popped and drained of fluid.

They were taking him to pieces, hacking at his armour with their jagged blades. He–

I lifted my fingers away. I'd seen enough, and the dozen enemy dead carpeting the earth told the rest of the tale. Rawthroat was still with me.

'How long was I unconscious?' I asked.

'How am I supposed to know? I spent most of the battle on the other side of the enemy horde, carving the bastards to pieces. What do you remember last?'

'The blade. I remember breaking the blade.'

Rawthroat removed his helm, showing a face pockmarked by old scarring. His hair was likely once black; now, from his thinning crown to the curving moustache linking to his sideburns, it was iron grey streaked with white. He seemed to pull his helm clear purely so he could hawk and spit.

'If that's the last thing you saw, you've been gone for most of the day. Almost eight hours, now. Even once the Great Beast fell, the battle raged on.'

He was looking at me, almost cautiously. 'What is it?' I asked.

'The way you broke the blade... That was...'

'Duty.' I moved away, seeking my other brothers among the slain. 'How many of my order have you found alive?'

'A handful. No more. We're surprised any of you are still breathing. Tough bastards, you sons of Titan.'

'You aren't even supposed to know we exist. It's strange to hear you refer to us like that.'

He shrugged. Such thoughts clearly didn't worry him.

I turned to look at him. 'What of Captain Taremar?'

Rawthroat shook his head. 'A hero's death, that one. I'll never forget the sight.'

Taremar was dead. I wasn't sure how to feel about it. I scarcely knew him; he'd seemed a cold and unwelcoming soul to call a brother, but his list of heroic deeds rivalled the Grand Masters of the Eight Brotherhoods. This would surely be the capstone to a knight considered a legend by future generations of our order.

I made my limping way over the blasted earth, seeking the others. 'Tell me what happened.'

'With your golden captain? He stood before the beast after you broke the blade. He fought it. He killed it. That's what happened.'

'How descriptive.' I looked back over my shoulder for a moment. 'The sagas on Fenris must be singularly dull.'

Rawthroat snorted. His scratchy, deep voice turned even that into a bass rumble. 'You asked. I told you.' He was flexing and tensing his arm, clearly sore from his own share of wounds.

Bodies carpeted the ground. I'd paid such little heed in the battle – focusing only on slaughtering the Neverborn – but red-clad Legiones Astartes warriors and corrupted human bodies lay in profusion among the bloody puddles. How many had we killed? Did such a number even matter, in the shadow of the Great Beast's banishment?

I found Enceladus a short distance away.

He was slumped in a graceless, lifeless crouch, his head lowered to his chest. A host of enemy dead kept company with his corpse, each one bearing the marks of death by sacred shells and infused blade. His sword – recovered somehow from the primarch's forearm – stood tall as a banner pole, impaling the breastplate of a fallen warrior from the desecrated World Eaters Legion.

Enceladus's slack hands rested in his lap, as if he merely sat in prayer. But for the shaft of a spear driven through his chest, he seemed almost serene.

My first instinct was to reach out and pull the weapon free, but I felt a sudden reluctance to touch him at all. I wasn't sure I wanted to see his final moments.

+Hyperion. My boy.+

I flinched back. Rawthroat went for his weapon, teeth already showing in a snarl.

'What? What is it?'

Enceladus slowly raised his head, meeting my eyes. The movement revealed the slit throat that had come within an inch of ending his life, even without the impaling spear.

+Malchadiel,+ he sent. +Malchadiel is still alive. I stood above him, as Galeo stood above you.+

I was scarcely listening, already voxing any Imperial forces for a trained medicae or a Wolf-trained Apothecary. I couldn't risk teleporting Enceladus like this. He'd never survive it.

'Hold,' I said to him. 'Help is coming.'

+Malchadiel,+ he sent again, straining now.

That's when I saw the silver gauntlet, streaked by blood, beneath three mutilated armoured bodies. The first I shoved aside with a telekinetic pulse, sending the dead World Eater rolling off the pile. Even that effort left me staggering, greyness threatening my sight. I went to my knees, physically pushing the other corpses away.

Malchadiel lay as I'd last seen him, collapsed on his front, one arm reaching out to one of his fallen swords. In the hours since we'd both fallen, the enemy hadn't left him untouched. His armour was a wreck beyond even mine – the entire back savaged and reduced to scrap. Chainblade wounds decorated the broken armour at his shoulders and back. His power generator was nowhere to be seen.

Worse, his left arm ended at the elbow, in a wound of violated ceramite, loose cables, and scabbed-over flesh.

Without power, his armour wasn't linked to my retinal display, stealing any hope of seeing life signs. It took intense concentration just to muster enough energy to reach out with my psychic sense, to see if my brother still lived.

'Were these both your brothers?' Rawthroat asked.

'Hush,' I snapped back.

'You're a miserable whoreson, Bladebreaker.'

'Be quiet, please.' It was no good. I couldn't focus. I had to pull Mal's helm free.

As soon as I worked the seals at his collar, freeing his blood-smeared face, his remaining hand slammed against my wrist. He gripped, and gripped hard, though his voice was a hurt whisper.

'Did we win?'

I looked over at the bodies surrounding us, and felt the hollowness where once Castian's presence had lingered in my mind. Enceladus was a fading whisper. Malchadiel was even fainter.

'I'm not sure.'

* * *

II

Back aboard the *Karabela*, the mood was unsurprisingly sombre. As soon as the bridge doors rattled open, I sensed the crew's unease, like a drifting scent. Some were grateful to see one of Castian still breathing; others didn't know any of us well enough to care one way or the other, but feared contamination from what we'd faced on the surface.

Talwyn Castor rose from his throne and saluted.

'Sir Hyperion.'

I waved him back into his seat. As I did so, a spark crackled from my damaged elbow joint. My wargear was in horrendous shape; Axium was going to lecture me for hours about it. Malchadiel's was no better, and Enceladus returned to the ship in wreckage that had had to be cut free.

'Justicar Galeo is dead,' I told them. 'As is Dumenidon. The prime enemy is destroyed, and his hosts are vulnerable. Orders will come from Jarl Grimnar within the next few hours – the *Karabela* will align its weapons batteries with the rest of the fleet and add its strength to the orbital bombardment taking place.'

Castor gave a crisp nod. 'Understood, sir.'

'That will be all. I shall be with the Palladium Kataphrakt for a significant duration. Summon me if I am required.'

'Sir?'

'What is it, captain?'

'Will you be making planetfall again?'

'I intend to, yes. The battle is over; the war is not.'

'May I ask how many of the order survived?'

I had to swallow before speaking. 'Thirteen. Thirteen, of one hundred and nine. I am still piecing together the full details myself, but I thank you for your concern.'

I meant it, too. Few of our servants would have thought to ask, and even fewer would've legitimately cared.

'One last thing, sir.'

'Speak.'

'Are you Justicar of Castian now?'

I hesitated. I'd not even considered that.

'Just... attend to your duties, Talwyn.'

III

Axium's perfectly contoured face regarded me with an exquisite imitation of sympathy.

'Hyperion,' he started. The entire workshop chamber seemed suddenly quieter.

'Save your words,' I said. 'Forgive me, Axium – I simply have no wish to discuss it at the moment.'

'As you wish.' He stepped back, artificial eyes running along my suit of armour. 'Oh,' he said at last. 'Oh, my.'

I detached my storm bolter, unlocking its bindings before resting it on the closest table. Every movement sent sprays of sparks from my elbow.

'Your left arm's olecranon servos are suffering to a terminal degree.'

I held the trembling arm before him. The neural links that made the armour so responsive were now giving me random muscle spasms, in my arm more than anywhere else.

'Oh,' he said again, watching my fingers twitching. 'That won't do at all.'

I dearly wanted to be free of this limping, constricting Terminator warplate. My own armour remained where I'd left it: in compartmentalised and sealed storage against the work-chamber's eastern wall.

Axium summoned several servitors to attend him. Like the adepts of the Palladium Kataphrakt, none of the augmented slaves possessed bionics cast from what Axium termed the 'vulgar metals': gold, bronze, copper, and so on. Every bionic implant was chromium, iron, steel or – in the rarest cases – solid silver.

They deployed digital tools and servo-arms, beginning the laborious process of machining me out of the armour plating.

A few minutes in, and they were pulling away ceramite plates sticky with blood on the inside. Axium paused, his silver eyes meeting mine.

'You are wounded.'

'Blades in the joints, and a spear through the thigh.'

'I am speaking of your face. You looked... pained.'

'I'll live. The pain is in my thigh.'

'Yes, yes, the joining muscle-cables around the adductor brevis muscle of your right thigh.' He leaned down. 'I see it now.'

'I'll live, Axium. Just get me out of this.'

Despite my weariness, I still sensed her coming. I looked up a few moments before the chamber's doors opened.

'Hyperion,' Annika said. She walked in alone, her warband nowhere to be seen. 'Blood of the Emperor, you look...'

'Alive?'

'Yes. Well. Throne, you're bleeding.'

The pressure in my head was immense, and she wasn't helping.

'The blood is old and the wounds are sealed.' I didn't enjoy others circling me like this, picking at me like vultures over carrion. As Annika came closer, the servitors extracted several more restraining bolts, freeing another layer of subdermal armour over my shoulders and arms.

She looked untouched. Tired, but untouched by the battle itself beyond the marks of wear and tear on her bodysuit plating. True to her word, she'd fought at the war's edge, holding back with the reserve regiments.

'Have you heard what the Wolves are calling you?'

'Yes.'

'Bladebreaker.'

'I said I'd heard.' Perhaps I spoke harsher than I'd intended. She flinched back, looking at me for a long moment.

'Hyperion...'

'Galeo and Dumenidon are dead.' I rolled my shoulders as the last of the armour there came free in two servitors' industrial clamps. 'Malchadiel and Enceladus yet live, though Enceladus will never wear armour again, such is the damage to his flesh. Mal's memory and spine no longer function.'

That made her blink. 'Malchadiel can't walk?'

I'd carried him off the battlefield myself. It was agony, to feel him questing to connect to the rest of Castian – and worst of all to feel him reaching for Sothis – and finding nothing. He was a blind boy, lost in the woods.

+Sothis?+ he kept sending as I carried him to the gunship. +Sothis? Sothis?+ I felt the name brushing across my consciousness, feeble as a cobweb across the face. +Sothis? Sothis?+

'His spine is shattered. I was unconscious after I broke the blade; I don't know what happened. It's possible the damage occurred when the beast broke our kine-shield.'

Annika took it in with admirable calm, her thoughts slowed by her weariness. 'I see.'

'The war isn't over. I'll get back into my armour, and face the enemy as the Emperor intended.'

She looked at me strangely. 'Alone?'

'Thirteen of us survived. Four of us are still able to fight. Axium will do what he can for Malchadiel, while our survivors return to the battles below.'

'The Great Wolf said you weren't to appear before the general population.'

'His orders mean exactly nothing to me, inquisitor. Impure

souls still walk down there. I am the hammer that will break them, no matter where they hide. More of my order will come, Annika. This world needs us. Mark my words, the Inquisition will call for more of us.'

She nodded, still looking hesitantly at me. 'I understand that. But… you look sickly. Wretched, even. Your wounds–'

'Enough.'

'But Hyperion–'

'Will you cease mothering me? I am a Grey Knight of Titan, not a child.' One of the servitors missed a pinning socket on my forearm, his drill bit scratching across one of the remaining pieces of subdermal armour. I backhanded the useless creature, and felt its jaw break. 'Get away from me. Axium, get the rest of this armour off. Now.'

The servitor I'd struck was struggling to rise. It was difficult to see through my blurring vision. A moment later, the ship tilted beneath my boots, causing me to stagger.

'We're under attack! Captain Talwyn?'

Voices pressed back against me. I couldn't tell them apart. Hands joined them, pushing against my armour. Annika was one of them. Axium was another. They were unimaginably tall.

I shoved them back with a focused pulse of kinetic force. Only… they didn't move a muscle.

+Sothis?+ Malchadiel's voice reached me from where I'd left him in the medicae bay. +Sothis?+

Was I on my knees? I was. I was on my knees.

'Help me up,' I said.

'…kind of cerebrovascular incident…' Axium was saying.

'…haemorrhage…' said a voice. A female voice. Soft. I wondered if she could sing. My grandmother used to sing to me, in another life.

'…into stasis. By the cog, get him into stasis…'

I laughed. *By the cog.* What did that even mean? Martian swearing made no sense to me.

+Help me stand,+ I sent in a vicious wave.

No one replied. Not even poor, broken Malchadiel.

'Help me up. I don't want to die on my knees, like Galeo.'

I reached for one of the arms in front of me. It was silver. In my grip, the forearm bent and warped, too soft and fragile for my fist.

From somewhere else, I heard Axium scream. I'd not even known he could. Blinking did nothing to clear my vision.

Someone said my name. I think it was Annika. Someone else said something about stasis.

'I am a Grey Knight of Titan,' I said. 'I... I am the hammer.'

And then, blackness.

EIGHTEEN

SCARS

I

I opened my eyes to the sterile blue lighting of an apothecarion. Not the medicae chambers of the *Karabela*; this was a fully-equipped apothecarion capable of tending to the needs of an entire brotherhood at war.

I knew this place. How could I not? This was the surgery chamber aboard the *Fire of Dawn*, flagship of the Eighth Brotherhood. Ranks of monitors and the shining steel of medical machinery lined the walls.

I sat up, pulling bio-monitor plugs and nutrient feed lines from my skin.

'The dead rise,' said a voice from behind me.

I knew him even before I saw him, and was saying his name even as I turned. 'Nadion.'

He was clad in a loose grey robe – the humble attire of an unarmoured knight, engaged in meditation or study. The sleeves were rolled up, leaving his arms covered only in gloves of clear, thin plastek to prevent accidental contamination or infection.

Nadion's shaved head showed no shortage of immaculately shaped bionics. Half of his skull had been replaced only a few years before I'd earned my armour.

'I'd not expected you to rise for another hour or so,' he said. 'How do you feel?'

Cataloguing my hurts seemed churlish. 'I've felt better,' I admitted, hoping that would be enough. 'I don't remember much of what happened.'

'Your executor primaris, Axium, saved your life. He interred you in a stasis chamber when you suffered a... well. Suffered a host of severe reactions to your psychic outpouring. I've prepared a list for you to access at your leisure. I hope you're prepared to read the words 'haemorrhage', 'embolism', and 'risk of neurological damage' a great many times. You were lucky to survive unleashing your powers like that. Had you been fully human, you'd have died before being able to hold the blade at bay for a second, let alone break it.'

'We weren't spoiled by choice, Nadion. I had to do something.'

'I wasn't criticising, brother. Still, I've recorded the bio-auspex results for you, as well. The damage to your nervous system and a host of blood vessels was almost terminal. Indeed, it was terminal, had Axium not locked you in stasis until my arrival.'

Throne, it was still so hard to think straight. I remembered losing consciousness. Barely. Even that felt as much a dream as a memory.

'When did you arrive?'

Nadion had the ageless quality of most warriors ascended into the ranks of the Adeptus Astartes. We told our age by the scars we wore. Those of us who fought on unscarred tended to look any age between twenty or fifty, with characteristics of youth and middle-age in equal measure.

The arcane genetics involved in our creation never really ceased to surprise me. Some things, you simply couldn't get used to.

The Apothecary keyed in several buttons on the hololithic projector by my slab of a bed. He was calling up the details of my surgery, answering as he cycled through visual archives.

'We arrived nine standard days ago. Others from the order reached here much earlier than us, of course. And I'll answer your next question before you can ask it. You've been unconscious for a hundred and thirty-one days. I've been tending to you for the last two days and nights.' He looked at me, his dark eyes unblinking. 'How is your head?'

'A hundred and thirty-one days?' I asked.

'Well, the repetition proves your hearing is functional, at least. Now please answer my question.'

'But what of the war?'

'The war's over, Hyperion. The war was over the moment you and Taremar killed the Blood God's princeling. All that remained was a purge of the lingering taint.'

I suspected the millions of people on Armageddon locked in battle for half a year would beg to differ with his appraisal, but it was typical of the order to see things in such a way.

I'd been with Annika too long, that I even considered the other possibilities.

'How many of the order have come?'

Nadion looked at me, no longer focusing on the bio-hololithic. 'Almost two hundred. Three battle-barges, including the *Fire of Dawn*. We came in force, brother, little by little, as soon as we were able. Imagine our disappointment to learn the heroism was already done, months before we arrived.'

'Don't make light of this, Nadion. A hundred of us died down there. A hundred. That thing... It went through us like a bladed wind. I've never seen anything like it. It was harvesting us, reaping our lives. No other words can describe it.'

'Forgive my levity. You know I meant no offence, brother. I grieve with you.'

I nodded, though the motion made me wince.

'I saw that,' Naidion said. 'I'll ask again, how is your head?'

'It throbs in time with my heartbeat. As I said, I've felt better.' My eyes drifted to the hololithic display, showing an image of my wounds and the resulting surgeries performed since lifting me from stasis.

I blinked at a blur of blackness taking up the left side of my flickering holo-image skull.

'That's...'

'Yes. It is. Hence why I'm asking how your head feels,' said Nadion.

I reached to touch my cheek, and my fingers bumped against cold metal. I wasn't sure what to say. Instead, I stroked across the metal, feeling for its edges. They blended with only faint seams where the metal met skin.

'The pressure in your head split your skull in these places...' Nadion was pointing at the hololithic, but I hardly needed a diagram to tell me where I was mutilated. I could feel it with my fingers.

'I wasn't that injured in the battle, Nadion. Why have you done this?'

'Be calm, brother. We are speaking of psychic pressure. And in case you're still blind to what I'm saying, believe me when I say you're fortunate your head didn't burst. You clearly aggravated the wounds further by using your powers after you woke on the battlefield.' He gave me a long look.

'That wasn't wise. That was, in fact, foolish beyond measure. You should have known.'

'I had to see how Galeo died.'

'Just Galeo?'

After Malchadiel had woken and the recovery gunship was inbound, I'd gone back to Galeo. I couldn't resist; I had to know. That much I remembered clearly.

I'd found Captain Taremar's corpse, as well. His death had been everything Brand Rawthroat had said it was – one man with a golden blade against a towering evil, though the vague flashes of insight I'd gleaned spoke of a brief battle. No man could stand against such a foe for long.

'No,' I admitted. 'Not just Galeo. A hundred of my brothers died while I was unconscious, Nadion. I had to see what happened to them.'

'Your brothers died while you were in a coma, fool. You were more than simply "unconscious".' He sighed, deactivating the hololithic. 'When you reached for them, did you see anything of worth? Were the images clear?'

Were they ever? The dead were always jealous of their secrets, even to those they'd once called kindred.

'No,' I admitted again. 'I saw little detail beyond the blows that ended their lives.'

'Well, I will not fault you for making the attempt. Three matters remain before I can release you.'

I looked at him while still feeling my face, exploring the geography of surgical reconstruction.

'An inquisitor by the name of Annika Jarlsdottyr has visited you a number of times. I have recorded her visits in a secondary file for your perusal.'

Bless her for her attention. She was a unique soul, that one. 'My thanks. What else?'

'A Wolf warrior has also visited you several times, reporting that he was checking your condition to report back to his Chapter. His name was–'

'Brand Rawthroat, I assume.'

'A fine deduction. It was indeed.'

'And the last matter?'

'Well, you are aboard the *Fire of Dawn*, Hyperion. What do you think the last matter might be?'

'Lord Joros wishes to speak with me as soon as I am able.'

'What an insightful fellow you are,' he said. For the briefest moment, I thought he was going to smile. I thought wrong.

'I sense something is going unsaid, Nadion. That doesn't bode well.'

'Indeed?'

'You've not told me of Malchadiel.'

'Ah, yes,' replied Nadion. 'Malchadiel.'

II

I found him in the flagship's port secondary hangar. He was, perhaps unsurprisingly, surrounded by what looked like scrap metal drifting in the air around him. The familiarity of the scene forced the beginnings of a smile on my lips.

The smile died when he turned to face me. He wore the same monastic robe as I did, though the long sleeves couldn't quite hide the black iron hand where his left arm had once been. His face was a patchwork of sutured flesh, leaving him looking more like Sothis in his mutilation than I'd ever believed possible. The biggest change of all came when he turned around fully. I heard the clank of heavy steel feet thudding on the deck, though he wore no armour at all.

The revolving metal scrap drifted down to the floor as he met my eyes.

'You look different,' he said.

Automatically, I reached up to touch the cold metal where

half of my face had been. It stretched from my left temple all the way down to my jawline, and round to the back of my skull.

'So do you.'

He came closer, with a thudding, awkward gait. 'Nadion took my legs. My spine was, to use his term, "mangled", so he replaced that, as well.' He said the words as though it were nothing at all. Then, a small smile. 'I can't run yet. In truth, I don't walk all that well, as you can see. But I'll adjust. We are Grey Knights. We endure.'

He lifted his left arm to show me. It purred and hummed in a chorus of smooth bionics. 'He gave me this, as well. It's easier to use.'

This... this was extensive augmentation. He was more cybernetic than human now, even at a casual glance.

'How do you feel?'

He shrugged. It was the little details like that that showed our age compared to the true veterans. They tended to forget tiny human touches like shrugging or nodding.

'It feels different. It also feels better than being dead, so I can hardly complain. It doesn't hurt, if that's what you mean.' His ruined face creased with a smile. 'I heard the Wolves are calling you Hyperion Bladebreaker now. A Fenrisian deed name? That has a heroic ring to it, don't you think?'

The words left my lips before I really knew why. I think his smile triggered them.

'You look like Sothis now,' I said.

He touched his face for a moment, with his remaining human hand. 'I suppose I do. To be honest, I've not looked at myself in the mirror a great deal. Have you spoken with Lord Joros?'

'Not yet.'

'Then I shall come with you. Give me five minutes to repair

this turret.' He turned back to his work, already bidding the
metal to rise. 'It's good to see you alive, brother.'

I sent him a hesitant pulse of returned feeling. He accepted
it, and the link between us was reforged anew. I heard his
thoughts again as I always had; the faintest background presence, ignorable unless I focused.

From within a deep, healing slumber across the chamber,
I felt Enceladus merge with the communion. His union was
wordless, weak, but undeniably there.

Even in this diminished form, Castian stood once again.

III

Joros, Knight-Lord, Grand Master of the Eighth Brotherhood,
was as much an example of the knightly ideal as Captain
Taremar or Lord Vaurmand of the Third. It isn't unfair to the
man to say he thrived on formality, and the *Fire of Dawn* was
as much monastery as warship. Walking its halls, you'd never
believe it had a crew of thousands. Such was the silence.

At capacity, the Great Hall had room for several hundred
warriors; far more than existed in a single brotherhood.
Woven banners and deed lists hung from the arched ceiling,
no few of which depicted the deeds of Castian through the
generations. For once, I felt no pride. I felt no awe, either.
The deeds of my predecessors failed to move me. I felt a similar insularity in Malchadiel, walking at my side as we made
our way along the central carpet.

It smote me to walk at his side, and I feel no shame in confessing it. His halting, ungainly stomp didn't seem to bother
him at all – he found the flaws curious, and blithely assumed
he'd adapt to his new legs and hips soon enough. Even so, it
wounded me to see him struggle. We were only alive because
of his kine-shield. To leave the battlefield as a cripple seemed
the poorest of rewards.

He didn't even have a ridiculous deed name, awarded by the Fenrisians. Not that I cared for my own.

Several times during the walk, Mal had stopped to lean against a wall, flexing his joints and making muttered notes about slight adjustments that he planned to make.

'A degree of resistance in the fibre-bundles mimicking the tibial collateral ligament,' he said at one point. 'It's nothing I can't rectify myself.'

'Shouldn't you ask Nadion or one of the Techmarines to deal with such things?'

'Only the parts I can't reach.' He'd moved away from the wall, testing his knee again. 'Come. Our lord awaits.'

That wasn't entirely accurate. Grand Master Joros wasn't waiting; he was in council with his paladins, while seated in his ornate command throne. Every figure in the chamber except for Malchadiel and myself wore dense Terminator plate. Even the knights by the marble pillars, standing at attention, generated a significant hum from their active, hulking suits of armour.

It all seemed a touch dramatic for honour guard duty, but it was also tradition down to the last detail.

One of them nodded to me as we passed. I almost stopped in surprise at informal recognition from a paladin.

'Well, well, well...' Lord Joros said from his throne. 'Look who has finally awoken.'

I came to a halt before him. Malchadiel did the same, though he had to lean on me for support. He'd clearly not mastered stopping with any grace yet. The receptors and nerve-bondings in his new legs hadn't settled enough.

I made to kneel as tradition dictated, but Malchadiel's bionic hand gripped my shoulder.

+I don't think I can kneel,+ he sent, clearly nervous about the fact. I looked to him, meeting his eyes. He gave a faint shake of his head, confirming his words.

+Then we'll stand,+ I sent back.

Respect had to be shown. I bowed as deep as I could while supporting Malchadiel, helping him do the same.

Lord Joros rose from his throne, taking several heavy steps forwards, looking down at us from the height bequeathed by his Terminator plate.

'Did your wounds wipe the traditions from your minds, my brothers?' His aquiline features seemed particularly hawkish in the shadowy half-light of so many candles. He presented us with his signet ring, cast in black iron and forged to fit around an armoured knuckle.

Malchadiel cleared his throat. 'I cannot kneel, Grand Master.'

The lord watched us both, showing neither amusement nor malice. He said a single word, through an emotionless facade.

'Try.'

I was reluctant to release Malchadiel. In the end, it was he who moved from my arm with a faint nod, going down on one knee with halting, stuttering movements. His knees ground and clicked, ticked and thrummed. They locked at one point, causing bolts of pain up his new spine.

I took a knee next to him. We kissed the signet ring in turn. It had the tangy taste of old blood and older metal.

'Rise,' Lord Joros said a moment later.

I did so. This time, Malchadiel refused my hand to help. He rose a little smoother than he'd knelt, though the tightness at his eyes showed how much it cost him to bite back the pain.

'So, then.' Joros returned to his throne, seating himself and draping his white cloak over the chair's side. 'Two of the last survivors of noble Castian – though the chances of Enceladus ever awakening are almost laughably low. It must be said, you are heroes, both of you.' He tilted his head in the barest nod. 'You've brought great honour to the Eighth Brotherhood. Especially you, Hyperion. The Wolves already name you Hyperion Bladebreaker.'

'So I've heard, lord.' Many, many times.

'The Eighth lost a single squad in the Ragged Brotherhood of Armageddon.' Our lord shared a glance with his nearby paladins. 'This tragedy has left us stronger than before. I find that intriguing. By comparison, the Third Brotherhood is reduced to half-strength. A moment of woe for them, no doubt. Yet it does rather eliminate Lord Vaurmand from nominating himself for the rank of Supreme Grand Master for a long while.'

Our brotherhood's strength was preserved purely by chance – that most of our warriors were too far from Armageddon to answer the initial call. That hardly struck me as a position steeped in honour.

Joros watched me closely, as he gleaned a fraction of my unguarded thoughts. He narrowed his eyes as he spoke again. 'I am not so macabre as to dance over the bones of my brothers, Hyperion. Put aside your morbid concerns. I am merely stating the situation as it stands. Should Supreme Grand Master Ocris fall, the honour will be disputed between myself, Llyr of the First, and Geronitan of the Fourth.'

I stood silently through my lord's ambitions, suspecting I knew what was coming. 'Castian stands on the edge of destruction. Enceladus, should he rise again from the wounds that have laid him low, has earned his place back as Sepulcar of the Dead Fields. I would never refuse him the chance to return, with all honours. However, neither of you are suited to take command. You are both too inexperienced to rise to the rank of justicar.'

'I understand,' we said in unison.

'The true fighting was over long before we arrived, which I should be thankful for. But we enter the aftermath now. This foulness is almost finished – only the cleansing remains. We'll be back at Titan's docks before another month or two. You have my word.'

When he spoke again, he lowered his voice. 'The Inquisition is preparing to take control of the ashes, now the Wolves have won their war. Given the extensive nature of the sanctioning that remains to be done in the wake of this madness, the ordos have ordered us to aid them. We need every knight, and every ship. You two will return to the *Karabela* and await further instructions.'

'As you command,' I said. 'What have the ordos revealed about the scale of the sanctions?'

Joros leaned forwards in his throne, suddenly kingly and weary in equal measure. 'None of us will enjoy the duties to come, Hyperion. But we are the blade, not the hand that wields it. Our place is to kill, not to question.'

'I don't like the sound of that, lord.'

'I would think less of you if you did. Return to your ship and await your orders. When they come, obey without hesitation. Do you understand me?'

We saluted, again, in perfectly unity.

'Once this reeking aftermath is behind us, you will both be honoured for your actions on Armageddon. It's the least the Eighth can do. Malchadiel, am I to assume you still wish to be sent to the Ring of Iron?'

'Mars still calls to me, lord.'

'Then it shall be so. Hyperion?'

'I ask only to serve, lord.'

'A noble answer, but we'll see. Back to the *Karabela*, then. And heed these words, brothers. *Watch the Wolves.*'

* * *

IV

Annika was waiting for us. Her companions ringed Captain Castor's command throne on the strategium, standing in disarrayed formation. Annika waited by the throne itself, fuming.

'Have you heard what the ordos have decided?' she asked.

Malchadiel was sweating, pained by his new augmetics, but remained at my side. I looked up to Annika, confirming what I'd suspected on entering. Yes, she was fuming.

'I'm fine,' I said. 'My thanks for asking.'

'This is no time for jokes, Hyperion.'

That was a perfect example of what I mean when I said I fail to understand most human humour. Timing is everything.

'I have heard nothing regarding the ordos' intent, mistress. We were instructed to return and await further orders.'

She leaned on the railing, looking down at us. 'There was a vote, among the Inquisitorial forces here. They voted to condemn the entire population of Armageddon.'

That wasn't a surprise. Her reaction, however, was.

'I fail to understand how you can't have expected this,' I admitted.

'The Great Wolf was adamant in his orders. Entire populations of some hive cities haven't even been touched by this war. That's why he ordered all Grey Knights out of the cities.'

'And there's been no contamination while I was wounded? Not a single soul saw any of my order, in these last one hundred days? None of those cities saw even the dust from an enemy army on the horizon?'

She scowled. That was never a good sign. 'This isn't a standard purge, Hyperion. They're rounding up the entire population of the planet. The people are to be sterilised and committed to labour camps. Armageddon will be reseeded with colonists drafted in to dwell in the empty cities.'

I looked at Malchadiel. He looked back at me.

+There's been a flaw in communication,+ he said. +That cannot be true.+

+Of course it can.+

+You don't think this is a rather extreme reaction for our masters to take?+

+I'm saying it doesn't surprise me. These people have walked the same world as one of the Great Beasts of Sanguinary Unholiness. Armageddon is only escaping Exterminatus because of its industrial value to the subsector's Imperial Guard.+

Annika was still looking down at us. 'I can almost hear you two speaking with one another. It's like... what is the word in Gothic? Tinnitus? A ringing inside my ears.'

+Interesting. Perhaps we've been linked with her too long, and too often.+

+Agreed.+ I turned back to the inquisitor. 'Mistress, how are the Wolves reacting to the ordos' decision?'

Captain Castor didn't bother to rise from his feet. 'I can answer that, sir.' He tapped several keys on his throne's armrest. 'The Wolves' flagship has been broadcasting this signal to our fleet for the last three hours, on automated loop.'

I listened as the Great Wolf's voice resolved from the static. '...sition vessels. The voice you hear is that of Jarl Grimnar. I request that you stand down from these plans of yours. Take this request in the spirit in which it's offered. It would be unfortunate if I had to repeat it as a warning. This is the Fenrisian warship *Scramaseax*, to all Inquisition vessels. The voice you hear is–'

'They don't sound happy,' Darford pointed out, from his place at Annika's side. His rifle was over his shoulder.

I ascended the steps to Talwyn's throne, taking my own place on the dais. 'We are dealing with a Chapter that has, on several occasions, suffered censure from various dioceses of the Ecclesiarchy, as well as come under investigation by members of the Inquisition itself. They're proud souls, and they have every right to be furious at how our masters are dealing with this world. But they're being naive if they think anyone will heed those words.'

Malchadiel followed me up, his awkward gait drawing eyes from all across the chamber.

'But what if they react... unfavourably?'

'They won't.'

'But if they do?'

I didn't want to consider it. That way lay madness. 'Talwyn.'

'Aye, sir.'

'Show me the fleet, please.'

'Aye, sir. Oculus, sweeping reveal across the fleet. Auspex to track, sing back every signal.'

It didn't take long. Even in the months since the Great Beast's banishment, most of the vessels to arrive had been long-haulage cruisers for Imperial Guard troops. There must be close to a million fresh soldiers on the surface, not even counting the several million survivors.

Seeing all those ships gave me a thought I couldn't shake free.

+What if we'd waited?+ I sent to Mal.

He laughed from across the dais, as if I'd said something amusing out loud. More eyes turned to him, which he devoutly ignored.

+So many answers exist to that question, brother. The flaw in such reasoning is that there are no wrong answers. You could say that the fallen primarch's very unholiness demanded we act as soon as we were able, to banish such corruption from humanity's empire – and you'd be right. Or you could say it was better to lose a hundred knights than a whole world of innocents.+

+I'd have said the same only a few months ago.+ I didn't turn to look at him as we conversed. One of the many advantages of telepathic communion was the ability to focus on other things at the same time. +But look at what the ordos are planning. Why did we rush into that battle and kill ourselves by the dozen, if the Inquisition was going to decide to sterilise and cull the population anyway? We lost one hundred knights for a populace that are doomed to misery and extermination, despite our sacrifice. I see no justice in that, Mal.+

+When you put it like that... It does rather make the blood run cold.+

+I think I understand what Annika means. In such a light, the Wolves' reaction – already noble enough – takes on another layer of righteousness. They've lost warriors, too. How many of them died in glory, only to learn now it had all been in vain, defending a doomed population?+

Malchadiel sent back the impression of a weary smile. +I have no answer for you, brother. I wish I did.+

I suddenly wanted to speak with Brand Rawthroat, though I doubted it would do any good.

Captain Castor announced his findings with a stern expression. 'The fleet numbers at twenty-eight vessels capable of void warfare, sir. Eight are Titan interceptors and warships, wearing the Chapter's grey. The *Karabela* brings the total to nine. A full sixteen are Fenrisian, belonging to the Wolves, including the capital ship *Scramaseax*. The remaining three are Inquisitorial cruisers, including the Imperial Navy vessel *Corel's Hope*, commandeered for this operation by Lord Inquisitor Ghesmei Kysnaros.'

So the Wolves outnumbered us in the void. Significantly. With sixteen ships, that surely represented almost half of their Chapter fleet.

'And the Imperial Guard troop ships?'

'Wallowing cogs and bloated whaleships, sir. Twenty of them. None are battle-capable. At least, they can fire their little guns all day and night, and not scratch us even on a gamble.'

If everything should somehow go wrong, the Wolf and Guard vessels outnumbered us three to one. Even with the troop transports being effectively worthless in a void war, the odds weren't in our favour.

I thanked him and looked back to Annika. 'Despite their protests, the Wolves are still collared by Imperial Law, mistress.'

She bared her teeth in something that wasn't a smile. 'I hope you're right, Hyperion.'

Annika departed the bridge, and her warband followed. Darford had a nod of acknowledgement for me, the Khatan a smile, and Vasilla a soft prayer. Clovon gave nothing more than a look, and Merrick refused even that. His cyber-mastiff stalked at his heels.

+How is your back?+ I sent to Malchadiel once they were gone.

+On fire. Don't worry about me, brother. I believe Captain Castor is about to ask you for...+

'Orders, sir?' asked Talwyn.

I watched Armageddon turn and burn on the oculus. Right now, even as we waited in orbit, entire city populations were being rounded up. What were they being told? What honeyed lies were being poured in their ears, to get them to go willingly into a program of sterilisation and forced labour camps?

I'd thought we were dying for these people. I'd believed we were selling our lives to purge this world of evil.

Instead, we'd fallen in droves, purely to preserve a planet's industrial infrastructure, so Armageddon could keep churning out ten million battle tanks a year in the care of a new colonist population. I wasn't sure that was worth so many lives, though I could almost imagine Dumenidon arguing with me.

The armies of mankind need those weapons, he'd say. What is the loss of one world against all those that would fall without Armageddon's armaments?

And he'd be right, but the truth would still taste foul. This was why Galeo forever advised us against questioning our leaders. Too many truths. It wasn't our place to choose the right one. It was our place to heed what we were told.

'We wait,' I said to Talwyn, 'and hope our masters have thought this through.'

NINETEEN

THE FIRST TO FIRE

I

The Wolves weren't fools. They knew what lay in store for the valiant defenders of Armageddon. Powerless on the ground, it still didn't stop them attempting to halt the herding of the population into wilderness labour camps. Reports started to reach us of Wolves threatening Inquisitorial storm troopers, and convoys of civilians never reaching their assigned refugee camps. If the Wolves were hiding them, they were doing so with a cunning that defeated orbital surveillance.

The *Karabela* was ordered to align its auspex scanners groundwards, and join in the search. I wasn't certain I wanted them to find anything at all. The scale of the purge felt wrong, and I was already weary of paying lip service to it.

I refused to walk the surface, and not only because Lord Joros's orders demanded I remain in orbit. I had no desire at all to stand with my brothers, or the legions of Inquisitorial storm troopers, corralling the deluded, innocent souls from their cities.

I learned the lies we were telling them, though. That, more than anything, left the foulest taste on my tongue. The truth came from Lord Joros himself, though he met my disgust with dispassion when we discussed the matter over the vox.

'The Inquisition is already at work,' he said of the herding. 'The cities are emptying under watchful eyes.'

'What lies are we feeding them, lord?'

'Be mindful of your choice of words, Hyperion.'

'I will, Grand Master. I would appreciate an answer, though.'

'They are being told the cities must be temporarily evacuated for sacred cleansing. Then the people will be allowed to return. Guardsmen will, of course, watch over their homes and belongings, sparing them from looters.'

I laughed at the falsehoods, not bothering to hide my bitterness.

Annika was the one to enlighten me about the sterilisation. I didn't thank her for it, either. She came onto the bridge almost a week after I had last seen her, and fixed me with her pale blue eyes.

'Would you like to know how the ordos are rendering an entire population sterile?'

No. I had no desire for that knowledge – none at all. How would it help?

'I would rather not know, mistress.'

'Injections,' she said. 'I've been down there. I've seen it myself. They're given injections upon entry to the work camps. Men, women, even the children. They're being told it's to protect against disease. Instead, it's ending millions of families, making them the last generation descended from this world's original colonists.'

'I told you, it is none of my business. My focus is the field of battle, not the aftermath.' I felt on the edge of losing my temper with her, and it was difficult to remember a show of anger would achieve nothing. She'd come back after a week on the surface, purely to throw these accusations at me. As if this was my fault. As if I could do anything about it even if I wished to. 'You're the inquisitor, mistress. Your brothers and sisters are the ones doing this.'

She spat on the bridge deck. Strangely, the gesture wounded me, that she would show such disregard for Castian and the *Karabela*.

'You're a knight, Hyperion. There is nothing noble or righteous in exterminating an innocent population, yet you stand by and do nothing. All of you.'

I turned away from her, feigning a sudden interest in a control console. 'If the deed is so objectionable to you, Inquisitor Jarlsdottyr, then perhaps you should do something about it. Venting your wrath at me serves no purpose, when you and the ordos hold all the power.'

'I've killed before, Hyperion. I've murdered to keep secrets. A whole city sector once died by my order, burning up in fire from the sky, because I had to be sure a single cult was eradicated. But this is genocide. A global purge, for the basest of reasons, convenience. The troop transports will leave within the week, Grey Knight. What will you do then?'

I turned back to her, speaking through clenched teeth. Armoured as I was, I towered above her.

'I'll open fire on them and consign those brave souls to oblivion, as the Inquisition will no doubt order me to do. I'll do my duty, Annika.'

'You will address me as Inquisitor Jarlsdottyr.'

'I will address you as traitor if you keep voicing heresy in front of me. The Inquisition speaks, and we act. It's the way of things. You lecture me for what? Preparing to obey orders? Should I teleport down there with Malchadiel limping behind me, resurrect my dead brothers through the power of wishful thinking, and slaughter my way through a hundred thousand Inquisitorial storm troopers? Is that what you'd have of me?'

She met me bark for bark, to use her own phrase. 'Think, Hyperion. What do you think Jarl Grimnar will do when the troop ships make ready to depart? The Wolves are weak on the ground, without the numbers to challenge the ordos. But in orbit? In orbit, where their fleet vastly outnumbers the Inquisition's?'

I shook my head. 'They wouldn't defy us. It would be madness.'

She snorted, undeniably feral, and her lip curled as she turned away. Without another word, Inquisitor Jarlsdottyr left the strategium. The Khatan and Vasilla remained for a moment, just long enough to impart their own unique brands of wisdom.

The Khatan, for once, didn't grin. 'Just when I thought you couldn't be any more useless at dealing with women, Two-Guns.'

What was I supposed to say to that? What did it even mean? 'Why do you talk to me like this? You know I have no idea what you mean.'

She shook her head and left, seemingly unimpressed by my answer. Vasilla looked as close to nervous as I'd ever seen her. She forced a shy smile and made to leave herself.

'Fortune be with you, Hyperion.'

That was no less confusing, for it had all the hallmarks of a farewell.

II

Three nights later, the first troop transport made its move.

The *Trident of Ilmatha* drifted into high orbit, the first step in readiness to leave the world of Armageddon behind. We watched it – Malchadiel, Talwyn and myself – on the *Karabela*'s oculus screen.

With no desire to increase the crew's tension, which was already palpable, Mal and I did our best to display no emotion. Captain Castor had no such reservations. He sat in his throne, linked fingers against his lips, staring to the point of forgetting to blink.

'Mark my words, gentlemen,' he said. 'This is about to become quite the shitpit of curse words and short tempers.'

The *Trident of Ilmatha* was a fat lady, modified for greater transport capacity according to the whims of the Administratum in whatever subsector it had first originated. Its capacity for void warfare walked the border between ignorable and laughable, with almost all its bulk given over to additional cargo holds, communal barracks and engine deck space.

I'd not seen many Guard transports, but she was singularly the ugliest vessel I'd ever laid eyes on, putting me in mind of a fat-bellied whale too awkward to swim unaided.

'Throne, she's an ugly bitch,' Talwyn said, from his throne nearby. 'It'd be a waste to shoot each other to pieces over a junker like her, wouldn't it?'

'It would be a waste to shoot each other to pieces at all.'

'As you say, Sir Malchadiel. Let's hope it doesn't come to that.'

The *Trident* rose higher, beginning its slow, slow turn to face away from the world. She'd fire her engines to break orbit in a minute, perhaps two. If something was going to happen, it was going to happen soon.

'What are the Space Wolves vessels doing?' I asked.

Shora, the heavily augmented mistress of auspex, shook her head back at us. 'Nothing, sirs. They're not moving at all.'

I watched the fleet for another few moments, unsurprised when the vox crackled live.

+Here it comes,+ Malchadiel sent.

'This is the *Fire of Dawn* to the *Karabela*.'

'I hear you, Lord Joros.'

'Hyperion, you are to escort the *Trident of Ilmatha* to the jump point past Pelucidar. Once it reaches the transit point and you're out of auspex range from the fleet, you know what to do.'

'As you command.'

'In the Emperor's name.' The link went dead. In the silence that followed, Captain Castor looked at me, his eyes laden with meaning.

'Orders, sir?'

'Ready the engines for escort formation. Open a channel to the *Trident of Ilmatha*.'

'Done, sir.'

'This is the *Karabela*, to the transport vessel *Trident of Ilmatha*.'

A male voice crackled back with a short delay. 'This Captain Farrisen of the *Trident*. We hear you, *Karabela*.'

'We will be your escort to the jump point. Acknowledge.'

'Negative, *Karabela*.'

Malchadiel and I shared a glance. +This isn't good,+ he pulsed.

'Forgive me, *Trident*. You have no choice in the matter. This order comes from the highest authority in the fleet.'

'We appreciate it, *Karabela*, but the *Runefyre* has already been chosen to escort us.'

+Kill the link,+ I sent to Captain Castor. He did so, blinking at my sudden telepathy.

'Done, sir.'

'Follow the *Trident*, despite its protests.' The ship shivered as it woke, the engines opening up.

On the oculus, I watched the fat-hulled troop ship accelerating with all the speed and grace of a wounded mollusc. At this rate, it would take eleven hours to reach the safe transit point past the world of Pelucidar. By comparison, the *Karabela* alone might have reached it in less than one.

'The *Runefyre* has fired its engines,' said Castor. 'They're shadowing the *Trident*.'

I watched it taking place on the oculus, as the Space Wolves frigate – a tiny thing in comparison to the troop ship – took up a protective formation.

'Don't do this...' I said.

'Orders, sir?'

'Maintain course. The *Runefyre* is no bigger than us. What are its capabilities?'

Malchadiel was the one to answer. 'It's a Gladius frigate, brother. Twenty thousand crew, perhaps a few thousand more. We outgun it, and could easily outrun it.'

'They're testing us.'

Malchadiel nodded. 'I believe so.'

'Open a channel to the *Fire of Dawn*.' Once it was done, I realised I wasn't sure what to say. The situation was unprecedented. 'Lord Joros–'

'We see it, Hyperion. We believe the Wolves are merely posturing. Keep to your orders.'

'With all due respect, lord... If they aren't posturing, what do you expect me to do?'

The delay was painful, and telling. 'I expect you to do your duty, Hyperion.'

'Grand Master, I cannot open fire on an Adeptus Astartes vessel. I will not be party to heresy.'

'You forget yourself, Hyperion. Letting these Guardsmen leave this system alive is the basest heresy of all. You know what they've seen. Their lives were forfeit the moment they witnessed it. If the Wolves refuse to see reason, then they will share in the necessary fate.'

The link blanked out, terminated at the other end.

'This is ludicrous.'

Malchadiel agreed with a nod. 'The Wolves hold the cards. We need more ships to face them. They won't stand down unless we offer a greater show of force.'

'How many Inquisition vessels are en route?'

'Impossible to know. It hardly matters, Hyperion. The evacuation of Guard regiments will be complete in a handful of days.'

I looked at the oculus again, watching the slow drift of stars alongside the corpulent troop ship. The *Runefyre* was a pale reflection of our own vessel, keeping pace on the larger ship's other side.

'Today is going to be an interesting day,' said Captain Castor.

III

We reached the transit point just over ten hours later. The *Runefyre* broke away in a sedate drift, putting minimum safe distance between itself and the *Trident*. The troop ship's engines began to power up hotter, harder, in readiness to break into the realm between worlds.

The transit point was, in reality, nothing more than a vast area of clear space past the outer world of Pelucidar. Routes in and out of solar systems frequently ended at such junctures away from the planets themselves – all the better for avoiding risk of collision between vessels in orbit, let alone the chance of Geller malfunction allowing a warp breach to infect a nearby world.

'You have our thanks,' voxed the *Trident*. 'Priming warp engines now.'

I sensed Castor watching me with a keen eye. 'Orders?'

'Prime weapons. Ready lance strikes at their engines.' I looked back at him. 'You're the captain. Prepare to do whatever it is you do, but open a channel to the *Runefyre* first.'

'Open, sir.'

'This is Hyperion of the Grey Knights. To whom am I speaking?'

Distortion couldn't quite steal all identity from the voice. 'I cannot help but notice you're running out your guns, Bladebreaker.'

'Rawthroat.'

'The one and only. You sure you wish to fight this fight?'

'The *Karabela* outclasses the *Runefyre* by any measurement, brother.'

He laughed, distorting the link for a moment. 'I didn't ask who'd win the fight. I asked if you wanted to fight at all.'

'You know I don't.' The *Trident* was powering up its engines, moments from tearing into the warp. 'Rawthroat, these souls are consigned to death by the order of His Holy Majesty's Inquisition.'

'And yet they send you here to pull the trigger, staining your conscience and absolving their own. You're serving scum dressed as saviours, Bladebreaker. What honour do you find in that, I wonder?'

'Enough pedantry. They've seen Sin Incarnate, and cannot be allowed to share the knowledge. I have to do this.'

'Go ahead, then. Do what you feel is right, brother.'

With the link silent, I turned to Castor. 'Kill the *Trident*.'

The captain leaned forwards in his throne. 'Gunnery, all weapons lock on the troop ship's engines. Await my order to fire.'

As voices called out in acknowledgement and obedience, one rose above the affirmative clamour.

'Captain, the *Runefyre* is priming its weapons batteries.'

+Void shields,+ Malchadiel ordered.

'Void shields, aye,' answered one of the helmsmen, without realising where the order had originated.

A transmission reached us from the *Trident*, suffering further interference distortion from our shields and its warp engines going live.

'*Karabela*... We're reading weapons lock from–'

Castor spoke over the voice. 'Fire.'

IV

I've never been comfortable with void war. I don't like the helplessness, the feeling of your life in the hands of another, with destiny decided by machines and trajectories of cannonfire.

The *Trident* never even had time to raise its void shields. Somehow, that made the massacre worse, though I couldn't say why. They never had a chance, either way.

'Make it quick,' I said. 'They deserve that, at least.'

'Aye, sir.'

Chain reactions burst along its engine housings, triggering explosions deeper within the ship's bloated hull. Contrary to the saga-poems, detonations in space are surprisingly sedate ruptures, with almost nothing in the way of light. Our lance strikes carved through the composite metals forming the most basic armour plating, pulling the ship apart from the rear. Its temperamental engines were the first things to go, bursting apart in a spray of wreckage. The *Trident*'s puncture wounds vented air, debris, crystallised coolant and flailing crew – and still we cut into it.

The *Karabela* broke off after its first attack run, coming about in an arcing turn to finish what it had started. I kept the communication link open the entire time, listening to the *Trident*'s crew's confusion become panic, and in turn become screaming. Duty demanded we never turn a blind eye to the horror in these deeds. Hearing their final moments was the least we could do.

When silence reigned, the *Karabela* coasted through the wreckage and past the drifting hulk. The auspex return several minutes before opening fire had read four hundred thousand souls. Now, it read none.

The *Runefyre* came alongside us at the end of our second strafing run. I was certain its greeting would come in the form of a weapons barrage. Instead, Rawthroat's voice rasped over the vox.

'I didn't think you'd do it. We have all learned lessons today, eh? Remember this moment, Bladebreaker. Remember it well.'

'I'm unlikely to forget it, Rawthroat.'

'Good. Whatever happens in the days to come, remember that you were the ones to fire first.'

TWENTY

FAITH AND GUILT

I

We'd failed the Wolves' test. They wouldn't risk a single ship again.

Imperial Guard landing craft rising from the surface turned the orbit above Armageddon thick with traffic, and we all saw what was coming. Under the pretence of organising the evacuation at the end of hostilities, Logan Grimnar was arranging for the bulky troop ships to make ready all at once. There would be no simple dispersion, allowing Inquisition vessels to prey upon those who must be silenced one at a time.

He'd scatter them in one throw, knowing we lacked the firepower to bring them all down.

'We may have had to surrender the population to your master's cold claws,' Rawthroat had said to me in the wake of the *Trident*'s destruction. 'But several million heroes still draw breath in those troop ships. They deserve to live after what they've conquered.'

At no point did I ever argue with him. What use would it be to tell him of the risks of apostasy, recidivism, and heresy from even one soldier who'd seen more than his fragile mind could handle? These men and women had looked into the eyes of things that should not be. With all the will in the world, an unknowable number of them were already tainted – be it through madness, enlightenment, or the cancer of corruption nestling in their hearts and minds from beholding absolute evil. Cults might rise. Worlds could fall. We acted to preserve lives, not merely keep secrets.

And when had the notion of fairness ever entered into war? In the Inquisition's long and bloody history, countless trillions had died to preserve the ordos' secrets. In the greater scheme of the galaxy, no one would miss these poor soldiers. Even their loved ones would eventually die and be forgotten; within a single century, no soul would ever remember any of these unwilling martyrs.

I told myself all of this, time and time again. As true as it was, it didn't quieten my uneasy conscience.

Annika and the others remained aboard the *Karabela*, as was their right. I didn't have the authority to demand she leave. I wasn't sure I wished her to, either – I had the creeping sense of disquiet that she'd do something foolish.

She joined us in the strategium five days after the destruction of the *Trident*. Armageddon was devoid of off-worlders, beyond the Inquisition forces setting up and maintaining the work camps full of newly-sterilised Imperial citizens. Just looking at the dark stains of these false refugee encampments away from the empty cities left a bitter taste in the back of my mouth.

The Space Wolves fleet had pulled back into high orbit, making room for the Imperial Guard transports to cluster together. Our own vessels, still outnumbered, were forced to hang back from the formation work taking place.

I could sense Annika trying to get my attention. She didn't make a public point of it, but I could feel her thinking at me, as if it would establish a psychic connection. I kept my eyes on the oculus, watching the Space Wolves preparing to betray the Imperium of Man.

+Inquisitor,+ I greeted her.

'Hyperion.' She was tense, but not quite nervous. '*I wasn't sure this would work. Could you hear me trying to reach you?*'

+Something like that. I'm surprised you stayed aboard.+

'*So am I.*'

+Aren't you worried about being on one of our ships if this escalates beyond tension?+

Annika smiled at me, and I felt the weight of judgement in her icy eyes. '*You still don't understand the Wolves, do you?*'

+No. Nor do they understand us. That's why this will not end well.+

The bridge doors rolled open to admit Malchadiel. He was walking easier now, after several long sessions of engineering and light surgery with Axium.

As for Axium himself, I'd only seen him once since awakening, and that was to apologise for mangling his arm as I passed out. He forgave me without a second thought. His new arm seemed little different than the first, though he'd smithed the new one in the *Karabela*'s forges, rather than on Deimos. I could see the seam where the new arm met the old silver, but declined to mention it.

On the bridge, Malchadiel paused at seeing Annika standing with me by the throne.

'Inquisitor,' he said.

'Hello, Mal.'

'Your presence is a pleasant surprise.'

Their awkward politeness was cut short by the vox. 'This is

Jarl Grimnar to the Inquisition vessels in orbit. Heed these words, all of you. Stand down from your murderous intentions, and this day ends without bloodshed. Any repetition of the *Trident* incident will be met with a degree of force you simply won't survive. I take no pleasure issuing this threat, but you've forced our hands. Now, give me an acknowledgement that you've heard and understood this message.'

Captain Castor breathed a low whistle. 'If they really lose their temper, we won't even have time to shit ourselves before we die. Even Lord Joros must recognise that.'

Malchadiel's eyes never left the oculus. 'Don't count on it, captain. Our lord is an ambitious man. How fine it would look on a roll of honour, to be the Grey Knight who stood firm in the Inquisition's name against the deviant Wolves of Fenris.'

+We're in trouble,+ I sent.

Malchadiel still didn't look away. +Yes, brother. We are.+

Lord Joros wasn't the one to reply. Instead, a new voice crackled back over the vox, broadcast across the entire fleet.

'Chapter Master Grimnar. I am Lord Inquisitor Kysnaros. At my right hand is Grand Master Joros of the Grey Knights Eighth Brotherhood. You are one man, Logan. One man protected by armour and misplaced pride. How many Wolves stand with you? Eighty? Ninety at most? Your fleet outnumbers us here, above this ruined world. But the Inquisition's reach is long, and the fleet of a lone Adeptus Astartes Chapter is but a raindrop in the storm. What can you hope to achieve? We'll still hunt down every ship that manages to flee, and when we do, entire worlds will have to burn in order to keep the secret from spreading even further. Every listening station that marked the ships' passage. Every world where the ships dock. Billions and billions of lives, Grimnar. So I ask you, in all humility, to think carefully before you act. What you do here will decide the fate of more than these soldiers' lives.'

'Fool,' breathed Annika.

I turned to her. 'This "Lord Inquisitor Kysnaros", do you know him?'

'Barely. I met him for the first time in the meetings to decide the population's fate. We didn't bond well, he and I.'

I took a breath. 'Be ready to prime weapons and raise void shields.'

'Aye, sir,' Castor replied.

Grimnar's reply was characteristically gruff. 'These soldiers fought for the Imperium. The Imperium will not turn its back on them. Your choices are simple, witch-hunter. Stand down and survive to breed twisted little children of your own one day, or keep threatening us and learn the limits of a Wolf's temper.'

Kysnaros was seething down the link. He was a man unused to being disobeyed.

'We are His Holy Majesty's Inquisition, you grisly savage. Our authority is absolute. We know what is best for mankind's realm. Your place is to obey. Nothing more.'

'Such mighty words from a man with so few guns. These people are untainted, inquisitor. Let them go, and this ends here.'

'I will tell you how this ends, Jarl Grimnar. It ends with you on your knees, as the first High King of Fenris to bare his throat to a foe's blade. Refuse, and suffer the excommunication of your Chapter and the Exterminatus of your miserable home world.'

My blood ran cold. No show of calm could entirely conceal my shock at those words.

+That… That's a threat beyond anything I've ever heard,+ sent Malchadiel.

+He can't be serious,+ I sent back.

+No? He's speaking a madman's bluff, then.+

Jarl Grimnar's response was several moments in coming. 'I admire a man with imagination. However, Kysnaros, the idiocy you speak will never reach fruition. I'm done sharing words with you, little hunter of warlocks. My fleet is making ready to move. We'll not fire unless fired upon, so let your own consciences guide you.'

In the silence that followed, I signalled to the several of the bridge crew in turn. 'Arm all weapons, ready the void shields and prime engines for attack speed.'

'The troop ships are powering their engines, sir.'

The vox opened up again. 'This is Grand Master Joros aboard the *Fire of Dawn*. All Grey Knights vessels, your targets are being uplinked now. Be ready to attack on my mark. Cripple your target, and move to the next. We can finish the remnants once they're helpless.'

Annika was leaning against the railing, watching the oculus. She hung her head with a sigh. Captain Castor stared at the hololithic image before his throne.

'The *Fire of Dawn* has ordered us to cripple the troop ship *Fortitude*.'

Annika's silent voice was soft and strained. '*Hyperion, we have to stop this.*'

+I have a lord inquisitor and my own Grand Master demanding it of me. Even my own conscience tells me the risk of taint is too great to allow these people to live. This is how the Inquisition has always worked. You of all people should know that.+

'*We've never purged loyal armies on this scale.*'

+You're one inquisitor ordering me to cease. How many are aboard the *Dawn*, or the battleship *Corel's Hope*, demanding that we open fire? A dozen? More?+

She didn't fight me. That battle had been fought and lost days ago, before the *Trident* burned. Now she just watched the oculus as keenly as the rest of the crew.

'I'm almost glad Galeo and the others are already dead,' I said aloud. 'This will be a singularly dishonourable way to die.'

II

The first to fire was the frigate *His Wrathful Choir*. One of the *Karabela*'s sister ships, a match for us in size and speed, it opened up with a precision lance strike that spilled luminescence across the *Tora's Bastion*'s starboard shielding.

Troop carriers are toothless in a void battle. Some are built with reinforced armour and overcharged shield generators, but even they rarely carry an impressive armament. These fat whaleships were deployed from necessity when Armageddon first called for help, and were hardly prize examples of the shipwright's craft.

The *Tora's Bastion* didn't even fire back, despite outweighing its foe by a vast degree. Its thin void shields shimmered under the lance beam, spreading a sunburst of riotous colour and rendering the shields themselves visible to the naked eye while they absorbed the abuse.

The *Karabela* accelerated away from our fleet, weapons locked on the sluggishly fleeing form of the *Fortitude*. No orders were necessary any more. Castor directed the ship's actions from the control consoles on his throne's armrests, paying heed to nothing beyond the hololithic overview casting its harsh white radiance across everyone's faces.

The *Fortitude* didn't get far. As with the *Bastion*, its weak shields buckled and burst under close-range lance strikes. From there, it took Castor less than a minute to direct precise cutting beams through the labouring vessel's engine decks.

To cripple a ship and move on to another target sounds like a bloodless order. It isn't, not by a long way. Even a small ship like the *Karabela* has a crew of over twenty thousand souls, and no matter how precise Castor's lances were, he was still sawing his way through the bowels of a ship carrying closer to half a million men and women.

I felt them die. Only as a dim, tactile sound – the caress of a distant shout barely reaching the ears. The outpouring of hope, fear, loss and panic couldn't be ignored by anyone with an iota of psychic sensitivity among the fleet. Even Annika, who was latently sensitive at best, had to grit her teeth.

The *Fire of Dawn* and *Corel's Hope* put all other destruction to shame. The true warships cut their way between the rising transports, immense weapon batteries screaming. They burst shields without effort, and smashed through the carrier vessels with nothing like the same precision our smaller vessels were showing.

The Space wolves ship *Runefyre* was waiting for us when we drew closer to the next whaleship in line. It arced before us, thrusting ahead and over the surface of the transport *Arkaine*. Our guns slowed, then fell silent.

Captain Castor was staring through narrowed eyes. 'They're fast, and their heading is impossible to predict. Every time I fire, I risk striking the *Runefyre*.'

It was a scene being repeated across the fleet. Several of the troop transports were wallowing in high orbit, crippled before they could flee. Most of the others were thick with Space Wolves escorts, and while the smaller frigates were merely a risk to aiming, the larger Fenrisian cruisers made targeting all but impossible.

'This is Hyperion of the *Karabela*, requesting clarification of orders.'

'You have your orders,' replied the voice of Inquisitor

Kysnaros over the bridge vox.

'The orders from my Grand Master are to cripple the Imperial Guard troop transports.'

'And the order from one who outranks your Grand Master is to destroy any ship that seeks to thwart the Inquisition's justice.'

'I am not opening fire on an Adeptus Astartes warship. Castor, hail the *Runefyre*.'

'Done, sir.'

'This is the Grey Knights warship *Karabela*. Acknowledge, please.'

'I hear you, Bladebreaker.'

'Rawthroat, you have to listen to me. This has gone far enough. The Inquisition will fire on you next. You've made your point, now back down.'

In the background, I could hear his bridge crew shouting orders and reports to one another. Our vessels were already firing, raining fusion on the Space Wolves ships to blast them aside.

He laughed. 'We're not making a point, Bladebreaker. We're doing what's right.'

'You can't know if every single one of these souls is free from taint.'

'The jarl has spoken, grey one. You're not allowed to massacre millions just in case a handful are corrupt. Look at yourself, knight, and tell me the Emperor wishes this of the Imperium's protectors.'

'Only a fool would threaten countless worlds in the name of optimism, Wolf.' I was almost shouting at his stubbornness. 'You'll bring censure against your entire Chapter. You cannot trade fire with Inquisitorial vessels and escape retribution!'

'Look to the skies around you, brother. Do you see us firing back?'

'I...'

+He's right,+ sent Malchadiel. +Look.+

'Castor, give me a full view of the fleet.'

The oculus showed us ship after ship, separated by the distances of protracted void conflict, though the Guard vessels had no hope of outrunning ours. Grey Knights ships, along with those of the Inquisition, still fired weapon streaks across the span. Several were punching home into limping transports, but most were left as spreading oil-stains across the shielding around Wolves ships.

None of them fired back. Not a single one. The flagship *Scramaseax* endured a twin assault from the lances of the *Ruler of the Black Skies* and the *Fire of Dawn*. Its shields were already dead under the pressure, yet it sailed on, adjusting its bearing to keep guarding a round-hulled transport ship.

'Hyperion of the *Karabela*,' Lord Joros's voice crackled over. 'You are hereby ordered to destroy the *Runefyre*.'

'At once, my lord.'

Annika was looking at me. Captain Castor was looking at me. Malchadiel was looking at me.

'Target the *Runefyre*.'

'Done, sir.'

'Rawthroat, can you hear me?'

Either he couldn't, or he chose not to answer. I drew breath to speak, without really knowing what I intended to say. Before a single word left my lips, the oculus exploded in light.

'Warp breach!' several crew called at once. The bridge vox bloomed into renewed life as a huge, battlemented war-barge knifed its way into reality through a hole in the universe. Great bronze emblems marked its armoured sides, each of them depicting a wolf howling high towards a black sun.

A fleet of frigates and destroyers bolted ahead of the main

cruiser, contrails of fiery light streaming from their engines.

Annika laughed, throwing her head back and howling. Several servitors turned to regard her in lobotomised stupefaction.

Jarl Grimnar's voice rumbled across the vox. 'Lord inquisitor, we invite you to welcome the Fenrisian battle-barge *Gylfarheim* and her fleet.' His pause was just long enough to add to the mockery. 'I assume you wish to cease firing at our vessels. Am I wrong?'

Another pause followed, this one significantly longer.

'This is Lord Inquisitor Kysnaros to all Inquisition forces, break off the attack. Repeat, break off the attack.'

Across our fleet, every vox-channel died to sudden static, before breaking into a long, triumphant howl.

The attacking fleet slowed – at first to a crawl, then to sit dead in space. We watched the Wolves escort the troop transports away, engines flaring hot all the while.

TWENTY-ONE
CONTAINMENT

I

Whether in matters of prevention, cure, or retribution, the Inquisition is nothing if not thorough. It also keeps deep and comprehensive archives on those who fall to its whims. Much of the aftermath of Armageddon I learned from sequestered Imperial records, hidden by virtue of their Inquisitorial seal; the rest I gleaned from the minds of my brothers or the inquisitors present at the time, who in turn had ridden inside the minds of those they were killing.

Annika often used a phrase that applied perfectly to the ordos' reaction after the Wolves slipped through our fingers.

Spill enough blood and any secret will die.

This was what we did. This was how the Inquisition had worked for thousands of years. To banish all trace of sin, so that none would ever know of it.

Annika didn't condone the massacres that followed Armageddon, but she was correct in her phrasing. No matter how far and wide something has spread, information can always be preserved in secret if the right number of lips are sealed. Containment is key. So said our masters.

The Wolves had thwarted us. You could look at that as the actions of a noble brotherhood, seeking to see the galaxy through a moral purity that simply didn't exist, even if it deserved to.

It would be more realistic, if somewhat less kind, to remember that the Wolves must have known how we'd react. The Inquisition was never going to sit idle while such a horrendous secret spread through the Imperium.

The Grey Knights and our Inquisitorial masters pulled every trigger in the months that followed. I would never deny that.

But the Wolves must have known what we'd do. The Inquisition's hand had been forced. It could be argued then, that the Wolves shared some of the blame for the billions of lives we ended after Armageddon.

I don't blame them, myself. They are Adeptus Astartes, bred to be weapons first and reasoning souls second. They would consider it the coward's way – the way of the immoral enemy – to prevent a greater evil by committing a lesser evil. There's honour in that. There's a simple, ignorant, honour.

They are, to be blunt, not pragmatic creatures. There's no room for pragmatism in honour.

But we were born, schooled, trained and sworn to see a greater picture, beyond personal honour and the lives of a few million souls. Our mandate was to defend the species itself, and the lives of billions were always of greater value than millions.

I admire the Wolves. I even forgive them for their narrow-minded, stubborn honour. I hold no grudge that their actions meant we were forced to silence ten billion innocent voices instead of a few million potentially corrupt ones.

But the Inquisition is not so forgiving.

* * *

II

The Ralas Meridian.

An asteroid belt, seven systems coreward from Armageddon and several weeks' warp flight for standard Imperial jump drives.

The asteroid belt was a host of worthless rocks, possessing no value in minable metals, and circling an uninteresting sun. For the sake of completeness, it seemed to be all that remained of a world destroyed by natural forces thousands of years before mankind first ventured among the stars.

The system's only value was to the Adeptus Astra Telepathica, serving as an astropathic relay station between worlds too remote for rapid or reliable transit.

Four days before its destruction, it tracked the Imperial Guard troop transports *Mankind's Birthright* and *Lucky Queen* passing through its sphere of monitored space, fresh from a campaign on the world of Armageddon. It also recorded several vox-messages between the two vessels, as well as the impressions of communion between astropaths on board both ships.

These recordings were archived and immediately forgotten, as meaningless and standard as they were.

On the night of its destruction, a single frigate appearing as a modified Adeptus Astartes Standard Template Construct pattern annihilated the lightly-defended relay station with a volley of broadsides. Afterwards, it hammered the asteroid base into gravel, all without even once broadcasting its intent.

Throughout the attack, the vessel refused all attempts to communicate, and matched no known transponder codes.

There were three hundred and forty-six residential staff and indentured servitors aboard at the Ralas Meridian station. None survived the assault.

With its duty done, the Grey Knights warship *Armistice* cut its way through the asteroid field and plunged back into the warp.

III

Jendara Quintus, in the Tremayne Sector, categorised by the Imperium of Man as a Gamma-class planet: civilised, but not teeming with the same masses of life that make up a hive world. Its main population centre was the city-state Illustrum (population: nine million) at the mouth of the Shuma River.

Many, many light years from Armageddon, the majority of its educated citizenry had still never heard of the distant world. The only souls to know of the planet's existence were those who'd served there, and those they'd spoken to upon returning home.

Jendara Quintus was protected by a blistering array of orbital defences, none of which activated when the Grey Knights warships *Ruler of the Black Skies* and *Fire of Dawn* entered the world's ionosphere.

The orbital defence array remained inactive even as the warships bombarded the cities from the heavens, never once replying to the screams for mercy rising from the surface.

Five days after its satellite defences failed to come online, Jendara Quintus was left alone in lifeless, silent peace. Beacons deployed in orbit warned any nearby vessels away from the dead world, citing the brutal xenos invasion that had swept the planet clean of all human life.

IV

Tybult – a world believed to be named for an ancient character from Eurasian legend. Despite its purpose as an agricultural supply world, it also provided huge tithes in the form of recruitment figures to the sector's Imperial Guard levies. At the close of 444.M41, it was in the process of founding the Tybultian 171st Rifles.

It was common for vessels on long warp journeys on nearby transit routes to refuel and resupply at Tybult's extensive orbital docks. Three ships were doing so on the eastern hemisphere morning of the planet's death – one of which was the Imperial Guard transport *Casus Belli*.

The dockyard installation exploded under multiple torpedo strikes originating from deep space. All three of the docked vessels went down with the docking station, burning up in the atmosphere several hours later, when they fell to the surface.

The crews of the three vessels – almost entirely on shore leave down on Tybult's surface – survived almost one hour longer than their ships. They died with the rest of the planet's populace, when the warship *Corel's Hope*, rearmed under Inquisitorial mandate, deployed air-bursting virus bombs above the main cities.

The virus matter contained within each globular incendiary was an artificial strain of cytotoxic agent, designed by ancient minds in service to mankind during the age of Imperial expansion. The merest contact ate all cellular life, in any organic form, from soil and trees to flesh, blood and bone – and the virus itself spread by damning everything it touched, even microbiotic life in the air.

The disease's hunger ages everything it touches, breaking it down at the cellular level. The end result for most biotic substances is to become a flammable, chemical-rich residue – not entirely unlike organic slime.

Amazing to think that the architects of the Imperium would design an artificial disease that rots and melts all life, degrading it into inert sludge. What enemies did our ancestors face, to warrant such foul genius in the Emperor's name?

Tybult burned that day. As the population corroded while still alive, along with the planetary ecosystem, the atmosphere thickened with volatile byproduct gases, as a result of dissolving matter.

A second bombardment, this time of the warship's plasma batteries, ignited the planet's turgid, poisonous air. Already a grave-world of biological ooze, Tybult was reaved clean of all life by the ignition of its atmosphere. A handful of hours after its arrival, *Corel's Hope* turned away from the world it had slain, leaving nothing but superheated rock and silent cities.

V

The Adeptus Mechanicus outpost Priam Novus was nothing more than a listening post at the edges of the Armageddon Subsector, primarily charged with the recording of Imperial traffic through the region's northern reaches.

Among its recent logs were notations relating to the journey of the bulk transport *Yulacese*, en route from Armageddon to the Helican Subsector.

Despite its modest role in humanity's empire, the Priam Novus deep-space installation was defended by a task force of Fury-pattern Interceptors. The Cyrus Omega XA-II Squadron was well-trained and experienced at repelling the assaults of void pirates.

When the Grey Knights destroyer *Flawless Reprieve* broke from the warp and rained torpedoes upon Priam Novus, Cyrus Omega XA-II Squadron scrambled with all haste. They survived longer than any of the three thousand souls aboard the station itself, as the warship ignored them completely. Once the destruction was complete, the *Reprieve* turned and boosted back into the warp.

The last member of Cyrus Omega XA-II Squadron to die

was Wing Commander Falana Deshivan. She, like the rest of her squadron, asphyxiated inside her cockpit when her oxygen reserves at last ran out, days later. It could be argued that was a mercy, as had any of the fighter wing survived a further three days, their deaths would have come in the form of freezing to death when their fighters' power cells were finally depleted.

VI

The troop transport *Maerlyn's Run* was safe once it reached the warp. Its captain, Argan Valoy, had thanked the Wolves for their timely assistance and breathed a sigh of relief as the warp drive whined its way to consciousness. In a burst of chaotic light, they were under way, safe from whatever madness had infected half the fleet in orbit around Armageddon.

Five weeks into their flight, their Navigator reported sighting silhouettes in the turmoil of warp space – impossible shapes cutting through the tides nearby. Captain Valoy was a careful man. He believed in all necessary caution, better safe than sorry. In this instance, he ordered *Maerlyn's Run* to drop from the warp and give time for the Navigator to rest, before pushing on.

As the enginarium decks began the process of balancing power within the warp engines to breach back into reality, the silhouette that Valoy's Navigator had seen made itself known. Protected by superior shielding and hexagrammic insulation against the horrors of the warp, the Grey Knights vessel ploughed through the filthy tides, ramming the transport amidships and buckling its hull.

With the ship open to the void the venomous matter of the warp spilled into the *Maerlyn's Run*, as the crew's nightmares became manifest among them. Those that weren't immediately killed by giving birth to daemons inside their own skulls were pulled apart in the following minutes by Never-born rampaging through the ruptured decks.

The *Maerlyn's Run* returned to real space thirty-three nights later, several subsectors spinward from where it had first entered the warp. An Inquisitorial purge-team found no survivors on the wreck, and the hololithic records of the crew's final moments were locked away under the highest authority, given over to our Titan monastery for safeguarding.

VII

The Wolves couldn't be everywhere at once. Perhaps they underestimated the Inquisition's true fervour, leaving so many possible targets outside their web of protection. I can't say, for I've never had the chance to ask.

But when they did defend their interests, they showed up in overwhelming force. *Corel's Hope* broke from the Sea of Souls on the outskirts of the Porphyr System, under Lord Inquisitor Kysnaros's orders. We were with the *Hope*, Malchadiel and I, and still in acting command of the *Karabela*.

Since Galeo and Dumenidon fell, entire worlds had burned or been put to the sword, all to preserve the secret of what we'd all witnessed on Armageddon. We'd attacked convoys ourselves, and destroyed void stations, all for the sin of over-hearing the wrong vox-message, or positively identifying a ship that should never have left Armageddon. Never before had a duty felt so hollow. Righteousness without morality is a sour victory, no matter the necessity.

Primarch. Such a word, laden with the resonance of mythology. Angron. Lord of the Twelfth Legion. The wider Imperium could never be allowed to know the Emperor's own sons turned against him, nor that the Grey Knights existed in the empire's shadows, fighting a war against creatures that couldn't be real. We spent so much sweat and effort ensuring even the most minor sins never reached the eyes and ears of Imperial citizens; the greatest heresies of all had long since passed into apocryphal legend.

Where they belonged.

Aboard the *Karabela*, I spent more time than I should standing in the medicae bay, speaking to the cryo-coffins of my dead brothers. Their sarcophagi were mounted and locked in the storage bays, yet I still found myself returning to them time and time again. Sometimes I'd apologise. Sometimes I'd ask for advice. Mostly, I'd just dwell upon the lessons I'd learned under their guidance, and wonder how in the infinite hells I was supposed to live up to such warriors.

More often, I'd speak with Enceladus. Once cut from his armour, he was an emaciated, broken thing of ragged flesh and wiry sinew. He drifted in an amniotic tank, breathing into a face mask, his eyes curdled in his skull. Even if he woke, he'd never see again. Armageddon had killed him, he just hadn't got round to dying yet.

+Wake up,+ I sent endlessly into his floating corpse, limbless with the removal of his bionics.

He no longer answered. That may have been a good sign – a sign of deep healing. It may have been exactly the opposite. Nadion wasn't sure, either.

Malchadiel would often find me there, and draw me back to the bridge. Annika would do the same. Only Clovon and Vasilla would remain there with me; the former watching impassively with his inked and scarred visage, the latter praying as I mused, and occasionally asking questions about my brothers' lives. Strangely, that soothed me. Speaking of them lanced the wound of their loss, making their absence in my mind a little less keen.

'Thank you,' I said to her, one night.

She didn't feign ignorance. She smiled her slow, patient smile – an expression far too wise for her tender years – and simply said: 'It's nothing.'

Garven Merrick visited me once, while I pored over the latest reports of our so-called 'cold war' with the Wolves. Each of these read exactly as they were: short lists of incidents where the Inquisition reported the annihilation of a colony, city or space station, balanced by incidents where Grey Knights or Inquisition vessels had arrived to face overwhelming Space Wolves blockades around the target.

There was little meat to the reports, and nothing in the way of actual conflict. The Wolves never waited for long, nor did they return fire when fired upon. Their desire was to evacuate every soul they could, and scatter them from our paths.

And it was working. Week by week, system by system, it was working all too well. Five months into the war of massacres, raids and running away, it wasn't difficult to see that we'd never catch every single loose end. The strands had frayed too far. Some of the souls who'd seen our secrets were going to escape. Hell, they already had.

The Barsavan Dragoons were the finest example in the records. The Wolves had scuttled the Barsavans' troop ship themselves after leading several of our ships into a deep-space chase, and proceeded to leave the survivors on random Imperial worlds across a number of subsectors. What hope was there to find a few thousand soldiers on a world with three billion people? What worlds should we even begin to target for investigation, let alone Exterminatus?

The Grey Knights realised the Wolves' game earlier than the inquisitors holding our leashes. On more than one occasion in hololithic transmission meetings, I'd been forced to watch Lord Inquisitor Kysnaros shouting down all counter-arguments offered by members of our order. He was still certain containment could be reached. It could, of course – logic dictates that it's true – but the cost in lives to reach containment was becoming ludicrous.

In truth, there's little of relevance to add to the archives. For every purge we completed as ordered, another elsewhere across the Imperium was failing due to the Wolves' interference. Never once did they let us bring them to battle. Never once did they let us catch them unawares.

Captain Castor once told me the majority of his life was spent waiting for something to happen. Even as overseer on a Grey Knights warship, he spent a significant portion of his time in warp transit, travelling for weeks on end at the beginning and end of every operation. And on the rare occasions the *Karabela* fought in a void battle, she easily outclassed most enemies, or was agile enough to flee if necessary. The months we spent chasing the Wolves and erasing all records of Armageddon exemplified Castor's boredom.

Do it enough, and even the immoral becomes the mundane. You acclimatise. You become desensitised. How many civilian targets, annihilated from above, could I mourn as fiercely as I'd regretted the first?

I was in Castian's communal chamber, reading through the last briefing reports, when Garven Merrick came to speak with me. As usual, he wore his battered, scratched enforcer armour, though without the heaviest plates on the shoulders and chest. His bulky shotgun was slung over one shoulder, as casual as a hunter out for a day's sport.

The cyber-mastiff walked at his heels, though perhaps a more accurate word for the way it moved would be loped, surprisingly close to a real canine in its movements.

+Hello, Faith,+ I sent to the mechanical beast. I wasn't sure of the creature's exact mechanics, but something in its artificial brain always seemed to register my silent greetings.

Still, it was never impressed. This time it regarded me for a moment with disinterested eye lenses, then went back to scanning its surroundings in a slow pan of its head.

'Sir,' Merrick greeted me. 'May I speak with you?'

These were literally the first words we'd ever shared, in over a year of operational duty together. Skimming his surface thoughts revealed that he wasn't sure if he should salute or not. Old habits from his years as a law enforcement officer died hard.

'There's no need,' I told him.

'No need, sir?'

'No need to salute.'

He scowled at that, clearly not liking me in his head. 'As you say, sir.'

This wasn't starting out well. 'Forgive me, I didn't mean to make you uncomfortable. Force of instinct. What did you need, Garven?'

'You know Inquisitor Jarlsdottyr well, don't you?'

The question unsettled me, mostly as I had no idea what the answer was. 'I don't know. I know her better than I know any other human.' I paused. 'Is that an acceptable answer?'

'Good enough.' Merrick was a man of few words, possessed of an unshaven awkwardness and a reluctance to make eye contact. I think that was why I found his company paradoxically easy to deal with. 'I don't pretend to understand your kind, sir.'

'And I don't pretend to understand yours,' I replied, forcing a smile to show it was meant as a jest. He didn't laugh.

'Be that as it may, sir… you and the inquisitor are friends, aren't you?'

I looked at him for a moment. 'You are adept at asking questions I find difficult to answer.'

'Never mind, sir.' He turned and made to leave.

'Wait. Yes, she and I are friends. At least we were.'

He turned back. 'She's angry. Furious, even. I'm worried about her. We all are.'

'Am I to assume she's told you our current orders?'

'Yes, sir. To link up with Kysnaros's armada at Haikaran, to offer terms to Jarl Grimnar.'

I nodded. 'And am I to assume Inquisitor Jarlsdottyr doesn't trust Kysnaros's intentions in this meeting?'

'I think you already know she doesn't trust him, sir.'

Whether he'd be comfortable or not, I subtly leeched from his mind. He was telling the truth: his fears for Annika were that she'd lose her objectivity, her patience, and her temper. He worried that she would do something rash, and get herself killed.

It also wasn't why he was here. It was a lesser truth to conceal a greater one.

'She is probably the most capable soul on this ship,' I replied. 'You know that as well as I do.'

'She's not immortal, though. And she has a temper, forgive me for saying so, sir.'

As if I didn't know that myself. 'I will watch over her, Garven. You have my word. Was there anything else?'

'No, sir. Well. Yes, sir. If you have time, that is. I was wondering if you'd ask the silver automaton to help me with something.'

'His name is Axium. What's wrong?'

'It's Faith. We've not docked in months, and I need new tools and parts to maintain her. The silver automaton might have them.'

'He may indeed. I wouldn't address him as "the silver automaton" to his face, however.'

'Sorry, sir.'

'It's fine.' I crouched down, and focused on the cyber-mastiff.

'Faith, come.'

'Faith, go,' Merrick said. The dog thrummed and whirred on active joints as she stalked closer to me. I looked at the scratches marking her jagged jaws, and the hazard striping marking her flanks.

She seemed fine to me, but I was hardly an expert on the matter. 'Malchadiel may be able to help you, as well. You should speak to him.'

Merrick actually went pale. 'No, sir. He'll… I've seen how he takes things apart with his mind.'

I had to smile. 'I see your point. I'll tell Axium you're on your way.'

'Thank you, sir.' He saluted, quite unnecessarily. Faith turned to regard me, and loped around her master's legs.

The ship shook around us a few seconds later, hard enough to threaten our balance.

'Rough ride,' Merrick said.

'That wasn't us dropping from the warp,' I said. 'Something hit us.'

The sirens began wailing, a backdrop to Mal's voice.

+Get to the bridge,+ he sent to me. +Kysnaros has started the war.+

VIII

We were already taking fire by the time I made it to the bridge. Castor was out of his throne, shouting at the helmsmen over the shuddering hull. Malchadiel was by the bank of weapons consoles, looking over the officers' shoulders.

The oculus showed a single vessel, the capital ship *Scramaseax*, taking a pounding no Imperial warship should ever have to receive. Void-fires ravaged its battlement-spine, while a visibly weak shield buckled and flickered in and out of existence.

I vaulted the railing and landed by Malchadiel.

'Throne, look at her,' I said. 'She's already half-crippled. Who fired first?'

Malchadiel's expression said it all. 'Hazard a wild guess, brother.'

I turned to Castor. 'Status report.'

'You're seeing it, sir.' Castor straightened his leather coat, brushing imaginary dust from a gold button with a casual swipe of his gloved hand. 'We dropped from the warp to link up with Kysnaros's armada. The fleet was already in battle.'

'Have we received any orders?'

'Only to open fire as soon as we reach weapons range.'

'How many other vessels are there in our armada?'

Malchadiel reached to manipulate the tactical hololith with the sensory pressure pads in his fingertips. He turned the star field, highlighting the vessels ship by ship.

'I count fifteen, including the *Karabela*.'

I watched Logan Grimnar's flagship turning and burning in the void, protected by a flawed and failing shield. As I watched the ancient flagship of a Space Wolves Great Company breaking apart, I felt it scoring its way into my memory. I'd never forget this moment. Never. This was supposed to be a truce on neutral ground. We were ordered here to stand by while Kysnaros parleyed terms, and brought the months of idiocy and frustration to an end.

For once, the Wolves were fighting back. In this case, too little, too late. The *Scramaseax* retaliated with insignificant weapon bursts, flailing back at enemies it was now too wounded to harm.

Malchadiel was distant, but not dispassionate, as he gestured towards the struggling cruiser.

'That ship is older than our Chapter, Hyperion. By killing it, we're spitting in the face of our own species' history.'

'Kysnaros has gone too far.' I didn't understand any of this. 'Why did the Wolves only show up with one ship?'

'They didn't. They showed up with five.' Malchadiel turned the starscape to a better angle. It was then that I saw the wreckage. This battle was hours old.

'Castor, get me a link to Lord Joros on the *Fire of Dawn*.' While I waited, I watched the beleaguered *Scramaseax* rolling in the void – a wounded animal baring its belly.

'*Karabela*?'

'It's Hyperion. What am I seeing, my lord? Grey Knights vessels opening fire on a First Founding Chapter. This… this is blasphemy.'

'Accelerate to attack speed and engage the enemy. Cripple that ship, Hyperion, and be ready to teleport to the *Fire of Dawn* at my order. We have the Wolf Lord by the throat.'

'Sire… We were told this was a parley on neutral ground.'

'It was.' His voice was breaking apart in vox-distortion. 'Lord Inquisitor Kysnaros suspected the Wolves of treachery. We opened fire before they had the chance.'

'And you believe that, my lord?'

He had the audacity to laugh, despite the gravity of the moment. 'Not for a second. But this is our chance, brother. We take Grimnar captive, and his Chapter will kneel in submission.'

'This is perfidy, Joros. It leeches any honour our order ever laid claim to.'

Castor shook his head. 'The signal's lost, sir.'

I stood in dumbstruck silence for several seconds, just watching the *Scramaseax* die.

The next voice I heard was that of Lord Inquisitor Kysnaros, over a fleet-wide address.

'Jarl Grimnar of the *Scramaseax*. Your ship bleeds fire, and your life is measured in mere moments. By virtue of the power vested in me by His Imperial Majesty, I am empowered to offer you a last chance to serve the Golden Throne. Lay down your arms and come aboard the battle-barge *Fire of Dawn*, if you wish to discuss the terms of your surrender. If you would rather die where you are, too proud to admit you're beaten, then by all means transmit any last words you have. We will honour your Chapter by ringing the Bell of Lost Souls once you're lost to history's pages.'

I didn't expect a response. I honestly expected them to die in proud silence, aboard their wounded flagship. I'd even have admired them for it.

'We will meet,' came the throaty reply. 'We'll meet and discuss terms.'

'Good, good.' Kysnaros was all smiles, even over the vox. There was nothing snide or petty in his tone, which only made it worse. He sounded happy, beaming, to have been able to enlighten a lesser mind into the perfectly obvious course of action. 'Today may have dawned in darkness, Jarl Grimnar, but the sun will set over a final peace.'

The Space Wolves ship's reply was a grunt of static, followed by silence.

'Mal,' I said. 'We need to get ready.' +Annika?+

'Hyperion? I'm on my way to the bridge. What's happening?'

+The endgame. Meet us at the teleportation platform.+

'I outrank you, Hyperion. I'd be coming whether you wished it or not. Nothing could keep me away.'

TWENTY-TWO
THE KNEELING KING

I

We stood in ordered ranks this time, under Lord Joros's keen
and traditional eye. With reinforcements from Titan and
across the galaxy, we numbered almost a full hundred again,
with countless more knights on their way, aboard a host of
ships.

The gathering was a grim reflection of the first time we'd
met the Great Wolf, aboard the *Ruler of the Black Skies* above
Armageddon. This time, we were reinforced by a full company of Inquisitorial storm troopers clad in black carapace
armour, faintly reminiscent of upright chitinous insects.
Annika and the other inquisitors were no longer content to
stand at the sides and allow a Grey Knights Grand Master to
deal with matters alone. They took centre-stage, with Lord
Kysnaros heading that particular group, very much the first
among equals.

By virtue of rank, Joros stood alongside the inquisitor,

towering above the humans surrounding him. His greying hair seemed touched by frost in the harsh overhead light of the hangar bay.

Logan Grimnar descended his gunship's ramp, his armour blackened and battered, with only three Wolf Guard at his back. Against all odds, I recognised one of them. Brand Rawthroat scanned our gathered ranks, and nodded once his eyes met mine.

I returned the gesture, risking a telepathic pulse. +It grieves me to see you here, brother.+

His smile was a curled lip, revealing a fanged incisor. *'I lost my ship months ago.'* I sensed his amusement at the moment. *'Now get out of my head, warlock. Watch how a Wolf surrenders.'*

Jarl Grimnar pulled his axe free once he reached Kysnaros and the Grand Master. Every inquisitor tensed, and several of their warband-warriors clutched weapons tighter. With no telepathic signal, we didn't move.

'That's far enough,' said Lord Joros. He made no move to reach for a weapon. He was, as always, possessed of a most admirable calm. Galeo had often considered self-control to be our Grand Master's most prized virtue.

Jarl Grimnar obeyed, halting ten paces away from the gathered Inquisitorial retinue. He let the axe-head slam onto the deck, and leaned on the inverted haft, scarred gauntlets resting on the black iron pommel.

'You betrayed an armistice,' he said in that voice so like spilling gravel. His tawny hair, white-streaked and singed in places, was a matted mess framing his gnarled-oak features. He wasn't ancient for a Space Marine, but he was certainly past his mid-life prime. Still, he emanated vitality even in his most modest movements; here was a tough old soul that wouldn't easily fall. Even now, he showed no sign of capitulation.

'Yes, we betrayed the armistice,' Kysnaros conceded. 'I pray you'll forgive me, in time. You have to understand, great jarl, that your Chapter's reputation with Imperial command hierarchy calls the worth of your sworn oaths into question. How many times have you come into conflict with the Ecclesiarchy? Or the Inquisition's lesser elements? I wasn't sure I could trust you.'

Grimnar smiled, showing old teeth in a nasty grin. 'You violated an armistice, killed thousands of my Chapter's servants, and now name us oathbreakers when you – as always – fired first.'

He looked back over his shoulder to his three remaining Wolf Guard. 'This is why we so rarely speak to outlanders, eh? No manners.'

The Wolves chuckled, as Grimnar looked back to Kysnaros. 'You wished to speak with me? I'm here, boy. Speak.'

Boy. It was difficult to dispute that judgement. This was my first time in Inquisitor Kysnaros's physical presence, and he seemed much younger than his poor-quality hololithic images had suggested. I had no doubt rejuvenat surgery played a part in his youth, of course. He couldn't truly be as young as he appeared; no man or woman in their mid-twenties could ever rise to the rank of lord inquisitor. Such ascensions usually took centuries, and a legion of allies, favours and supporters.

He wore nothing in the way of armour, and carried no weapon beyond a golden sceptre of office. If anything, he seemed more preacher than inquisitor, robed in deep reds, with a silken hood pulled down to reveal his features.

When he spoke, his voice was similarly youthful, lacking the brazen edge so obvious in the throats of all the augmented warriors present.

'It would have been faster to teleport here, would it not?'

Grimnar shrugged, the massive wolf pelt on his shoulders seeming to shrug with him. 'We rarely trust teleportation. Only in hours of direst need. Now speak. Why did you beg me for an audience?'

'Beg you? Not quite, jarl. We wish to negotiate the terms of your surrender.'

Grimnar nodded, as if such words were the wisest sounds ever to leave human lips.

'I see. And if I wish to name you an oathbreaker, a lying viper with piss for blood and an idiot boy swimming too far from safe shores – what then would you say?'

Kysnaros closed his eyes for a moment, shaking his head, the very image of patient benevolence. At his side, Lord Joros smiled, enjoying the jest.

'Logan,' the inquisitor replied. 'Come now, it's over. Will your Chapter really fight on without you?'

He laughed, the sound a brutal bark. 'Of course. Just as your Grey Knights would. We are brothers, us and them. If only one Wolf was left alive in all of mankind's Imperium, he'd still defy his enemies until the last breath fell from his broken body. Your knights are the same. I saw it in their eyes when we first met. I saw it when they duelled the Great Beast of Armageddon. I see it in each of them now. They know the value of blood and tears. You...' he nodded to the diminutive inquisitor, '...do not. And I wonder if you realise how you scar your Grey Knights' hearts against you, by committing them to wars they don't wish to fight.'

I felt my mouth open, and closed it quietly. Throne aflame, he made it hard not to admire him.

+He reads us like a scroll,+ Malchadiel sent.

+He really does.+ My eyes flicked to Lord Joros, his hands resting on his sheathed blades, much in the same way Jarl Grimnar leaned on his axe. +Well, some of us.+

Kysnaros was fast losing his feigned patience. 'Your flagship is lost.'

'We have other ships,' said Jarl Grimnar.

'Your Chapter cannot hope to stand against us.'

'No? Hmm.' The Great Wolf looked back over his shoulder at his men. 'The boy-lord says we can't stand against him.'

'Strange, my jarl,' replied one of the scruffy Wolves – a balding warrior with shaggy sideburns. 'We were doing well before they wiped their arses with an honourable oath of armistice.'

'Aye,' Rawthroat agreed. 'We were. Perhaps we should invite them to Fenris, jarl. They'd find a warmer welcome there.'

Grimnar nodded to their words, turning back to Joros and Kysnaros. 'Tell me, which one of you whoresons gave the order to open fire on our shieldless, weaponless vessels?'

'It was I,' said Joros. 'It gave me no pleasure, but the deed was done for the greater good.'

The jarl nodded. 'I've marked your face, knight. I'll remember it from now until the Wolftime. You have my word on that. No Fenrisian ever forgets one who violates the laws of sheathed blades and bared throats. Once those laws are broken, all rules of decorum and honour are abandoned. To betray a betrayer is never counted as a sin.'

Kysnaros tied his long blond hair into a ponytail, keeping any stray strands from his face. 'Enough of this. The Imperium's woes will not bide while we stand here and make superstitious promises. Chapter Master Grimnar, you will surrender as agreed, and your Wolves will stand down.'

Jarl Grimnar gave us his canine smile again, showing wet fangs. 'That,' he said, 'will not be happening.'

II

Lord Joros of the Eighth Brotherhood had ruled with a cautiously ambitious hand for seventy years. He was respected

by those of us in his brotherhood, though scarcely loved; a
warrior admired but rarely emulated.

The list of his deeds was more impressive than his unap-
proachable exterior might suggest. While he lacked a great
many commendations for command, as a duellist and a
front-line fighter, it was acknowledged across the order that
few could match his reputation and skills with two falchion
blades. A vital aspect in any blademaster's repertoire is the
ability to read an opponent's movements, and react with
greater speed than they can act in the first place. Joros was a
master, and his reflexes were renowned.

And yet, his blades had scarcely cleared his scabbards
when Logan Grimnar's axe of blackened steel and burnished
gold cleaved into our Grand Master's breastplate and throat,
ending a worthy, respectable life of service with a single
crunching chop.

Joros went down, felled by the axe blow and dead before
he hit the ground. The Great Wolf's axe – named Morkai after
some heathen Fenrisian superstition about a god guarding
the Halls of the Dead – ripped back out, blood sizzling on its
active metal surface. In the time it had taken me to look back
from Rawthroat to his liege lord, my own Grand Master was
slain. That should explain, at least partially, how quickly the
High King of Fenris moved.

'Hold!' Kysnaros screamed above the rattle and clank of a
hundred Grey Knights raising weapons; three hundred storm
troopers shouldering their hellguns; and a host of inquisitors
ready to react each according to their own proclivities.

None of us moved a muscle. None but Grimnar. The Great
Wolf swung his axe once, a casual arc to spray us with flecks
of our lord's blood.

'That's for my ship,' he said. 'Do you have yet more worthless words to babble, or are we finished here?'

'Logan... Lord Grimnar, your ship is lost and you have hundreds of weapons aiming right at your heart.' Kysnaros stepped around the slumped, bleeding body of the former Eighth Brotherhood Grand Master. 'It's over. Even you can see that it's over.'

Grimnar took a step back. 'The only thing I see is that oath-breaking son of a whore bleeding all over his own deck. I ask again, do you have more words, more threats, to share? We both know you need me for what you intend.'

'Surrender,' the lord inquisitor said softly.

'So you can use me as a banner of submission, to wave before the Wolves and pray it will force them to their knees? Tell me you're not foolish enough to think that would work.'

Kysnaros sneered, adding petulance to his array of expressions.

'Don't make me kill you.'

'Don't make me laugh.'

The teleportation flare flash-blinded several of the storm troopers closest to the aura of dispersion, and caused the deck to shiver beneath our boots.

But we were ready for it. Joros had told us to stand in readiness, and the moment had come. As the distant machinery aboard the *Scramaseax* pulled at the physical forms of Jarl Grimnar and his men, we threaded our powers through the veil between worlds, and pulled back. It felt like trying to hold water between my fingertips; I had no idea if it was even working.

The teleportation mist thinned and faded. Grimnar, Raw-throat and the other two Wolf Guard remained in place. I could see the jarl's reaction in that moment – how his fingers tightened around the haft of the axe, how his eyes narrowed as his mind raced. Like an animal backed into a corner, he was ready to fight no matter what. Beneath the instinctive readiness was a deeper intelligence – he was more than a warrior, he was a general calculating how much destruction he would wreak amongst his foes before finally falling to their blades.

I had no doubt he'd fight us even as we cut him to pieces. He'd gut a dozen of us before he breathed his last.

Any hesitation at all would have seen them dead or captured. We were already moving forwards, already marshalling our efforts to pin them in place with kinetic force, when Jarl Grimnar's storm bolter barked a single cry. His three Wolf Guard fired with him, each in different directions.

The explosive bolts smashed against ceramite in a chorus of detonation, preceding a moment of gruesome silence. Four knights crashed to the decking, each of them killed outright, holes blown through their throats.

'Hold!' Kysnaros cried again. 'Bind them!'

We released the power we'd gathered, but even as a mere piece of the whole communion, I could feel the weakness in our shared grasp. Grimnar had known how best to hurt us. Four justicars lay dead, with their squads reeling in the bond-broken moments of psychic fallout. Their squad leaders no longer channelled their powers into a unified force. Worse, I could feel each knight struggling against the onset of pain and anger threatening to overwhelm them.

Jarl Grimnar and his Wolves burst out of existence in a storm of light. I had a momentary glance, through the shielded hangar bay doors, of the wounded *Scramaseax* coming about and trying to make her final attempt at an escape.

Kysnaros looked at the four dead knights, then at Joros murdered at his feet.

'Let them go,' he said quietly.

TWENTY-THREE
ARMADA

I

None of us really understood Kysnaros. His thoughts and the reasons for his actions remained equal mysteries.

As time passed, it became clearer to all of us on the fleet's fringes that the lord inquisitor had earned his rank and title from a punishing series of small-scale crusades and street-level purges. Admirable work, no doubt. But he was ill-suited to managing a campaign of containment – especially one that was failing so catastrophically.

Worse, we'd driven the Wolves to show their teeth.

The Grey Knights destroyer *Blade's Fall* drifted back to the inquisitor's growing armada, reporting an inability to destroy its target: one of the troop vessels from Armageddon now docked at the Kyrius Expanse refuelling station. A Space Wolves cruiser patrolled around the installation hub, finally leaving with the transport when the whaleship was due to depart.

By that point, the hundred thousand men of the Uruvel Outriders had scattered across seven other vessels, departing for other warzones on other worlds. A lone Grey Knights ship had no chance of catching all of them, let alone destroying them all before they reached their destinations.

This was a story we came to hear a dozen times, each time with a different retinue of vessel names. And now, when the Wolves outnumbered and outgunned our pursuit ships, they let us know in no uncertain terms how the game had changed. The *Xiphos* and the *Makhaira*, sister ships to the *Karabela*, limped back to the armada's mustering point in the same week, both reporting Space Wolves vessels not only firing on them, but firing first.

We lost contact with the *Kaskara*, the *Spatha* and the *Glaive of Janus*; the latter serving for almost ten thousand years as the flagship of the First Brotherhood. The *Karabela* was one of the ships tasked with tracking it down, and to my eternal regret, we succeeded.

The night we found her, Castor broke from the warp at the edge of the Corolus System, tracking what both Malchadiel and I could only describe as a 'heartbeat in the warp'. Just hearing it gave me a headache – this insistent, throbbing pressure against my temples.

I knew the feeling, having sensed it once before.

'It feels like Armageddon,' I said to Annika. 'It feels like dawn on Armageddon, when the battle was won and a hundred of my brothers were gone in a moment of blood and fire.'

Locating the *Glaive* took no time at all. She was a hollow hulk orbiting an untouched Adeptus Mechanicus listening post, serving the priests of the Machine God as a bountiful source of scrap metal if the salvage crews crawling all over her were anything to go by.

'Kill them,' I'd ordered. 'Kill them all.'

Malchadiel shook his head. 'Belay that order, Captain Castor.' My brother stood before me, blocking my view of the parasites at their macabre work. 'Do you wish to be responsible for making this worse, Hyperion? Really? Don't make the Inquisition's war your own.'

We'd solved the mystery of the heartbeat in the warp. We'd been drawn by the sound, the pressure of the sensation, only to learn it was the lingering consciousness of over fifty of our order's most powerful knights, slain in a single blow.

'That,' Malchadiel had said, 'was why it felt like Armageddon. It was the very same thing.'

II

We rejoined the armada sixteen days later, coming home to find Kysnaros's fleet had grown yet again.

+Throne of the Emperor,+ Malchadiel pulsed when we saw what awaited us on the oculus.

'All stop.' Castor was out of his throne, straightening yet another brocade jacket. 'I said all stop, damn you.'

The screen was filled by the battlements of a vast battle-barge, drifting in slow patrol. Along its red-armoured hull, white skulls were painted in unity with the stylised black 'I' of the Inquisition.

'Identify yourself,' the vox crackled, 'or be destroyed.'

'That seems a trifle theatrical...' Castor said, before looking over at the both of us.

'Identify yourself,' I replied.

'This is the Adeptus Astartes battleship *In Sacred Trust*, serving the Holy Ordos of the God-Emperor's Inquisition. I repeat, identify yourself.'

Malchadiel looked at me. 'God-Emperor?'

I took a breath. 'Fanatics.' Rare were the Chapters that

ever considered the Emperor a god. Such belief was for
the deluded masses we were sworn to protect. 'This is the
Grey Knights frigate *Karabela*, returning to the armada as
ordered.'

A pause. Perhaps a relay of identification information,
passed from ship to ship in search of clearance. How things
had changed. We'd never before broadcast our actions across
the fleet network, in keeping with our codes of secrecy. For
all Kysnaros's fervour, he was damning every human to a
mind-scouring purely for the fact they'd witnessed our ships,
let alone seen us in the flesh. I wondered if he was as blind
to his own hypocrisy as he seemed. You could never tell with
inquisitors; no other creed of human being is as apt to twist
their perceptions to suit their own desires.

'Proceed, *Karabela*.'

'Identify your Chapter, if you please.'

'We are the Red Hunters, and deeply honoured to serve our
lords alongside the Knights of Titan.'

I didn't reply. Castor terminated the vox-channel with a
single switch click, and raised his immaculately trimmed
eyebrows.

'I have a question, and one I believe is relevant to the situation at hand.

'Ask it.'

'Your Codex Astartes lists that a Space Marine Chapter shall
number one thousand warriors, does it not?'

'It does.' Among a million other regulations and rituals.

'Auspex readings indicate almost twenty ships in Red Hunters colours have joined the armada. That would suggest we're
dealing with...'

I looked back at the oculus. Malchadiel joined me at the
railing, as we cleared the bulk of *In Sacred Trust*, and bore
witness to the war-fleet beyond. It was suddenly much easier

to see why Kysnaros and his allies commanded such power and influence within the Inquisition.

'Their entire Chapter is here. Kysnaros has summoned an entire Chapter.'

III

We'd been back two days before the order finally came. Another five ships were reported destroyed or assumed lost, and although his voice was thickened by reluctance, Kysnaros appeared before every officer and knight in the fleet via hololithic image.

At the end of the cold war's eighth month, with the Terran standard calendar ready to turn from 444.M41 into the new solar year 445, Lord Inquisitor Kysnaros finally ordered us to abandon pursuit of any vessel tainted by the Armageddon conflict.

None of us were surprised by his admission of defeat. After seven months of harrowing interception duty, destroying undefended outposts, annihilating civilian transports, and exchanging brief, passionless butchery with the Wolves, we'd expected his eventual capitulation.

We were wrong.

'Fenris!' The robed, life-sized hololith spread his arms in beneficence. 'We shall make all speed to Fenris, home world of the treasonous Wolves. There we shall give them the ultimate choice: to serve loyally once more, after a penitent crusade of appropriate length... or to enter the sequestered archives as sinners never to be spoken of again.'

Fenris. The fortress-monastery of a First Founding Chapter. This was no longer a matter of skirmishes and sporadic void battles. Malchadiel looked at me in disbelief.

+Civil war,+ he sent from the other side of Captain Castor's throne.

What could I say to that? I nodded in agreement, unwilling and unable to lie to my brother.

IV

For the first time in months, I went to Annika before she could come to me.

I didn't wait on ceremony or manners – I didn't even knock on her chamber door. The bulkhead rolled open at my psychic pull, and I walked right inside.

During the more than a year of our companionship, I'd grown closer to Annika than I had to any other human I could recall. Not counting my former life, she was practically the only human I'd ever conversed with in depth, beyond a few long discussions with Captain Castor over games of regicide.

I'd touched minds with her a thousand times and more – at times both apt and awkward. Once, she'd been painting a scene of her home world with an amateur's eager hand, and had refused to speak to me for days after I'd distracted her at a crucial moment. Another time, I'd touched her mind the same moment as Clovon was touching her flesh, and I'd immediately recoiled with my skin crawling. On yet another occasion, I'd interrupted her in a fistfight with Darford, and my voice in her mind had interfered enough with her focus that she'd had her nose broken.

I'd trained with her myself, watching the play of her muscles as she sparred, and smelling the scent of her sweat from across the room. Even a healthy animal like Annika tired so much faster than a knight ever did. I found that fascinating, to see the differences of Adeptus Astartes physiology highlighted in such stark, visible terms. It's one thing to be considered divine. It's quite another to see comparative evidence.

I'd also listened to her speak of the ordos and their politics. I'd heard tales of her past purges and operations that went awry. I'd learned Fenrisian curse words from her lips, and taught her many of the myriad ways of blocking incoming blows with a quarterstaff.

On more than one occasion I'd stood with her and her warband in the communal showers after training, blind and numb to any sensation of desire, watching her wash her hair and listening to her speak of serving in the sweltering jungles of Voroxis, killing heretics who spilled from a downed rogue trader vessel.

Bizarrely, the Khatan had declared, upon seeing me wash myself, that my ascension to knighthood was 'a great shame'. Captain Castor had explained the meaning to me several months later, though I still didn't see the humour in it.

Inquisitor Jarlsdottyr had grown colder to me since Armageddon's aftermath, only reinforcing her natural stubbornness. She was Fenrisian, and she was on the edge of war with her own High King. Beyond that, she was an inquisitor. She answered to no one.

Tonight, I decided she would answer to me.

Still, for all our shared experience, there was one thing I wasn't prepared to walk in and see.

Malchadiel stood in her chamber, armed and armoured as always. Axium was next to him, flanked by several of his senior tech-priests. Darford, Clovon, the Khatan, Vasilla, Merrick and Faith all stood in a loose crescent with the others – each of them armed and in their eclectic clash of uniforms and armour.

The oculus monitor on her wall showed a quad-screened display of four faces: two female, two male, each of them an inquisitor I recognised from the hangar bay when we'd captured Jarl Grimnar. Present in hololithic form were seven

– seven – Grey Knights, four of whom were of justicar rank, from a variety of brotherhoods. Their flickering holo-avatars were projected from the imagifier table against one wall.

Annika stood at the heart of this gathering, her Cretacian bolter slung over one shoulder, hanging by its worn strap. Her dark hair was swept back in a spiralling braid, and her face was marked with fresh tribal hunting paint. She'd clearly been in the middle of addressing everyone.

'Hyperion,' she said.

I stood in silence. I may have blinked. Either way, I'm certain I looked as foolish as I felt.

'Is there something you need?' she asked.

I looked over the gathering one by one. 'I'm going to kill Lord Inquisitor Kysnaros,' I said.

She didn't miss a beat. 'Come in, then. Your ideas are as welcome as anyone else's.'

'How long as has this been going on?'

'Long enough.' Annika grinned.

'Forgive me, brother,' Malchadiel said quietly. 'We feared to bring you in among us.'

'In the Emperor's name, Mal… why?'

Annika was the one to answer. 'We thought you might say no.'

TWENTY-FOUR
FENRIS

I

They say Fenris breeds cold souls. One had only to look at the world from orbit to see why.

From above, no world looked bleaker – not the thirsting wastes of Tallarn, nor the tropical chaos of Volaxis. Fenris was a world at war with itself. Somewhere in the twisted trails of its history, something had aggravated the planet's very soul. The sea warred with the land, swallowing continents whole, every decade or two, only to disgorge new landmasses – rank with soil poisoned by seawater – elsewhere on the globe. These sour landscapes battled the sky, punching mountains heavenwards in breathtaking ranges unmatched anywhere else in mankind's galaxy.

Even from orbit, it was clear Fenris could never sustain civilised life. Cities would sink at the whims of the drowning seas, and what few landmasses seemed stable were earth-dead from eternal winter. Agriculture didn't exist on that world.

No Fenrisian was ever born a farmer, and none ever became one later in life. The people who called the world home were reavers, raiders, hunters and sailors. It must be said, they made excellent stock for an Adeptus Astartes breeding world.

I'd read that Fenrisian myth blamed their world's instability on a great kraken – a creature of the deepest seas – that wrapped its tentacles around the planet's core and strangled the world's heart. The human imagination never ceased to fascinate me. Against all reason, a human man or woman could convince themselves of anything.

We watched the world turn beneath us, dotted by occasional storms over the frost-choked land, but existing in slow ignorance of its potential death that we carried in our warships' weapon bays.

'It looks so different,' Annika said, staring at the oculus. 'The islands I knew even a handful of years ago are already drowned, and new ones have risen, with new wars and new raids fought to claim them.'

She sounded almost wistful.

Fenris, like any home world of the Adeptus Astartes, boasted a legion of defences. A network of orbital missile platforms and weaponised satellites ringed the world with incendiary teeth, while the Wolves' fortress-monastery, known variously as the Aett, the Fang, and a host of other names, was hewn from a great range of mountains, and reached high enough into the sky that its tallest spires linked with the orbital dockyards. In a galaxy of wonders, Fenris from orbit managed to take my breath away. Nature at its most tectonically savage, blanketed in neverending winter.

The sternest deterrent to any souls brave or foolhardy enough to lay siege to a fortress-monastery world was the Chapter's battlefleet. Our ramshackle void campaign had taken care of that last, best line of defence better than any of us had predicted. The Wolves' ships had been called away in packs – first to bear troops into the meat grinder at Armageddon, then over a span of months to defend escaping troop ships or isolated void stations from predation at our hands, across any number of sectors.

The Wolves were only one Chapter, stretched thin and bled dry. Honour, they possessed in abundance – but honour doesn't build ships or breed Space Marines. Honour doesn't defend a world without warships in the sky.

A lone vessel suckled at the cold comfort of its home world's orbital docks. A lone strike cruiser, docked at the Fang's apex, scarred from its own crusades and badly in need of repair. Such a ship would usually have an escort of frigates and destroyers, though none were in evidence. Perhaps they'd risked even those out in the aftermath of Armageddon, trusting in the Aett's impregnable defences.

But we had no need to besiege the fortress itself, when we could pull the world apart beneath its very foundations.

Kysnaros shared nothing of his intent. He was a hololithic presence among us – a ghost on every bridge – watching and keeping his own counsel. Occasionally, a Red Hunters captain would materialise next to him, speaking of fleet formations or angles of effective planetary bombardment, before shimmering back out of existence.

Nor did he reveal the extent of his ties to the Red Hunters.

'I've found nothing,' Annika admitted. 'Kysnaros lives and serves outside the ordos. His power and influence are from a past he chooses not to share, rather than laid bare in a paper trail others can follow.'

The armada spread across the Fenrisian heavens, ringing the Fang's spires and turning all weapons down to face the planet. Kysnaros waited until every vessel was in place, according to his preset coordinates, before appearing before us.

A servo-skull projected his image. The skull of a human male – jawless and augmented by anti-gravitic suspensors – floated along at approximately human height. That brought it to my chest. The drone bobbed and weaved through the air in a calm drift, its right eye socket clicking and ticking as it projected Kysnaros's image.

Talwyn was less than amused. I don't think he liked being watched on his own bridge.

'Does every ship in the fleet have one of these now?'

'I believe so,' Malchadiel replied.

I said nothing. I merely watched Kysnaros. For once, he wore a suit of contoured power armour, sculpted to resemble the musculature of a slender, healthy human male. A cloak of wolf fur completed the uncharacteristically militant look. I didn't want to know how he'd come to be in possession of such a thing. The idea that he'd stolen it from one of our captives was abhorrent, as was the possibility he'd looted it from the dead.

Despite his new, lordly attire, his hololithic avatar was formed from pelucid, thin light, as it walked among the crews gathered on every bridge deck.

I didn't hate him. I wanted to, but I couldn't muster the requisite depth of emotion. None of us hated him, not even Annika. Hatred thrives on familiarity and intimacy, and struggles to grow in less fertile hearts. He wasn't a figure of loathing and lies, cackling at the notion of genocide for bloodshed's own sake. He was merely a man, one we scarcely knew, who turned our talents to unwholesome ends. Pragmatism moved him above all else. In that regard, he was no different from any one of a thousand other inquisitors. He was no worse than any one of a hundred Grey Knights, either. Many of our order might even have admired him for his conservative behaviour in the aftermath of Armageddon.

The oculus painted a bleak picture. Fenris was as close to undefended as it might possibly be. A lone strike cruiser in orbit seemed a custodian of sorts, perhaps here by chance, perhaps assigned in perpetuity to watch over the world below. I learned much later that it had sustained significant damage mere weeks before, aiding an Imperial Navy patrol in the local region in a suppression action against a pirate fleet. At the time, I merely saw the burn marks tiger-striping its pockmarked hull, and wondered if this, truly, was all the Wolves had left in the vicinity, with their fleet engaged elsewhere.

And our ships were faster, by far. Even had it come down to a race to reach Fenris, the Wolves were weeks behind. Were several Fenrisian warships even now bolting through the Sea of Souls to reach their home world and form a bulwark against invasion? Probably. Likely, even. By the time they broke from the warp, it would all be over, one way or another.

I watched the warship's engines open up, the booster housings rolling back to breathe hotter, wider, whiter into space. Once under way, the warship rolled and turned in a precise drift, until it came abeam of *Corel's Hope*.

'Why have you not answered our hails?' came a voice from the ship's command deck.

'In all honesty,' Kysnaros replied, 'I've been seeking the right words. I never meant for it to end this way. I still pray we might finish this lamentable conflict without further bloodshed. Tell me, noble Wolf of Fenris, do you know why we've come? Do you know why I've brought this mighty fleet into the stars above your world?'

Captain Castor paid no attention to the exchange. His focus rested on the screeds of data uploaded from the lone vessel.

'They're running out their guns,' he said. 'And charging their void shields, though the damage they're showing means they won't last six seconds against even a tenth of our fleet.'

'We know why you've come.' The voice held less warmth than a stone. 'You've come to see Fenris bleed, to soothe the shame of your own black heart. Kill every man, woman and child who knows of your cowardice, and you can go back to feigning bravery. Aye, inquisitor. I am Taurangian the Cutter, and I know why you've come.'

Kysnaros's reply was heavy with abject regret, all the more repellant because of its aching sincerity. The lord inquisitor was a soul forever speaking as if the weight of the Imperium's worlds rested upon his shoulders.

'Is there none among your Chapter that can wield reason and wit as well as an axe? Must every confrontation end with recrimination?'

'What do you want from us? We will never bend the knee to you. We will never bare our throats to end this war. What do you want that we would ever willingly give?'

'An end to this. I want to speak with one who can end it, before it truly begins.'

The answer was almost a minute in coming. 'Aye, lord. There's one among us like that.'

Kysnaros's hololith was flickering in and out of focus, strangled by interference from so many ships close by. 'Your world and your Chapter stand on the very edge of ruin, Taurangian. If you have one who can speak for the Wolves, then bring him forth. I pray only that he uses wiser words than your High King did. Both sides must compromise, and forgo yet more attempts at heroics.'

'Give us four hours,' replied Taurangian.

'You will have it,' promised Kysnaros.

His avatar turned, looking with slow care around the bridge – around every bridge, I assume. He stared right through

Malchadiel, Annika, Castor, and a half-dozen crew officers.

'Hyperion,' his hololith said, without warning. The flickering image was looking directly at me.

'My lord?'

'You are the one the Fenrisians name Bladebreaker, aren't you?'

'One Fenrisian named me that, lord. I cannot speak for all of them.'

'But you broke the primarch's blade.'

'I did, lord.'

He nodded, and looked away into the middle distance. 'May I speak with you, please? On board *Corel's Hope*?'

II

He stood within an ocularium, alone but for the monitors lining the walls, which were so numerous and dense that they reminded me of scales along a reptile's hide. Each screen displayed a view from the command deck of one of the fleet's ships, letting him see through the eyes of his servo-skulls.

He smiled when I entered, and blanked the screens with a vague wave of his hand. A psyker, then. Formidable, surely. As powerful as myself or Malchadiel? Unlikely.

+Don't be so certain.+ He smiled again as he sent the words.

'You summoned me, lord?'

He shook his head, the smile fading. 'Quite the opposite. I asked you to come.'

'Of course.'

'I wished to speak in private, Hyperion. We have to end this, and end it now. Wait. Let me finish. I already see resistance in your eyes, but listen for a moment. Mistakes have been made. I shoulder the burden of blame. But there's still time. The Wolves can escape destruction, and the Inquisition will leave them in peace. We simply need to guide the process.'

I looked at him in disbelief. 'You've brought an entire Chapter, and a battlefleet, into the skies above their home world. Even if you turn tail and run right away, they will never forgive the Inquisition.'

'There are two sides to every coin. Have I mustered an entire Chapter in support of this fleet? Yes, but only to show the Wolves they cannot claim the moral high ground as members of the precious Adeptus Astartes. Not when another Chapter stands in opposition to them.'

'The Grey Knights already stood with you, against them.'

He shook his head, meeting my eyes. 'Out of a tenuous loyalty alone. Many more of your brothers could – and should – have joined us by now. Do you not think it strange that they haven't?'

'The galaxy is a vast place, lord. We are only a thousand men. Little more than eight hundred now, in the aftermath of Armageddon and the Months of Shame.'

'The Months of Shame.' Kysnaros gave a small snort. 'How strange to hear the name history will remember you by. No worse than I deserve, admittedly. But you're right. The Grey Knights have a greater, wider calling than this debacle. Which is why I've not summoned them. I could have. Many inquisitors would have by now. But I have no desire to pull them away from their other duties. Even if I did, it presupposes the Grey Knights will actually fire if I had to give the order.'

He looked at me for several heartbeats. 'And will they?'

'Some may.'

'Exactly,' Kysnaros replied, raking his hands through his long hair again. 'Some may. Most will not. This is not your role, and not your place. I am guilty of dragging you away from your Emperor-sworn mandate, and into the politics of the Imperium. For that, I apologise.'

'It… surprises me to hear you speak this way, lord.'

'I'm sure it does. The Red Hunters are a blunt instrument to the Sons of Titan's scalpel. They will fire, Hyperion. And they'll count it a great honour to do so. Even so, I brought them to make my point with their presence, not their warships' guns. The Wolves must stand down. The alternative is too grotesque to countenance. Skirmishes in the void are one thing. So what if a little pride gets wounded and a handful of men lose their lives? That means nothing in the scale of the Imperium. Savaging a First Founding home world is a different and darker tale. It's far beyond sanity. But the Wolves must stand down. They cannot question the Throne like this. It cannot be allowed. What can I do?'

This wasn't going the way I'd expected. I'd been so certain I'd come here alone, safe in the knowledge he'd be dead once I left. I said nothing. I simply watched him.

Kysnaros laughed. 'Yes, well, murder is a bold move, but I understand why you feel forced into it. If I haven't dissuaded you yet, I hope to have done so by the time you leave.'

I guarded my thoughts tighter, closer, behind a wall of concentration. There are certain deceptions to learn, a wealth of simple exercises that can shield one's thoughts when willpower alone will not suffice. I focused part of my attention counting the beats of my heart, and trying to count his at the same time.

'Very nicely done.' He smiled again. 'Now all I hear are the numbers accruing in your mind. A child's trick, but a timeless one. I've used it myself often enough.'

'Why didn't you force Jarl Grimnar to heed your commands? You're powerful enough to do it through psychic imprint alone.'

He sighed, shaking his head. 'Some stories have no villain, Hyperion. Merely a mix of souls, each seeking to find where the answers lie. Help me, damn you. Stop staring at me with your eyes full of judgement and help me. How can we end this? Shackling Grimnar to my will would damn him in the eyes of his Chapter. They'd declare war on the Adeptus Terra, and how many Chapters would join them? Even one would be too many. I will not preside over another Horus Heresy, a reliving of the Reign of Blood, or a second Nova Terra Interregnum.'

'What did Lord Joros advise you?'

'Poor Joros. Noble to the last, taking the blame for my orders.' Kysnaros paced the room. 'He advised threatening them, showing them our own strength, drawing comparisons to alpha male animals in the wild. It sounded right, Hyperion. It felt right.'

'The Wolves aren't animals. No beast is bound by honour, nor does it sacrifice itself for others outside its pack.'

Kysnaros knuckled his tired eyes. 'And how well I've learned that lesson. But there must be some answer, somewhere. Joros gave me little counsel, beyond swearing he could arrange for his men to fire when the final order came. He suggested we posture, so we did. He assured me the threats would work, so we threatened. He swore taking Grimnar captive would end the war, so we ambushed and betrayed them at an armistice. The blame is mine and mine alone. I will not hide from it, and I've recorded my culpability in the archives myself. But I'd never even met one of the Adeptus Astartes before. Joros was a mutual commander and advisor in the face of the Wolves' intolerable independence. He was difficult to work with, but what could I do? As I said, I have no desire to demand more resources from Titan's fleet. I couldn't demand another leader for so few Grey Knights, when they had a duly elected one already here.'

We didn't elect most of our commanders – Joros was a

Brotherhood Champion who ascended over our last Grand Master's body on the battlefield – but now was hardly the time to duel over the details.

'We stand on the edge of civil war, lord. What would you have of me?'

'The Fenrisians respect you, do they not?'

'One of them did. I should add, that was before we betrayed him and his High King.'

'No, your tale has spread more than you imagine. You're the right choice, I know it. You have to do this thing for me, Hyperion. The Wolves will send their ambassador to us in less than two hours. I need you to meet with him, alongside me. We can end this. We will end it. We can't let pride and stupidity push us past the point of no return.'

I could still kill him. I could kill him now, and end this with a single lost life. One murder was all it would take. One instant of casting aside all honour, all righteousness, for the sake of expedience and pragmatism. One sin to spare thousands of lives. Joros would be proud to hear me think it.

'Hyperion.' The lord inquisitor looked at me for a long moment, meeting my stare with his green eyes. 'I have a question.'

'Ask it.'

'No Grey Knight has ever fallen. No Grey Knight has ever served the Archenemy, or tasted the taint of the Ruinous Powers. No Grey Knight has ever succumbed to mutation, or corruption, or any heresy of thought and deed. Will you tell me why?'

I searched his face for any signs of mockery. More than that, I searched his soul. I wasn't gentle, either. It was a ransacking, a violation; the wards I held around my mind crumbled as I slipped free of my own consciousness, and rifled my way through his heart. I sensed a thousand fears, hopes, concerns, joys... but no mockery, and no sour tang of deception. None aimed at me in that moment.

He smiled, barely, as he allowed my painful intrusion unopposed. 'I'm glad you see my sincerity. Perhaps I can explain the question better.'

'Please,' I said, and withdrew from his consciousness like a blade unsheathing from a wound. He grunted at another stab of pain, and wiped his bleeding nose.

'You stand before me here with murder in your eyes. Such deeds, such emotions, pull at the Dark Gods' attentions. But no Grey Knight has ever fallen to them. Are you free to act with impunity, forever protected purely by genetic divinity? Can you revel in bloodshed and sin, knowing you cannot be corrupted?'

He raised a finger, cutting off my answer. 'Or,' he continued, 'is it a struggle to always remain pure of thought and deed, against the madness and malice that would stain all other souls?'

I wasn't sure how to reply. 'You're asking the fundamental question that lies at the heart of our order. We ask it ourselves, from the moment we first don the grey and silver, to the night we inevitably die in battle. Philosopher-soldiers among our ranks have written treatises on the subject for millennia.'

Kysnaros nodded. 'And do you have the answer? Hyperion, what is the Emperor's Gift? A license to do as you please, safeguarded against the evils that wrack our species? Or is it a sacred charge, a responsibility you have to live up to, fighting every second to remain purer than the species you're sworn to defend?'

'I don't know. None of us know.'

He was still meeting my eyes. 'But what do you believe?'

What did I believe? Did I even wish to share it with an

outsider? Annika had asked me it herself, on countless occasions. Each time I'd changed the subject, or simply walked away.

'I believe each of us makes that choice ourselves.'

Lord Inquisitor Kysnaros stepped closer to me, and lifted my gauntlet in both his hands. He aimed the storm bolter on my forearm directly at his heart. I had only to close my fist to fire the weapon.

'Then choose,' he said.

TWENTY-FIVE
ABOVE THE STORM

I

'We can't trust him.'

When Annika was adamant about something, there was no arguing with her. Galeo might have convinced her through dignified arguments punctuated by meaningful silences, but she rarely listened to anyone else with the same grace.

'We can't trust him.' Those were her first words upon leaving our Stormraven, once Malchadiel had flown her over. I'd told her everything, then waited for her response. 'We can't trust him.' She turned to Kysnaros, who stood at my side. 'We can't trust you.' Annika had never been shy about speaking her mind to people's faces.

The hangar bay's noise killed any hope of polite conversation. She was practically shouting over the sound of a Lightning fighter plane being craned and winched into place, while Kysnaros's smile was so false it might have been painted across a face of blank, tanned flesh.

'I understand your reservations, Annika.'

She shushed him with a glare. 'You understand nothing about me. Nothing. I know why you've changed your song, Ghesmei. You know there are elements in the fleet ready to move against you. You fear them. So now you'll try anything to crawl out of the fate you deserve.'

Kysnaros made no effort to deny it, though neither did he betray any evidence of agreeing. From what I'd sensed of his mind, there was no trace of deception, but arguing with her was as fruitless as demanding the sun refuse to rise.

'Killing me now will change nothing,' he said.

'No?' Annika's pale eyes were thin slits. 'I don't trust your judgement in that, either.'

'Annika...' I said, with an edge of warning. We didn't have time for this, and even if we did, it would serve nothing. 'The Wolves have summoned us to meet their ambassador. Come with us. Speak for the ordos. We can end this while it's still a series of awkward skirmishes that shame us all. Warriors become proud of wars – even those that shouldn't have been fought.'

She looked at me as if I were speaking another language. 'You have no idea who the Wolves are sending, do you?'

Instinctively, I pushed into her mind, but she hid the answers well. 'No,' I confessed. 'Do you?'

'I can guess. I only hope I'm right.'

II

We met above the storm. That's how high we were.

The Wolves agreed to meet on a landing platform close to the Fang's peak, which put us below the atmospheric crest but far above the clouds. I watched the storm from above – a blanket of charcoal smoke, hiding the entire world beneath us – feeling myself a little mesmerised by the sporadic flashes of lightning. Every burst cast a spear of sharp light through the black heavens.

The air was thin enough that I had no desire to test it. I breathed slowly, tasting my suit's recycled oxygen supply. I'd been in my armour since just after Armageddon; the ceramite suit's link-ports chafed where they bonded with my skin, and the internal air supply was beginning to taste of my own sweat.

While power armour was built to be worn for days, weeks, even months if necessary, that didn't mean it was pleasant after a few weeks. Waste was minimised by regulating intake, but the real trouble came in the form of rashes on the skin, which couldn't be cleaned or disinfected without the armour being unplugged and detached, segment by segment.

We came down by gunship – Annika, Kysnaros, myself, and Malchadiel piloting. Darford had no shortage of complaints about being left behind, but the others merely wished us luck.

It was cold on the aerial platform. I knew that from my retinal display's temperature gauge, though it was obvious enough from the howling wind and the diamond-dust layer of frost coating the tower's walls. Malchadiel and I were immune to the cold in our armour, as was Kysnaros in his contoured suit. Annika wore a rebreather, but other than that, did nothing more than throw a cloak over her thin body armour. When I'd given her a questioning look, she'd rolled her eyes.

'I was born here.'

That settled it, then.

We waited on the platform, facing the wind, not far from the shadow of our Stormraven. It was difficult not to tense when the tower's bulkheads began to unlock on loud hydraulics. There was no way Jarl Grimnar could have reached

Fenris by now, but the ambassador serving in his place was likely to be just as stubborn. War would come, without both sides compromising. Kysnaros spoke for an Inquisition that needed an untrustworthy ally to kowtow to its wishes; the Space Wolves ambassador would speak for an independent army devoted to the Imperium's people, not its laws.

Annika was right. It would be simpler just to kill Kysnaros.

With a storm hurling hail at the fortress below us, and the wind blasting through the tower tops, we faced the opening bulkhead. Dull red lighting did nothing to illuminate the figure within, but I knew what it was as soon as it started walking forwards. The platform shivered with each step it took, and once it was out in the moonlight, its riveted, armoured hull was unmistakable.

Annika burst into tears. I'd never seen anything like it – one moment she was composed, staring daggers at Kysnaros; the next she was weeping softly, her hands up to her rebreather mask, the tears freezing into silver trickles down her cheeks.

I turned from the advancing war machine to glance at her. 'Mistress?'

She was already sliding down to her knees, still weeping, staring up at the approaching figure.

'He's real,' she said in a whisper over the vox. 'Don't you understand? Don't you see? He's real.'

The Dreadnought stomped closer, drawing to a halt some ten metres away. Moonlight became bladed lines on the edges of its dense armour plating. Tribal paintwork marked its old, old hull. One of the war machine's arms was a heavy, brutal rotary cannon – lowered and aiming away from us. The other arm was closer to humanoid, ending in a curved, vicious array of metal talons.

I looked at the sarcophagus fronting the armoured walker, showing ivory and bronze carvings of wolves, Fenrisian runes, and talismanic scripture. Rising from the thing's back, flapping in the wind, was a faded war banner depicting a lone Wolf in armour of pale grey, his left hand rendered as curving claws of white fire. He stood proud, facing the setting sun in the west, with one boot on a pile of ancient helmets. I recognised the colours of the Bearers of the Word, the Warriors of Iron, the Lords of the Night… Those most ancient of foes, forming the Legions of the Eye.

Annika wouldn't stop weeping. It wasn't a display of undignified wailing – but the soft, muffled weeping was becoming unnerving. They were a pilgrim's tears, shed in a temple at the end of a long journey.

'You're real,' she whispered to the towering war machine.

'**Of course I'm real.**' The Dreadnought's voice was bionic thunder. '**Get up off your knees, foolish girl.**'

Kysnaros looked between Annika and the war machine, his face behind the rebreather betraying his confusion. He dearly wished to begin negotiations, but suddenly had no idea how.

'I am Ghesmei Kysnaros,' he said to the Dreadnought. 'A ranking lord in His Holy Majesty's Inquisition.'

I was only peripherally aware of their conversation. The name inscribed on the sarcophagus couldn't be real. If it was, it meant…

Oh. Throne of Terra.

'My lord,' I said, as I went to one knee myself.

The Dreadnought turned slightly on its waist axis, with a low growl of sacred mechanics. '**Enough of this. Get up.**'

'…and a duly appointed representative of the God-Emperor…' Kysnaros finished, still unsure where to look.

'**God-Emperor?**' The Dreadnought made the sound of gears slipping, grinding together. From the booming augmetic tone, I assumed it was supposed to be laughter. Either that, or an internal weapons system reloading. '**Calling him a god**

was how all this mess started.'

Kysnaros was wrong-footed again, thrice now in a single minute. 'What do you... I don't–'

'Nothing. Times change, and that's the truth of it.' The war machine turned again, facing all three of us. **'Now. What brings you into the night sky above Fenris, and why shouldn't I break your little fleet into pieces with this castle's many, many guns?'**

The lord inquisitor straightened his back at that. 'Please name yourself, sir, as I have done. Then negotiations may begin in good faith.'

'Are you blind, little man? It's written on my coffin.'

I couldn't let this go on any longer. Not only was it blasphemy, it bordered on excruciating.

+His name is Bjorn, called the Fell-Handed. First Great Wolf of the Chapter, and second High King of Fenris after Jarl Russ, the primarch himself. They woke him to deal with us.+

Kysnaros's eyes never left the armoured shell, and the black iron coffin bound on its front.

'You... You walked in the Age of the Emperor?'

Bjorn made the gear-grinding chuckle again. **'Walked, ran, pissed and killed. I did it all. I met the Allfather, you know. Fought at his side more than once. I do believe he liked me.'**

Kysnaros slowly, slowly went to his knees.

'Oh, for... Not you as well.'

III

The Dreadnought turned to me, when Kysnaros had explained the story of Armageddon.

'Is that true?' he asked, unashamedly blunt. **'You broke the Black Blade?'**

I looked at the sarcophagus bound to the hulk's front, connected by adamantite bonding clamps and cable-linked life support feeds.

'It's true, Jarl Bjorn.'

'Just Bjorn. I don't sit on thrones any more, and I no longer rule anything at all. I saw Angron, both before the Change and after it. Breaking the Black Blade is no mean feat, knight. I fear you earned yourself your own walking coffin with that deed.'

The thought turned my blood to ice. 'I would rather sleep in the Dead Fields, alongside my brothers.'

'There speaks a man who believes he has a choice about such things. Heroes never do. Heroes get to be immortal, awoken every few centuries for another war, or to share the Old Tales with yet another generation.'

As if for emphasis, he took a lumbering step forwards. His claw could have wrapped around any one of us with ease, so to see the gentleness with which he touched Annika was almost heartbreaking. The war machine rotated his wrist servos, rattling and grinding as he rolled his claw. Then, with the flat of one savagely sharp talon, he tilted her head to one side, then the other, showing the tears of ice on her pale cheeks.

'Enough tears now, little maiden. You have the look of the frostborn about you. What tribe, huntress?'

'The Broken Tusk, Great King.' Her voice was a mouse's, no louder than that.

'I still remember them. Vicious bastards, every one. A blessing in a battle if they were on your side, and a curse if they weren't. Awful sailors, though. That's the sad truth.'

The Dreadnought stepped back, releasing her cheek. 'No finer sight on any world than a frostborn maiden. Especially a beauty with black hair. Rare back when I had eyes to stare, and surely even rarer now.'

I stared at the towering figure, wondering if there was some difference in the process by which gene-seed was once culti-vated compared to the method now. He seemed to be able to determine that Annika was attractive. I wasn't sure I could make that perception myself, and I had a thousand other questions to ask: about the warrior's experiences in the age of the Heresy; about witnessing the Emperor in person; about the classes of vessels that once sailed the stars and now no longer saw use...

'So,' the Dreadnought interrupted my reverie. **'Move ahead to the part that convinces me not to destroy your little fleet. Or I might just slay you, and end this with no effort at all.'**

Kysnaros bristled, but held his temper. 'Others will come, Jarl Bjorn. Doz–'

'I told you. Just Bjorn.'

'I... yes. But... Dozens. Hundreds. I didn't come to see Fenris burn, but mark my words, this world will die if the Wolves don't compromise. Too many inquisitors view this as the perfect chance to rein in that famous and inconvenient Adeptus Astartes autonomy, and silence a troubling voice once and for all. The Wolves are beloved by the people of the Imperium that know of their existence, but the institutions of the Adeptus Terra are far less well-disposed towards the Sons of Fenris.'

The Dreadnought seemed to consider this. **'Small men with small concerns. Make your case, inquisitor.'**

'A penitent crusade would appease the Inquisition. A cen-tury... Perhaps two.'

'You want us to send an entire generation of Wolves out into the stars, cloaked in shame, to appease fools who fail to serve the Imperium half as well as we do.'

'It's the only compromise that allows both sides to endure without conflict.'

'You remind me of a remembrancer I once knew.'

'I don't know what that is, Jarl Bjorn.'

'A remembrancer is a parasite paid to remember things. This one had a tongue like a snake and the heart of a weasel. He'd seek to convince everyone that his poems were works of genius, and that all critics were simply too foolish to appreciate him. That's what you remind me of. The same failure of conviction. So try harder.'

Kysnaros was drawing breath to do exactly that, when a sickle-shaped Trecenti warning rune flashed white on my retinal display.

'Wait. Something's wrong.'

Kysnaros reached a hand to his ear, re-tuning the vox-bead there. 'The... the Wolves are back. Their entire fleet just broke warp.'

'How is that possible?' I asked. Behind us, Malchadiel was already powering up the gunship's engines.

'I don't know. But they're inbound, and...'

'And they can see an enemy fleet with its weapons aimed down at the Fang. Your move, inquisitor.'

TWENTY-SIX
KINDRED

I

By the time we reached *Corel's Hope*'s strategium, the Wolves
fleet was in vox-range. The battleship's bridge was a nightmare of activity and sound compared to the *Karabela*'s stately
operation, though I was guiltily grateful my presence sent
crew scurrying away from me. Too many humans, too many
smells, all too close. I wasn't made to be paraded in public.

Even appearing in front of these officers had set them in
line for a mind-scrape at best, and an execution at worst. My
skin crawled each time I felt one looking at me. With four
hundred serfs, servitors, officers and slaves – my skin never
stopped crawling. The noise of their minds was a distracting
miasma of emotion, and not for the first time did I wonder
if humans simply felt things stronger than we do. Once we
receive the Emperor's Gift, does it dampen our capacity to
feel and sense as a normal human did?

Maddening, to think of such things now.

Kysnaros tore off his rebreather, leaning both hands on the railing of the central raised dais.

'Is the channel open?'

'Yes, sire,' came a nearby officer's reply.

'This is Lord Inquisitor Kysnaros to the Space Wolves fleet. Negotiations have begun in good faith. Divert your course and hold off from engaging us.'

The voice that replied was thunder given guttural, unamused life. 'I am Jarl Grimnar of the Wolves, lord of that world's sons and daughters, and defender of the Fang. No more lies, coward. No more tricks. Our Rune Priests laid down their lives to bring us back here and paint the walls of our fortress with your sick blood. You *dare* warn me to back away from my own birth world? Are you blind as well as mad, weakling? This is Wolf space, and we are Wolves. Leave now, before we feed our oceans with your bones.'

Kysnaros glanced over to the battleship's usurped captain; a portly man in his fifties, in an immaculate uniform from one of the many divisions within Battlefleet Solar.

'How long until they reach weapons range?'

'Less than a minute, lord. They're coming in hot.'

Coming in hot. A bizarre dialect. I wondered what world he was from.

'Why so calm?' Annika asked from my side.

'I can't say for sure. I think I've accepted the fact we're unlikely to survive any of this. I accepted it weeks ago.'

Kysnaros was already speaking again, for whatever good it would do. I watched him surrender to panic, moment by moment. He'd pushed the Wolves too far, brought too much threat into their skies, and broken any chance of a peaceful resolution. I knew it. He knew it. He just didn't wish to face it.

'Move the fleet into a defensive formation. Keep the guns

aimed at the Fang. They have to realise we will fire.'

'They realise it,' I interrupted. 'And they no longer care. Inquisitor, break the armada apart. Run. It's over.'

'No. No, there's still time.' He turned back to the vox-mic hanging from the ceiling on a twisted cable. 'They have no hope against our armada. They must realise that, at least.'

I mounted the stairs, feeling a fist forming, and doing my damnedest not to raise my arm and fire.

'You've threatened the Fang in front of the High King of Fenris. We had a chance with the Fell-Handed, but now? With the Wolves' entire strength bearing down on us? Inquisitor, you will never leave this system alive. The remnants of the armada might, but the cost in life will be catastrophic.'

'Hyperion,' he said, as if I could possibly help him. 'Hyperion...'

'Surrender, lord. Surrender before the first shot is fired.'

'They must see reason!' He was on the edge, now. I could see the whites around his eyes as he grabbed the vox-mic. 'Jarl Grimnar... This doesn't have to end in war–'

'You brought us here,' the voice crackled back. 'You sowed the seeds of this harvest. Now reap it.'

'A penitent crusade would absolve your sins, Logan. We can end this without bloodshed–'

The only reply was a laugh. A laugh that became a howl.

II

The fleets crashed together in the sedately brutal way of the most vicious void battles. Warships so often duelled over vast distances, waging war with calculated weapon strikes, that it wasn't uncommon for a captain to have never once come face to face with another ship prepared to ram his own.

Only a commander's madness or hatred could bring warships within ramming reach of one another. Too much could go wrong with no room to manoeuvre; with no space to come about; with no hope of escaping if something went wrong.

The Wolves crossed into weapons range, howling all the while. They came closer, closer, and closer.

The panic threatening to claim Lord Inquisitor Kysnaros only moments before drained from him in a cold flood. In a true trial, his qualities made themselves plain. He pointed from station to station dispensing orders in absolute calm, phrased with perfect clarity. Ship by ship, the armada received its commands.

'I want half of the fleet to focus all its fire on the fortress-monastery. All use of atomics and cyclonics are disallowed, but traditional bombardment *mustn't cease*. The rest of the fleet, focus on their capital ships.'

'Aye, lord,' called back several officers, moving to relay his commands.

'Shields to variable cycling,' he ordered, already moving from the void shield station to the gunnery platform. 'Do you see the Space Wolves ship *Gate of Garm*? All ahead full, interception course. Order the *Helana* and the *Consecrator* to come about and use us as cover while they manoeuvre. We'll take the *Garm*'s assault on our starboard shields. As soon as we pass by, fire one-third of our broadsides at the *Garm*'s aft section, aiming for the armour plating around its primary thrusters. Then align with the *In Sacred Trust* for an attack run against the *Scramaseax*. Get the Aquiliania escort squadron to herd the *Scramaseax* so that it's forced to plough between both battleships. We'll cripple her with our laser batteries.'

He moved around the deck, never ceasing, only stopping his stream of orders to hear another status update from elsewhere in the armada.

'Order the *Farwall* and the *Bloodghast* to protect the *Redoubt* until she can get her engines back online. You. Second lieutenant. Order the *God of Us All* to break off from its out-rider arc and commence immediate bombardment of the Fang.'

Annika looked lost in the chaos, her eyes never settling on any one officer or station. 'Are we safe here?'

'The *Corel's Hope* is the biggest, most heavily defended ship in the armada,' I replied. 'But no, we're not.'

'He's firing at the Fang.'

'I know.'

Kysnaros moved back to the railing, clicking his fingers as he concentrated on maintaining a second-count.

'Now,' he said softly. The deck shook beneath us as the first of our weapons released into the void.

The command deck was drowning in shouting voices. I was struggling to filter them out from each other. One, however, stood out above all others.

'Boarding pods!'

'Details…' Kysnaros called back.

The tactical hololithic superimposed over the oculus, projected from the roaring mouth of a gargoyle sculpted into the ceiling. Every ship among both fleets, many of which were sailing perilously close to one another, was a winking rune of red or white.

'Boarding pods fired from every single Fenrisian warship.'

'Tell all afflicted ships to brace and stand by to repel boarders. Order the Red Hunters to begin counter-attacks on every single Space Wolves vessel that has launched its warriors. Board them in turn, and kill them from within. Order Chapter Master Daemar to deploy his elite companies via teleportation to take hold of the *Kerberaus* and the *Sky's Hammer*.'

The deck shook again, savagely enough to throw some of the crew from their feet.

'Taking heavy fire,' a servitor mumbled to itself, from its new position on the deck. It rolled from side to side, too damaged from a concussion to stand back up.

On the oculus, I watched one of the most uncomfortable sights I'd ever had the misfortune to witness. The grey iron battlements of the *Scramaseax* drifted past in a slow, beautiful slide, countless firelight-winks along the walls and towers showing the anger of individual turrets.

Corel's Hope groaned in protest at the other vessel's proximity. Throne, we weren't just close enough to see individual windows, we were close enough to reach out and touch the warship's bruised armour.

Detonations speckled the ship's spine as our own laser batteries and lesser turrets returned the unwanted attention. The lances at the ship's prow kicked hard enough to breed a second shudder, almost as violent as the first. Ahead of us, displayed on the panning oculus, a Space Wolves ship I couldn't name rolled away even as it crumbled. Our final lance array ignited its plasma core, briefly blinding the oculus with a retinal blurring of painful colour.

The next vision was of a Red Hunters strike cruiser, the *Purity of Loyalty*, blackened by burn markings, struggling to come about on dying engines. I watched it trembling, coming apart as it caught fire in Fenris's atmosphere. Escape pods sprayed from its hull in a scattering of doomed seeds.

Yet another vision filled the oculus. One of our ships, the Grey Knights cruiser *Solemnity*, was driven back from the armada, out of formation. The ships harrying it veered away, just in time for the Fang's own defences to open fire now *Solemnity* fell into range of its tower guns.

'Shields?' I heard Kysnaros yelling. '*Shields?*'

They were down. I could tell from the way we were shaking under the *Scramaseax*'s guns. They'd punched through the barrier, and were pulling us to pieces with their dense turret batteries.

Kysnaros was no less aware. 'Shields! I want them back up before they–'

A second blinding light flashed across the command deck. The first had been from the outside, and easy enough to look away from. No luck, this time. It was close enough to feel, and it was a feeling I knew so very well.

III

I'd never seen a warrior sprinting in Terminator warplate. He ran through the fiery mist of a teleportation storm, with no hint of the sluggishness I'd felt on Armageddon. Impossible as it was, I swore I could hear the pounding of his boots, and the screaming whine of protesting servo joints, over the ship falling apart around us. Sparks burst from every racing step he took.

I couldn't even conceive of the power and rage it would take to force Terminator plate to react against its will like that. I fired at him. Malchadiel fired at him. Our storm bolters crashed and boomed and blasted chunks of ceramite away with no effect at all.

In the middle of his sprint, the grey warrior leapt onto a control console, smashing it beneath his armoured boot, and kicked off with a jump high enough to bring him down on the central command dais. Despite his speed, there was nothing of grace or agility in his movements, merely anger and ferocious strength, pushing his armour's joints to the absolute limit of the sacred ceramite's endurance.

Malchadiel and I moved in the perfect unity of those whose minds are meshed as one. The Wolf's axe felled Mal in a heartbeat, cleaving his legs out from under him. I brought my stave around in a whirling parry, to block a blade that didn't exist. The immense axe blade was a blur, coming from the wrong angle to crash against the side of my helm hard enough to throw me off the raised platform. I felt something crack in my face, and fell back over the railing, dropping the six metres to land on the deck in a heap of numb limbs.

I looked up, half-blinded by blood and disoriented enough to lose all sense of balance. Just standing was a struggle I wasn't sure I could win. My face was broken again. Some part of my skull was screaming.

Insignificant las-fire burned scorch marks on the old warrior's suit, all going utterly ignored. Several beams of laser fire even managed to punch home, drilling hot into the flesh beneath the plate, earning no more notice than the rest.

The three Naval armsmen died in turn, their lasrifles falling silent. The first and second died from bolt shells to the chests; the third from an archaic throwing axe slamming into his face and leaving him to jerk on the floor like an abandoned automaton.

Annika bared her teeth as she reloaded her bolter.

'Ayah! For the High King! For the Aett!'

Kysnaros faced the old warrior, weaponless and clad only in ceremonial power armour. He said nothing. He never had time to whisper a single word.

The old warrior's axe didn't even slow down going through him. Lord Inquisitor Kysnaros's head fell from his shoulders, rolling and banging down the steps. The body toppled a second later, collapsing back into the command throne.

Logan Grimnar raised the axe Morkai in one hand, roaring a howl to the burning bridge around him. For every crew member reaching for their sidearms, two dozen were abandoning their stations for the escape pods.

+Hyperion. Hyperion, help me.+

+Mal.+

I hauled myself to my feet, staring back up the stairs. Malchadiel, his new bionic legs severed from the thighs down, was dragging himself across the deck. His ceramite breastplate squealed along the gantry as he crawled.

Jarl Grimnar stalked closer to him.

+Mal!+

He rolled, raising his storm bolter, but the axe ended his arm in a silver blur. His forearm spun away, and the mounted bolter with it.

I fired. I fired my storm bolter until it clicked dry, staring in disbelief as every single shell burst apart against the relic axe blade. Seven bolts fired, for the pathetic victory of staining the embossed golden wolves a dirty, burned black.

Jarl Grimnar raised the axe again, pressing a boot down on Malchadiel's chest. I started running.

'So will be the fate of every treacherous snake's son in your honourless Chapter.'

No. *No.* I'd lost Galeo. I'd lost Dumenidon. I'd lost Sothis, directly because of my own weakness. Enceladus was lost within a coma, likely never to wake again. I wouldn't lose Mal. He was the last; my only brother; my one chance not to fail the oaths I'd sworn in the name of unbreakable fraternity. The energy nodes on my backpack crackled and spat witch-lightning in response to my helpless anger.

Annika moved in front of me. I hurled her back with a torrent of kinetic force, smashing her back against a burning wall. Other Wolves – warriors I'd never even seen teleport aboard – fired at me from where they'd been killing the crew at the chamber's sides. Every impact sent me staggering, choking on the smoke of my own dying armour. I cried out as the axe fell, just a wordless, fevered shout of shameful denial.

In the same second, I threw myself into the hell behind reality.

* * *

IV

The axe crashed down.

I stared at Jarl Grimnar, eye to eye, both of us baring our teeth into the face of the other. His axe trembled, the blade locked tight against the haft of my black stave. I could feel ghost-flame filling my eye sockets, bleaching and burning all colour from my vision. Even through the pale fire, I saw the unease in the Great Wolf's dark stare.

+*No.*+

His fangs scraped his lower teeth as he grunted. If it was a reply, it was a weak one.

+**No.**+

The old warrior tensed, pressed harder, and his grimace became a predator's toothy smile. My stave – the Trecenti runes along its black sides flaring white-hot – started to shiver as he forced me down. I couldn't stand against his strength in Terminator plate. I felt the fire streaming from my eyes begin to cool.

+Brother,+ came Malchadiel's fading voice. +Finish him.+

+I… I can't…+

+You shattered the cursed blade of a daemon-god's son. Finish this mortal, mongrel bastard.+

I smiled back, teeth bared again, almost laughing. My voice was nothing more than a guttural snarl through the protracted effort.

'Do not speak to me of honour…' White warp-fire sidewindered in hissing coils around my fists. 'You… are as guilty… as we are. This is the Imperium of Man, Old Wolf, not a fabled empire of bliss and joy. *We* are the Emperor's Gift. *We* know what must be done. *We* never let stubborn pride and misplaced kindness blind us to the real enemy.'

The axe cracked. A thick, black crack split the ancient relic, severing one wolf's head from its shoulders.

'We are *both* guilty in this war.' I spat the words into his grizzled, bearded face.

+Behind you!+

I heard Mal's warning the same moment Jarl Grimnar's eyes flicked to glance over my shoulder.

I couldn't turn. I tried to hurl the jarl back, but even with every iota of energy, it was no different from trying to move a mountain.

I knew who it was. I sensed Brand Rawthroat's presence and personality, charged with anger and savage amusement, clear enough to almost feel the axe in his hands.

A wave of kinetic force crashed into me, smashed into all of us, hurling us all from our feet.

+Just run.+ Malchadiel's silent voice was scarcely a whisper. I sensed his signature in the psychic release. +Just run.+

I stood above him – my legless, one-armed brother – and summoned my stave back into my fists from across the deck. Spinning it in my hands, I turned to face Rawthroat and his unkillable jarl.

Only, I didn't face two Wolves.

I faced twenty.

They closed just as their namesakes would, in a unified pack, never blinking, teeth on show the moment before they tore into their prey.

+Come closer,+ I sent to all of them at once. +I can't kill you all, but some of you will never return to that freezing hell you call home. Who wants to be first?+

This time, the flash of light and air displacement heralded the arrival of something truly huge. We all turned to regard what could possibly have joined the fight at this last stage.

Every Wolf went to his knees. They knelt among the mutilated dead, bowing their heads to the towering war machine.

I alone remained standing, and I confess, even I felt the temptation to kneel.

'Enough,' boomed Bjorn the Fell-Handed. '**Enough of this madness.**'

'First Jarl,' said Grimnar, pausing only to spit a gobbet of blood aside.

'**Enough.** *Enough.* **The Fang is aflame, burning hotter than it ever did under the black magic of Magnus One-Eye. Three Imperial ships have crashed into our walls, pulling them down and opening our hearth-halls to the Fenrisian winter.**

'**Our orbital docks are wounded unto death. Our fleet is in ruins.**'

Logan Grimnar surged to his feet, aiming at me with his axe. 'First Jarl–'

'**You will watch your tongue with me, young one.**'

Despite the fleets tearing each other apart beyond these burning walls, despite the ship itself shaking as it was still being fired upon, several of the Wolves laughed to hear their jarl being called young.

'**This is over. Grimnar, you have acted with all honour, but the time to bare our throats has come. Pride and right-eousness will take us all to our graves. I know that better than any of you. Call off the attack. End the war howls.**'

The Dreadnought turned to face me, its waist axis grinding. '**Who speaks for you?**'

'I… I am not sure, lord.'

'I do.' Annika Jarlsdottyr, her clothing wet with blood, moved to stand next to me. 'I speak for the Holy Inquisition.'

'**Then remember these words, little maiden. Be sure that every soul to carry your order's sigil hears these words. If an Inquisition ship ever darkens the skies above Fenris again, we will pull it from the sky and feast on its iron bones. Do you hear me?**'

She bowed her head. 'I hear. As will others.'

The ancient Dreadnought moved away from all of us, its stomping tread shaking the deck as much as the incoming fire.

'**I have never, in all my years, stepped into a teleporter until now. No wonder Russ hated it so much. If I had skin, it would be crawling.**'

He rotated back, his claw and assault cannon both aimed at me. '**One last thing. You. Hyperion.**'

I swallowed at the way he said my name, as I crouched, tending to Malchadiel as best I could. After all this time – after months of hoping it would end – it now took all my strength not to ignore the awkward ceasefire and hurl myself back at Grimnar.

I could see the same thing in his face. That same beast-at-bay anger in his eyes. We both knew he'd kill me in a heartbeat, but when has reason ever played a part in actions born of spite or rage?

Reluctantly, I broke eye contact first, and looked over at the Dreadnought.

'Sire?' I asked him.

'**Before you are allowed to return to wherever it is you dwell, I want you to walk the halls of the Fang and speak of your order. The Wolves will never be scoured of this memory. No more secrets, Grey Knight. We know you, now. The Wolves will always know you, from this day forth.**'

To end a war, both Chapters would break their laws. But what choice?

I went to one knee.

'Aye, jarl. It will be so.'

'**And you both speak for the Inquisition? With authority?**'

Annika met my glance with her own. There was nothing of warmth there, not any more.

'We can be convincing,' she said.

EPILOGUE
ECHOES OF SURRENDER

I

I will end this account with a truth rarely told. Two, in fact.

The first took place six hours after the guns fell silent. The second took place three weeks later, when only the *Karabela* remained in orbit, off-shore from the floating hulks of a warship graveyard.

II

We stood before the surviving inquisitors, those who boarded the crippled *Corel's Hope* in order to hear the words spoken at the battle's end.

I waited in silence as Annika walked back and forth before them, relaying the words of a warrior who'd once waged war at the Emperor's side. The war room aboard the ruined battleship was lit by infrequent flashes of the flawed hololithic projectors, and the white eye of Fenris rolling past the observation window every time the wounded, near-powerless ship completed another revolution in its drift.

When Annika trailed off, her last words hung in the air between the gathered agents, nobles and officers, with no one replying right away. I scanned the crowd – the former enforcers of Imperial law now exalted to the hidden ordos; the spire nobles now draped in Inquisitorial panoply; the preening lordlings clad more in self-importance than righteousness; and the earthy, battered warriors who eschewed grand trappings in favour of the quieter, subtler work.

Inquisitors, all. Not a single soul carrying anything in common with his or her kindred, but for the emblems they swore oaths to.

'No,' said one of them, at last.

'The battle is over.' Just speaking made them flinch back. I shook my head, taking a step forwards. 'The battle is over, and before it could become a war.'

But the inquisitors shared glances, and I knew they'd soon be sharing secrets.

'We will explore alternate avenues against this Chapter,' a bruised, dreadlocked man said through an augmetic vocaliser mounted in his epiglottis, replacing half of his throat like a torc.

Several others nodded.

'Perhaps the next time Fenris comes under siege by the Archenemy, Battlefleet Solar will be slow to react. What a shame that would be.'

That earned a few murmurs of agreement, and even a chuckle.

'What do we know,' asked a robed Biologis adept, 'of Space Wolf gene-seed?'

III

There are some moments in life you will always regret witnessing. The insipid scheming of the Inquisition after the battle was one of them. The bitterness of the Wolves was another. Both sides were justified in their anger, but validation didn't render it wholesome.

We lingered in orbit, the *Karabela*'s guns adding to the Fang's as we scuttled the wrecks too broken to serve as scrap iron. Each dead ship was sent to the surface of Fenris as an asteroid of burning metal. We'd stand on the bridge, Captain Castor and I, watching each one tumble into the black seas.

With Annika gone, and Malchadiel taken aboard the *Ruler of the Black Skies* back to Titan, Talwyn and I were almost alone. We were barred from setting foot on Fenris, of course. I obeyed the letter of that command, while violating its spirit.

Fascinating, to drift from mind to mind within the Fang's bleak walls. I spent an hour as a thrall; a failed aspirant, physically enhanced but ruined by my own defeat, indentured to a dead warrior and now with no arms and armour to repair.

I spent a whole evening as a servant – nearly blinded by the eternal gloom in which I lived – working in secret, sacred forges that had never seen the sun. I watched bolter shells being shaped, rune-carved and blessed. I watched muscled artisans beating iron and steel into blades. Only after several hours did I realise why I was having such trouble hearing anything: I was seeing through the eyes of a woman who'd been near-deafened by a lifetime of toils in the underforges.

I will not lie. I touched the minds of a hundred and more Fenrisian servants, never allowing my presence to be detected, sharing their chores and pleasures through vicarious curiosity. I learned much, but cared little. There was something in particular I wanted to see.

I found it, weeks after the void battle.

From a raised gantry overlooking a stasis containment chamber, I watched through the red-tinted eye lenses of a cowled and heavily augmented thrall. In place of hands, coiling cable-tendrils rolled and unrolled from my elbows. In place of legs, I moved on dense, slow tank treads, rumbling over the metal deck.

Logan Grimnar, High King of Fenris, stood before a wide circular elevator, his axe in his hands. At his side, his remaining Wolf Guard mirrored his stance. I recognised Brand Rawthroat, but resisted the temptation to see the ritual through his eyes. This was enough of a trespass.

The armoured form of Jarl Bjorn rotated its weaponised hands, rolled its bulky shoulders, shifted its immense weight – testing every point of locomotion one last time. Hundreds of cables and wires already linked to the Dreadnought's coffin and hull, some from the machinery concealed beneath the elevator, others stringing up to the humming generators hanging from the ceiling.

Everything was in readiness.

'Sleep, First Jarl,' said Logan Grimnar. The Wolf Guard raised their weapons in salute. 'Until Fenris once more calls.'

The Dreadnought fell still. Slowly, the elevator began to lower into the pit, with all its subterranean generators. Frost-mist made diamonds on the war machine's blue-grey armour plating.

'Fenris. Always. Calls.'

'Always. But rest well, for now. Preserve this tale among the sagas, jarl.' Grimnar's voice was a measured counterpart to the dragging, weary drawl of the slumbering Dreadnought.

'Remember. The Inquisition. Will not. Leave us. In peace.'

Jarl Grimnar nodded, as solemn as I'd ever seen him. 'I know.'

'Watch. The. Skies. Brothers.' The Dreadnought descended into the mist, and a bulkhead in the floor started to seal closed above it. 'Howl for me. When. They. Come...'

CHAPTER X
LOST SOULS

IMPERIAL DATE: 498.M41

I

I met him at the Pinnacle-Seyta-V landing platform. The Thunderhawk gunship came in low, silver in the night, gleaming in the liquid methane rainfall. It touched down with almost ludicrous perfection, graceful from the height of its approach vector to the moment its landing claws rested on the rockcrete platform.

As the gangramp descended, I stood straighter, letting my targeting reticule flicker across the gunship's armoured panels.

I didn't know what to expect. In all honesty, I'd done my level best to banish any expectation. Fifty-five years was a long time, even for those of us destined to live for centuries.

He descended the ramp, boots sending shivers through the plasteel. His armour was changed to a monumental degree. Layers and layers of densely packed ceramite girded his chest and limbs. The storm bolter on his arm beamed a permanent, thin beam of red-dot aiming light, as did a fist-sized targeting cogitator mounted on the side of his helm. Instead of an Interceptor teleportation backpack, he had an immense plasma cell generator on his back, with four thick, multi-jointed servo arms curled closed. Each of them ended in tight, packed industrial claws, doubtless capable of wrenching a tank's armour apart, or lifting it completely off the ground.

He looked to me, his helm tilted slightly. In curiosity? Surprise? I didn't pry into his mind to find out for sure.

I saw myself as I must look to him. Gone was the unadorned armour of a young knight. I stood clad in my ceremonial plate, the silver ceramite encrusted with myriad runes in Trecenti and High Gothic – meaningless in terms of pure language, but each one a sorcerous benediction of hope against the blackness behind the veil. A hood of riveted, consecrated gold reached over the back and sides of my helm, linked to my armour through dense black cabling.

At my hip was a sheathed force sword. On my back, a mag-locked staff; the same weapon I'd carried through the two short years I'd served in Castian. I still carried a pistol to complement my storm bolter, though no one had called me Two-Guns in a long time.

Our suits of armour held only two similarities now, and the first was simply that they both remained unpainted in the Grey Knights' eternal tradition. The second was the inscription of a chained wolf on our left bracers – the mark of surviving that bloodstained dusk on the killing fields of Armageddon over half a century ago.

When he walked closer, I offered my hand. He ignored it and embraced me. The contact lasted only a moment, though I heard his chuckle over the vox, and felt the warmth from his mind.

'Hyperion,' he said. 'My brother. It is good to see you.'

'Welcome home, Mal.'

'You look… different.'

I smiled at that. It was strange, speaking with my teeth and tongue for a change. I was so used to the effortless ease and instantaneous comprehension found in silent speech.

'As do you. Come.' I led him inside. The bulkhead whirled closed and locked behind us.

'I cannot speak of Mars,' he said, apropos of nothing. 'So do not ask. Suffice to say, one can grow weary even of seeing a new wonder each day. Duty called, and I could no longer ignore its cry.' He gestured to my armour, most notably to the psychic hood shielding the rear half of my helm. 'Tell me of that,' he bade me.

'There are things I can't speak of, either,' I replied. 'We keep more lore hidden within this monastery than you would ever believe, brother. Behind arcane locks, a thousand secrets lie untold.'

He nodded, sanguine and unsurprised. 'I would like to walk the Dead Fields before I am assigned back into duty.'

'Of course.' Sothis. He wanted to see Sothis, and our brothers sleeping beneath Titan's surface. 'We'll go there now.'

Serfs bowed and moved aside as we walked the monastery's cold, quiet halls. I sensed he was building up to a question, but didn't know how to frame it.

+Just ask,+ I sent.

'This promotion of yours,' he said. 'Prognosticar Hyperion. You serve with Torcrith now? Truly?'

'Torcrith went to sleep within the Dead Fields nineteen years since. But we served together for a time.'

'How did he die?'

I shrugged a shoulder. 'The same way we all die. In pain.'

'And it's your task to train others?'

I nodded. 'As Torcrith trained me. Hopefully, I'll find it easier than he did. I wasn't a quick student.'

Malchadiel gave a muted smile. 'I'm sorry to hear of your loss, though it pleases me to see your talents recognised, brother. So yours is the voice that advises captains and Grand Masters. Except now you stand alone.'

'We both stand alone, Mal.'

'True enough,' he conceded. 'It makes my eyes ache to look upon you, Hyperion. Your soul is so very bright. But I've missed the unity of purpose within a squad. Haven't you?'

There was no sense lying to him, of all souls. 'I miss it still. But it's better this way.'

He knew of what I spoke, and it wasn't pride at a promotion through the ranks. 'I sense your guilt lingering behind those words, Hyperion.'

'Time heals all wounds but those we most need tending. And it's not just Sothis, Mal. I was always supposed to be alone in this. I think we both were.'

He nodded to that. 'What of the others?'

He'd see Galeo and Dumenidon soon enough – they slept beneath the surface of Titan, next to Sothis. I knew he didn't mean them.

'Inquisitor Jarlsdottyr hasn't filed a report with the ordos in seventeen years. She is believed lost during the Jaegra Ascension, slain by the Archenemy.'

He glanced at me as we walked. 'Jaegra?'

'Cretacia's largest moon. It's a long story, brother.'

'Did you ever see her again? After the Months of Shame, I mean.'

'Yes. Yes, I did.' He sensed from my tone that the subject was best left alone.

'Why did you meet me up there?' he asked. 'I'm glad you did, but I confess I'm surprised.'

'Because we have unfinished business, you and I.'

He looked at me, and I sensed his interest grow sharper, more hesitant. 'Oh?'

'It can wait until after the Dead Fields.'

Malchadiel nodded. 'As you wish.'

When we reached the end of the steps descending down into the Dead Fields, we were greeted before reaching the first grave.

'Look at you both,' said a voice softened by age and infirmity. A man so thin he bordered on skeletal limped closer on smooth, silver bionics.

'Enceladus,' Malchadiel greeted him. 'Still alive, old man?'

His scarred face twisted into an elder's smile – all wrinkles and time's lines. 'For a little while longer, I'm sure. How was Mars, my boy? And don't hide behind secrets. I have enough of that these days from Hyperion.'

II

We left the Dead Fields after three hours. I will not share the words of regret and oaths to fallen kin we spoke there. Such things have no place in any archive outside the human heart.

Worldrise, on Titan. We'd made our way to one of the monastery's countless battlements, standing armoured in the poisonous, freezing air as the sphere of Saturn rose above the mountainous horizon.

Malchadiel was quiet. He'd said little since we left the Dead Fields.

'Brother,' I said to him. 'Come with me.'

He looked around. The howling wind flapped at his tabard, and tore a scroll from my pauldron.

'To where?'

'To Terra.'

'Hyperion, is this a jest?'

+No. As I said, we have unfinished business. There's something I still owe you.+

III

The Imperial Palace is a nation in itself, covering a significant portion of Holy Terra's surface. Thousands of minarets, towers and spires rise from the golden skyline and breach the world's ever-thinning cloud cover.

One of these towers is black. One, and only one, standing out from its gold and marble kindred. They call it the Tower of Heroes.

At the summit of this vast architectural spear is a bell tower. The belfry itself is the size of a cathedral, and houses a single bell of un-assuming, commonplace metals, given over to the stains and patinas of time's eroding touch. This lone bell is the size of a Titan, and attended by hundreds of men, women and servitors whose existence is devoted to maintaining the instrument's function.

It rarely rings. When it does, all resident servants must be evacuated and sealed within reinforced shelters to prevent the annihilation of their eardrums – and subsequent death through lung rupture and embolism.

And when it does ring, the tolling can be heard across half of Terra. The rest of the world hears it anyway, as all communications fall silent, replaced by a channelled transmission of the sound.

This is the Bell of Lost Souls. Among its many legends is the holiest of all; that when the bell rings, the Emperor hears the sound even in His slumber upon the Golden Throne, and sheds a single tear.

As His genetic inheritors and mankind's most valued protectors, the Bell of Lost Souls rings once each time a Grey Knight falls in battle. It's said that this is our reward for the recognition we will never receive from a galaxy that must never know we exist. Galeo once stood at the base of the tower, when he was the last of his Castian brothers, and pulled the levers that set the great, arcane mechanisms to work. Minutes later, the bell tolled nine times – once for every fallen brother. All of Terra knew that the mighty had fallen, and the Imperium was a darker place because of it.

I'd stood there myself, in the very same place, in that sacrosanct control chamber surrounded by reverent slaves and burning incense. I'd tolled the bell twice: for Galeo and for Dumenidon.

But never for Sothis. When the time had come, I'd chosen to wait a little longer. Despite my desire, there were other, worthier hands than mine who deserved to ring that bell and speak Sothis's name.

Malchadiel was with me now, though neither of us were there in the physical sense. Instead, I made our presence known through subtler means.

A robed slave looked up, and without hearing any order, began the laborious process of automated lockdown, broadcasting vox-transmissions to send the belfry attendants into their bunkers.

Another slave started working the controls to awaken the continental communications relays.

Another slave, this one an overseer, keyed in the one hundred and three ciphers to unlock the safeguards that would allow his menials to access the deeper systems.

Ah, the Imperium's bureaucracy. A wondrously complex thing to behold.

This took me almost eight hours, with feather-light touches on almost ninety minds. At no point had anyone within the Palace given the order for the Bell of Lost Souls to be tolled.

When all was in readiness, Malchadiel and I shared the

mind of a single servant. One hand rested on the ornate control console, the other on the lever that would activate the myriad mechanics within this monument to honour and misery.

+Do it, Mal.+

The serf gripped the lever, whispering a single name as two tears made a slow journey down his cheeks.

'Sothis.'

The last lament of Sothis of Castian rang out across mankind's birth world, ignored by none, heard by all – and humanity's empire mourned another fallen hero.

ACKNOWLEDGEMENTS

Thanks to my editor Nick Kyme for having the patience of a funny-talking Northern saint, and to Rachel Docherty, Ead Brown, Graeme Lyon and Nikki Loftus for their invaluable opinions. A huge Ta to Liz and John French for the last-second, deadline-defying use of a laptop and their spare room.

Also, sincerest thanks to Marvin Minsky's *The Society of Mind*; Cornell University's 'Curious About Astronomy'; the online resources of physicist and astronomer William Wheaton; NASA's very detailed website; and BBC's *Wonders of the Solar System*, *Wonders of the Universe* and *Horizon* for the information about space, temperature, physics in vacuum, eidetic memory – and (of course) Titan.

A portion of this book's proceeds will go to Cancer Research UK and the SOS Children's Villages charity, for orphans in Bangladesh.

ABOUT THE AUTHOR

Aaron Dembski-Bowden has written several novels for Black Library, including the Night Lords series, the Space Marine Battles book *Helsreach*, *The Emperor's Gift* and the *New York Times* bestselling *The First Heretic* for the Horus Heresy. He lives and works in Northern Ireland with his wife Katie, hiding from the world in the middle of nowhere.